Molly Hopkins was lucky (or mad) enough to work as a tour guide on the European coach circuit for over fifteen years. She visited Paris, Amsterdam, the Loire Valley and many other fabulous destinations, always with no fewer than forty people in tow. She now lives in a picturesque village in Middlesex with her husband and two teenage children. *It Happened in Paris* is her first novel.

Coming soon

It Happened in Venice

IT HAPPENED in Paris

MOLLY HOPKINS

PARIS

sphere

SPHERE

First published in Great Britain in 2011 by Sphere

Copyright © Molly Hopkins 2011

The moral right of the author has been asserted.

*All characters and events in this publication, other than those
clearly in the public domain, are fictitious and any resemblance
to real persons, living or dead, is purely coincidental.*

A CIP catalogue record for this book
is available from the British Library.

ISBN 978-0-7515-4459-6

Typeset in Bembo by M Rules
Printed and bound in Great Britain by
Clays Ltd, St Ives plc

Sphere
An imprint of
Little, Brown Book Group
100 Victoria Embankment
London EC4Y 0DY

An Hachette UK Company
www.hachette.co.uk

www.littlebrown.co.uk

In memory of my beautiful friend Sarah Ward

PARIS

Acknowledgements

Thank you to everyone at Little, Brown, especially Rob Manser for believing I'd written a publishable tome, and passing it to Rebecca Saunders, who was sure of it. And to Manpreet Grewal, who should write a book on how to write a book.

Thank you to Karen Browning and Julie Manser for their support, encouragement, and liquid lunches, and to my friend Sue Besser for staying in posh hotels all over the world and telling me all about them.

Thank you also to my friends, past and present, in the travel industry (you know who you are) for providing the material that gave me the inspiration to write in the first place. Your secrets are out but your identities are safe, I promise! And to my precious nieces, Becky, Lauren and Katie Coombs, for being the best unpaid editors a writer could wish for.

And finally a big thank you to my family, Peter, Elise and Jack, for living on Pot Noodles whilst I was writing this book, and to my dog, Paxie, for taking himself on walks.

Everyone contributed.

PARIS

Chapter One

OK, I've cracked. I'm leaning against the fridge, glass in hand, in a state of blissful relaxation. My heart has been racing all day with the pressure of enforced wine deprivation; I conceded defeat at seven o'clock. I would've had a heart attack otherwise. Last week my doctor told me that anyone who drinks more than eight units of alcohol a week is in danger of becoming alcohol dependent. Brandishing a plastic beaker, he illustrated what amounted to eight units. It wasn't enough to drown a wasp. To be honest, I suspect I may already be alcohol dependent, but I don't care, because I depend on all sorts of things, like make-up and credit cards. No, alcohol dependency doesn't bother me at all. What does bother me is the fact there are hundreds of skinny alcoholics out there. How do they stay slim *and* snorkel wine? I wouldn't mind being a skinny alcoholic. I wouldn't mind being a skinny anything.

I swirled the glass under my nose. This drink is medicinal and so much better for me than drowning myself, which I'd considered this morning. I've been made redundant from the advertising agency where I've worked for the past ten months. OK, so this in itself may not necessarily be deemed a life or death issue, but in celebration of being employed, I have amassed an overdraft of nine grand. I wish I'd been the victim of fraud. It would have been so much cheaper than me spending my own money.

I ambled from the kitchen, glass in hand, jack-knifing back for the wine bottle. So, I'm unemployed and overdrawn. I owe the bank nine thousand pounds. That's nine hundred ten-pound notes. I swallowed a lump of panic and swiftly replaced the mental picture of an enormous stack of ten-pound notes with a neat little bundle of fifties, and immediately felt better. Put like that, it's nothing.

Sitting on my bed, I opened last night's *Evening Standard* with a flourish.

'OK, Evie. Mission Employment: find a job,' I told myself, but, typically, the Job Vacancies page had been shredded by the letterbox, and so I found myself pondering the Lonely Hearts ads.

'Thirty-something.' Yeah right. Forty-four next birthday, more like. I slurped my wine.

'Fun-loving.' Hah, a pisshead. I flipped the page over with a dramatic sweeping gesture.

'Seeks knight in shining armour.' Husband's buggered off with someone else. What she seeks is anything male with a pulse.

'Enjoys eating out.' Can't cook.

'Adventurous.' A slut.

I tore out an advert headed 'Hypnotism combats alcoholism', threw the newspaper neatly on the floor, and decided for the first time in my entire life to clear out my bedroom.

I'd just thrown open the wardrobe when my flatmate, Lulu, arrived home from work. She thumped down on the bed, kicked off her pumps and tucked a pillow behind her head. I tossed her a fleeting look. She squirmed against the headboard, legs straight, ankles crossed. She wore her navy nurse's tunic with the dinky upside-down watch and white trousers. Arms folded with exaggerated purpose, she looked at her fingernails.

'Good day?' I asked her, sensing the opposite was likely the case.

She shrugged and went into dream mode.

'So,' I tried again. 'What did you get up to?'

She gave a despairing sigh.

'Remember I told you about David, the new doctor at my surgery? I've fancied him since the creation of time. I've positively adored him and, well, I thought he might be the one,' she said, in a whiny, sorry-for-herself whimper.

If I'm not mistaken, he'd actually only worked at the practice for two weeks.

'Mmm, I do. He—'

She flapped a silencing hand.

'I stayed at his flat last night.'

The whiny whimpering was now punctuated with watery blinks.

'We slept together.'

I dumped a jumble of clothes, hangers and polythene bags on the bed.

'Lucky you,' I said, massaging my forearms. 'I'm jealous.' As well I might be, I thought. I haven't had sex for twenty-eight days.

Lulu sucked her knuckle, her face clouded over. 'He came before me!' she shrieked, vaulting from the bed.

I jumped.

'He finished before I'd hardly started . . . twice!'

Demented with rage, she paced the room.

'We did it twice and both times the same thing happened. It's fraud!' She squirrelled in her pocket, whipped out a tissue and blew her nose. 'It's not acceptable behaviour, not on a first date.

3

Perhaps after, after, five years of marriage, or on his birthday, or, or, if I'm knackered and I say he can, but, but . . .' she stuttered.

Privately, I thought it charitable of her to have given the guy a second chance. Twice!

'He didn't even fancy it at first. He was watching *Deal or No Deal*. I broke a nail tugging his belt off. Look.'

Her hand shot out in front of my face. She had indeed broken a nail. I winced.

'He wanted to wait and see what was in the last box.'

She snorted in fury.

'"Sod the last box," I told him. So, he got going, and guess what? Guess what!?' She shook her head forcefully. 'Bet you can't guess. Never in a million years.' She gave me a millisecond to speculate, and then rushed on. 'He went into some sort of trance. I thought of that scene in *Ghost* when Whoopi Goldberg was possessed by spirits. I hoped he'd been possessed by a horny marauding Viking kidnapper, but no. I think he must have been possessed by a Victorian train driver, because he literally *chugged to a halt*. And then it was over.'

Her hands twisted and knotted in despair. 'I thought I might have been possessed myself, by the Boston strangler, because I wanted to kill him. And what makes it worse is that it was my idea.' She pounded her chest with a clenched fist in emphasis.

Horny marauding Viking kidnapper. Gosh, I wouldn't mind one of those myself, I mused. Imagine a gorgeous hunk of a man, hair in a ponytail, six o'clock stubble, brandishing an enormous sword. He'd wear a leather skirt and a fur cape, and smell of Chanel for Men. He would easily be able to lift me up to put me in his boat, and I'd look dead slim next to him. I frowned. But what would I be wearing?

I'll Google 'Vikings' for images.

Lulu stamped her foot in temper. 'Do you have an opinion

or not?' she snapped. 'I've just been sexually insulted and you're acting like nothing's happened.'

'Er, well, don't upset yourself,' I told her. At least you've had sex, I thought. 'It happens, you know.' I tilted my head in sympathy as she marched past.

'Not to me it doesn't!' she yelled. 'I'm good at what I do.' She tossed her hair in a circle, and folded her arms so tightly, her fingers turned white. 'It's just like being a fat aerobics instructor. Tell me, have you ever wondered why they bother? Huh, have you?'

I gazed at her. Aerobics instructors? Had I missed something?

'Fat aerobics instructors might as well get fatter and fatter. What's the point of working your backside off if your arse is the size of a bus and stays that way? Well, I should just have watched *Deal or No Deal.*' She jabbed her finger in my face. 'Do you get my point?'

I nodded knowingly. Too bloody right I got her point. I've been to aerobics once.

'Oh well, the next one can only be better,' I offered, improvising.

'Men like him should be deported,' she snapped.

'Where would you suggest they be deported to?'

'Out of London for starters.'

I held a dress in front of me, gazed in the mirror and wondered how many vinos I'd had when I bought it. It was neon green. I tossed it on the 'to go' pile on the floor, and delved back into the wardrobe. This tidying-up lark is exhilarating. Why hadn't I thought to do it before? It takes no time at all, I'm finding things I'd forgotten I had, and with fewer clothes cramming the rails I can see what's what. Yes, there was definitely a semblance of order taking shape, and it was pretty damn rewarding.

'I've made a decision,' Lulu said, resolute.

'What's that then?'

'I am not sleeping with a man unless he's taken me out on three dinner dates. So, if this ever happens again, at least I'll have enjoyed three pleasant evenings in fabulous restaurants with exquisite food and fine wines.' She bounced back onto the bed.

'And,' she crossed her arms triumphantly, 'I told Esme the surgery cleaner what a crap shag he is, which is the equivalent of a BBC news flash, so his reputation's shot to bits.' She nestled back against the headboard and tucked a strand of long blonde hair behind her ear. 'I buried his mobile phone in a pot of chilli con carne on my way out of his flat as well. It's not as though I want to hear from him again, is it?' she reasoned, smiling at her Tiffany ring. I turned from the wardrobe to face her.

'Why did you finish with Marcus?' I asked. A guy she'd dated for three months before finishing with him on Valentine's Day. She tapped her finger on her cheek, thinking hard.

'Do you know, I can't remember. Marcus was willies and willies ago.' Her attention drifted. 'What are you doing?'

'What does it look like? I'm clearing out my wardrobe.'

'Why?' she asked, giving a bewildered shrug.

'Why do people normally clear out their wardrobes?'

She polished off my wine and studied the bottom of the empty glass.

'Haven't got a bloody clue. I don't see the point myself.' She wafted gracefully from the bed, pulled her tunic over her head and wriggled out of her trousers. 'Do you think we should go to a slimming club?' she asked, tugging on my arm. 'Take your clothes off, and stand beside me, in front of the mirror.' I stepped out of my shorts and pulled my T-shirt over my head.

'Not bad,' she said, drawing in her tummy. 'I mean, we're not size zero, but, well, we don't have wobbly bits. And we are twenty-six, we're not eighteen any more.' She flashed her bum to the mirror. 'I hate those new pants, the low-cut briefs. I prefer the high-leg. I couldn't find any in Marks and Spencer yesterday,' she complained. 'Do you think the nation's lingerie designers are of the opinion that the entire British female population have developed square arses?'

I nodded, scrutinising my own figure and wishing my boobs were smaller.

'You're fine. I mean, you're a C-cup, I'm a D, so of course I'd think you're fine,' she said.

Lulu is beautiful. As well as thick blonde hair and huge brown eyes, she has long sweeping eyelashes and amazing high cheekbones. But in fairness, and she would be the first to agree, I'm not too bad looking either, with my unusual combination of dark brown hair and pale blue eyes. We both have slimmish, longish legs we tend not to appreciate and size twelve backsides which we're prone to obsess over.

She's a district nurse. It's mind-blowing, because I know her for the drunken party animal she is. The only bedside manner I can associate with her is condom related. But apparently she's the most popular and hardest-working district nurse in her practice. Her appointments are booked in ten-minute slots. She says she loves her job. Secretly, I think she enjoys whipping down knickers and stabbing as many buttocks an hour with a needle as she can.

'We're out of toilet paper, bread, bin bags . . . in fact, everything. We need to do a food shop. And we're down to our last four bottles of wine,' she said, still studying her profile. She prodded the cellulite on her thighs, sighed, and knelt to scoop up her clothes. 'Get dressed. We'll go now.'

'What about this lot?' I asked, flapping my hand towards the mountain of clothes on the floor.

'Stick it back in the wardrobe,' she suggested, with a dismissive backward wave.

I am not sticking it back in the wardrobe, I thought, indignantly. I'd never get round to clearing it out again. I've started getting this place into shape and I'm determined to complete the task. I tucked the clothes under the bed. I suppose I could sort it out properly another time, there's no real rush.

'Ready?' Lulu hollered from the front door.

Chapter Two

Lulu and I share a ground-floor garden flat in a three-storey Victorian building in Tooting, south-west London, the initial purchase having been hugely financed by my parents. The view from our lounge window is three green wheelie bins and a bus stop. On this beautiful July afternoon, our six-foot-square patch of grass was awash with colour, as our one and only rose bush flourished with two beautiful flower heads, both of which Lulu knocked off with her handbag rushing towards the gate.

Lulu's driving terrifies me. She reversed out of the driveway onto the main road. I buried my face in my handbag. It took a seven-point turn, but she was glossing her lips at the time, so she did brilliantly considering she could only use her left hand. As the car shot forward, my neck snapped back and my feet instinctively stamped in search of the non-existent dual controls. I gripped the roof handle, otherwise I'd end up nosediving her crotch when she turned right.

'You might like to listen to the engine,' I hedged, noticing she was pushing fifty and still in third gear.

'The engine? Why listen to the engine? Let's listen to Beyoncé,' she suggested, switching on the CD player. 'AAAAHHHH!'

My innards churned.

'What!?' I shrieked, gripping my chest with fright.

She covered her eyes with her left hand whilst her right hand piloted the steering wheel.

'I thought that lorry was going to hit us. I couldn't watch,' she panicked.

My heart was going like a bongo drum. I threw her a sideways glance. Near collision over, she studied her eyebrows in the rear view mirror.

'Remind me to borrow your tweezers when we get home. Don't let me forget. I look like Animal from the Muppets,' she grumbled.

We arrived at Tesco and she strode purposefully through the car park, leaving me to jog behind her.

'Come on, hurry up,' she tossed over her shoulder.

I quickly doubled back to squash some money in a Salvation Army collection box. I'd had a chat with God in the car. Firstly, I'd asked for safe deliverance to Tesco, and secondly, I'd asked him to make me slimmer or, failing that, to make Lulu fatter. I'd be devastated if she could fit into my Diesel jeans and I couldn't. I'd promised to donate to good causes if he helped me out.

Lulu could make an Olympic sport out of pushing a shopping trolley.

'We don't need chocolate spread. And biscuits are fattening. Buy low-fat cheese. I'm aiming to lose half a stone this week,' she prattled.

She trolleyed, torso bent, at high speed towards the Wines and Spirits aisle.

'Kate Moss is a pipe cleaner and she likes a drink. Grab the leaves,' she added bossily, meaning the salad.

'Buy one bottle of Pinot Grigio, get one free. So we might as well buy five to get five for nothing, and six bags of Walkers crisps. I can't be a saint all the time. Oh, oh,' she gasped, falling to her knees in worship of the sparkling Prosecco. 'It's expensive, but we deserve it.'

'Er, thought you wanted to lose half a stone this week,' I reminded her.

'Well, I will if we've got bugger all else to eat but crisps and salad, won't I?' She stole a French stick from an unsuspecting woman's basket.

'Put that back,' I hissed, my eyes darting a quick left and right in fear of witnesses.

'I'm doing her a favour. She's got an arse as big as Brighton; I need that French stick to keep me sober and there's none left in the bakers,' she justified, marching forward.

Back at home we opened a bottle of wine and unpacked the shopping.

'I've got a surprise for you,' Lulu announced. 'Guess what I bought?'

'A giant bar of chocolate?' I replied, hopeful.

Grinning, she sipped her drink.

'Nope, it's much better than that.' Putting down her glass, she delved into the last of the shopping bags.

'A decent bottle of wine that wasn't on special offer?'

'Nope, better than that too.' She hopped from one foot to the other.

'Well, if I can't eat or drink it, I don't want to know.'

'Yep, you do,' she insisted. 'You do.' She whipped a couple of boxes from behind her back. 'Da da, da da,' she sang.

I glared at them. 'They're fitness DVDs,' I said flatly. She nodded.

'I bought them when you were at the cash desk and I popped over to pick up some magazines. We're going to have a night in and do a workout. Change into your gym kit and meet me in the lounge.' She placed our empty wine glasses in the sink with exaggerated care and ushered me through the kitchen door. 'Come on,' she cajoled. 'Chop, chop.'

Lulu has frequent mad notions. Subsequently, we have a hall cupboard full of rubbish. We have ice skating boots, squash and tennis racquets, Italian language tapes, bowling shoes, two crash helmets for a moped she never bought, a fold-up mountain bike that has never seen daylight (in fact, it's never been unfolded) and a set of twenty-five A-Z encyclopaedias.

I strolled into the lounge. Lulu was leaning against the cast iron fireplace, examining the DVDs. I snuggled comfortably in the corner of our navy chintz sofa and took a second to admire our recent handiwork. Lulu and I had decorated the flat. After three days of raucous arguments, and testing twenty-eight sample paint pots, we'd decided on magnolia in the bedrooms, magnolia in the lounge, magnolia in the bathroom and magnolia in the hallway. And thanks to my chums at Visa, we'd splashed out and laid a spongy powder-blue carpet throughout.

There's a distressed (to the point of falling to bits) chocolate leather armchair in the corner, a Mexican-pine coffee table in front of the fireplace and a matching dining table in the window alcove, which doubles as a computer desk. A huge bronze chandelier dominates the centre of the room. It's stunning, but bounces off the skull of anyone taller than a troll. There are also nineteen church candles of various heights and girths looming on, over and across the fireplace, thanks to some pissed Internet shopping by Lulu. The overall effect provides the perfect setting for a rampant Black Lace session, or a wake.

'Right, let's get this show on the road,' Lulu boomed with authority. 'Mel B looks amazing. Shall we try hers?' She waved the box to illustrate the slender and toned Melanie.

'Well, we don't need to lose weight; we just need to tone up. Let's try the Geri Halliwell one, *Geri Body Yoga*,' I suggested.

'I want to lose a bit of weight from my boobs. Is there a DVD to help with that?' she asked, tossing the boxes to me, one at a time. I eyed her D-cups and laughed. Surgery was surely her only option. 'I'd appreciate it if you could take this seriously,' Lulu sniffed. 'Diet and exercise play a crucial role in maintaining a healthy and well-balanced lifestyle. Sometimes I despair at your slothful attitude.'

Slothful? I thought. She's the one with coffee cups and wine gums soldered to her dressing table.

We agreed on *Learn to Step* and stood side-by-side, eyes fixed on the television. It was torturous, complicated and, in my opinion, dangerous. I was wilting and sorely tempted to suggest we watch *Friends* instead. And Lulu, who was eagerly adding a bit of bounce to her lunges, was nearing physical collapse.

The end of the warm-up flashed on the screen.

'Shall we take a break?' I wheezed, bent double.

With forced reluctance she agreed, and we both flopped down on the sofa.

'Do you think we should watch it for a bit? We don't understand the technical terminology, do we?' I pointed out lamely. 'When she says "horseshoe" or "step-touch", we have to stop and watch to see what she means so we end up missing the beat.'

Lulu dabbed a line of sweat from her top lip with one of our new cream cushions.

'Yes, yes, of course, I was thinking exactly the same thing myself. We should definitely familiarise ourselves with the routines first.' She swiped her brow with the back of her hand. 'I'll fetch us a drink. We don't want to dehydrate.'

She returned with a bottle of wine propped in an ice bucket and two glasses.

'OK, we'll watch it through once and then do it ourselves,' she stated decisively, handing me a full-to-the-brim glass. She settled on the sofa next to me and stretched her legs alongside mine, on the coffee table. We sipped our wine as our heartbeats steadied, and studied our trainers.

'So,' she sighed, 'you need a job. Have you registered with an agency?'

'Well, no.' I gave a throaty cough. 'I've, well, I've decided on a career change to be honest, so—'

'A career change!' she interrupted.

I already had a speech prepared. I adopted Miss Moneypenny tones.

'We spend all our money on eating, pissing it up and going on holiday—'

'At least no one can accuse us of wasting it,' she reasoned.

'Exactly. But, well, I started thinking about how great it would be to do all those things and get paid for it.'

She wiggled curious brows. 'So you're looking for a job as a fat, wine-guzzling ice cream seller?'

I hid behind my glass.

'No . . . I want to be a tour guide,' I told her.

She swivelled to face me.

'Oh, you do?' she said.

'Yes, I do,' I replied, matter-of-fact.

'Since when?'

I faltered. 'Since, well, since . . . since we've been watching the holiday programme on a Monday night,' I admitted.

'We watch that forensic science programme on a Tuesday. Why don't you get a job as a coroner and start chopping up bodies. Start with the doctor I slept with; he doesn't need his flute.' She jabbed the remote control, switching the television off. 'You don't know the first thing about being a tour guide!'

'What is there to know?' I shot back.

Lulu slurped some of her wine. 'I don't know what there is to know, do I? Because I'm a district nurse, and you don't know because you studied Media.'

'I want to travel, meet lots of new people and get paid to do it.' I squirmed. This sounded obtuse and hollow even to me.

'In that case, have you considered a career as an astronaut? You,' she said, pointing an accusatory finger, 'are the last person I'd put forward for a job as a tour guide.'

I tucked my legs beneath my bum and rounded on her.

'Why? It's not as though there's such a thing as a degree in Touring, is there?'

She thumped her glass on the table and began counting on her fingers.

'One,' she reproached, 'you have no sense of direction. Two,' she stared at me with unblinking brown eyes, 'your suitcase was the subject of a security-controlled explosion when we went to Spain, and we ended up in custody in Malaga for eleven hours until your dad bailed us out. Three,' she shivered and addressed the ceiling, 'and the worst experience of my life by far, was when the police were called to our hotel in Turkey. Fourteen silk carpets were delivered to our room because *you* were practising your Turkish or Arabic or French or whatever that language was that you made up with the old man in the shop. You thought he was talking about his fourteen children! The carpets beat us back from the market! I thought you were dead clever and multilingual, and all the while you were talking out your arse. And I was doing lots of nodding because I wanted to look dead clever and multilingual as well.'

'You,' I reminded her smugly, 'cried your eyes out in Turkey.'

'Too right I cried. I've seen that film, *Midnight Express*. We were ambushed by three policemen, the hotel manager, that

15

lunatic dwarf carpet salesmen, and his two seven-foot heavies.' She reached for the wine bottle and discovered it was empty. 'I thought we were never going to get out of that one. I nearly wet myself when that policeman took his handcuffs out of his pocket.' She heaved a sigh and shuddered. 'And don't you ever forget that you have me to thank for your freedom, because if I hadn't passed out with fright and the British Embassy hadn't gotten involved, we'd have been done for. I couldn't speak for two days! Remember you thought I'd gone mute so you bought me a writing pad and an Etch A Sketch?'

'Anyway,' I said, dismissing her sarcasm with a wave of my hand, 'I think I have a natural aptitude for socialising and creating a jolly party atmosphere.'

'Yeah, you do,' she agreed forcefully, 'but then you pass out and wake up with a hangover twelve hours later. Do you mean to tell me that you're contemplating taking responsibility for escorting people to a foreign land with the aim of bringing them back in one piece? It just won't happen, trust me.' She emptied her glass. 'If you bag a job as a tour guide, someone will sue you, or you'll end up on News at Ten, or God knows what. You're the least suited candidate for a job like that.' She stood to tidy the table. 'You couldn't organise a piss-up in a brewery.'

She *does* exaggerate. My brain whirled for something to fire back with. It didn't take long.

'Hah,' I blurted, 'look who's talking.' I pointed an accusatory finger.

'What?' she retorted, bristling.

'You booked us on that nightmare City Slickers Break. How could you mistake a shop-till-you-drop extravaganza for a long weekend in the desert?'

'The website was misleading,' she insisted hotly.

'Misleading?' I spat. 'We both had an allergic reaction to the fleas or bugs or whatever creature it is that hover around a horse's arse. We suffered horrific, and what we worried might have been permanent, constipation because our backsides refused to have a number two in the open air.'

Her fingers whispered over now-flaming cheeks.

I was on a roll ... 'We had to borrow smelly clothes from smelly men, which were ten sizes too big for us, because we'd packed smart-casual and evening wear. We arrived at that revolting ranch wearing Chloe stilettos. Remember? Eh? And that hag of a cook had to lend us shoes and they looked like dead ferrets. In fact, we don't know that they weren't dead ferrets,' I chided. 'And you shagged that cowboy! You kept calling him Hawk, when his name was Hank, and I had to sleep in our tent *all by myself*, which was terrifying. I even started wondering who I could shag, just for the sake of a bit of company, so I let that dingo, hyena thing sleep with me, because I thought it was a dog, only to discover I was lucky not to have been eaten, and—'

She raised the flat of her hand. 'We each lost half a stone, if you remember,' she interrupted defensively.

'Yes, we did, but only because we were ravaged by disease and malnutrition from living in the wild like, like, savages.'

'We were not living in the wild.'

'What were we doing then?'

'Camping.'

'Exactly ... camping! Why, since the invention of hotels, would anyone want to do that?' Lulu tossed her hair over her shoulder in a sharp jerky movement. I ploughed on. 'And remember the rash? The rash we had that kept us locked in this flat together for nine days?' Her face crumbled at the memory. 'You turned all the mirrors to the wall, and sat in the bath crying for hours on end. And I got that massive lump on my head when I fainted on your bedroom floor because you had so much calamine lotion on your face that when I came in with a cup of tea I thought you were dead and rigor mortis had set in.'

Her mouth formed an indignant rosebud. 'Let's have a gin and tonic before we go to bed,' she suggested pinkly.

As usual, we drank too much. Despite this, I still didn't manage to get much sleep. The piercing wail of the timer on the cooker woke me three times. On cue, Lulu leaped out of bed, belted down the hallway, thundered into the lounge and dived onto the computer. She's bidding for a chaise longue on eBay. She tells me it's George IV, circa 1825, with scrolled foliate decoration in pure gold leaf and upholstered in crimson damask. I pointed out it won't fit in the cupboard under the stairs with the rest of her crap if she hates it. In anticipation of winning the auction, she's bought a huge crystal fruit bowl and filled it with red grapes and green apples. I think she fancies herself as a naked Renaissance slut, draped over her antique chair, brushing her long hair. I've made it clear that I refuse to sit in the lounge watching *Friends* if she's in the scud lying next to me.

I bolted upright and bashed the quilt.

'Can't you use your mobile as an alarm!?' I shrieked.

'I left it at work. Only five minutes of bidding to go.'

I shuffled to lie on my face and stuffed my head under the pillow. Sean Connery and I . . . no, not Sean Connery, he's a living relic. I'm not even sure he's still alive. Er . . . who can I have? George Clooney? No, he's as grey as a badger. Let me think . . . I can't even have Antonio Banderas because he'll be drawing his pension before I'm forty. I don't want to find myself wiping slobber from my husband's face, even if he is a world-famous actor and multimillionaire to boot. So, I'll have . . . And just as I was deliberating who to bonk for the night and eventually marry, a big lump landed on top of me.

'I got it, I got it! Amazing, it closed at three hundred and fifty quid. It should have cost four times that. I'd make money just by putting it back up again.'

'Fabulous,' I said, with a weary sigh.

'Yes, fabulous,' Lulu echoed, leaping from my bed and skipping out of my room.

I could have Brad Pitt, couldn't I? Wait! What am I thinking? My Viking! Yes, I'll have him. Why not? We can be naked tonight until I have time to Google up a couple of outfits.

PARIS

Chapter Three

I decided to have a day off from both my diet and spring-cleaning, and concentrate all my efforts on finding a job. I sauntered down the High Street to the newsagents where, on the recommendation of a ten-year-old rocket scientist, I bought the *Travel Trade Gazette* and *Travel Weekly*.

'I'm sure these are the most likely publications to assist in your pursuit of employment,' he had informed me.

'You think?' I'd replied in a chummy fashion, squinting lop-sidedly at the magazines tucked under his arm: *Mathematics Grade III* and *Plus Maths*. This kid is bright, I'd thought.

It was a beautiful sunny day, exactly what you'd expect for early July. I settled on a pavement table at Bar Thea, the wine bar opposite the flat, which is the perfect location if you don't mind perfume à la car exhaust or the Great Unwashed Male striding past en route to Tooting Broadway tube station. Costas, the waiter, frisbeed a latte in front of me, and then hot-footed after a girl wearing a skirt as wide as a hairband. I would have pre-ferred a cappuccino but I knew that while he was on the totty trail, nothing short of standing on a chair and doing a bit of semaphore would bring him back. I spread my newspapers on the table and sipped my coffee meditatively. My spirits rose; there were loads of ads for jobs within the travel industry. I wiggled my pink highlighter aloft and scanned the page.

My friend, neighbour and owner of the bar, Nikki, materialised beside me. He picked up a chair, spun it around and straddled it. I felt my happy smile fade. I'd hoped for a bit of privacy while I was job hunting. Nikki has black shoulder-length hair, which he wears tied back, and chocolate almond-shaped eyes, fringed with thick black eyelashes. He's a born and bred Londoner of Greek descent. Handsome, I'll admit, but you'd have to execute a nationwide search to find a more lecherous slut-bucket. Mind you, it's not entirely his fault. It's pathetic to watch the way women dribble all over him. All he has to do is coquettishly wiggle one eyebrow at them, and they're frothing at the mouth and whipping their knickers off in no time. That's the end of the courtship, and the beginning of a relationship that lasts anything between three hours and two days, depending on how long it takes his shag-a-barometer to locate another throbbing G spot.

Right now, he was trying to persuade me to go to the gym with him.

'Nikki, I don't fancy it,' I said impatiently. 'Go annoy someone else.' I lifted my newspaper from the table and hid behind it.

'Evie, you have no hobbies. Come with me, just this once.'

My face creased in annoyance. I gave an irritated sigh.

'If you don't like it, you don't have to come again,' he said.

'Why do you want me to go?' I asked.

'Because I'll get three months' free membership if you join,' he admitted.

'I won't join.'

'You might.' He swiped my newspaper and whipped it behind his back. 'Evie, it'll do you good.' I doubted it.

He linked his arm through mine. 'Sweetheart, give it a go,' he pleaded.

'Nik, *n-o*,' I punctuated.

He pinched my cheek, he pulled my hair, he blew a raspberry in my ear, he walloped my knee with a spoon, he dropped an ice cube down my T-shirt and he sat on my lap. I caved in.

'OK,' I agreed reluctantly. 'Now, give me my newspaper back.'

He brightened as he handed it back to me. 'We'll go this afternoon. Make sure you're ready by four o'clock.'

I felt a flurry of panic. 'Err, I was thinking along the lines of next Friday or Saturday,' I backpedalled. 'Not today. I mean, I'm busy. I've got a lot to do, and—'

A beefy bicep clamped my neck tight. Nikki tugged my head towards him and gave me a noisy kiss on the cheek. 'Be ready,' he warned, slowly standing. 'Oh, you're not working, are you?' he asked, gesturing to my newspapers on the table. 'Can you help out in here a week on Thursday? My dad wants the day off.'

'Me? I've never worked as a waitress.'

'It's a slave I want. You'll learn,' he said, and I suspect he wasn't entirely joking.

I grimaced. 'Nik, I don't think I can. I'm busy job hunting and—'

He gripped my chin between his thumb and forefinger, lowered his head and eyed me shrewdly. His breath was warm on my cheek. 'Do you want to tell an old man he can't go to his hospital appointment just because you refuse to give me a couple of hours of your time?' He swivelled my face towards his dad, who was sitting on the adjacent table, sucking greedily on an inhaler, massaging his chest. He gave me a cheery wave. I swallowed.

'OK,' I heard myself say.

'Don't mind if I take my leave, do you? The bar's getting busy.

Evie,' he said, eyeing my newspaper. 'You don't need to find another job. If you turn out to be a good little slave, I'll keep you,' he added, giving me a devilish wink.

After Nikki left, I highlighted quite a few ads, made some calls and, would you believe it, I only managed to secure an interview for a guide's position. It's scheduled for the day after tomorrow with Insignia Tours, a tour operator based in Trafalgar Square that specialises in European city breaks. Elated, I finished my coffee and crossed the road to the travel agent where I picked up a selection of City Break brochures. I also popped into Blockbuster to see if I could find any travel-related DVDs. I needed something relatively educational, so I chose *Alfie*. I mean, how hard can this be? And Jude Law is a ride.

Back at home, I snuggled on the sofa, studied *Vogue Paris* and watched my movie. I must say, this all seemed incredibly straight-forward. Much jollied by my newly acquired expertise and understanding of the travel industry, I arrived at the conclusion that I may already be one of the best tour guides on the circuit, although technically, I admit, undiscovered.

Nikki turned up at the flat at four o'clock on the dot. He kept his finger on the bell until I answered the door.

'I'm not bloody deaf,' I yelled, marching down the communal hallway.

He stood by the garden wall, arms folded and legs apart, watchful. I closed the door and trudged down the path behind him. I was knackered just walking to the Sports Centre. When we arrived, he spun the revolving door with the flat of his hand. I missed the exit and was left circling inside. Helpfully, he reached in and hauled me out by the hair.

I gripped his meaty arm and leaned against his shoulder to steady my heartbeat as he flashed his membership card to the lusting receptionist. Ah! An oasis of sorts, I thought, when I spotted two armchairs in the corner of the reception area. Perfect, I decided, shimmying round him. I'll have a rest. My backside was seconds from touchdown when a commanding grip clamped my elbow and shot me into orbit down the corridor and through the doors of the gym.

'Right, take those out for a start,' Nikki said, pointing to my earrings. 'And double knot your laces.' I unclipped my earrings. He thumped his palm on the handrail of the treadmill. 'Get on and I'll show you what to do.'

I sighed and ambled forward. 'Nikki, we've walked here from the flat,' I protested, handing him my earrings. 'I don't really think I need to go for a walk on a machine as well, do you?' I held his gaze, dropped my chin and raised my arms to tighten my ponytail.

'You're not walking,' he said forcefully. 'You're running. Get on.'

Oh well, I brooded, I'm here now. I might as well show him what I'm made of. I stepped robustly onto the treadmill. I am, after all, young, strong and healthy. I readied myself with poise and gave Nikki a confident 'ready when you are' nod. He switched the machine on and I started to jog, then trot. Rather stylishly, I might add. Every inch the Bond Girl. I bobbed my ponytail, breathed evenly and, when I was confident I wasn't going to scooter off the back, I let go of the handrail and added a bit of elbow power. On and on I darted, at speed. And then, blow me if I wasn't sprinting. Gosh, I'd always dismissed the marathon, thought I couldn't do it, but here I was running for my life. I breathed laboriously – in, out, in, out. On and on I raced, like a human bullet. Ah, I decided, I'll move the ironing pile from our treadmill at home and run for an hour or so every night. Yes, I will, I will. If only I hadn't left it so long. This is so invigorating, and energising, and stimulating. Oh! A sharp pain! It's just a stitch, I told myself. I pushed on. I can do it, yes I can. Actually, I was starting to feel a bit nauseous. I gulped, panted and gripped my side. A little blip, I mused. On I zoomed. Nikki stood like a sentry at the head of the machine.

'How many minutes have I done?' I gasped, exhilarated. I mopped my feverish brow.

'One,' I thought I heard him say.

On and on I sprinted, feet pounding and arms pumping. My ponytail spun like a windmill sail.

'How many minutes, Nikki?' I managed, breathless. The bile rose in my mouth and there was a ringing noise in my ear.

'Still one,' he said nonchalantly.

I bashed my ear. The ringing stopped, but a buzzing started. 'Nikki, it cannot still be one minute,' I wheezed. 'Impossible.'

'It is,' he said, studying his fingernails.

I gripped the handrail. I felt sick. Beads of sweat trickled down my neck. I reeled and swayed, then bent double, resting my forehead on the handrail. My feet kept running. God, I was on the point of death. My head lolled loosely from side to side and I tried to fill my lungs with air. A wounded high-pitched howl filled the gym. It was me. I clutched my chest.

'Aggg, I'm having a heart attack!' I yowled.

The machine stopped. I gasped, and then, just like an Olympic gold medallist, I gave in to tears. Nikki sighed indulgently, circled my waist, lifted me off the machine and dropped me onto the floor.

'Off you get.' He glanced at the clock. 'One and a half minutes. Not bad,' he said.

I sniffed and wiped my nose with the back of my hand and let him lead me towards the torture implements in front of the mirror. He offered a brief demonstration on each apparatus before I had to do it myself.

'I'm tired. I want to go home,' I wailed.

'I'll keep the weights down for you,' he smiled, squeezing my arm. 'Sweetheart, you're doing really well,' he lied.

I rubbed my eyes with clenched fists. 'Nikki, I can't do this.'

'You can.'

'I don't want to.'

'You do.'

I followed him, the will to fight and live fading. He dragged me from one torturous contraption to the next. I huffed, puffed, staggered and grunted.

'One last machine,' he encouraged through gritted teeth. I sniffed.

'Nikki, I don't want to do it. And I'm not joining.'

'I don't want you to join. I'd rather pay double the membership fee than see you in here again.' He grabbed my wrist, forcing me to totter unsteadily behind him. 'But you're here now, so you're finishing the circuit,' he said sharply.

He stood behind me, snaked an arm around my waist and lifted me so I was straddling the bench. With the palm of his hand he pressed between my shoulder blades, forcing me face down.

'The quicker you get started, the quicker you'll finish.' He lifted my legs onto the bench. 'Right, hold onto the handles at each side of your head and straighten your legs.' My nose was squashed against the bench. I raised my chin to look for the handles. 'OK, the weights on your ankles will make it harder for you to lift your legs. This machine is good for firming up your backside. That said, your backside looks pretty good to me, but I suppose there's always room for improvement. Do twenty reps,' he ordered.

I snarled inwardly, squeezed my eyes shut and pressed my

heels towards my backside. This is the last one, this and then I can go home and have a glass of wine and a bag of crisps. Two reps and my thighs ached. I hate this gym, I thought, and I hate Nikki. I'd get my own back, somehow. Four reps and my ankles throbbed. Five reps. I had a stitch again. I grunted. Six reps. Seven. Mmmmmm. Wait . . .

I heaved. Is that . . .? No, it can't be. My groin was tingling. My eyes flew open. It was the unmistakable, yes, the unmistakable warm pre-orgasm tickle. I'd know it anywhere. Well, you would, wouldn't you?

I wriggled my hips into the bench. I swivelled my head so I faced the window rather than Nikki's groin. A breathtaking ripple-prickle shot to my tutu. I was right! Bloody hell. It must be the angle of the weights or maybe the seam in my leggings. God knows, and who cares, because it was definitely there. This was, unquestionably, my favourite exercise. Nikki counted. I quickened the pace, lifting my legs faster and higher. I should get a membership. Yes, an annual membership, nothing less would do. Nikki was right to bring me here. I'd make the effort and spend all my spare time working out. Didn't I have plenty of that at the moment – spare time? Yes, I should keep fit. I now understand the need to stay in shape.

'Uggggh,' I grunted, when a sharp pain shot up my nostril. I perched on my chin, to stop my nose gouging a dent in the bench.

'Well done, Evie. You've managed twenty reps,' Nikki boomed from somewhere in the distance.

I kept the pace. Oh. My. God. I must buy one of these machines for the flat. I can't wait to tell Lulu.

'OK, Evie. Off you get,' Nikki commanded. 'That's enough. You'll strain yourself.'

I inhaled ecstatically as a succession of jiving worms travelled south.

27

'Get off!' Nikki bellowed.

'Leave me, leave me, I'm fine,' I gasped, breathless. 'I'mmmm fine.' I think I'd managed about seventy-two reps.

'No,' he spat angrily. 'The last thing I want is for you to injure yourself.'

'Nikki, leave me alone.' I was no more than five seconds from ecstasy . . . four seconds, three, two . . .

'Evie, stop it. Stop it now.'

My body jerked and twitched like a landed trout as I was overcome by wave after wave of pleasure. And then I slumped forward and shuddered, luxuriating in the after-tickles.

Nikki pounced.

'Get. Off.'

I sighed. I'd forgotten about him.

'Off.'

He lifted the bar from my ankles and hoisted me to standing. My legs wobbled. I gripped Nikki's arm for support. I felt light and floaty and happy.

'Do what I tell you next time. You're not used to exercise,' he snapped, shaking me by the elbow.

My groin throbbed, which was lovely, but so did my thighs and that was agony. My knees buckled. I landed on the floor with a thud, nose jammed in Nikki's belly button.

'What's got into you? I told you to do twenty reps because twenty is more than enough to begin with.' He gripped my elbows and helped me to my feet. 'Up you get.'

'I liked that machine,' I told him, deciding that keeping fit wasn't as tedious as I'd imagined. In fact, I'd recommend it.

Nikki took a step back, eyed me levelly, smiled and held my hands by my side. 'OK, but you have to be careful. You're too keen.'

PARIS

Chapter four

Back home, after my workout, I was sipping my second gin and tonic when Harry, our next-door neighbour, popped over with his dog, Lucsie, a white, long-haired Jack Russell.

In the last few months Harry has found walking his dog ever more difficult. When he knows I'm home, he'll often ring the bell and ask me to walk Lucsie for him. I don't mind. Harry is getting on a bit, and well, we're all going to grow old one day. I'm happy to help. It's nice to be nice, after all.

'Sure, Harry. I'll walk Lucsie,' I told him, accepting the leash from his outstretched hand.

'You're a good girl,' he praised, nodding appreciatively.

I closed the door and tugged Lucsie down the hallway. His furry face creased and wrinkled as he resisted the leash. He's a little devil, I thought, he knows what's coming. I tied the leash to the handrail of our treadmill, flicked the switch on and, tally-ho, he set off on his brisk walk around the park, along the riverbank, through the fields or wherever his doggy imagination chose to take him. His small pink tongue hung loosely from his mouth as he padded on reluctantly.

'Let me fix myself another fizzy drink and then I'll join you.' I might be unemployed, I thought, shaking the dregs from the gin bottle into my glass, but I still don't get a minute to myself.

I hadn't long taken Lucsie back to Harry when I heard the unmistakable sound of screeching brakes and Beyoncé.

'Hullooooo,' Lulu yodelled, as her key twisted in the lock of the door.

'In the lounge,' I shouted. I was sitting at the computer in the window alcove, studying the Insignia Tours website.

'Do you want a drink?' she asked, coming into the room and kicking her shoes behind the sofa. I squinted at my empty glass.

'Why not?'

Bloody hell, I fretted. I've never even heard of some of the cities this company promotes. I was suddenly grateful that my interview was for a position as a guide on their Paris breaks. At least I knew where France was. The tour company wanted a copy of my CV in advance of the interview. I frowned and peered worriedly at the screen. The stumbling block when you venture on a new career path is that you may have to embellish slightly about previous relevant experience. I sighed, twirled a strand of hair into a jaggy point and brushed my cheek. I might not get the job, I thought grimly. I wasn't qualified. But presidents don't have diplomas in, well, in President Training, do they? I mean, Ronald Reagan was an actor before he got the President's job. I sat upright, suddenly understanding. He lied, he lied big time on his CV. I smiled, congratulating him on his initiative. Yes, I bet he told some blinding whoppers. Inspired, my fingers danced over the keyboard.

Lulu elbowed the lounge door, cradling the wine bucket. 'What did you do today?' she asked, scraping the bucket on the edge of the dining table.

I told her I had a job interview lined up.

'If you're offered that job, without a shadow of a doubt

Missing Persons will become the busiest department in Scotland Yard.' She sloshed wine into two glasses, and moved towards me. I didn't want her to see what I was doing so I splayed myself across the PC screen. She lifted my arm.

'Sociology! Italian! German!' she shrieked. 'Have you had a brain transplant since leaving school that I know nothing about? Advanced Red Cross First Aider! You can't just credit yourself with medical qualifications.' She gestured with her glass towards the computer. 'Make yourself a doctor, why the hell not? Then you could apply for a surgeon's job in Harley Street.'

I rounded on her. 'You can talk! You put "Stamp Collector" and "Flying Instructor" on your CV.'

'They were hobbies, *not* qualifications. I could hardly list my hobbies as shopping and going down the pub, could I? And no one is likely to ask me to fly a Boeing 747 at the surgery, are they? So I won't get caught out.'

I dismissed her with a backward wave. 'Oh, they're only little lies,' I said, attaching my CV to an email saying how much I was looking forward to the interview.

'Mark my words,' she warned, 'this will all come back to bite you in the arse.'

I changed the subject and told her about my fabulous afternoon down the gym. Her eyes glistened with the promise of possibility.

'*Really?*' she said slowly. 'That is just what we need.' She bumped me off the edge of the chair and took over the keyboard. 'We'll buy that machine,' she said, cheeks flushed.

I frowned, surveying the lounge analytically. 'But where would we put it?' I asked.

Head bent, she bashed at the computer like a demon. 'What?' she mumbled, distracted.

I waved my hand randomly. 'Where would we put it?'

She tossed me an irritated glance. 'We'll chuck the bloody sofa out if it's as good as you say it is,' she snapped.

After an hour surfing the net she still hadn't found it. She was becoming fraught, agitated and pissed, having topped up her glass three times.

'Do you think it's hot in here?' she asked, flapping the mouse pad. She undid the top four buttons on her tunic. Her 34Ds jiggled as she typed at breakneck speed. She had eBay, two American gym-supply companies and three UK sites open. Shoulders hunched, she clicked the mouse manically. 'I mean, this is the kind of thing I've been looking for: an exercise routine I can enjoy and wouldn't mind sticking to. Something that would trim up my backside, tummy and legs.'

'We couldn't do without the sofa,' I pointed out lamely.

'Of course we could,' she snapped. 'Show some enthusiasm. I'm doing this for your benefit as well, you know.'

Eventually, she reluctantly conceded defeat.

'I'm so disappointed,' she sulked, almost tearful. 'I was looking forward to a new fitness regime.' She splashed the last of the wine into our glasses. 'OK,' she rallied, 'shall we defrost the Weight Watchers shepherd's pie?'

I moved to the sofa.

'So, what do you think of me having an interview lined up for a tour guide's job?' I asked.

Her brown eyes held mine. There was a beat of silence before she did a so-so gesture with her head. 'Oh, that. Yes, well, make sure you check the company profile on the web. You might end up kidnapped and forced into slavery in Yemen or whoring in King's Cross,' she said crisply. 'And anyway, wait until they meet you. Five minutes and you'll blow your own cover. I bet you won't even be able to find their offices.'

Chapter five

My sister Lexy rang early the following morning.

'You're still in bed, aren't you?' she challenged. 'I *know* it, because you took for ever to answer the phone.'

I peered blearily at the ceiling. I'd picked up on the fourth ring. 'So what's wrong with that?' I asked, massaging my temple with the heel of my hand. Pulling back the quilt, I swung my legs over the edge of the bed and stood up. My knees buckled and I slumped to the floor. There was a loud thwap as my cheek hit the carpet. Incredibly, I still held the phone to my ear.

'You've not forgotten I'm having my hair cut and that you're taking the twins to a birthday party, have you?'

'Of, of course not,' I winced. 'I'm, I'm looking forward to it,' I panted gamely, clawing up the side of my chest of drawers. I'd forgotten I'd worked out yesterday. I was certainly paying the price now.

'Are you shagging someone? You sound breathless,' she quizzed.

'No! Of course I'm not.' I wobbled, stumbled backwards and flopped back onto the bed.

'Don't be late,' she said and hung up.

I spent twenty minutes massaging my legs with body lotion

before attempting to stand and stagger to the bathroom. I dressed with care and put on a purple silk mini dress, matching slingback sandals and a fitted denim jacket. An exploration of my newly accessible wardrobe produced a black velvet shoulder bag with lilac trim. Silver hoop earrings and my purple leopard print silk scarf completed the outfit. A party is a party after all. I rushed from the flat, scarf billowing, jumped in my car and made it to Hampton in twenty minutes. Lexy stood sentrified in the doorway of her Victorian vanilla-painted detached house, tapping her watch impatiently.

'I've got ten minutes to get to the hairdresser's. I was about to report you missing,' she complained.

My sister is two years older than me. We were occasionally mistaken for twins when we were younger, but not any more, because now we look nothing like each other. In fact, these days, she doesn't even look *human*. She paid four hundred and fifty quid to have her eyebrows modelled and tattooed so now she looks like a Vulcan from Star Trek. And by the state of her fringe you'd think she cuts it with a knife and fork. It's a short, jaggy, spiky mess but she insists she doesn't care if she looks like Lucifer's slut, so long as you can see her eyebrows.

'Here.' Lexy slapped a key and a sheet of paper in my hand. 'You might arrive back before me, so take the spare key. I've drawn you a map to the party,' she said, spinning on her heel, her Prada bag clutched to her chest.

I love looking after my three-year-old nieces. My two angels stood side by side in the hall, looking gorgeous in their pink party dresses. Lauren is shy, loving, caring and sensitive, with a warm, generous nature. She has striking emerald eyes, fringed with long eyelashes, and shoulder-length wavy brown hair. The perfect child. Becky is equally beautiful, with golden curls and indigo blue eyes, but – and this is a *significant* but – there's something *not quite right*. She's selfish and spiteful. She scrubs her face with her sleeve if you kiss her and wriggles out of your grasp if you try to give her a cuddle. I reckon she'd leave home and live on her own if she could. I look at her sometimes and wonder if perhaps there was a mix-up at the hospital, whereby this wicked baby sprite was foisted onto our family when in reality she's actually an evil changeling of *Omen* proportions.

Becky tilted her blonde head upward and proffered a demonic grin. The hair on my neck prickled as it often does when she looks at me. I cranked up a wobbly half smile in return. Long ago, I'd decided to be nice to her just in case she does possess evil powers and decides to get even when she's older. Perhaps I should pop into a church with her one day, sit in the pews and see if her head rotates or if she self-combusts. At least then I'd know. Of course I've never said anything to my sister. Obviously Lexy thinks Becky is normal. Well, she would, wouldn't she?

'OK, girlies. Party time,' I said, searching Becky's hairline for any tell-tale signs. You know, like the odd satanic tattoo.

I brushed their hair and sprayed a smidgen of Chanel No 5 behind their ears. 'Let's go,' I said brightly.

I tossed a loving glance over my shoulder. They waddled behind me, clutching a birthday present each. I wondered if my sister would mind if I took them to the jeweller's to have their ears pierced, but changed my mind when I remembered that I'd fainted when I'd had mine done.

I know there's no real need to dress up for a kids' party, and maybe I'd pushed the boat out a little bit too far but, honestly, some of the mothers might as well have come out wearing their dressing gowns. Baggy tracksuit bottoms are designed for the gym or the house, flip–flops are for the beach, and T-shirts covered in vomit and coffee are for the washing machine, so why anyone would venture out in public dressed in the whole hor-rific ensemble is, frankly, beyond my understanding. I introduced myself as 'auntie' and pretended not to notice several porridge-coated hair bangs. My priority was to entertain my precious babies, and so I propelled myself full throttle into party mode.

The twins didn't win anything at Pass the Parcel. I was furi-ous. The brat who won cheated – I saw him. He had one eye on the volume control knob of the CD player the whole time. I did holler 'Cheat! Cheat!' but no one cared so I was delighted when I saw that the gift he received wasn't really worth having. Becky was the last to guess at Pin the Tail on the Donkey, and she won. I'd cunningly nipped a slit in the eye mask. Fortunately, she's as devious as me and cottoned on straight away. I was so proud of her. She fumbled around blindly, little arms out-stretched, lips puckered in consternation, and then, hey presto, she pinned the tail in exactly the right spot. I nearly fell over clapping. Honest to God, how clever is she? She reminds me of myself.

During Musical Statues I managed to keep the twins in the game until the finish, as it was my job to decide who was 'out'. And so I made sure everyone was out, except them. There was a bit of a Steward's Enquiry when one little girl denied moving her arms, but my decision was final. It's only a bloody game. The twins were delighted when they were pronounced equal win-ners, by me. They each won a coloured whistle that was in the shape of a beautiful robin redbreast. I was so proud of them, especially Becky as she'd won two games out of three. Lunch was a revolting affair and I ate nothing. Suffice it to say, I'll never be buying Quavers or Skips again.

We sang 'Happy Birthday' to Samantha, the birthday girl, party bags were distributed and gratefully received and finally it was time to leave. Sally, Samantha's chubby, grim-looking mother, thundered down the hallway and flattened herself across the front door, blubbering that she'd found chewing gum in the party bags. She looked terrified. Bloody hell, I thought, we're only talking about a bit of bubbly, not puff or weed. She blamed her Swedish au pair. Privately I thought that the most pressing issue requiring her attention should be sacking her Swedish au pair and hiring a dumpy-frumpy Mrs Doubtfire. I smiled, thanked her for a delightful and enjoyable afternoon and shimmied down the hallway and out the door, a child gripping each hand. We skipped and sang 'Doh a Deer' all the way back to the car. I felt like Supernanny.

I was *sick to death* of the robin redbreast whistles before I'd even driven to the end of the road. What a stupid present to give a toddler. I was so demented by the ruckus that I slammed on the brakes at a green light, and caused two drivers behind me to swerve. One mounted the pavement and one veered to the other side of the road. They blared and honked their horns.

'Arse!' one driver bellowed.

'Legal braking distance applies!' I hollered back. I failed four driving tests, so I'm something of an expert on braking distance.

Becky tugged on a lock of long blonde hair. 'Arse,' she whispered conspiratorially to Lauren.

I swivelled around, almost garrotting myself with the seat belt. 'Give the birdies to auntie, darlings,' I pleaded through gritted teeth, arm outstretched. They handed over the whistles, then busied themselves rummaging through their party bags.

'Birdies fly,' I sang over my shoulder, catapulting the whistles out of the car window and into the bushes.

My heart was racing. The combination of traffic, kids, whistles and London drivers had completely eroded my patience. I closed my window and sighed heavily. I was shattered, and still *parked* at the front of the queue at the traffic lights, which were once again green. I checked my rear view mirror, expecting to see a fist-waving, pissed-off London cabby. Instead I was delighted to see the driver in the car behind screaming into her phone and glossing her lips. I shot forward just as the lights turned amber.

Halfway down Hampton Hill High Street I spotted Threshers and a bottle of Shiraz popped up in a think bubble before my eyes. I straightened my arms, squeezed the steering wheel and screeched from fourth gear down to stationary. I piloted the kids into the shop, grabbed three bottles of wine, paid with cash for speed and engineered the tricky assault course back to the car, past bottles of beer and stacked up boxes of cheap champagne glasses.

I strapped Becky in the back of the car. As I turned to lift Lauren I noticed a large gummy blue mess on the back of her head. I peered more closely and realised it was a blob of slimy bubblegum, about the size of a small table coaster. It was matted in Lauren's silky brown curls, which were beyond repair.

I ground my teeth. That airhead au pair, I cursed, and kicked the wheel of the car. I eyed the bottles of wine. I was tempted to swig straight from the neck, but I was too busy wrestling Lauren's hands from her hair.

'Don't touch your hair, darling. It's a weenie bit sticky.' I bound her wrists with my leopard print scarf, then frisked Becky's party bag to confiscate her bubblegum.

'Mine!' Becky shrieked, clutching the blue chewy bar.

'Not now, it isn't. It's mine!' I yelled. 'Giveittomegiveittome giveittome.'

Once we were all settled comfortably (well, I was comfortable: Lauren was tied up and Becky was howling), I drove to the end of the High Street and parked outside the card shop. I flicked a glance in my rear view mirror. The pair of them sat wide-eyed and expressionless.

'Out,' I ordered, heaving myself from the driving seat.

I was fast changing my mind about them being my precious angels. In the card shop I borrowed a pair of scissors to cut the bubblegum from Lauren's hair. I am *not* having my sister think I can't supervise and survive a simple outing to a children's party. If she notices that a portion of Lauren's hair is missing I'll just explain that Becky pulled it out. As I was chopping out the last couple of matted clumps, I spotted Becky cramming her pockets full of pencils.

'Put them back, Becks,' I warned.

'Mine,' she informed me.

'Becks. Put. Them. Back!'

She grabbed a handful of felt-tip pens, toddled towards me and jammed them in my pocket.

'We share,' she offered.

'Put them back!' I yelled.

She pouted, gathered her plunder and dumped the lot in a bin of cuddly toys. I struggled for calm.

'All finished, darling,' I said to Lauren with a sigh, as the last of the hairy bubblegum dropped to the floor. She slipped her tiny hand in mine and snuggled into my hip.

'Tank you nanty. Love you,' she said, emerald eyes dancing.

Unexpectedly, I felt nippy-eyed. I sniffed and blinked hard. I was drained. I'd had these kids around my feet all day. You have to experience it for yourself to know what it's like. It's all so, so stressful and exhausting, and me being single makes it a million times harder. I have to do everything myself. I don't have a partner to help, do I? It's just me on my own with these kids. They're self-centred, bloodsucking parasites that sponge every ounce of strength from you. I caught sight of my reflection in the glass display-cabinet, and felt a jolt of horror. My hair was limp and stringy, my lips anaemic and my eyes sunken and blank with misery. I sniffed. Now that I thought about it, I hadn't touched up my lipstick, sprayed perfume, brushed my hair, eaten or had a drink since I'd left home this morning. I can honestly say I have a tremendous respect for mothers of small children. I looked around at my little demons wretchedly. It was time to go.

Back in the car, I fastened the girls' seat belts. Engine on, two minutes' drive, and home, I thought thankfully. I felt like kissing the doorstep when we arrived. I almost pulled the gate from its hinges as I ushered the twins down the garden path. Lexy answered the door, swishing her head from side to side.

'Do you like my hair?' she beamed.

'Yes, it looks, erm, amazing. I'm in the biggest rush,' I said, prodding the kids through the doorway. She raised her tattooed eyebrows and fingered her Vulcan fringe.

'Why? Where are you going?' she quizzed. 'I thought you had the day to yourself?'

'Man coming to mend the washing machine and Lulu is working late. Can't live without my washing machine.' This was a big fat lie, but I'm so traumatised. Yes, that's the perfect word: traumatised. And I'm so exhausted and under threat of becoming unhinged that I suspect I might start to cry. Lexy agreed I couldn't live without a washing machine, but was reluctant to let me escape. She lurched forward and grasped my hand.

'I'm not sure about my hair,' she said. 'I've had layers put in.'

'It's lovely, really nice. I love it,' I enthused. 'You look like Princess Vulcan now, not just an ordinary Vulcan.' She rolled her eyes.

'Come in,' she pleaded. 'I'll put some make-up on, then perhaps I'll like it better. I'll make you a coffee, and I bought jam doughnuts. You like them, don't you?'

I prised her fingers from my wrist, prepared to break one if she didn't release me. A coffee was the last thing I needed. I was suffering from alcohol deficiency.

'Would love to, but I must dash,' I shot back. She clasped my forearms.

'I wish you didn't have to work. It would be lovely having you around during the daytime. You could help me with the kids,' she said. I think she meant it.

I bestowed big kisses all around and bounded like a gazelle to the car. Lauren stood in the doorway rubbing the back of her head, showing off her new haircut to her mum. Thankfully, Lexy was too busy checking her own reflection in the glass door panel to notice or care. My Renault Clio rocketed forward on take-off as I accelerated from nought to sixty. I needed Tooting, my dressing gown and a glass of Shiraz sharpish. And a job, I thought, as I caught sight of the kids waving in my rear view mirror. I simply must get that job. I can and I will.

Chapter Six

Running late for my interview, I clattered through Tooting Broadway station, cursing my black stilettos. I jumped onto the train and scanned the carriage. There was one remaining empty seat. A young backpacker was headed towards it. I beetled forward, shimmied behind him and gave him a discreet little hip bump. He tumbled forward, helped by the weight on his back. I scrambled into the seat, and made myself comfortable.

I heaved my Baedeker Paris guidebook from my bag and flicked through the pages trying to commit as many facts and figures to memory as I could. I felt jittery, nervous and sweaty-palmed. I *wanted* this job. And it's not as though I can be myself. Obviously, that's the last person I should be, because *myself* stood no chance whatsoever of getting this job.

Oh, for goodness' sake. I'm not auditioning for *X Factor*. I sat up and crossed one leg over the other. Who's better than me? I thought, twisting the strap of my bag into a leather blob. 'Who's better?' I muttered aloud, feeling the onset of diarrhoea.

I got off at Charing Cross and marched with a determined stride through the station, down the Strand, across Trafalgar Square, towards Cockspur Street, all the while chanting 'yes I can, yes I can'.

Very impressive, I thought, as I pushed the heavy smoked-glass door of Insignia Tours. Black leather sofas were placed either side of a large glass coffee table, prints of various European cities adorned the walls and large artificial palm trees flanked each of the three elevators on the far wall. I clip-clopped across the polished marble floor to the reception desk and gave my name to the security guard. He snorted in greeting, handed me a name badge and jerked his head towards the seating area. Two minutes later, a slim blonde girl about my age, wearing a green trouser suit, walked towards me. I stood up with a contrived sure-of-myself smile, and extended my hand.

'Evie Dexter,' I said officiously.

'Tina Williamson,' she replied, blinking like a drowsy tiger. 'Would you like to follow me?' she asked, turning with exaggerated care.

OK, now I'm on a high. Things have taken a definite turn for the better. Tina Williamson has a raging, wicked *hangover*, I realise. This changes everything. I'm looking forward to this now because I will be interviewing her from a lofty, sober disposition, whereas she would be interviewing me with a big bass drum banging in her head. I whizzed the strap of my bag up my arm. This was all suddenly looking very positively positive. Tina tottered with hunched shoulders towards the stairs, with me following dutifully behind.

'Oh my God!' I enthused, taken aback. I pinned her to the wall as I burst into the interview room. 'Oooooh,' I gushed, overwhelmed. 'What a marvellous view.' Five purposeful steps and I stood by the window. I clutched my bag to my chest and gasped at the magnificence of Trafalgar Square.

Tina smiled feebly and lowered herself into a chair at the head of a beautiful oak table. The view was amazing. It's not often I bother to take the time to admire my surroundings.

London is my home, and home is usually taken for granted, but this was, well, unbelievable. Nelson's Column rose from the centre of the square, piercing the clouds like a glittering silver needle. I stepped back when I realised my nose, palms and lips were flush to the glass. I turned to face Tina.

'It's fabulous. The fountains look fantastic from here,' I raved.

She slowly dragged a manila folder in front of her, opened it and closed her eyes. I tore myself from the window and screeeeeeeched my chair along the wooden floor, sitting composedly opposite her. She sat, elbows on the table, chin on balled fists.

'OK,' she sighed wearily. 'Paris.'

I gave an eager attentive nod.

There was a confused silence.

She peered at the folder.

I wondered if I was supposed to peer at it as well so, to be on the safe side, I did. I gave the folder an admiring wide-eyed stare.

'Paris,' she exhaled. 'How well do you know it?'

'Like the back of my hand,' I amazingly heard myself declare. And I launched into a chronicle narrative that would have bored the backside off Robinson Crusoe, and he was starved of company for years. I regurgitated the index, synopsis and entire contents of my Baedeker guidebook. And thank God I'd let Lulu drag me along to see *The Da Vinci Code* because my all-encompassing knowledge of the Louvre and French art was attained as a result of watching that film. In fact, I was starting to bore myself, that's how much of a show-off I was. I sounded like a contestant on *Mastermind*, speciality subject: talking rubbish.

I whacked my hand on the table causing a loud thwap when I suspected Tina had dropped off. Her neck snapped back and her eyes flew open. Yes, I had her attention now. I tossed my hair over my shoulder, crossed and uncrossed my legs, and rushed on, recapping on a *Vogue* feature I'd read about Paris Fashion Week. Except I pretended I'd been there. And, warming to my theme, I even told her I'd had a VIP pass to see the Versace Collection.

She was wilting. I didn't care. I was on a roll. This was *me* I was talking about.

'And,' I started. I was about to morph myself into Florence Nightingale and beef up my first aid qualification, when Tina held up both hands in a 'don't shoot' gesture.

'Eh, eh,' she said, breathing laboriously. 'Yes, you seem to know your stuff.' She scratched her nail down the list of names on the right-hand side of her spreadsheet.

'Not all of our Paris Weekend Breaks have been allocated to guides yet, so we're keen to enlist a few more for the summer season. We . . .' She paused for a moment, closed her eyes and swallowed, head bobbing loosely. I smiled. I'm no doctor but I can diagnose Internal Bouncing Vomit Syndrome when I see it.

'We . . .' She broke off. 'That is . . .'

I rummaged in my bag and whipped out a can of Diet Coke. I slid it across the table towards her. She tore at the ring pull and gulped greedily.

'Erm,' she spluttered.

A belch like a clap of thunder took us both by surprise. Her eyes widened. So did mine.

'I think I might have a throat infection,' she lied unconvincingly.

'Really?' I sympathised.

I offered her a Polo mint, which she snatched, crunched and gobbled.

'Do you have any questions you would like to ask me?' I enquired from my sober seat.

'No, I'm sure we've covered everything,' she hiccuped. 'Oh yes,' she recalled quickly. 'Could you start tomorrow?'

For a moment I thought I'd misheard. But no, she was scribbling my name at the bottom of her diary. I felt a worm of excitement tug at my tummy and barely managed to suppress the desire to whoop.

'Yes, of course,' I squeakily confirmed.

'Super,' she replied, and snapped the folder shut. 'Give me a few minutes to fetch your paperwork,' she said, already heading for the door.

I stood up from the table, walked regally to the window, opened it and spread my arms wide and told the crowds below that Pope Evie had just got the job. And that Lulu was a cheeky gobshite.

Tina returned a few minutes later, brandishing a rather official looking file.

'Everything you need is in here: itinerary, hotel vouchers, passenger lists, insurance documents, contact details for your local guide, client questionnaires, cash float, emergency traveller's cheques, briefing notes and de-briefing forms. Do you have any questions?'

In truth, I had about a million. I hadn't the faintest idea what she was talking about. But do you know what? I didn't give a toss. I'd got the job! Surely that was the hardest bit. 'Nope, everything seems crystal clear to me,' I heard myself singsong.

She finished by asking me to call her when I returned on Monday to confirm all had gone well. If it had, I would be contracted until October.

I walked smartly through the marble-floored reception area, swinging my tour file. I flashed a beaming smile at the friendly, chatty security guard I'd met earlier and skipped into the afternoon sunshine. I raised my face to the sun and spun around, à la Julie Andrews. I didn't swear at a cab driver who almost ran me over and I even let someone beat me to a seat on the train.

Chapter Seven

'So you've been offered the job and you start tomorrow? That's incredible!' Lulu congratulated. 'I'm pleased for you. I feel sorry for the people you'll be looking after. But, hey, at least you'll enjoy a free weekend in Paris before you get sacked on Monday.' I was perched on the edge of her bed, as she got ready to go out on a date.

'I was offered the job on merit. I studied, researched and put myself out there. I do know what I'm talking about,' I boasted.

She swiped a sheet of vanilla hair behind her ear. 'Well done. I take my hat off to you. I would've had a panic attack, blagging away and prattling on, trying to sound as though I had half a brain. I'm stunned. You amaze me,' she complimented. 'Honestly, I'm soooooooo impressed.'

I gave a self-appreciating shrug, and for some reason felt compelled to add: 'She questioned me in French for the final ten minutes of the interview, so that was a trifle nerve-racking.' Lulu twisted around from her make-up mirror, beaming widely, mascara held aloft.

'Evie, you're a marvel. You are so, how can I put it? Resourceful. You're a, a chameleon, yes, that's what you are. You can turn your hand to anything. I'm soooooooo proud of you.' She bowed

47

her arm around my neck and kissed my cheek. 'You were always good at French at school.'

I glowed, and caressed my tour file. She's right. I was good at French, but that was because I sat next to BO Brenda, and she let me copy.

'You'll mess up, wait and see.' She patted my knee. 'But by all means make the most of it while you can.'

I sighed and snatched my Nars lipstick from her dressing table. I'd been considering letting her keep it, but she didn't deserve it.

Her jovial tone faded. 'OK, enough about your job. Let's talk about my date. I know we've gone over this ten times but do you know what you have to do?'

I gave a despairing sigh. 'I don't understand why you agreed to go out with this guy Vic, if you can't remember what he looks like. You gave him your number, didn't you? You wouldn't have done that if you hadn't liked him. Would you?'

Lulu tossed her mascara into her bag and walked over to the wardrobe. 'I met him in Club 100, after I'd been to that huge bash laid on by one of our pharmaceutical suppliers. I was plastered. Don't you remember? I put my Chinese takeaway on the doorstep to get my keys out of my bag, and then I searched the place high and low for it and phoned the police to see if anyone had handed it in. I was cautioned for wasting police time. He could have been a revolting sales rep with a face like a barnyard animal and I gave him my number because he bribed me with the promise of freebies.'

She had a point. We have a hundred tubes of suntan lotion, two hundred shower caps, twenty boxes of tissues, fifty bottles of calamine lotion and a ten-year supply of various remedies for colds and flu stuffed and packed into the bathroom. All accrued as a result of Lulu's liaisons with sales reps.

'Right,' she asserted bossily. Her lips twitched as she attempted to fasten the zip on her jeans. It was hopeless. 'Let's go over it once more.' She grabbed a wire coat hanger from the wardrobe, looped the end through the tip of the zip and heaved with the will of the Gods.

'You ... answer ... the ... door,' she gasped. The zip was slowly cooperating. 'I'll ... be ... hiding ... behind ... the ... lounge ... curtain.' She panted, air obviously in short supply, but in fairness the zip was definitely travelling north, and then, yes, it was up. She unhooked the coat hanger and flattened herself against the wall to catch her breath. Then with an iron will she set about fastening the top button. I congratulated her inwardly when she managed it, and was tempted to give her a round of applause, but I didn't because that would have started our 'who's the fattest' fight.

'If I like him, I'll signal the thumbs up, and if I don't, I'll give the thumbs down, in which case you tell him I've been called to attend an emergency Caesarean delivery.'

'You're not a midwife.'

'Don't nit-pick,' Lulu snapped. She leaned forward, unclipped my earrings, turned back to the dressing table mirror and put them in her own ears. 'Can I borrow your short Juicy Couture necklace? My pendant sits like a rosette on my cleavage. Your Juicy seems to highlight my slender neckline. And, well, it sort of takes the emphasis off my boobs, hides them even,' she said, delusional.

A string of kippers around her neck wouldn't hide her D-cups, but I knew better than to say anything. I handed her my necklace, and jumped when the doorbell rang.

'Showtime,' she announced darkly.

She towed me down the hallway, side-stepping on tiptoe into the lounge to take her place behind the curtain. I swung open the front door.

'Hello,' I said smiling, initially half-heartedly before breaking into a genuine welcoming grin. The game of charades was over. Not because Vic was particularly handsome, but because there was a red Aston Martin parked behind my white Renault.

Lulu bounded down the hallway.

'Don't wait up,' she said, giving me a backward wave.

I made myself some coffee and studied my Paris paperwork. I was due to meet the coach at Victoria at 9am on Friday. We would then drive to Dover, before boarding the late morning cross-Channel ferry to Calais. From the French coast we'd continue the journey by driving to Paris, where we would be staying three nights in a four-star hotel. I marvelled at how much I was beginning to sound like a tour guide already, simply by reading the itinerary out loud. I gave an excited giggle, crammed the file and my passport into my handbag and dragged my suitcase from under the bed.

As I was only going away for three nights, I cut back on the packing. I would have to make do with seven pairs of shoes, two pairs of boots and twelve outfits. The last thing I popped into my toilet bag was Milk Thistle capsules. Lulu once told me that any randy pisshead of a Roman emperor worth his toga would take Milk Thistle to help him keep up with the pace at the weekly orgy down the local temple. I know that there aren't many orgies in Tooting, and Lulu is a vacant drunken excuse for company, but every now and then she comes up trumps. Apparently she hasn't had a hangover for weeks and swears it's all due to the liver-regenerating qualities of this wonder drug. It's worth a try. Sometimes after a night out with the girls I feel like I'm having an out of body experience.

Job done, I decided on an early night. I'd just puffed my pillows and snuggled into bed when Lexy rang.

'Congratulations again! I still can't believe you got the job. Remember I told you in confidence that my neighbour Mary suspected her husband of having an affair with one of the teachers in the school where he works? Shite that he is and respected Headmaster to boot! Well, I told one of the mums from the nursery, in confidence obviously, and she told her mother-in-law, in confidence, who happens to be a dinner lady at the same school. Well, sod's law, the mother-in-law slipped and fell at work and has been in hospital for four days. She's been babbling on morphine, and ended up spilling the beans. Now Mary is blaming me! It's an outrage! Tell the truth, do you think it's my fault? Mary and I had the biggest argument. I mean, I don't even *know* this stupid dinner lady!' she ranted. 'Oh! Nearly forgot. Can you leave your Whistles jacket on your bed? I'll pick it up while you're away because I want it for Saturday night. Must dash, can't sit gossiping away to you all night. Bye.'

I hadn't opened my mouth once. I put the phone down. I can't wait, I thought excitedly. A lovely weekend in Paris, just the fifty of us. That's forty-eight passengers, the driver and me. I'm going to give it my all, I just know I'll be good at this. I mean, it can't be any more taxing than living with Lulu, looking after the twins or avoiding Nikki, can it?

Chapter Eight

I rang a local cab company.

'Twenty-five quid for a cab to Victoria!?' I yelled, horrified. 'At least Dick Turpin wore a mask. This is extortion! It's only a straight line through Balham and Clapham. I will not fall victim to your commercial voracity,' I snapped, hopping into my shoes.

'Does that mean you want the cab or not, love?' the controller asked, disinterested.

'I most certainly do not. Ply your trade elsewhere, you greedy man.' I accused him of being a thieving bandit and threatened to expose him to *Watchdog*. This left no alternative but to travel by tube. I didn't mind, it was a matter of principle. Twenty-five quid is, after all, twenty-five quid.

I checked my appearance in the mirror for the tenth time. I wore my Karen Millen navy suit with a shorter-than-I-would-normally-wear hemline, my white Conrad blouse, which Lulu pointed out had cost more than our television, and Lulu's new Russell & Bromley navy stilettos, which she'll probably spend the entire weekend looking for. Yards of shiny brown hair fell down my back. Well, to just past my shoulders actually. Nars Chelsea Girl lip gloss, a pale lilac Bobbi Brown eye shadow with a smattering of blusher and a light coat of mascara completed

the look. Buoyed by the excitement of venturing forth to ter-
ritories unknown, waking up without a hangover and this being
a slim day, I couldn't wait to get going.

I chewed my bottom lip as I eyed my Samsonite case. It was
pretty big. I reckon with a bit of engineering I could fit Nikki
in it but, on the plus side, it had wheels. I managed, with difficulty, to manoeuvre the case out the door of the flat and trundle
it behind me down the narrow communal hallway and out of
the building. Exhausted and not yet as far as the garden gate, I
dreaded the ordeal of dragging it across the street to the tube station. Perhaps twenty-five quid for a cab wasn't as expensive as
I'd first thought. Let's face it, what can you get for twenty-five
quid these days? And the cab driver might have three hungry
kids and need the money. What kind of person would begrudge
the price of a Benefit eye shadow pallet if they had the opportunity to feed an entire family?

Hopeful it would be a different guy on control at the cab
company, and having decided to fake an American accent if it
wasn't, I dropped the handle of my suitcase so I could ferret my
phone from my shoulder bag. It took a couple of seconds, perhaps even a whole quarter of a minute, for my brain to process
the fact that my shoulder didn't have a bag draped over it. I
frisked my chest, hips, and backside and ran my palms up and
down my thighs. No bag. I felt sick.

'No bag, no bag,' I chanted. My heart sank all the way to
Lulu's navy stilettos. My bag with my money, phone, passport,
keys, passenger lists, guidebooks and make-up was on my bed.
My head pounded, and there was a weird ringing sound in my
ears. I swallowed hard, feeling as though I was under water. I
kicked the front door and, like a demon, set about punching all
three doorbells. The entire queue of nosy commuters at the bus
stop outside our gate stared, eyes out on stalks.

'What are you lot gawping at?' I bellowed, eyes shining with madness. They scarpered like rats clamouring for a seat on the 220 bus to Shepherd's Bush.

The other tenants in the building are locum doctors, and they were obviously either out saving lives, or pissed and in bed. Even if I managed to get into the building I would still be locked out of the flat. I slumped against the door and bashed my forehead with the ball of my hand. Right, think. Get from Tooting to Paris, that's all I have to do. How hard can that be? I gave a nervous snort of laughter. It's not as though I have to perform a triple heart bypass operation. I sat on the garden wall and breathed deeply. Actually, I'd rather perform a triple heart bypass operation . . . I leaped up. Be positive, I thought. I can do it. I slumped down. I can't, I can't. I want my old job back. I jumped to standing. For God's sake, this is what I do. I'm a European tour guide, I told myself with conviction, innards growling.

I dragged, kicked and pushed my suitcase across the street to Tooting Broadway station. 'Help!' I bleated. 'I need help.' My eyes flashed around the station like a laser beam at a Black Eyed Peas concert. I spotted a station guard. I lunged forward and rugby tackled him against the ticket kiosk. Thwap! His hands and face hit the glass.

'Aahhhh,' he grunted, sandwiched between my 36Cs and the kiosk door. I flipped him around, grabbed his lapels and pulled him towards me.

'Haaavve got to get to Victoria . . .

'No handbag . . .

'No money for a ticket . . .

'No passport . . .'

He gave a sympathetic nod as I bounced his head against the kiosk window.

'New job . . .'

He blinked madly, his jaw dropped and his eyes grew wide in understanding. I swiped my dribbling nose on his shoulder.

'Nine grand overdraft, need this job, desperately need this job . . .

'Lulu takes the piss . . .'

I hammered his head against the glass rhythmically. We had an audience.

'Whaaat are you staring at?' I screamed at a short man with a flat face and shiny bald head.

He bolted, and so did the guard the minute I loosened my hold on his jacket. I was about to grab him again when he somersaulted over the barrier and opened the gate. I tossed my hair over my shoulder, and lifted the handle of my case.

'How kind,' I panted. I clattered through the barrier and thundered down the escalator, sobbing uncontrollably.

There was one remaining seat when I got on the train, and only myself and a dapper-looking pinstripe heading towards it. I gripped the back of his jacket and catapulted him down the centre of the carriage. To be honest, I think he welcomed the distance between us. I thumped into the seat. Everyone avoided eye contact. I do the same thing myself when there's a fruit cake on the loose. An elderly lady sat next to me. She eyed my suitcase and placed her soft wrinkly hand over mine.

'Listen dear, men are good for nothing. You're doing the right thing leaving him. I wish I'd been blessed with courage at your age. But it was different back then.' She smiled and nodded reflectively.

I hugged myself, sniffed loudly and rocked back and forth, tears cascading down my cheeks. I felt an overwhelming surge of relief that leaving him was the right thing to do.

'I'm doing the right thing, I'm doing the right thing,' I

hymned. I gripped her bony hand and searched her eyes urgently. 'Am I? Am I really? Am I really doing the right thing?' I asked her. I squeezed my eyes shut, and tried to remember who I was leaving.

'You're a beauty, dear. You won't be on your own for long,' she said, wriggling her hand from my desperate grasp.

'D'you think,' I sobbed, then rushed on, 'I'll meet someone soon?' I was fevered and delirious. She prised my fingers from her wrists and stood to leave.

'Oh, yes,' she said wisely. 'Definitely.'

'No, no, no!' I yelled as she moved towards the door. 'I'm not leaving him! I remember now. Don't go!'

She left, and so I belted out the whole sorry tale to an amazed carriage of commuters. And d'you know what? Not one of them could think of a solution to my problem.

At Victoria, I heaved and tugged my suitcase off the train and along the platform. With mad eyes and hair like a gorgon, I marched towards the guard at the barrier, one arm outstretched, bawling and hiccuping. I was psyching myself up to explain my predicament when, without persuasion, he bolted away from me, and opened the barrier.

I hauled my case through the station exit and around the corner to Bressenden Place. Right, find the coach. I sighed. I'd expected only one coach to be waiting but there was a whole line of them. Shit, I cursed and ploughed on tearfully.

The first driver I spoke to was going to Amsterdam, the second to Paris but not for Insignia Tours. What was the name of the coach company? I dropped the handle of my case and massaged my temples. Think, it began with an H or a D, no a P . . . Patterson's, I think. Yes, that's it: Patterson's Coaches. No, no, an H. It was Harrison's.

I hobbled on, my case rumbling behind me, and saw three

gleaming maroon coaches lined proudly on the bend, all displaying the Harrison's logo in bold gold letters. I swooned with relief when the driver of the second coach asked me if my name was Evie.

'Hi,' he said, eyes sparkling in welcome 'Pleased to m—'

I dropped my case and stumbled towards him, chin and bottom lip trembling. His forehead buckled into anxious creases. I burrowed my nose into the knot of his tie.

'No mooooooooney. No passssssssssport.'

He held my forearms lightly.

'No maaaaaaaaaaake-up!' I wailed, inconsolable.

'OK, calm down. We'll work something out,' he soothed, rubbing my back woodenly. I wiped my nose on his shoulder. He cupped my face. Flint-blue eyes held mine. 'Crying won't help,' he said, eyes smiling. I snorted in understanding and howled and howled and howled. He ground his thumbs into my cheeks. 'Don't,' he said, with a nod of encouragement. 'Don't,' he repeated.

I gazed at him wide-eyed, and after a couple of minutes of slow, unified eye-to-eye head nodding and him chanting, 'calm down, calm down' I stopped crying.

'That's better,' he whispered softly.

I held my breath. He still cupped my face.

'Don't worry about money, I have money. I'll buy you make-up. This isn't the end of the world,' he told me with a confident smile.

I sniffed and hiccuped and sniffed and hiccuped and sniffed. I was starting to feel better.

'Our only problem is your passport,' he added bleakly.

And like an aircraft engine, I revved . . .

'Don't,' he warned.

I bit my knuckle. He scanned my face.

'Do you have your driving licence with you?' he asked. There was an expectant silence.

'No,' I managed, chewing a slobbery fist. He held my chin like the teeth of a trap.

'Listen to me,' he said firmly.

I was all ears. I am, after all, in charge of this trip and this driver is in my employ.

'When we arrive at Dover Docks Immigration, the passengers have to leave the coach to walk through Passport Control. You and I have to stay on board and drive to the checkpoint where we deliver the passenger declaration forms and have our own passports checked, so this is what we'll do. You hide in the coach toilet, I'll hand in the forms and say I'm working alone. We'll rejoin the passengers at the Customs exit and drive down to board the ferry.'

A frisson of hope scurried in my chest, like when I watch the National Lottery live, clutching my ticket, excited, animated, optimistic.

'Do you think, do you think that'll work?' I squeaked.

'Why shouldn't it?' he asked. 'Now, we've got twenty minutes before the passengers are due to arrive. I'll put your suitcase on the coach and buy you a coffee.' His hands were still holding my face.

'You're hurting my jaw,' I complained.

'Am I? Sorry,' he said, giving me a blokeish shoulder smack.

A few minutes later, we were sliding into an alcove booth in the Italian coffee shop on the corner, opposite the coach. He handed me his copy of the passenger list, together with his clipboard and pen.

'How well do you know Paris?' he asked.

'Err, I have been, but I was only eight at the time. I sort of exaggerated my experience at the interview,' I confessed, embarrassed. He gave me a penetrating look.

'I see.' He paused. 'How long have you been a guide?' he asked.

'Um, about an hour,' I admitted.

'So you don't know the city and you don't know the job?' he quizzed in a tone I couldn't quite identify.

'No and, er, no.'

'Right,' he said, finishing his coffee. 'Fine.' He rattled his empty cup onto the saucer and leaned across the table with folded arms. 'As the passengers arrive, tick their names off your list and tell them to give their suitcases to me to load onto the coach. Let me know when your list is complete. On board, advise everyone the journey to Dover takes two hours and explain the procedure for clearing Customs and boarding the ferry. You might want to walk up and down the coach to make sure everyone is comfortable.' He gave me a reassuring smile. 'Got it?' He stretched across to squeeze my hand. I gave a curt nod.

'Got it,' I said, trying for a smile.

'Good girl. Come on, let's go.' He stood up.

'What do I call you?' I asked.

'I'm Rob. And you're Evie, right?' he asked, smiling warmly.

I gave a tight nod and clutched the clipboard to my chest.

'Well, Evie, time to go,' he said, smile widening.

I felt a flutter of panic at the word 'go'. I would have been happy to sit in the café until Monday night, and then go home and tell Lulu I'd had a blinding weekend. Rob placed a hand gently on my back and guided me towards the door.

The passengers arrived steadily over the next half an hour. Everyone was in high-spirited, holiday mode. I got quite animated myself at one point, until I remembered that I had bugger all to be happy about. Likely I'd be fired in two hours' time. Rob bantered with the passengers as he loaded the suitcases. He had a kind word and a warm welcome for everyone. Every now and then he caught my eye and gave me an encouraging wink or a reassuring smile.

Once my passenger list was complete, I jumped on board to execute a final count, and then walked around to the side of the coach where Rob was closing the luggage flaps.

'We have everyone,' I told him, innards jumping as a fresh wave of panic swept through me.

'Now, don't worry,' he said confidently. 'I've told you, it'll be fine. Trust me.'

'Has this happened before? I mean, you've smuggled someone and succeeded?' I asked, hopeful that his reply would be along the lines of 'it happens every week'.

'Nope, never,' he admitted. He slammed down the last two luggage flaps. I chewed my thumbnail nervously.

'How can you be so confident?'

He drew in his breath sharply. 'The last thing I want now that I've met you is to spend the weekend in Paris without you.' His voice was soft and he tucked a loose strand of hair behind my ear. He put his hand on the small of my back. 'Come on, let's go. You'll be fine.'

I settled down in the crew seat adjacent to Rob and lifted the microphone from its cradle. As he indicated so he could pull out of our parking space, I addressed the passengers with poise and confidence. In my old job at the ad agency I'd often had to pitch to clients and mostly I'd be lying or exaggerating, so it was nice to be telling the truth for a change.

'Good morning. My name's Evie and our driver for the weekend is Rob. Our journey to Dover should take no longer than two hours. For your convenience, there are toilet facilities in the centre left-hand side of the coach. At some point during the journey I'd like you all to check that you have your passport in your hand luggage, ready for inspection at Dover. If anyone has mistakenly packed travel documents in their suitcase please let me know. For now, all you have to do is sit back and relax.' I replaced the microphone in the cradle and glanced cagily towards Rob. He gave me a sexy wink.

In theory, I should have been manically suicidal but guess what? I felt a surge of desire, and it left me breathless. I took a minute to study Rob. He had thick, dark blond hair tinged with the odd burnished copper highlight, turquoise eyes framed by long eyelashes, high cheekbones and a well-formed, almost chiselled jaw. He looked dashing in a navy blue jacket with gold buttons and a small gold motif on the breast pocket.

I craned my neck to get a better look at him. His legs were open as he sat comfortably at the steering wheel. I gawped at his thighs. They were big. Not fat, no, not fat at all, just, well, big. No belly hanging over his belt, so he's probably not a lager swilling type of guy. That'll make a nice change, I thought. His fringe flopped lazily across his forehead and a small shadow appeared on his cheek whenever he blinked. I watched, transfixed, as he checked his wing mirror and casually blew his hair from his eyes. Mmmm, I thought, definitely over six foot and he's probably about twenty-eight.

I inched forward in my seat and gripped the armrests for stability. Involuntarily my eyes travelled down the length of his tie towards his crotch. Gosh, what can I say? I wondered briefly if he might be wearing Abercrombie boxers. They're usually bulky under the trousers, aren't they? They pad a boy out a bit and can give a girl a bit of a false impression. I leaned forward a smidgen more.

'Evie!' Rob bellowed.

'Aaaaargh! Whaaaat?' I shrieked.

'Sit back! You'll fall out of that chair in a minute if you're not careful,' he warned. 'You're right on the edge. What're you doing?'

'Oh, sorry. I was just looking, er, I was looking, um, in the window of Army & Navy,' I lied, mortified.

'Well, don't. You'll end up on the floor. Put your seat belt on and sit back.'

'Yes. Sorry. Seat belt, yes.'

I managed to make it from London to Blackheath without drawing any more attention to myself, but I was restless. By the time we joined the motorway, I was rocking back and forth on my chair. Some geriatric crooner was warbling away on the sound system. Barry Manilow, I think.

'I should check to see if everyone is all right,' I eventually told Rob. He nodded and eyed me encouragingly.

I gingerly mounted the three steps to the elevated passenger section. Safe in the knowledge that Rob didn't have eyes in the back of his head, I had another good old leer at his crotch. Blimey, it can't all be him, can it? I smiled optimistically. Did I say optimistically? I mean, I smiled automatically, because I always smile. After all, I've only just met him . . .

'OK. Shout if you need me,' he said kindly, eyes fixed on the road.

Two elderly ladies, who had been the first to arrive, sat in the front seats directly behind me. 'Hello,' I greeted.

A blast of lavender fumes stung my nostrils. 'Hello, dear. I'm Doris and this is Ellen,' Doris said, extending her hand.

'Have you been to Paris before?' I asked sweetly.

'No, never,' Doris replied. She patted her friend's knee. 'Have we, Ellen?'

'No, never,' Ellen echoed, popping a sherbet lemon into her mouth.

They had identical large shiny patent handbags perched on

their laps, and the same shade of pale blue rinsed through their hair. I chatted on.

'Oh, so this will be a nice change for you.'

'Oh, yes,' they chorused and nodded. Doris tugged her cardigan tightly around her and leaned forward conspiratorially.

'Tell me, dear: do the seats rotate?' she asked gravely.

Now, the coach was comfortable enough, probably one of the finest and most modern I'd ever seen, but to expect the seats to rotate was frankly outrageous. This isn't the bloody tea cups at Thorpe Park. I rolled my eyes. I had to deal with this as politely and as diplomatically as I could. I smiled indulgently.

'No, Doris, I'm afraid the seats don't rotate,' I replied. 'But they do recline,' I offered by means of consolation.

Doris's eyes glazed over and she frowned. I put the befuddled expression on her face down to old age. She had probably forgotten what she'd just asked me. Ellen wore the same dazed expression. I smiled reassuringly, and glided on regally to chat to the couple behind them. I thought I'd dealt with that quite well, even if I do say so myself.

Ah, these two have obviously had some sort of a disagreement, I thought. Maybe I can smooth things over. He was staring out of the window whilst she tried to spark up a conversation with the side of his head. She turned huffily from him when she noticed me standing next to her.

'Hello, love. Duncan's sulking.' She inclined her head towards her husband.

'Oh, I'm sure you're wrong,' I said cheerily.

'No, I'm not. He's always sulking.' She gave him a dig in the ribs. 'Aren't you, Duncan?'

Duncan was an enormous bulk of a man, with a mass of thick red hair, bushy eyebrows, slate-grey eyes and broad shoulders. He grunted and kept his face fixed to the window.

'Sod you then,' she snapped, giving his shoulder a punch. 'Anyway, love, I'm looking forward to this weekend. I've been to Paris a few times, but he's out to spoil it, so if you could arrange for someone to drown him in the Channel, anywhere between Dover and Calais, I'd be grateful. By the way, my name's Alice,' she said brightly. She pinched Duncan on the knee, making him wince. 'Duncan is from Inverness and I'm from Harrogate. We've been posted down south for the last couple of years though, because he's a training officer in the Army.' Alice prodded Duncan in the ribs. 'He was in the Gestapo but they drummed him out for cruelty,' she said, bursting into gales of laughter, delighted at her own wit.

'Don't lisin t'her. She's a professional pest,' Duncan rumbled, in a thick, deep Highland brogue. He gave me a welcoming smile and stretched across Alice to shake my hand. 'Have ye any room to put her in wi' the bags and let me have a bit of a sleep on the way to the docks?' he joked. Alice grabbed his hand, kissed him lightly on the cheek and chuckled.

'Look, love, you've done the trick. He's talking again.'

I beamed and nodded benignly. I'm really good at this, I thought, brightly. Yes, I definitely seem to be a natural at this kind of thing. I'm already pacifying old ladies and sorting out marital disputes.

A lady adjacent to Alice was vying for my attention. She tapped me lightly on the arm and whispered timidly.

'Evie, dear, I wonder if I could ask you a few questions?'

My smile buckled. I wanted to do the talking. I didn't want a question and answer session on account of the fact that there's a limited number of questions I know the answers to.

'Of course,' I replied grimly.

Her face creased with worry.

'I've never been on a ferry before. Should I change my

money after breakfast or will the queue at the bank be shorter before breakfast? But will the bank run out of money if I wait until after breakfast? And if I change my money first, can I pay for my breakfast with euros, or do you think it's cheaper to pay with pounds? Also, my daughter would like to call me at the hotel. Do you have the telephone number? And how long are we actually at sea for?'

She shuffled towards me, and discreetly did a quick left and right checking for eavesdroppers. I felt compelled to do likewise. I bent my head to hers. She dropped her voice cautiously, and hastened on, her breath warm on my cheek.

'Has an English ferry ever sunk that you know of, and are there enough lifeboats for all of the passengers? I've seen *Titanic*,' she said with a knowing wink. She patted her silver curls. 'Oh, and my name's Patricia.'

'Err, excuse me one moment, Patricia. The driver appears to be trying to catch my eye.' I turned and tapped Alice on the arm, who was reading a magazine. 'Alice, could you have a chat with this lady? Rob needs me, and Patricia has a few questions.'

Alice beamed. 'Yes, love, of course. You go attend to that Adonis of a driver of ours.' She threw her magazine in Duncan's lap and leaned across the aisle to chat to Patricia.

I hot-tailed it back to the sanctuary of my chair.

'Evie,' Rob said quietly.

'Uuh.'

He crooked his finger. 'Come closer.'

I leaned towards him.

'Seat rotation means the clients move every day. You know, two seats back or two seats forward. It gives everyone the opportunity to sit at the front.' He gave me a fiendish wink. 'It doesn't mean that the actual seats rotate,' he motioned a circle with his index finger, 'like so.'

I cringed. 'Well thanks for letting me know,' I replied, embarrassed.

'Don't mention it,' he said, grinning broadly.

I turned to look down the aisle at my forty-eight comfortably seated passengers. Doris and Ellen were clutching their patent handbags and humming along with Barry. The others were munching contentedly on boiled sweets, gossiping, reading newspapers, playing Travel Scrabble or deliberating over crosswords. My heart pounded. Patricia's interrogation had thrown me. What am I doing here? I asked myself. As I watched the beautiful Kent countryside speed by, I sank deeper into my seat, and tried to stop myself from throwing up.

Chapter Nine

As we approached the docks, I was seized by contractions of terror. I glanced fretfully at Rob, who appeared to be ignoring me. But then, I reasoned, he is driving and doesn't have an eye protruding from his left ear, so perhaps I'm being paranoid. My stomach cramped viciously. Rob handed the ferry ticket out of the window to the security guard. The ticket was verified, and we were directed to Immigration. I was having trouble breathing. For some reason, air seemed in very short supply. I massaged my heart and tried to work a smidgen of saliva into my mouth.

We stopped at the Customs Hall where the clients shuffled off the coach in a crocodile line, passports in hand, emitting copious amounts of pre-holiday excitement. I stood at the foot of the coach steps with a fixed grimace on my face until the last happy soul had disappeared through the door. Rob gripped my elbow and pulled me back onto the coach.

'I can't do this,' I wailed.

He prodded me down the aisle of the coach, jabbing my back with his keys. 'Get in the toilet,' he told me in a no-nonsense tone.

I gripped the armrests and dug my heels into the floor. He cannoned into me.

'Go and hide in the toilet now,' he snapped, exasperated. He prised my fingers from the seat and nudged me forward.

'I feel sick,' I moaned, shooting him a haunted look.

'Not another word. This is a needs–must situation.' He bundled me down the central aisle steps into the toilet, and closed the door firmly behind me. 'Stay there until I come back for you,' he warned.

I flipped the seat cover down and sat glumly in the dark, wondering if criminals waiting to be executed felt like this. I bet they didn't feel this bad. They had months, sometimes years, to adjust to their situation, whereas I'd only forgotten my handbag a couple of hours ago. No one had ever spent a mere two hours on death row, had they? No, this was much worse.

Suddenly, the coach lurched forward. I had a quick chat with God. I explained Lulu's weight was no longer a pressing issue. I wanted him to pull strings here, immediately. I was making all sorts of irrational promises: I'd go to church; I'd stop swearing; I would take Lucsie on proper walks; I'd—

There was a purposeful thud on the door.

'It's OK. Come out.'

I slumped against the wall, relieved. Then I had a quick pee in celebration.

'Come on!' Rob shouted, rapping the door. 'What the hell are you doing in there?'

I ran my hands under the tap, and then fumbled for the door latch.

'Oh, Rob. You're so clever,' I said, scrambling up the steps. My eyes shone with tears of relief.

He smiled warmly. 'Don't cry. You've got nothing to cry about now, have you? We're through. Come on, welcome everyone back on board,' he said briskly, clapping his hands in a let's-get-this-show-on-the-road gesture.

I sniffed and blinked owlishly.

'No time for this,' he said softly, reaching for my hand. 'Come on, everything's going to be fine.'

'Yes, yes. Just coming,' I rallied. 'You're absolutely right.'

We drove to the end of the Customs Hall, where the now-familiar cheery crowd crocodiled back on board. Everyone busied and bustled to sit comfortably and then we lumbered slowly down the ramp to join the long queue of coaches waiting to board the ferry.

Having relaxed and calmed down, I took a minute to appreciate the beauty of my surroundings on this sunny July morning. Seagulls swooped and jived over the glittering English Channel, which was flanked by the breathtaking vista of the stunning White Cliffs of Dover, a summit of flourishing flora and luxuriant green hills. And then I remembered I didn't have any make-up and thought, never mind the flora. Where the hell are the shops?

'We'll buy make-up on the ferry,' Rob assured me, as the queue of coaches inched forward.

'Are you sure?' I panicked. 'I mean, positive sure?'

'Positive sure,' he echoed.

We drove onto the ferry and parked on the lower deck. Rob told me to ensure that everyone took careful note of our deck number and parking bay. I was also supposed to tell them to pay special attention to the on-board public announcements on arrival in France, which detailed when they needed to return to the coach. Thank heaven for Rob. You might think that jotting down your deck number and parking bay is simple common sense but I'm here to tell you that it wasn't exactly at the fore of my mind, and I'm a sensible enough person. Left on my own, I probably would've lost all forty-eight people on the ferry.

Finally, everyone disembarked and we were alone.

'Hungry?' Rob asked.

I watched as he expertly flicked this switch and that. The coach dashboard resembled the cockpit of a small aircraft, nothing at all like my Renault.

'Yes, I am actually,' I replied, smiling.

He stood in front of the rear view mirror and straightened his tie.

'That's better!' he said brightly.

'What's better?'

'You smiling.' He picked up my jacket, gave it a shake and held it up like a matador's cape. 'Come on then. Let's go and eat. Pick up my folder, there's maps and brochures in there that'll help you.'

He led me from the coach, along the car deck and up a narrow service staircase to a dining room reserved for drivers and guides. We ate quickly, and after our plates were cleared, he spread the map on the table.

'Voila, Paris!' He stroked his jaw with his thumb and forefinger, smoothed his tie and looked at me steadily.

'OK,' I said. 'Point out our hotel and the route we take into the city.'

He highlighted the map with meticulous care.

'Fantastic. Now I'll know where we are and what we're passing en route, so I'll know what to say.' I smiled gratefully and scribbled down a few details about the landmarks we would be passing.

Rob eyed me studiously. 'We're due to arrive at our hotel at approximately five-thirty. Allowing time to check in and unpack, we should be ready to go back out by seven-thirty. I know a restaurant we can take everyone to. The group rate for the meal is thirty euros but you can charge fifty-five,' he said casually. He handed me a sheet of paper detailing the menu selection. 'On Saturday evening we'll take everyone on an Evening Illumination Tour of the city with free time for dinner in the Latin Quarter. You can charge thirty euros per person and we can keep and share all of it.'

Now, I don't want to boast, but I've always been a bit of a boffo brain at arithmetic, especially when it relates to money. Namely, my money.

'So,' I muttered, astonished and mentally calculating the potential profit margin. 'We can make approximately two thousand, five hundred euros based on achieving a hundred per cent sales?'

He gave a condescending chuckle. 'It's highly unlikely that everyone will reserve places. I have *never* known a guide to sell to a whole group, and I'm referring to guides that have worked the circuit for years.' He patted my hand. 'Think along the lines of fifty per cent,' he added, matter-of-factly.

What the hell would the other fifty per cent of the group want to do that's better than coming out with me? I wondered. I am their guide and mentor.

In the tax-free shop I picked up mascara, two lipsticks, an eye-liner, a trio box of eye shadows, a blusher, foundation, a bottle of Chanel No 5 perfume and a make-up bag.

'Thank you. I'll pay you back,' I told Rob as he took his wallet from his inside jacket pocket. My eyes widened in confusion as he handed the assistant a fifty-pound note. I wondered briefly if he was thinking of paying for each item separately.

'No need. It's my pleasure,' he nodded, hand outstretched waiting for his change.

'Errrr,' the sales assistant addressed him timidly. 'The total is one hundred and forty-nine pounds, not forty-nine pounds.' He looked taken aback. Stunned, he offered his Visa card as his cash was returned.

'Luckily my skincare products are in my suitcase,' I told him.

'Lucky's right enough,' he said.

'Oh, I need a guidebook,' I quickly reminded him, pointing to the bookshelf.

'So you do,' he agreed and handed one to the sales assistant to add to the bill.

Thankfully Rob led the way back to the coach. After all my sound advice to the passengers, I'd actually forgotten to take note of the deck number and parking bay myself. The overhead lights hadn't yet been turned on, so the car deck was in darkness. I had to grip the back of Rob's jacket to negotiate stepping over the large steel cables that were holding the tyres of the coach to the floor.

'Come here,' he offered. He held my arm and shuffled me in front of him. 'I don't think those heels you're wearing are suitable. Do you?'

'Obviously not,' I grumbled, tentatively watching every step.

Back on the coach, I threw my clipboard on the dashboard and took off my jacket. I felt a ripple of excitement, the way you do when your holiday flight is about to land. Club 26-94 here I come. I gave a little round of applause.

'Evie,' Rob said casually, 'you still have to get through French Customs.'

'Huh?' I spun around to face him.

He eyed me warily.

'What?' I shrieked. 'You're telling me I have to go through all that again?'

He sighed.

'And I could be deported,' I wailed.

'Highly unlikely,' he replied calmly.

I rounded on him. 'Why didn't you tell me this before? I thought I'd nothing more to worry about?'

His face clouded. 'Because you were in a bad enough state. I thought one step at a time was best,' he said sharply.

'I can't hide with all the passengers on the coach this time, can I?' I buried my face in my hands.

He tugged my wrists and forced me to look at him. 'No, you can't.'

I gave him a watery stare.

'Don't start crying. Tears won't help,' he admonished.

I blinked madly. 'What shall I dooooooooooooooo?'

He led me to my seat and knelt before me. 'Listen to me,' he said softly. 'You tell French Customs you mislaid your passport on the ferry. I'll back you up. Tell them you need to enter France because you're responsible for the group.' He raised his eyebrows in question. 'How's your French?'

'Err, schoolgirl-ish,' I faltered.

He sighed, exasperated. 'Did you give any thought whatso-ever to the responsibility you were taking on? If anyone loses a handbag or their passport, has an accident or a heart attack, it's down to you to sort things out. Did you not think of that?' he asked firmly.

I floundered. Privately, I thought lost property would be a doddle to sort out, and as for accidents and heart attacks, well, there would be the emergency services and funeral directors to offer assistance and support. All of that seemed fairly straight-forward. But here I was, being thrown in at the deep end, with no passport of my own. How many guides had to cope with that on their first trip?

Rob patted my knee. 'Look, we'll manage,' he encouraged softly. 'Just do as I say. Customs will board the coach to check the passports. They're rarely thorough. At a push they'll check less than half. We'll play it by ear.'

My bottom lip trembled.

He chuckled. 'Be fair. You blagged your way into the job in the first place. Surely you can do this?'

I sniffed. Put like that, I suppose I could.

A faint rattle on the door heralded the passengers' return. They chatted animatedly as they shuffled back on board. My stomach growled with terror as we drove off the ferry and queued for Passport Control. Rob deliberately avoided eye contact. I couldn't blame him. What on earth must he think of me? I couldn't have got things more wrong if I'd tried. I could see the two French customs officers on the coach in front. They looked normal enough. Quite human actually, not the type of men to drag me away screaming and handcuffed. Behind me, Doris and Ellen were bickering.

'Four bottles of gin between us and not a splash of tonic to our name,' Ellen grumbled.

Four bottles! They're worse than Lulu and me.

'If you hadn't spent so long looking at the perfume, we would've had more time for duty-free,' Ellen complained. 'And, as usual, you didn't buy anything. Honestly, Doris, make-up at your age.'

I fingered the duty-free carrier bag in my lap.

All of a sudden, I was inspired. Make-up! My tummy flipped in excitement, and my heart skipped a beat. I threw my hands up and marvelled that the idea hadn't occurred to me before. The two custom officers were engrossed in conversation and slowly stepping down from the coach in front. One removed his box hat and tucked it smartly under his arm.

'Lock the doors, Rob. Lock them out,' I ordered, pointing at the two French officials.

He blinked uncomprehendingly. 'Whaaaaat?' he gasped, elbows resting lazily on the steering wheel. 'Are you mad?'

I shot from my seat and pressed the red button on the dashboard. The coach doors closed, I scrambled forward and snatched the microphone. Beaming, I faced my audience, my back to the windscreen.

'OK, everyone. There's the longest queue here, and probably upwards of twenty coaches behind us. Could you all hold up your passports please?' I gave an overhead wave in demonstration. 'Yes, that's it,' I encouraged, as one by one they obediently raised their passports. 'Now give them a wave so the customs officers can see that we all have one. Steady on, Doris! You don't want your arm to fall off,' I chortled.

Rob eyed me anxiously. The two officers stood directly in front of our windscreen. I smiled and blew them a kiss. They grinned bashfully and one of them blew me a kiss in reply. They could see everyone on the coach waving their passports and began to laugh. So did I. I threw back my head and cackled like a wicked pantomime witch. Nerves obviously, I'd only meant to chuckle. They waved us through.

Rob released the handbrake, slipped into gear and drove through the barrier towards the exit. I sank into my seat, exhausted.

'What were you waving? What was the red passport looka-like in your hand?' Rob asked acidly.

'My new Clarins blusher, of course.'

'Is that so? Clever you,' he said, expressionless.

75

PARIS

Chapter Ten

I'm in France. To be honest, I knew all along I would be. As Lulu observantly put it, I'm resourceful. What sort of a tour guide would I be if I couldn't even get myself through Immigration? Nope, I never doubted my abilities for a second. And here I am, at the helm and in charge. All I have to do now is babble to my heart's content on the microphone, study my guidebook and set my mind to the matter most pressing, which is selling the excursions and collecting all the generous donations towards my overdraft. First thing first, though. I had to put my face on. All the wailing and howling had taken its toll. I looked like I'd died three days ago. Luckily the suspension on the coach was super smooth, so foundation, blusher and eye shadow were easily applied.

'Errrr, Rob, do you think you could slow down a little to give me a chance to put mascara on?' I asked.

'How long do you need?'

'Not long enough to delay our arrival into Paris.'

'Looks like you're in luck, because we're stuck on red for a bit,' he said, nodding at the traffic lights.

I felt something brush by my face, and was about to swat what I thought was a wasp when Doris spoke.

'Lovely colour, dear. That eye shadow you're wearing, could I see it?'

'Sure. Give me a sec to finish my mascara and lippie. I need the mirror on the box,' I told her.

'I love make-up. I know I'm too old to wear it but I adore browsing the cosmetic counter just the same,' she said dreamily, with her chin resting annoyingly on top of my head.

'Doris,' I said firmly, 'there is no age limit on a box of eye shadow. If you want to wear it, then you wear it.'

'Oh, it's been about twenty years since I bothered. I'm eighty-two now. Don't think I remember how.'

I turned around, and knelt on my chair. 'I'll put it on for you,' I offered.

'OK then,' she said, closing her eyes and tilting her head.

Bloody hell. I hadn't meant right now. I'd meant at some point over the weekend, but when I looked at Doris's upturned face, framed by a halo of fluffy pale blue hair, my heart melted.

'OK, Doris. Lean back and give Ellen your handbag to hold.'

And whilst Rob negotiated our exit from the docks, I gave Doris a makeover.

'Oh,' Ellen trilled, as she inspected my handiwork. 'Do me. Do me.'

And so I did.

'Sit down,' Rob complained.' All I can see in my left wing mirror is your backside.'

George, an elderly chap with huge white twisted whiskers sitting directly behind Rob and travelling alone, sniggered. 'I've got the same view as you, son,' he said, with a chuckle. 'But I'm not complaining.'

'You lech,' Doris scolded, stretching across the aisle to dig George in the ribs.

Rob cast me an admiring glance. 'Don't get me wrong, I'm

enjoying the view myself,' he said, grinning. 'But it would be handy if I could see where I was going.'

'Have you finished with the eye shadow?' Alice interrupted. 'Pass it over, love. In fact, hand it all over. I've never used Clarins myself.'

'Cement and a chisel is what ye need,' Duncan bantered.

Elaine, a middle-aged lady two seats behind Alice, shuffled to the front of the coach to admire Doris and Ellen's new image.

'Oh! You look lovely,' she praised sincerely. 'Beautiful. It's so tasteful and subtle.' She clapped her hands and sat down in the empty seat next to George.

Doris and Ellen glowed. There was a fair bit of buttock shuffling and preening as they accepted Elaine's hearty compliments.

'Evie, do you think you could find the time to do me?' Elaine pleaded hopefully.

'I'll do you,' Alice offered. 'You're sitting behind me, aren't you? It'll give me something to do.'

'I'll move,' Duncan said, scowling. He heaved himself to standing and sat beside Elaine's husband.

Right, I had things to attend to. Now that I had my face on, I felt a million times better. I tugged my fingers through my hair, reached for the microphone and stood in the centre aisle, with an all-encompassing view of my audience.

'Good afternoon and a very warm welcome to France. May I have your attention for a few moments please?'

And lo and behold, forty-eight people obediently stopped what they were doing and stared at me, transfixed. I'm brilliant at this, I thought. I felt fabulous, I felt powerful. Yes, that's the word: powerful. This must be how Paul McKenna feels when he hypnotises an audience and makes people snort like pigs and eat onions and admit to having shagged their best friends' husbands.

'Can you sit down?' Rob asked sharply.

I ignored him, cleared my throat and preened professionally. 'We're due to arrive at our hotel at approximately five o'clock this evening. Check-in should take no longer than thirty minutes and then the rest of the evening is yours to spend as you please.'

Doris and Ellen fought silently over a large hand-held mirror.

Rob tugged on my sleeve and hissed at me to sit down. I twisted his ear. He yelped.

'Tonight, Rob and I will be dining at an extremely popular and well-known restaurant. It's our favourite haunt in Paris. We've been eating there together for years and we simply wouldn't dream of recommending anywhere else. It's located beside the Panthéon and is owned by a couple of very dear friends of ours. The chef,' I stuttered momentarily, trying to think of a French name, 'Pierre,' I decided quickly, and rushed on. 'Pierre was head-hunted and poached from the Paris Ritz,' I announced informatively. I was warming to my theme. 'Yes, Mohammed Al Fayed was livid. And tonight he'll be cooking for us.'

There was a collective rumble of excited undertones.

Rob coughed.

I beamed.

'And I believe Pierre worked briefly for Tony and Cherie,' I nodded, wide-eyed, whilst this impressive piece of gossip sank in.

Why the hell not? I thought, someone must've cooked for the Blair bunch. Why not Pierre from the Ritz?

'Sit down,' Rob snapped.

I continued excitedly. 'A delicious champagne aperitif will be served on arrival. There's live music and *unlimited* fine wines, together with a wide selection of French beers and a mouth-watering four course meal including frog's legs, or snails for the adventurous.'

Doris, who was still admiring herself in her mirror, grimaced and mouthed 'frog's legs?' to Ellen.

'Unlimited wine,' Ellen twittered, unblinking and attentive.

I pushed on. 'The menu consists of prawn cocktail, French onion soup or a house salad to start. Entrée options include poached salmon, fillet steak, coq au vin or lamb cutlets, followed by a selection of delicious desserts, and a cheese board with coffee and chocolates. Transport to the restaurant and back to the hotel will be provided, as our handsome chauffeur will be taking us.'

Alice let rip a wolf-whistle that would have done her justice at a Chelsea versus Manchester United match. Duncan scowled, and smacked her fingers from her mouth.

'And,' I purred, sashaying my hips slightly, 'I will be your personal escort.'

Duncan whistled and Alice scowled.

Rob leaned back and grabbed my wrist. 'Sit down,' he ordered sharply.

I wobbled on the step precariously. 'Excusez-moi, our debonair, hunky driver selfishly wants me to himself for a minute,' I broadcast, grinning wickedly.

There was a communal rumble of laughter, and a rather loud 'Don't blame him, who wouldn't?' from some gruff bigmouth sat at the back. I smiled sweetly and tottered down the steps to speak with Rob.

'Shut up! I am *not* sitting down. I need to see the whites of their eyes when I'm selling. It's a form of combat after all,' I spat venomously. I walloped his hand sharply with the microphone to release his hold on my wrist, causing a loud thwapping sound which reverberated throughout the coach. This was followed by a high-pitched howl from Rob. I scurried back up the steps to face the passengers.

'Sorry,' I continued. 'There appears to be a feedback problem with the microphone. Now, where was I? Oh yes! We were discussing where to go this evening. There are, of course, hundreds of restaurants in Paris, so you needn't come out with us, but should you decide to go it alone,' I paused to shudder, 'I want you to be *very* careful of pickpockets,' I warned, eyebrows raised, shaking my head despairingly. 'Don't wear jewellery that's easily stolen, such as necklaces. And take your streetmap to avoid the possibility of becoming hopelessly lost.' I turned to Rob. 'We never did find those two ladies from Bristol. Did we, Rob?'

'Huhh?' he muttered.

With authority, I carried on. 'If you're thinking of travelling by Metro, please plan your journey *carefully* before leaving the hotel, as the Metro system can be confusing. Be vigilant when crossing the road, as cars rocket towards you at high speed from the left and, of course, beware of unsavoury looking gangs of youths that may be up to no good. Still, I'm sure your evening will be pleasant enough.'

There was a frozen silence.

'Ohhhhhh!' I heaved a huge meaningful sigh. 'It's an urban jungle out there, but then any strange city is. The crime rate,' I began. 'No, no we won't go into that.' I trailed off, and waved my hand dismissively. 'Safety in numbers, I think. Let's stick together.'

Forty-eight pairs of eyes widened in unified agreement. Doris and Ellen hunched forward attentively, clutching their handbags, as though expecting to be robbed from the sanctuary of their prime front-row seats. They sipped gin and tonic from two very nice crystal glasses, complete with a slice of lemon and, can you believe it, ice. I wouldn't have been surprised if one of them pulled a table lamp from her handbag. I pushed on.

'On Saturday evening Rob and I will be having dinner in the Latin Quarter, where there are numerous bistros, cafés and restaurants, many of which have spectacular views of Notre Dame. The Latin Quarter is mainly pedestrianised, so it's the perfect spot for a leisurely stroll. Our evening will continue with the highlight of the weekend: a breathtaking tour of Paris by night. We'll circle the Arc de Triomphe, drive down the romantic Champs Elysées, stop at the Place de la Concorde and pass through the courtyard of the world-renowned Louvre to see the illuminated pyramid.'

I paused briefly to make sure I still had a captive audience. I did.

'We will also take you to the Red Light District, past the Moulin Rouge, so you can see the ladies of the night.' There was lots of giggling, a silent smirk from Duncan and a horrified gasp from Rob. 'Or,' I finished quickly, with a shoulder-shrugging gesture of indifference, 'you can go out on your own and pay a fortune for cabs.'

I glanced fleetingly towards Ellen and caught her camouflaging a bottle of gin with a purple neck scarf, whilst Doris hacked at a lemon with a rather lethal looking key ring.

'I'll give you a few moments to decide what you'd like to do and then I'll come around to take bookings, collect payment and answer any questions you might have.'

'The Red Light District?' Rob mouthed, as I stretched over to the dashboard for my clipboard.

'Well, yes, that's what I said, wasn't it?'

He prodded my hip, and looked at me, enraged. 'We *cannot* take forty-eight people to the Red Light District.'

'Why not? Do you prefer to go there on your own?' I asked caustically. Pen poised over my passenger list, I drew two columns, one for each excursion. I was ready for action.

'We'll discuss this later,' he reprimanded.

'We won't,' I retorted.

'Evie, poppet,' George called excitedly. 'We definitely visit the Red Light District?'

'We most certainly do,' I confirmed in newsreader tones, walking towards him.

Rob made a snorting noise.

George's bony hand gripped mine. 'Will we get off there at all?' he asked urgently.

'George, you're pushing your luck.' I found his name on my list. 'Now, are you coming with us or not? Hurry, George. I've got forty-eight people to attend to.'

After twenty minutes I dashed to the front of the coach, winked at Rob, grabbed my tax-free carrier bag and rushed back up the centre aisle. I spent the best part of an hour and a half taking bookings, chatting, cramming cash into my bag and gossiping. Cynthia, one of my forty-eight new friends, tapped me gently on the arm.

'Evie, the driver is trying to get your attention,' she said, nose-bagging a family-sized bag of crisps.

'Oh, thank you,' I replied, delighted for the chance to escape to my seat.

'We're ahead of schedule. I'll pull into the next service station and we can stop for half an hour or so. Is that OK with you?' Rob asked.

'Err, of course,' I confirmed. 'I was thinking exactly the same thing myself.'

At the service station, Rob sat with his elbows on the steering wheel, chin resting on clenched fists. He sighed. 'Could you do me a favour?'

'Sure, what?' I asked brightly.

'Could you stop asking me if we're nearly there?'

I turned on him. 'Why?'

'Well, apart from me, you're the only other person on the

coach that should know exactly where we are, and that we are *not* nearly there. And you've asked me about fifteen times.'

I shimmied in front of his rear view mirror and tousled a bit of life into my hair. 'Fine,' I snapped. 'I won't ask again!'

He nodded. 'And, it's too late now because you've sold it, but I can't believe you've committed us to taking forty-eight people, more than two thirds of whom are seniors, to the Red Light District. I could kill you,' he scolded.

I gave a rueful shrug. 'I don't know why you haven't taken people there before. Everyone's so excited and delighted to be going.'

Rob sighed, exasperated.

'Including me,' I quickly added.

'Well, I'm sure the odd one or two would be delighted,' he admitted grudgingly, 'but our job is to think of everyone.'

'That's just it. Everyone *is* delighted. It's only you who's moaning,' I told him.

He switched off the engine, stood up, straightened his tie and reached for his jacket. 'How many do we have for the restaurant tonight?' he asked petulantly.

I consulted my clipboard although I already knew the answer. He opened the door, jumped down the steps and turned to help me off the coach.

'All forty-eight,' I informed him proudly. 'Actually, we have all forty-eight coming out with us on both evenings,' I added smugly.

He eyed me cynically. 'Well, I'm not surprised.'

'Is that so? And why are you not surprised? Because you told me to expect no more than a fifty per cent take-up.'

'Uhuh,' he grinned. 'But that was before I realised you were a conman.'

'Is that what I am?' I pouted in pretend annoyance. 'A conman?'

'Yep,' he said, grabbing my hand and hustling me towards the entrance of the service station. 'That's exactly what you are.'

Just before the passengers were due to return to the coach, I stood rooting through Rob's sorry-looking collection of CDs in search of something to play for the last hour of the journey.

'Do you by any chance have at least one CD where the artist is still alive?' I enquired sarcastically. 'Honestly. Dean Martin, Frank Sinatra, and what the hell is this?' I asked brandishing a CD cover decorated with rabbits. He sat on the dashboard with his back to the windscreen.

'I'm not interested in modern music,' he mumbled, leafing through a newspaper.

I decided that the radio was probably the best option. I had just started fumbling with the frequency control when the clients began to trickle back on board.

'Oh, Rob. You are a wonder, single-handedly challenging those louts who tried to break into the coach,' Elaine proclaimed loudly. She gripped his hand. 'Well done.' She patted his cheek affectionately. 'I know I'm safe if I'm with you. There's safety in numbers right enough,' she said, over her shoulder, as she walked down the aisle of the coach.

Rob grinned, stiffly.

Duncan walked decisively towards us and slapped Rob's arm. 'Fantastic,' he boomed. 'Ye're a marvel, catchin' those pickpockets. I'd ha chased them maself,' he said, giving Rob an approving nod.

George tweaked his whiskers. 'Rob, dear boy, there's not many as brave as you.'

After a few more hearty compliments for his famed heroics, Rob stared at me, his neck pink and his cheeks blood-red.

'Would you have any idea why our passengers are under the impression that I'm some sort of a superhero?'

I pushed past him and scurried up the steps of the coach.

'Evie! I want a word with you,' he hissed between clenched teeth. 'Come here.'

'Not now,' I mumbled. 'Aren't we in some sort of a hurry?' And with that, I shimmied up the aisle to check that we had everyone.

Just after five o'clock we drove through the streets of Paris towards our hotel. I bounced in my chair babbling away ecstatically. I remembered a fair bit from Rob's induction course and my Paris guidebook, but to be honest, I was making up most of what I was saying.

'What's that big building on the left?' George asked.

'Ministry of Defence,' I replied expressively.

'But it says Samaritaine on the side.'

'Oh, yes. Sorry, George. I thought you were pointing to the building next door,' I lied merrily.

I'm in Paris, the capital of France. How cool is that? As we pulled up outside our hotel I felt a kind of giddy recklessness. Home sweet home, I thought. I've arrived. So far so good.

Chapter Eleven

'OK everyone!' I hollered, pitting my voice against the rabble in the hotel lobby, where forty-eight people jostled around me. 'You have your room keys and your bags will be delivered within the next twenty minutes. Let's meet back here at seven-fifteen, ready to leave for tonight's excursion.'

I slumped against the reception desk, breathless, and swiped my forehead with the back of my hand. Paris was bloody baking, and this checking-in business wasn't as easy as I made it look. I was exhausted. I'd spent half an hour screeching out names and room numbers, then searching the sea of faces for a 'yes, that's me'. And people had kept chatting amongst themselves, which had really pissed me off because no one seemed to be listening to me. I could feel a tantrum brewing. I closed my eyes, rocked on my heels and counted to ten. OK, I told myself, every job has its downside. This is obviously the bit that every tour guide hates.

A show-off Italian guide wafted gracefully through the lobby with a box of room keys tucked under her arm. She pushed the swing doors open with the flat of her hand, skipped onto her coach and picked up her microphone. I seethed. Why hadn't I thought to hand the keys out on the coach? Inwardly, I blamed Rob. He could have tipped me off. We're supposed to be a team.

Eventually the lobby thinned out as a flurry of angora cardigans, Jaeger skirts and taffeta petticoats headed towards the lift. A gust of lavender hit me like a football in the face.

'Evie.' Doris tugged on my sleeve. 'Where can we buy tonic water?'

'Tonic water will be in the mini-bar in your room,' I told her.

'Are the hotel prices expensive?' she fretted. 'We owe George a couple of cans.' She patted her blue curls absently.

'Yes, the mini-bar is likely to be fairly pricey.'

Her face folded in an anxious frown.

'Hang on a second,' I said. 'I have an idea'

She eyed me expectantly. I pivoted on my stilettos and searched the lobby.

'George!' I shouted when I spotted his unruly mass of frizzy-white hair. 'Can you come here a minute please?'

Rob appeared, having finished parking the coach. I didn't appreciate the way he was kicking my suitcase along the marble floor. I opened my mouth to say so but snapped it shut when I realised that I might end up carrying it myself. Besides, he looked hot, angry and agitated.

'I have our keys. We're next door to each other,' I told him.

He gruffly accepted his key from my outstretched hand.

George materialised.

'George, tell me. How long will it take for you to get ready for dinner?' I asked.

He shuffled awkwardly, balancing a pack of lager on his hip. 'Two minutes.'

'Good! Will you go to the supermarket and buy some tonic water for Doris and Ellen?'

'Of course I will,' he replied, transferring the lager from one hip to the other.

Doris blushed.

'There you go, Doris. Your knight in shining armour will help you. In return, he expects your company for pre-dinner drinks.' Doris giggled at George, who twirled his whiskers provocatively.

Finally, the lobby cleared.

Rob and I sidled into the elevator. His breath whispered on my ear as he bent to pull my bag through the door. In the confines of the lift he seemed taller and broader. As the door closed, he relaxed with his back against the wall. I felt my cheeks burn when his gaze caught mine.

'Would you like to go for a walk?' he asked, grinning broadly. 'I've been sitting down all day. I need to stretch my legs.'

A walk! I *never* go for walks. I don't see the point in them. I sincerely hoped the destination was the bar in the lobby.

'Erm . . . yes, yes. I'd love to.' I nodded keenly, as though he'd just hatched a plan of outstanding brilliance. 'That would be nice. I love walking,' I heard myself say.

'Do you?'

I bobbed my head and smiled. 'Yes. My flatmate and I often take ourselves off on long walks,' I flapped my arm towards the four corners of the elevator, 'you know, around town.'

Which is true. Topshop on Oxford Street is enormous and the last time we were there the escalators were out of order so, technically, we had gone climbing as well.

Rob eyed me doubtfully. 'You *do* surprise me.'

My smile faded. I felt a prickle of annoyance. Had he just called me a liar?

We arrived at our floor. I breezed out of the elevator.

'Are you sure you can manage that little carrier bag of money and make-up?' he asked sarcastically.

I swivelled around.

Splayed and squatting, he was about to be concertinaed by the elevator door. I charitably pressed the hold button.

'Thank you very much,' he said.

My room was bright and breezy with huge louvre windows, fluttering lemon curtains and a cream carpet. There was a double bed with a yellow quilt and faux-leather headboard. A mini-bar sat next to a nerve centre of sockets and adaptors for laptop users that was inlaid on the desktop of a pine unit which twinned as a dressing table. I hadn't long finished showering when I heard a faint knock on the door.

'Won't be a minute,' I shouted. I hopped into my pink trackie bottoms, straightened my T-shirt, whipped my hair into a pony-tail and gave myself a quick once-over.

There was a second, more urgent knock.

'Coming!' I yelled.

I arranged myself provocatively against the doorframe, chewed my lips to make them plump, juicy and sexy, and then opened the door.

'Hi,' Rob said with a cheery smile.

He was leaning gracefully against the wall, looking devastatingly handsome in cream chinos and a pale blue shirt. I grinned and stood back to let him in. As he walked into the room, I quickly tore the hairband from my hair, shook it loose, then hastily undid the top two buttons on my T-shirt.

'I've had second thoughts,' he said softly. He slowly turned to face me.

'You have?' I sighed. What the hell does he want to do now? A walk is about the most boring activity you'll get me to agree to.

He stood by the bed, wearing a mysterious smile. 'I thought we could stay in and have a drink instead,' he suggested.

I slammed the door a little too enthusiastically. He jumped with fright. I tried to look nonchalant.

'A drink,' I echoed. 'Oh, I was looking forward to going for a walk.'

He produced a bottle of champagne from behind his back. 'I suppose we could drink this some other time,' he said casually, 'if you'd rather go out?'

I shook my head, and batted my hand flippantly. 'No, no. Now that I think of it, my fitness instructor said I've been doing too much lately,' I boasted. 'He went so far as to say that I should take it easy.'

'Really?' he replied, moseying towards the mini-bar.

'Mmm, he did. I, erm, spend too much time on the treadmill apparently,' I babbled to his broad, beautifully formed shoulders.

As Rob opened the champagne and slowly poured the drinks, I marvelled at his perky bum. But hey, his bum's not smaller than mine. No, no, his bum is definitely *not* smaller than mine. Lulu says it's a proven scientific fact that a relationship is seriously disadvantaged if the guy has less money or a smaller bum. And I believe her.

An overwhelming surge of desire caused the breath to thicken in my throat. I swallowed and perched on the edge of the bed, knees together, feet apart, arms outstretched behind me, hair loose and bust slightly raised. This was how I looked my slimmest, skinny even. I felt hot, nervous, vibrant, excited and, if I'm honest, as horny as a stoat.

'Do you carry bottles of champagne in your luggage for just such an occasion?' I asked, tossing my hair back, Miss Piggy fashion.

'No, I don't,' he said lightly. He handed me a glass and sat next to me.

This was the tricky bit, accepting the glass whilst maintaining my Marlene Dietrich pose. I managed, though. I've done it lots of times.

Blue eyes held mine. 'I bought it downstairs in the bar,' he said.

He tugged gently on my hair, twirling a long strand around his index finger. A spasm of excitement squeezed in my chest as his thumb traced the line of my jaw. I breathed heavily, and gritted my teeth to stop myself licking his hand. I *really* wanted to lick his hand.

What's come over me? Rein it in, girl. Sip, sip, down the hatch. Two swigs and I was nursing an empty vessel. Rob immediately did the honours. I wrinkled my nose in my glass and studied him. He reached out and touched my cheek.

'Thank you,' I managed.

He started the hair-twirling again. I nuzzled my cheek into his palm.

'Thank you for what?'

'For assisting in people trafficking,' I said.

He smiled and shook his head in a don't-mention-it gesture. 'My pleasure.' Flint blue eyes twinkled with amusement.

'I'm grateful for all your, your help,' I stammered.

His smile widened. He shuffled back on the bed to rest on one elbow and gently coaxed me back to do the same. 'Do you have a boyfriend?' he asked.

The hair twirling stopped. I eyed his hand wistfully and noticed that my glass was empty again. His nose explored my neck, as he reached across me for the champagne bottle. I closed my eyes, and ... well, I sniffed him. It was just a little sniff, I doubt he even noticed.

'No,' I managed. 'Do you have a girlfriend?'

'No, I travel too much. Who'd want a boyfriend who's away from home every weekend?'

'I suppose I may well have the same problem myself from now on.'

Rob placed his hand over mine. I stared, transfixed. It was a beautiful hand, big and strong, covered with a smattering of stiff gold hair.

'Unless of course you become romantically involved with, say, the hotel manager, here in Paris, or the barman downstairs, or, well, you never know ...' He trailed off, persuading his glass between my lips. I sipped on autopilot as his gaze burned into my face. I noticed that he'd hardly touched his drink, but then I realised that he was driving later. He plucked my glass from my hand and placed both of our glasses on the bedside table. 'Comfortable?' he asked.

I was wide-eyed and mute.

He bent his head and lightly brushed his lips over mine. My arm conveniently buckled. I collapsed onto my back and lay staring up at him. I chewed my bottom lip, my heart hammering and my breath coming out in short sharp bursts. From a distance of only six inches, he was even more handsome. He tucked his arm behind my neck and pulled me towards him, and closed his lips down hard on mine. His mouth felt warm, soft and familiar, as though I'd kissed him before, which of course I hadn't. He pushed my hair from my face and started nibbling my ear. It may have been the champagne or his aftershave, or because it was a Friday night, or perhaps it was my recently enforced celibate status, but I knew that I had to have him, *right now.* He lay above me, weight on his elbows. I gripped his hips and tugged him towards me.

'Evie,' he breathed. 'I don't want to behave out of turn ...'

He cupped my face, his strong thumbs massaging my cheeks and kissed me urgently. My tummy flipped. I know we've only just met, but if he's *the one*, then, technically, I've waited a lifetime already, haven't I?

'I know we don't know each other very well ...' he whispered.

He kissed me again. I was fit to burst with want.

'I mean, it hasn't been that long. We only met this morning, and I know it's early in the day ...'

He gave me another kiss, more forceful this time, and extra lengthy. I shuddered.

'And, well, I—'

I interrupted, panting with need. I've never been one for lengthy courtships.

'It's not, it's not early in the day at all. It's after six and we're going out at seven,' I said.

His erection stabbed my groin, which made concentrating impossible. Well, except for concentrating on his erection, of course.

'Right.' He cocked a quizzical eyebrow. 'Right, great. So ... Shall we? I mean, can I?'

'Yes and yes,' I rasped, as my fingers worked the buttons of his shirt.

Afterwards, I lay back feeling wonderful. I stretched and sighed contentedly. Rob was amazing, absolutely a-m-a-z-i-n-g, but then fair's fair, so am I. And no, it wasn't bulky Abercrombie boxers. Yep, it's all him. Not quite an elephant's trunk, but not too far off. I studied his lovely bare bum as he padded into the bathroom to run the bath. I quickly grabbed the hotel telephone keypad and sent a text to Lexy and Lulu.

> Just shagged my coach driver, 2 orgasms, now getting ready to go 4 dinner. Must dash, duty calls. Don't reply am not interested in spiteful jealous comments. Lulu, ha ha, suppose you've spent your day wiping geriatric chins and arses.

I pulled on Rob's shirt and quick-stepped after him.

I am *not* joking, and I am *not* exaggerating, and yes, I tell lies sometimes (OK, quite a lot of the time), but honest to God, I'm not lying now: his naked back profile was the image of Brad Pitt in *Troy*. You know, the scene where Brad slips off his leather warrior skirt, and flashes his bum? Well, I was looking at that very same vision of perfection right now. It was perfect, just perfect. I'd go so far as to say his arse is better looking than his face. I chewed my thumbnail elatedly and wished that I had my camera phone. I could have sent a picture to Lulu and Lexy. They'd have vomited with jealousy.

The sight of Rob dolloping my Jo Malone oil in the bath brought me down from planet orgasm.

'Do you know how much that costs?' I snapped, rescuing the bottle. 'And I usually don't share it, so if you're thinking of getting in the bath with me, consider yourself honoured.'

'I am honoured. Arms up. I'll buy you another bottle,' he offered, grinning as he pulled the T-shirt over my head.

We climbed in the bath and giggled as a torrent of water spilled over the edge. He relaxed back, positioned me between his legs, folded his arms across my chest and cradled my head against his shoulder.

'I could fall asleep like this,' he said meditatively.

'Mmm, me too.'

He tightened his arms around me, and sighed. I deliberated which of my post-sex tête-à-têtes to regurgitate. It's very important you know, post-coital conversation. All the magazines say so. I decided to try a new one.

'Rob, I, um, want you to know something,' I stuttered. 'I, er, don't usually ... I mean, I don't normally jump in so fast. Things have moved, um, quickly here. Ordinarily I would take time to find out more about you and, you know, meet your

95

family perhaps, see if we have anything in common. I usually insist on at least three dinner dates before, well, before . . .' I trailed off.

'We had coffee this morning, breakfast on the ferry and tea in the service station,' he said in a gravely relaxed voice. 'So there you are. Three dates.'

'Yes, well,' I said bashfully 'But I, erm, felt—'

He kissed my cheek noisily. 'I know what you're trying to say, but don't worry. I think I'm a good enough judge of character to determine what kind of a girl you are.' He stretched his leg and turned on the hot tap with his toe.

'Right,' I smiled, pacified. I leaned forward to soap my legs but he pulled back my forearms and took the soap from my hands.

'Steady on there. That's my job.'

Apparently protocol dictated that Rob wear his uniform whenever he's driving, so he quickly popped next door to his room to change, which gave me just enough time to decide what to wear. Consequence of a mini fashion show, I put on a white silk halterneck mini dress, gold sandals and gold hoop earrings, and left my hair loose. Yes, I reflected, as I twirled in the mirror, every bit the sexy Roman mistress. I was applying a third coat of mascara when Rob tapped on the door.

He cupped my face and kissed me tenderly. 'You look beautiful.'

'So do you,' I said, nibbling his lip.

'I don't want you carrying a large amount of cash around in a flimsy carrier bag, so give me enough money to pay the restaurant and leave what you don't need in the safe,' he said.

I glanced at him sideways as I counted out the notes. He was frowning at the mess in the room. Well, I had moved in a couple

96

of hours ago, I justified to myself. That's more than enough time to trash the joint.

'Here you are,' I said, and handed him the cash.

He tucked the notes in his jacket pocket. 'Thanks,' he replied, still appraising the mess.

Chapter Twelve

The lobby was heaving.

'Love, over here!' Alice yodelled from the bar. 'Come and have a tipple before we leave.'

She looked *très chic* in a tight red knee-length dress with matching slingback shoes and a black sequinned bolero jacket, complemented perfectly by her short black bobbed hair.

Rob squeezed my elbow, and whispered in my ear. 'I'm parked around the corner so I'll bring the coach to the main entrance. Keep your eye on the door. *Don't* keep me waiting,' he commanded.

I nodded inattentively, already trotting in Alice's direction.

'Love, you look stunning! And,' she added chuckling, 'totally loved up.'

I flushed.

'Ahaaaah, I knew it! You two *are* an item. I told Duncan, and he, being a man and stupid and a bloody know-all-know-bugger-all-type of person, insisted that you'd only just met.'

I blanched.

'What would you like to drink, love?'

'A gin and tonic would be lovely,' I replied.

'Duncan, a gin and tonic for Evie, and a vodka and coke for

me. Make them doubles!' she yelled, chin raised, head bobbing as she searched the bar for Duncan.

'Am right behind ye, Alice,' Duncan snapped, and patted her shoulder. He turned to me. 'Good evening, lass. Ye look beautiful.' He signalled to the barman who materialised instantly. 'Where's Rob?'

'Gone to fetch the coach,' I explained.

'Coooooeeeeeee!' A now familiar high-pitched voice vibrated through the bar. I swivelled.

'Hello, Doris. You look stunning,' I flattered, admiring her pale blue twinset, matching hair and string of pearls.

'Thank you, dear,' she said brightly. 'Do you have your make-up with you?'

I waved my little bag.

'Bless you. Could you touch me up?' she asked, head tilted expectantly.

Duncan held my drink aloft. Doris plucked it from his out-stretched hand.

'What is it?' she asked.

'Gin and tonic.'

'Oh, thank you very much, dear,' she said, guzzling greedily.

I saw Rob pull up outside the main door, so I clucked around the bar, gathering the gang and ushering everyone out through the lobby. A kaleidoscope of floaty chiffon scarves, rustling taffeta skirts and tailored linen suits wafted past me in a fog of sandalwood and lavender as, one by one, they trooped onto the coach.

The drive across Paris took about half an hour. I warmed to my own rambling narrative, crossing and uncrossing my legs, tossing my hair from side to side and throwing in the odd French word.

'On the right side,' I trilled, mistakenly waving my hand to the left, 'you can see the, er, the ...' I stammered, suffering temporary memory loss. What is that? 'The, um, the ...' I tapped the microphone on my cheek, thinking hard.

'Champs Elysées,' Rob offered flatly.

'Ah, yes. *Le Champs Elysées*,' I chimed, and everyone missed it because they were looking in the opposite direction.

'Ah, ah, ah, to the right, *La Tour Eiffel*,' I continued informatively.

'Beautiful,' Doris enthused, a sentiment echoed by Ellen.

'You're very clever, dear,' Ellen said, leaning over my shoulder. 'You're the image of Audrey Hepburn. Has anyone ever told you that?' She twirled her pearl earring. 'And you're very good at your job.'

I wondered how many gins she'd had, but then confidence often implies intellect and I was oozing confidence. I'd taken to this guiding business like a duck to water.

Rob crooked a finger. 'Come here,' he whispered in a confidential rumble as we bypassed the National Assembly and headed towards the Latin Quarter. I switched off the microphone and shuffled from my chair to sit on the step beside the driving seat.

'What is it?' I asked.

'I'll park next to the Panthéon. That's as close as I can get to the restaurant. You'll have to walk everyone the rest of the way.' He paused. 'From where I leave you, you walk straight on, take the first left-hand fork and the restaurant is about eight doors down on the left.'

'Fine,' I replied, with a nonchalant shrug.

'You do *not* want to get lost with forty-eight people following you,' he emphasised in clipped tones.

He had my attention now.

'Oh, right. I see. OK, you're right of course. I don't ... Say that again,' I said, all ears.

★

At the restaurant, I was welcomed by Delia, *le patron*. She was skinny, tall and glamorous with waist length brown hair and wore a yellow micro skirt, a tight black top and multi-storey gold stilettos. You'd have to be born in France to get away with an outfit like that, I thought jealously. She hugged and kissed me as if she'd known me for years. Trays of aperitifs had already been prepared and everyone was urged to help themselves before taking their seats. I plucked two glasses from the tray and swiftly knocked them back. My nerves were shot to bits. I'd missed the restaurant and walked all the way to the bottom of the hill. I'd had to about-turn the troops in the middle of the road and a pizza delivery motorbike had almost killed George.

Once the clients were settled, Delia led me to a long table where several people were already seated. '*Tout le monde, je present Evie,*' she gushed, doing a Grecian sweep.

The occupants of the table smiled wanly and offered unassuming gestures of welcome. There were two German drivers, both huge men and both sporting dark bushy moustaches, and two female guides, also huge and also sporting moustaches. I nodded and grinned at them, then gingerly sat next to one of the guides who introduced herself as Katya. Delia placed an earthenware carafe of white wine on the table then scuttled off to attend to the diners.

The restaurant was comfortably informal with a slate floor, dark pine tables, cream painted brick walls, and a jumble of coloured Paris prints adorning the walls. Every table was occupied, with our group lining the left-hand wall and a German group of equal size on the right. An Omar Sharif lookalike musician weaved among the tables, sashaying his hips and bashing away on an accordion. Doris and Ellen, hands clasped to their chests, swayed and crooned to every note.

Rob arrived. He looked magnificent, tall and broad shouldered with freshly combed hair, his eyes sparkling wickedly. He weaved through the tables, laughing and joking with the clients, hugging the accordionist who was delighted to see him, and kissing Delia fondly. He placed an arm around my shoulders, and brushed his lips on my forehead as he pulled out his chair.

'You found it then?' he joked, groping my thigh beneath the table. I was about to return the gesture, when he was whipped around and bodily hoisted from his chair in greeting by Frau Thunder Buttocks, Katya, who had been nose-bagging the bread basket and hadn't noticed him strut in.

'Ya, Rob, iz wonderful to zee u,' she ambushed, rubbing her moustache affectionately along the side of his ear. Thunder Buttocks then stumbled backwards and for one terrifying moment I thought she was going to fall on top of me. Taking no chances, I dived for safety. Quick as a flash, she deposited Rob in the chair I'd bolted from, placing him between us, the crafty hairy monster.

The German drivers spoke little English, and of course I spoke no German, so the conversation was limited. I can't imagine what on earth Thunder Buttocks had to say of interest, but whatever it was seemed to have captured Rob's full attention. The Germans drank beer and Rob sipped orange juice, so it was down to me to polish off the wine.

'Skol,' grunted one of the drivers.

'Skol,' I boomed, crashing my pitcher of wine against his gallon tanker.

He performed a bit of gymnastics and entangled both of our arms, which resulted in me slurping his beer. Seconds later, Delia appeared. She perched her size zero bum on the edge of the table and deposited two crystal glasses of champagne between us.

'*Cherie, quarante-huit personnes! Mon dieu! Et votre premiere visite! Fantastique!*' she said delightedly, ricocheting her flute against mine.

'Bottoms up,' I slurred, and burped into my glass.

The starters and main courses were delicious. I noticed that everyone's plates were returned to the kitchen empty, which was a good sign. Rob was still in animated conversation with TB, as I now lovingly called her, which left me on my own, tossing back the second carafe of wine. A guitarist and a singer had joined the accordionist and all three musicians were gyrating and cavorting around the tables, flirting unashamedly with the clients. Ellen was, frankly, embarrassing, as was Cynthia. In fairness to the musicians, though, the restaurant was rocking with a considerable amount of foot stamping and ya-ya-ya-ing from the Germans, and enthusiastic handclapping and tra-la-la-la-ing from our group. I even had a tra-la-la-la myself.

'Evie.'

I turned to see Doris swaying behind me.

'I owe you a gin and tonic, dear,' she said, and handed me a glass. 'I'm having a ball! Are you? Oh, Evie dearest, you don't mind, do you, dear?' she ventured, snatching my make-up bag from the table and toddling off to the ladies.

I sipped my drink and studied the back of Rob's head as he chatted to TB. I squinted around his shoulder, mesmerised by her moustache, and wondered if I should enlighten her to the existence of wax strips. Let's face it, if she's sporting facial hair we're talking hairy pits and burst couch to boot. I hiccuped, and hiccuped, and hiccuped.

OK, old girl, you're getting personal, I told myself. Best slow down on the drinkies, the night is still young. I sighed. I was pissed. I'd meant to stay sober for three reasons: (1) I was working; (2) I fancied Rob to bits but I can't be bothered to shag when I'm hammered; (3) I talk a load of shite and can't remember a bloody word I've said, which could potentially mean the end of my career.

I lifted my glass, swayed to standing and decided to go walkies through the restaurant. If no one was talking to me on my table, then I'd find somewhere else to hang out. I walked over to where the musicians were and, in greeting, the singer buried his moustache in my cleavage. There seemed to be a lot of them around tonight; moustaches, not singers. He hugged and kissed me, well, he groped me actually. I wondered briefly if I knew him – had slept with him perhaps? – such was his familiarity.

'Love, this is the besht evening I've had in years,' Alice slurred, tugging me from the clutches of my pygmy admirer. 'Duncan, give Evie your chair and pour her a dwink.'

Duncan surrendered his seat and pulled himself another from an adjacent table. 'My pleasure, lass. Ye've done well tay bring us here. It's a bargain, drinkin as much as ye like, especially if yer as greedy as Alice. Here lass, try this.' He handed me what looked suspiciously like a urine sample.

I sniffed the glass and eyed him boozily. 'What is it, Duncan?'

'Calvados.'

'What's Calvados?'

'Brandy.'

'Cheers,' I gestured, and downed it in one.

George appeared. He gripped my arm and babbled in a chummy fashion. I beamed drunkenly, struggling to articulate. What was he saying? I bashed my ear with the heel of my hand.

'Are you having a nice time, Evie?' he asked kindly. 'Sorry, I was showing off, practising my German. It's not often I get the chance. I thought it might have been one of your languages.'

Thank God for that. I'd thought I was too pissed to understand English.

'Mmm, thanks, but it's you that's here to endwoy yourself,' I warbled.

'Oh, I am. I'm loving it,' he said and sauntered off towards the gents.

Hell, it's hot in here, I thought, sinking into the chair next to Rob. I felt light-headed. I wasn't quite myself. I origamied a fan from the menu and flapped it wildly in front of my face. Dizzy . . . yes . . . I felt dizzy, not at all like me to feel dizzy. Perhaps if I relaxed for a moment, I'd feel better. I folded my arms, closed my eyes, and dropped my chin onto my chest. *What if I start snoring?* Give yourself a shake, I told myself. You can't fall asleep here! I squared my shoulders and opened my sweaty eyelids. The German driver opposite me grinned toothily. He rocked back and forth, zooming in and out of focus. I wished he'd sit still. I remembered him being unattractive, but I didn't remember him having four eyes. I gripped the edge of the table and peered at him curiously. Sure enough, four eyes jostled for space on his forehead. Poor bugger, what sort of a syndrome is that? I wondered. To the right, Rob still had his back to me so I turned to my left, and almost jumped out of my skin in abject terror. There were no longer two groups of fifty; there were now hundreds and hundreds of people, all tussling for room. Twenty, no, thirty people squashed around each table, heads on top of heads. Monsters all of them, some had two mouths, others several noses. I could see two Alices and they were both pissed. And three Ellens. I felt nauseous and I was in shock. Yes, I'm suffering from shock. Oh God. Date rape drug. That's it, I've been drugged. I eyed my glass suspiciously. No need . . . no need to date rape me. I remembered being up for it. Am I going mad? I trembled fearfully.

'Help,' I bleated.

Nothing happened. My right hand groped blindly for Rob whilst my left hand held onto the edge of the table.

'Help,' I croaked.

I found Rob's hand and squeezed. He turned to face me, zoooomed into focus and clamped my chin. He raised my face to his.

'What the hell!?' he barked.

Rob's face loomed inches from mine. He'd morphed into a one-eyed ogre. I shrank back in horror. I would *never* have shagged someone with one eye in the middle of his forehead. No, I wouldn't. I'm sure of it. Never, no more than I would have shagged Shrek. I need new contact lenses, that's it! I'm going to be all right. Not going mad.

He was saying something, but what? Was he pointing? He jabbed a finger in my face. My hands flew to my mouth. Was something wrong with my mouth? I clenched my jaw, and didn't hear the comforting sound of teeth smashing against teeth. I appeared to be all gums. Had my teeth all fallen out? I crammed my fingers in my mouth, and sure enough, it was just a big empty hole.

'On your feet!' Rob bellowed angrily.

I swayed. 'Gummy,' I hiccuped. 'No teeeeeefff?' I howled.

'Get up. Now!'

'My teef,' I bleated, 'where are my teef?'

'Up now!'

Up, yes, fabulous idea, I thought. But how to go about it? All I needed was a second or two . . . Oh, oh, I'm on the move.

Rob gripped my forearms decisively and hauled me to my feet. He clamped an arm around my shoulders and half-marched, half-carried me to the back of the restaurant, through the kitchen and into what I assumed was the staff bathroom.

106

'On the floor.' He pressed down on my shoulders and my knees buckled.

'I can't! Don't feel horny at all. Maybe later . . .' I sniffed hard. 'You . . . Aaaaaaaaggggg,' I groaned as my backside made contact with the cold tiled floor. Delia hovered nervously in the doorway and handed Rob a glass. Surely she wasn't still drinking? Rob knelt beside me.

'Right, drink this,' he ordered sternly.

'No, no. No more drinks. I'm, I'm full. Don't fancy . . . Aaaaaaaggggg!'

He cradled my neck, tilted my head back and tipped a glass of revolting warm salt water down my throat.

'Finish it!' he boomed, locking my jaw open when I tried to shut my mouth.

He reached over, flipped up the toilet lid and then, unceremoniously, wrapped my hair around his fist and thrust my head down the bowl. A projectile fountain of champagne, white wine, calvados, gin, coq au vin and *pomme frites* burst forth.

'A disgrace . . .'

'Irresponsible . . .'

'I'm furious!'

Well, I had a few things to say to him as well, just as soon as I could speak. He was the one who'd plied me with champagne to seduce me. And seduce me he had. He'd taken advantage of me, of my vulnerability, integrity and innocence. I'm too trusting, obliging and . . . coercible. Then he spends all night drooling over his sexy little Deutsch chick leaving me to fend for myself in a foreign country. I started to sob at the injustice of it all. How could he treat me like that? I took two gigantic gulps of air, and I was about to give him a piece of my mind, when my head shot back and my jaw cracked as a large forefinger and thumb forced my mouth open a second time. I shook my head manically from side to side.

'Drink it!' Rob bellowed.

'Naaaaaaaaaa,' I gurgled, drowning as another deluge of salt water sloshed my tonsils. Fountain number two emerged.

Satisfied that my body was as devoid of alcoholic fluid as it possibly could be, Rob yanked me back from the toilet and slammed down the lid.

'Wait here,' he ordered.

I slumped, drained, onto the tiled floor. Time lapsed, minutes or hours; I couldn't tell. I slept, I think. Suddenly I was aware of a fleshy member moving about in my mouth . . . I seemed to be partaking in oral sex. I had to clear my head for a minute to try and remember who with. There was a considerable amount of activity going on in my mouth without too much effort from me. I must really like him, I thought, what girl wouldn't, he's a sexual gymnast. Unexpectedly, an infusion of spearmint hit my taste buds. A spearmint coating, what a wonderful idea. I wondered if it had been me that had thought of it.

'Look at me,' a gruff voice commanded furiously.

And against my better judgement, I opened my eyes. Rob, enraged, wriggled his toothpaste-coated finger in my mouth. He clutched my elbows and lifted me up from the floor.

'What have you got to say for yourself?' he challenged, turning to the sink to wash his hands.

'The Milk Thistle,' I wailed. 'It waterproofed my liver and all the booze was diverted to swim around my head.'

He looked down at me, gripped my wrist and led me abruptly from the bathroom.

'Milk Thistle,' he snapped, incandescent with rage. 'What are you talking about?'

'I never see gin goblins. Honestly, I don't, but Lulu does. She sees them all the time but I never have. No never.'

He pushed the kitchen door with the flat of his hand, tugging me behind him. 'You're talking gibberish. You're going to sit in this kitchen and drink a whole pot of sweet tea. You have forty-eight people to see safely back to the hotel.' He dropped me into a seat at the kitchen table.

I paled. 'You're driving, aren't you?'

'Of course I'm driving but you still have to do your bit.'

Delia stood armed with a canary yellow tea pot, steam swirling from the spout.

'Yes, yes. Sweet tea, that would be lovely,' I lied. The only time Lulu and I drink tea is when we're climbing the walls with cystitis.

I opened my mouth to speak but Rob turned and strode back into the restaurant. I shrugged, I'd forgotten what I'd been about to say anyway. With rubber fingers, I fumbled through my make-up bag, while simultaneously slurping from a mug of sweet black tea. The steaming liquid whooshed through my veins and fast tracked to my brain. Feeling giddy, I slowly circled my lipstick over my lips.

'*Cherie*, happen to me, yes, before many times,' Delia commiserated.

I don't mean to sound bitchy, and I'm not calling her a liar, but how can anyone expect me to believe that they piss it up as much as I do and still fit into a size eight micro skirt? Honestly.

She bobbed her head and smiled benevolently. '*Bien sûr*,' she clucked. 'Ees true,' she said, sloshing more tea into my mug.

'I'm fine,' I warbled shakily. 'Perfectly fine.'

'Call me, *oui*, if you need me,' she offered, squeezing my hand, before sliding gracefully from the table and sashaying through the swing door.

My vision was starting to clear. I sniffed hard and dabbed foundation under my eyes. It would be a long time before I had another drink, I can assure you of that.

'Evie!' Rob bellowed, coming back into the kitchen. 'You've had over an hour to recover. It's time to go. How d'you feel? Now listen to me. Walk out there, round them up and meet me where I dropped you off, OK?' He strode purposefully towards me, gripped my chin and tilted my head to his. 'You on planet people yet?'

'Of course I'm on planet people,' I insisted, affronted. I stood and smoothed down my dress. He grabbed my hand, and kissed the tips of my fingers.

'Good, about time. Now come on,' he said, turning and barrelling back through the swing doors.

In the restaurant, the sandalwood and lavender fog had converted into a cloud of brandy fumes. Somehow I managed to communicate that it was time to leave and a staggering crowd of inebriated revellers linked arms and formed a wobbly line to the door.

'Er, Alice, can you remember where we left the coach?' I whispered discreetly, conscious of the fact that there was a sizeable people jam forming behind me.

She clutched the doorframe and peered out into the street. 'What coach, love?' she hiccuped.

'It's up the hill. I can see the headlights,' George obligingly pointed out.

'Follow me, everyone,' I instructed, zigzagging out of the door, waving a white napkin aloft. I'd seen other tour guides wave things around so I thought I'd give it a go.

The fresh air hit me like a brick to the back of the head. If I'm honest, I didn't feel very well. I leaned heavily against George as we lumbered up the hill. I didn't care that he was well into his eighties and wheezed like a gas boiler. What I needed was a zimmer frame, and lacking that, George would do.

Back at the coach, Rob was sitting behind the steering wheel, rubbing his hands together briskly. 'Have you counted the passengers? Do we have everyone?' he boomed soberly. He started flicking switches on the cockpit control panel. Reeling slightly, I gripped the dashboard.

I had wandered up and down the aisle of the coach three times, but I'd kept losing count. I'd had a fourth go but lost the plot at ten, when I'd run out of fingers.

I turned on Rob. 'Don't you think I've been asking myself exactly the same question?' I retorted sharply. 'What do you think I've been doing for the last fifteen minutes? You try doing a head count when people won't sit still.'

'Evie,' Rob snapped authoritatively. 'We have forty-eight passengers and a fifty-seat coach. It isn't necessary that you count to forty-eight. Just look for two empty seats.'

I stared at him blankly. 'I was just about to do that,' I shot back.

He looked at me doubtfully.

I set off. Two empty seats, why hadn't I thought of that?

Returning several minutes later, I carefully negotiated the three steps from the elevated passenger section.

'I thought you'd got lost. What kept you?' Rob asked grumpily.

I gripped the armrest as I took my seat.

He sighed impatiently. 'Well, do we have forty-eight passengers or not?' he asked.

'Yes,' I said, crossing my legs triumphantly.

Doris perched her chin on the crown of my head. 'I'm wankered,' she said wearily.

'You're what?' I asked.

'Wankered. It means tipsy, it's a new word. My grandson taught me. He's an angel, such a good boy,' she said dreamily. 'He was twelve last week, blessed little lamb that he is.'

'I'm wankered as well,' Ellen said groggily.

Two minutes later, they'd passed out. Yep, Doris and Ellen were well and truly wankered.

Three minutes later, I'd passed out too.

Rob nudged me awake when we arrived at the hotel. Apparently I'd been snoring down the microphone. Honestly, he hasn't stopped moaning since I've met him.

I lifted the microphone. 'OK, everyone,' I said, stumbling to my feet. 'Tomorrow morning we meet in the lobby at nine o'clock.'

Forty-eight people groaned. I considered the possibility of a lie-in. Perhaps we could get up lunchtime-ish. I put my hand over the microphone and turned to Rob. 'Erm, perhaps a trifle later?'

His nostrils flared. 'The local guide arrives at nine,' he warned.

'Of course she does,' I said professionally. I sighed, and continued: 'So, good night everyone. We've had a long day, but I'm sure after a good night's sleep we'll feel refreshed,' I managed half-heartedly.

Glancing at Doris and Ellen, I wasn't so sure. Duncan heaved the pair of them out of their seats and escorted them into the hotel. George followed dutifully with the gin-depleted hand-bags, and Alice waltzed a confused doorman through the lobby. Finally alone, Rob closed the door of the coach and indicated to pull out.

'Where are we going?' I asked.

'I can't park here. I'm blocking the exit.'

'Drop me off and go and park on your own.'

He cast me a rueful glance. 'You're coming with me. The walk back will do you good.' And with that he pulled into the line of traffic.

'I am never coming to find a parking space with you again!' I shrieked, five minutes into our march back to the hotel. Rob held my elbow like the teeth of a trap. 'And slow down! You're making me trot! My feet are killing me. It's all right for you. You're not wearing four-inch heels.'

He halted for a second and grabbed my hand but I snatched it back. We had a childish hand-slapping scuffle, which resulted in him securing a firm grip on my wrist. Impatient for a break in the traffic so that we could cross the road, Rob shuffled from foot to foot.

'Let me go! You, you bully!'

The traffic lights changed and he bolted forward, tugging me behind him. 'Romantic, isn't it? Holding hands like this?' he tossed over his shoulder, pitting his voice against the blaring horns of the evening traffic.

At the hotel, I slumped against the wall in the elevator and kicked off my sandals. Rob bent down to pick them up when we reached our floor.

'Yours, I believe?'

I snatched them wordlessly and padded to my room. I couldn't manage a reply: I was hyperventilating with exhaustion. Rob took the key from my bag, unlocked the door and held it ajar.

'In you get. I'll be back in a minute,' he said, smiling.

I bowled my sandals into the room. One bounced off the wall

113

and the other landed on top of the dressing table. I wiped my sweaty eyelids with the ball of my hand. 'Where are you going?'

'To get my bags and move in here. I assume I can use the wardrobe as your clothes are lying all over the floor.'

I gave him a backward dismissive wave and hobbled into the room. 'Do what you like. I'm taking a shower. I'm not used to orienteering,' I carped.

He pinched my bum and chuckled. 'Won't be long.'

'Take your time,' I shouted to his retreating figure.

In the bathroom, I stripped off and stuffed my hair into a shower cap. Too tired to stand, I sat cross-legged in the bath and turned on the showerhead. I leaned back to rest on my hands, and luxuriated beneath the sharp jets of piping hot water. It was heaven. I relaxed back further onto my elbows and closed my eyes. Might as well lie flat, I thought. I adopted my man-in-the-bath pose: on my back, hands behind my head, feet together, and knees apart. My shower cap slipped over my eyes. I couldn't be bothered to move it.

'OK, out you get! You don't want to dissolve or shrink,' Rob thundered. He whipped back the shower curtain.

'Ah, a vision of elegance,' he proclaimed jovially. He hauled me out of the bath, wrapped me in a towel, rubbed my back and then spun me around and led me from the bathroom into the bedroom.

'Bedtime,' he said, pulling back the quilt.

Heaven, I mused, to be horizontal as opposed to vertical and marching. I whipped off the towel, tossed it on the floor and then burrowed into the mattress, pulling the quilt up to my chin. I was knackered and sober. Well, OK, not a hundred per-cent sober, but I wasn't far off.

Rob snuggled in beside me. 'Wanna spoon?' he asked.

I grunted in reply.

He teased me onto my side, enveloped himself around me and tucked my head beneath his chin. I nestled my bum in his belly and he sighed with contentment. I felt myself slip into a semi-conscious state.

'Rob,' I ventured, in a syrupy tone, 'when did you first realise how you felt about me? I knew how I felt about you almost immediately.' I sighed reflectively. 'Think of the time we wasted by not, well, by not being honest with each other. By not, you know, expressing our feelings.' I turned to face him and nibbled his lips. 'By not laying our cards on the table.'

'What are you talking about?'

'*Us.*' I smiled. 'I'm talking about us.'

'I met you at eight-thirty this morning and was shagging you by six o'clock. The only time we wasted was the time we spent driving here.'

I faltered, blinking in surprise. 'This morning? We only met, um, this morning?' I stammered. 'Are you sure? I thought I'd known you for longer than that.'

What *was* I talking about? See what I mean? I talk a load of shite when I'm pissed.

Rob pressed his lips to my forehead. 'But now that you mention it, you're right. There's no point in wasting any more time, is there?' he said, diving under the quilt.

PARIS

Chapter Thirteen

The following morning, there was a considerable amount of bad-tempered slamming of doors and rattling of drawers as Rob crashed around the bedroom unpacking. I sat at the dressing table blow-drying my hair. He tossed our now-empty suitcases on top of the wardrobe. I threw him an irritated glance.

'Surely there's not much point in unpacking? We're only here for another two nights,' I grumbled.

His face blazed with exertion. 'There is, otherwise finding anything is impossible.'

I swept an arm around the tidy room. 'I won't be able to find anything now, will I?'

He gripped my shoulders, lifted me to standing and gave me a delicious lingering kiss. The hairdryer and brush clattered to the floor as I snaked my arms around his neck.

'Dresses, jackets and blouses are in the wardrobe; underwear is in the drawers; toiletries are in the bathroom.' Blue eyes twinkled into mine. 'I'm going to fetch the coach. See you downstairs in half an hour. Don't be late,' he said firmly, kissing me again.

I circled his waist as he hurriedly thrust his arm into the sleeve of his jacket.

'And . . .' he began.

'What?'

'Tidy the dressing table before you leave the room.'

I sniffed out our local guide as soon as I entered the hotel foyer. It wasn't difficult. She had smack-me-in-the-face Parisian Dazzling Chic written all over her. She was tall, elegant, and stunningly attractive, with short bobbed black hair, oval shaped brown eyes and a wide mouth. She stood beside the reception desk, gold-rimmed bifocals perched on the tip of her nose, contemplating the lobby. She introduced herself as Carla.

'You tell me ze route?' she asked, raising two perfectly shaped black eyebrows.

I frowned. 'Ze what? I mean, the what?' I floundered.

Carla sighed heavily. 'Ze route,' she repeated, plucking at a chiffony scarf looped through the strap of her shoulder bag.

I massaged my temples in consternation. Route? Surely she knew where we were going? Was I supposed to do and know everything?

'Do you 'ave a preference of route for ze city tour? I can, of course, accommodate your preference,' she explained, inattentively painting a slash of bright red lipstick across her lips.

I felt a swell of relief. The route, of course. As in the which-way-to-go kind of route. For a bum-clenching minute, I was worried that I might have been expected to do a spot of map reading. We'd have ended up in Belgium.

'No . . . er . . . no . . . Just do the basic Paris run-around,' I said jokily, circling my forefinger on the palm of my hand.

'Ruuuun-a-rownnnd?' she echoed, head tilted in enquiry.

'Yes, you know, um . . . be sure to incorporate all of the principal buildings and monuments.'

Her face clouded. '*Mais bien sûr*,' she shot back, throwing her

117

lipstick in her handbag. 'Does ze driver know ze city? Tis not always so.'

'Yes, he does,' I pounced. 'Very well.'

She looked at me doubtfully, and flicked an imaginary speck of fluff from her skirt. 'We shall see,' she said in a wary tone. With that, she pivoted and glided through the lobby towards the washrooms, balancing expertly on towering slingback sandals.

I felt a gentle rat-a-tat on my shoulder.

'*Bonjour, ça va?*'

I spun around. A startlingly handsome man with wavy black hair and charcoal eyes grinned down at me. I smiled and was about to offer one of my many flirty sexy retorts, when (a) I remembered I was already shagging someone else, and (b) he sped past me, athletically vaulting up the central spiral staircase, where he disappeared into the elevator. The hotel receptionist leaned across the desk and gazed after him dreamily. She tapped my hand.

'Ze manager.'

'Very nice,' I remarked, devotedly deciding Rob was more attractive.

She gave a wistful sigh. 'Es sex, for sure.'

'Quite,' I agreed with a vigorous nod. A ride's a ride, after all.

I hurried through the lobby, out the main entrance and positioned myself on the pavement next to the coach. I tucked my clipboard under my arm and smiled invitingly as everyone trickled on board. Doris and Ellen arrived, arguing.

'I'm telling you, Ellen. My grandson caught a virus from his computer. He did. I heard our Mavis telling Larry. I don't know if he came out in spots or anything, but he definitely caught a virus,' Doris insisted with a defiant pout.

Ellen sniffed, disbelieving, and crammed a Kola Kube into her mouth. 'Not swine flu, I hope,' she sniggered.

'Morning, ladies. How do you feel?' I asked them.

'Fine,' they chimed.

'Lovely day, dear,' Doris continued, tilting her face to the sun and patting her blue curls.

Duncan dragged his heels as Alice towed him along the pavement. He shook his big red head like an angry lion. 'Ye've been to Paris before. Ye could have missed this damn tour and had a lie-in. Nothin' much has changed in the last four hundred years. What makes ye think it's any different from the last time ye visited?'

'Hello, love,' Alice greeted. 'You look rested.' She hugged my arm and snuggled close, whispering conspiratorially, 'My head is banging, but I wouldn't admit it to Duncan. Grey blobs keep skidding in front of my eyes. I'll likely snore my way through this tour. And, love, I swear to God, I know I had a fair bit to drink, but . . .' She broke off when she spotted Carla swaying towards us, bifocals pushed onto the top of her head, lips scarlet, short black hair gleaming in the morning sunshine, bare midriff and micro skirt nudging her gusset.

'Allo,' Carla trilled as she elegantly negotiated the steps of the coach.

Alice sank her nails into my forearm and growled. 'That,' she hissed, 'is attention seeking.' She stabbed a finger at Carla's perfect backside. 'Too skinny. My dining table has better legs.'

Duncan chuckled. 'Er, Alice, thought ye said there was no such thing as too skinny or too rich and yer bust couldn'y be too big? Yer just jealous!'

She rounded on him, fists balled by her sides. 'Shut up, Duncan. You simply do *not* parade around, dressed for a night club, in the middle of the day. I am *not* jealous.'

'Ye are.'

She scrambled up the steps of the coach. 'I'm not.'

'Ye are!' he hollered to her disappearing figure.

Laughing softly, he laid a fatherly arm across my shoulders. His beard tickled my ear as he spoke. 'She's hungover but willna'y admit it. Likely she'll snore her way through this tour. How are ye this morning, lass?'

'I've got a bit of a headache, and I'm starving, but I feel better than I should. Rob took me orienteering last night. I think it helped.'

'Aye, well, ye should have taken Alice,' he confided as he boarded the coach.

Carla was going to conduct the tour from my chair, so I was temporarily evicted to one of the two empty seats in the middle of the coach. As I walked up the aisle, I could hear her flirty warbling.

'Oh la la, I zink we will be working very well together,' she yodelled, her hungry gaze lingering on Rob.

'I'm sure we will,' he disloyally agreed.

The coach lumbered down the wide cobbled Champs Elysées, which was flanked by tall leafy trees offering welcome shade to the melee of Parisians enjoying breakfast alfresco. We drove past the Grand and Petit Palais, and then continued towards Place de la Concorde, where we slowly circled the Luxor Obelisk. I scribbled down everything Carla said as we rumbled along the banks of the Seine. Taking notes from her spiel was certainly easier than studying a tedious guidebook. I have to admit that she's as bright as a button and she's obviously very proud of her city. She's witty, interesting, and bursting with fascinating historical facts and figures, and she's on the ball with all the local and regional news. She also has a soothing musical voice, and I respect her professionalism, and . . . *hang on a minute!* I tapped my pen on my clipboard. How come I've got time to write all of this down? What's she doing? She hasn't said anything for ages.

I crooked my neck and peered down the centre aisle and watched as the scheming harlot snaked her hand forward and clutched Rob's knee. I groaned inwardly, and gnashed my teeth as her hand travelled up his thigh. Alice glared at Carla, bounced angrily in her seat and whizzed around to face me. Skinny trollop! she mouthed.

I jerked my chin towards Rob. 'He's no better,' I hissed.

Alice was about to agree when a bag fell on her head from the shelf above her seat. She gave a startled shriek, and sloshed her lemonade down the front of her blouse. Duncan eyed her heaving wet cleavage and sniggered into his Paris map.

Alice rounded on him. 'What are you laughing at?' she challenged.

'Nothin, ye imagined it. I never laughed,' he lied.

'You did.'

'I did'ny.'

'You did,' she snapped, tossing the remains of her drink down his shirt.

'Fan-tas-teek chauffeur,' Carla brayed.

I rolled my eyes. I could see Rob's reflection in his rear view mirror, his cheeks fit to burst as he lapped up the praise. Carla squeezed his forearm. I sat, pen frozen over my clipboard. Rob caught my eye, gave me a sexy wink and blew me a kiss. I cranked up a corner of my lips into a twitching half-smile. Carla turned her head, following his line of vision. She cleared her throat, glared at me knowingly and, not before time, got on with the tour.

We stopped briefly at Notre Dame for an internal guided visit. I scudded to the front and elbowed the throng, beavering my way to the head of the group to make sure I could hear every word. Afterwards we drove along the Right Bank, bypassing La Conciergerie and Les Invalides en route to the Eiffel Tower, where Alice and I had a quick cup of coffee, a hotdog, two Beroccas and a paracetamol, an almond and chocolate croissant, a tube of chocolates, an ice lolly and a family bag of crisps to share. Carla finished her tour at The Madeleine, where a spotty, long-limbed hippy guy was waiting for her in a spanking new Peugeot 207. I peered out from behind the curtain and watched as they embraced. He's either heir to a multimillion-euro Champagne Dynasty or she's been given the wrong prescription for her bifocals, I decided.

'He looks like a stoat,' Doris said observantly, peering out from behind the same curtain as me.

We drove on to the Opera House and parked opposite Galeries Lafayette, one of the largest city department stores. Comfortably reinstated in my seat, I realised I'd missed the sound of my own voice. I plucked the microphone from its cradle with a zealous swipe, and stood to face my audience. Forty-eight pairs of eyes twinkled expectantly.

'OK, troops. The afternoon is free to spend at your leisure. Enjoy lunch! Go shopping!' I singsonged. 'Or backtrack on the tour and revisit some of the fabulous sights we saw earlier. I have a selection of city maps laid out on the dashboard so please help yourselves to those. Have a fan-tas-teek afternoon, as our lovely local guide, Carla, would say. And I look forward to seeing you tonight at seven-thirty in the hotel foyer, ready to depart on our spectacular Evening Illuminations Tour.'

There was an audible ripple of troubled undertones, with no one appearing overly keen to leave the coach. Doris and Ellen fidgeted, and George seemed uneasy.

'What's wrong?' I asked, nonplussed, microphone swinging loosely over my arm.

Doris hunched forward gripping her knees protectively. 'We were chatting,' she said, circling a hand towards her fellow passengers, 'about the nasty things that have happened to other people.'

There was a collective rumble of agreement. My eyes widened as I patrolled the sea of anxious faces. Rob harrumphed, leaned back in his seat, folded his arms across his chest, and stretched one long leg onto the bottom step of the elevated passenger section.

'Er, well, it's not too bad in the daytime. It's in the evening that you have to be careful,' I counselled assertively.

'Yes, dear, but we might get lost,' Ellen fretted. She tucked a wisp of blue hair behind her ear. 'Or, or robbed . . . or, or worse.'

There was an uncertain silence. Rob gave a little snort.

'OK. No problem,' I said brightly, flicking my eyes the length of the two rows of worried faces. 'We'll pick you up from here in exactly three hours. That'll give you plenty of time for lunch and a spot of shopping. How does that sound?'

Two minutes later, forty-eight happy holidaymakers, in a jumble of cameras, tote bags, walking sticks and maps, edged forward in an impatient column and shuffled from the coach, leaving me alone with one grouchy driver.

'You've made a rod for your own back with your horror stories,' Rob grumbled.

I stood by the dashboard tidying my Paris notes. 'I don't mind coming back in three hours. What else would we do?'

'Well I can think of lots of things we could do, but none of them are here in town.' In two purposeful strides, he was standing behind me. I shivered as strong hands gently, yet firmly, massaged my neck and shoulders. He pulled me against his chest and chafed his chin along my cheek. 'Let's go back to the hotel,' he said in a brittle tone, his voice warming my ear.

'I must buy a handbag,' I told him, shaking my head. 'I'm lost without one. I still can't believe I left it at home.' I'd also been planning on visiting the Louvre. I really should see the Mona

Lisa. I am, after all, striving to be a learned and accomplished European tour guide and, as such, I must set about acquiring an all-encompassing knowledge of art history, European politics, current affairs and, well, everything really. But then, if you were given the choice between trooping around a baking hot museum looking at dusty old portraits of bleary-eyed dead people or spending the afternoon boffing the bum off a gorgeous hunk of a man, what would you do?

Rob raised my arm and waltzed me around to face him. He covered my mouth with his and teasingly probed my teeth with his tongue. I circled his waist and snuggled against him. He chuckled through his kiss and rumba-ed his hips into mine. I slipped my hands inside his waistband and down the back of his boxers and slowly massaged his backside. His body gave a jolt and he groaned. I shuddered when he—

'Evie, do you know where the nearest toilets are?'

Rob jumped back like a scalded cat, leaving me dreamily kissing fresh air.

Doris stood on the bottom step of the coach, wobbling perilously with her legs tightly crossed. She tugged the hem of my skirt. I clutched Rob's forearm for balance.

'I'm desperate!' she shrieked.

'There's a toilet in the bar on the corner,' Rob told her, jerking his head in illustration.

'Thank you, dears. And sorry!' she shouted. Doris penguined off, with Ellen quick-stepping behind her.

Rob tilted my chin and gave me a peck on the tip of my nose. 'Where were we,' his gaze drifted to my cleavage, 'before we were rudely interrupted?'

'I really need to buy a handbag, and I'd planned to visit the Louvre as well.'

He folded my hands in his and kissed my knuckles. 'We'll

dash out, buy a handbag and quickly grab a sandwich,' he said hurriedly. 'If we get a move on, we should be able to get back to the hotel with about an hour and a half to ourselves, and sod the Louvre ... well, for this week anyway. We'll go next week if you want.' He grabbed my shoulders and gave me a kiss on the forehead. 'Agreed?'

'OK,' I heard myself say. I could always look Mona up on the net, I thought. No need to meet her face-to-face.

Rob locked the coach and gripped my hand. We had two false starts and were almost mown down by a police car before there was a lengthy enough break in the traffic for us to scooter across the cobbles to the other side of the road. Rob, with me in tow, elbowed his way through the crowds, jack-knifed around the corner and sprinted along the pavement towards Galeries Lafayette. Inside, I tore my hand from his, padded breathlessly along the wall, and leaned, chest heaving, against a pillar. I felt sick. Rob stood with his hands clasped behind his head, his eyes scanning the store.

'OK, a handbag! Is that haberdashery?' he asked.

My breath was coming in short, sharp bursts. I had to sit down. My lungs were on fire, and my legs were jellified. I breathed slowly, in and out, in and out. I slid a glance left and right looking for a seat.

Oh my God! My chest swelled and suddenly I had energy. I felt floaty and weightless and happy. I was standing in front of *the most* impressive collection of costume jewellery I'd ever seen. I clapped my hands excitedly as a kaleidoscope of sparkling gems danced and glittered in front of my eyes.

'Come on,' Rob snapped. He took hold of my elbow and tugged me along the marble shop floor.

Scudding past, I lunged to finger the softly lit glass display boxes. My head snapped around as we jogged past the world's most amazing shoe collection. Rob stopped for a minute to pogo.

'Bags, bags, bags,' he chanted, jumping up and down.

I stood, limp and speechless, and gazed in awe at the imposing Neo-Byzantine coloured glass dome in front of me. And to tell you the truth, I felt quite emotional, a bit wobbly-lipped and nippy-eyed, the way you do when you hear the National Anthem, and you come over all gooey and dreamy and proud to be British. And, momentarily, you forget that you live on a tiny, freezing island in the middle of the North Sea, where fags, bevy and petrol all cost an arm and a leg.

An iron vice clamped my wrist. 'Come on. We're here to buy a bag. Nothing else! I've spotted them,' Rob said, advancing our march.

And then I noticed there was a sale on, and I felt a bit depressed. OK, I'll be truthful: I was on the verge of tears, because I didn't have my credit cards with me. And there was no chance of opening a store account. My situation was hopeless. Everything was marked down by fifty per cent. Imagine that. I could potentially have saved thousands because there were clearly lots of things in here that I sorely needed.

We skidded to a halt outside the customer toilets. Rob jerked his head towards a couple of million euros' worth of Louis Vuitton, Gucci, Prada and every other designer label you could think of. He tapped on his watch forcefully.

'You've got ten minutes tops. I'm starving. And horny,' he added. 'Grab a bag. I need a leak. I won't be a minute.' He gave his balls a handshake and disappeared into the toilets.

I limboed quickly through the throng of shoppers. Sod him, I thought. If he's got time to have a pee, then I've got time to look around. In the cosmetics section a Sergeant Major on the Lancôme counter ambushed me into a chair. She lassoed a black cape around my neck and wiped the make-up from my face with a damp tissue. I felt a prickle of excitement. I love makeovers. Sergeant Major Lancôme chatted away merrily. Her numerous thick gold bangles jingled as she sponged a scented foundation on my face. I gazed again in wonder at the beautiful glass dome and snuggled comfortably into the soft leather chair. I'm being paid to do this, I thought, closing my eyes. How cool is that? I sucked in my cheeks as blusher was applied. Best job ever, I decided, trying to remember the relaxation exercises I had learned in the one yoga class Lulu and I had gone to but, to be honest, I'd fallen asleep quite early on so I couldn't actually think of any. It didn't matter though because I already felt relaxed and pampered and privileged and happy. I wriggled deeper into the spongy leather chair. And radiant, and—

'What're you doing?'

I almost fell off the chair with fright. My eyes pinged open. Rob stood before me, face on him like the Anti-Christ.

'Won't be long,' I mumbled.

'You're right. You won't. I'm hungry,' he snapped. He lifted the cape from my lap to look beneath it. 'Where's your bag?'

'Haven't got one yet,' I mouthed with difficulty, as a gorgeous coral pink lip gloss was applied.

'I'm fuming!'

'I can see that.'

'We're leaving.'

'Give me a minute. You can see I'm busy.'

He whipped the cape from my neck, and tossed it carelessly at Sergeant Major Lancôme, who caught it with a practised flourish. She smiled at me conspiratorially, as he levered my arm.

'OK, I'm coming,' I said.

'Yes, you are,' he retorted, already beating a path towards the door.

'Er, we need to stop for a bag.'

'You can do without a bag.'

'But—'

'No buts.' He shot me a fearsome look. 'You have no idea how much I hate shopping.'

'Oh, I think I've got a rough idea.'

And with that he placed the flat of his hand on the revolving door and ushered the pair of us out into the street. There followed a fraught scuffle as we were roughly marshalled back inside the revolving door by two burly, menacing looking security guards. Rob, thinking we were being mugged, gallantly cradled me against his chest, grabbed one of the guards by the collar and pushed him back inside the door for another spin. Two more guards appeared, ensnaring Rob in a painful looking arm lock. I winced.

'What's going on?' he bellowed, nostrils flaring.

'Er,' I tried, as he whizzed past me on tiptoe, with an escort of three. I hotfooted behind them with a rather a handsome guard of my own.

It was all a huge misunderstanding. Rob hadn't given me time to pay for the cosmetics I'd chosen. Fortunately a replay of the store security camera, together with my extremely effective and seductive re-enactment, resulted in us being released without charge. Unfortunately this whole process took almost two hours. Now pushed for time, I snatched a denim shoulder bag from a stall outside the store, which, frankly, I was less than happy with. We then had to scurry to grab a couple of baguettes, finally arriving back at the coach fifteen minutes late.

Bedlam would be a pretty apt interpretation of the scene that greeted us. Forty-eight bewildered tourists were being roughly hustled against Crédit Lyonnais by mounted traffic police in crowd control fashion. Sweating, snorting, braying big black stallions were bullying and herding everyone together. Alice was semaphoring with a couple of carrier bags.

'Hullloooooo, love.'

Bent double, I managed a wave. We'd run all the way and my lungs were aflame.

'I bought four dresses,' she shouted over the noise of honking cars and police whistles. 'What did you buy, love? Aaahhhhhhh!' A horse whipped her cheek with its tail, she stumbled blindly and bashed her head on a lamppost. On the rebound, she smashed into Patricia and sent her sprawling towards Ellen. Ellen, who was absently rooting in her handbag, dominoed into Elaine, who lost her balance and ended up with her nose flush against a horse's penis. Doris was elbowing her way forward, likely to ensure she commandeered her beloved front seat. Her startled eyes grew wide as Duncan grabbed a handful of her blue hair and swung her behind him, narrowly saving her from being hoofed to death.

Rob sank his fingers into my arm. 'I have never, ever been late. This is so unforgivably unprofessional,' he said in sharp clipped tones.

I felt a flicker of irritation. We weren't *that* late.

Shamefaced, and mumbling apologies, Rob unlocked the door to let everyone on board. I, typically, was left to handle and pacify the police. And I must say, my French was pretty damned good, considering I hadn't used it since school. A few words here and there with Sergeant Major Lancôme had given me the confidence to parley, and I was parleying away rather nicely. I enjoyed the chat. In fact, everyone was on the coach and settled when Rob bellowed out the door to ask me how much longer I would be. I waved bye-bye to Pierre, Jean Paul and Maurice, my three new policemen friends, and climbed the steps.

Rob indicated, and slowly pulled into the line of racing kamikaze afternoon shoppers. I gave a final cheery wave to my mounted chums, and switched on the microphone.

'Sorry for being late,' I began ruefully, 'but . . . unfortunately, Rob's wallet was stolen and we had to go to the police station to report the theft for insurance purposes.'

There was a unified outburst of horrified outrage. Well, there would be, wouldn't there?

'Fortunately he had very little cash in it.'

The coach sagged as forty-eight people expelled huge sighs of relief.

'But the wallet was of great sentimental value.'

There was a voluble oration of heartfelt sympathy and commiseration. Rob's nostrils flared and a pink stain travelled the length of his neck to his cheeks.

'So, as I said, we apologise profusely for having kept you waiting. It's unforgivable, I know, and we—'

I was annoyingly interrupted by a collective thunderous denial of any inconvenience whatsoever. I had just been about to add a few precious trinkets and perhaps a love letter from a deceased loved one to the list of stolen items. Imagine that, an old girlfriend or favourite aunt had written a letter, on her deathbed, knowing nothing more could be done for her. How brave. I sniffed loudly, feeling sad and a little tearful. I sniffed again. Doris leaned forward, squeezed my shoulder and handed me a tissue. I blew my nose.

Rob's brow creased in concern. 'What's up?' he asked.

Then I remembered it hadn't actually happened. 'Nothing. I've got something in my eye,' I said lightly, combing my eyelashes with a tissue.

'They should bring back the birch,' Doris said forcefully.

'Yes,' I agreed, wondering what trees had to do with it.

That settled, I flicked through Paris *Vogue* and munched my cheese baguette, whilst Rob battled and honked his way through the throng of afternoon traffic.

Back at the hotel, we shagged a marathon. That shut him up, I can tell you.

Chapter Fourteen

That evening, everyone snaked noisily onto the coach, ready for another night on the town. I smiled at Rob and took my seat.

'You look nice,' he complimented with a grin that made my heart flip.

'So do you,' I told him. And he did, he looked gorgeous. The sun scuttled out from behind a cloud, sprinkling his blond hair with burnished copper highlights, and a shadow danced on his strong chiselled cheek as he blinked. He's so handsome, I thought mushily.

Doris squeezed my shoulder. 'He has a fine form, dear,' she complimented, jerking her head towards Rob.

'Mmmmm,' Ellen agreed, 'He looks just like, like ... What's his name?' She tapped a finger on her chin thoughtfully. 'Errol Flynn!'

'He does not!' Doris blustered. 'He's the image of, of ... What's his name?' She tried to shake the memory out of her head. 'Flash Gordon! Look at the forehead and chin on him.'

Rob blushed.

'Was Flash Gordon a stud then?' I asked.

'Absolutely,' they chimed.

I smiled at them and turned back to the business at hand,

making a mental note to check out ridey Flash Gordon on the net when I got a chance. I knew my stuff as far as the evening city tour was concerned. I'd read the guidebook from cover to cover when Rob had taken a bath. This was my first real chance to show off and I couldn't wait. I switched the microphone on with a theatrical flick of the wrist.

Doris jabbed my shoulder. 'Mutton dressed as lamb,' she said, pointing at a lady standing on the street corner.

'Better than mutton dressed as mutton if you ask me,' Ellen retorted with a snuffle of laughter.

Doris heard my exasperated sigh. 'Oh sorry, dear. You carry on,' she said, flapping her hand at the microphone, which I have to turn off *every time* she leans over my headrest.

I took a deep breath and began. '*Bon soir tout le monde,*' I said in a singsong voice. 'I must say you all look incredibly chic, very *Vogue*-ish. You've obviously been shopping, but then who can resist such fantastic bargains and beautiful clothes?'

'Duncan can resist, love,' Alice shouted. 'He keeps his money in his pocket, folded in a mousetrap.'

I gave a silent snort. Am I ever going to get a chance to speak?

'Aye, right Alice. So I do,' Duncan scoffed.

Doris turned and popped her head over the back of her seat to face Alice. 'Does he really? What a good idea! It would snap the fingers of a pickpocket, wouldn't it? Just like that!' She clapped her palms in illustration.

'Aye, but that wouldn'y be all it would snap, though, would it?' Duncan retorted gruffly, eyeballing Doris.

Doris's jaw dropped. 'Oh,' she squeaked. 'No, I . . . I suppose not,' she agreed, slinking into her chair, for once silenced. Ellen gave her a reproachful look.

'Ahim him himhim.' I gave a cough and tapped the microphone for silence.

Doris lurched forward. 'Sorry, dear. You were saying . . .' she apologised, stroking my hair.

I pushed on. 'Tonight is our second night in the City of Lovers.'

George leaped to his feet. 'Where?' he roared.

I rolled my eyes. Give me strength, I thought.

Ellen levered her bust with folded arms. 'He was asleep,' she told me conspiratorially.

George stood in the centre aisle. Forty-seven pairs of eyes looked on expectantly. 'Are we there? Don't tell me we've already been,' he panicked.

I leaned over my armrest. 'Been where?' I snapped, chest heaving with impatience. I was trying to make a speech, a speech which, if I do say so myself, will be quite dynamic.

'The Red Light District?' he asked anxiously.

'No, George, we haven't been. We go there after dinner. Now, can I get a word in?' I begged.

'Sorry,' he said, massaging his heart. 'Sorry,' he repeated, turning to address the rest of the group.

Forty-seven pairs of eyes contemplated the skylight in silent annoyance.

He sighed with relief and stumbled back to his seat.

I'd forgotten what I was about to say. What was it? I watched a girl on the pavement yell into her mobile phone and it struck me that I'd been phone-less for over thirty-six hours. I gulped. Lulu and I sprint around the basement of Selfridges and race around the whole of Harrods, because of poor or non-existent signal. That's harrowing enough, but at least it's fairly short term.

I'm un-contactable, I thought. Why hasn't it occurred to me before? What've I been doing? I've been working my arse off, that's what I've been doing. What kind of a job is this, where there's not a single bloody minute in the day for myself? No one's heard from me, and I haven't heard from anyone, and because I've been so busy dancing attendance on all these people, I've—

'Evie! You were saying?' Rob stormed.

'Huh? Oh yes, yes. I was, wasn't I? Yes. OK.' I fumbled for the microphone, which I'd dropped in my lap. 'Tonight we visit the Latin Quarter, named after the intellectuals and scholars who studied there and spoke Latin in favour of French. The Latin Quarter is proudly dominated by the imposing cathedral of Notre Dame, a twelfth-century masterpiece of Gothic architecture. Today, tourists flock there to wander the cobbled streets that are lined with shuttered balconied villas, canopied nightclubs and pretty boutiques. They go to be entertained by belly dancers, musicians, jugglers and mime artists, or to sample any one of the numerous trendy cosmopolitan bistros, smart cafés or Michelin starred restaurants.'

Doris leaned forward so her cheek was level with mine. She looped her fingers under the spaghetti straps of my top and gave a little tug. 'They're too tight,' she whispered. 'I'll loosen them.'

Ellen appeared at the other side of my face. 'I'll help,' she offered, crunching a boiled sweet. 'You carry on, dear.'

I squeezed my eyes shut, prayed for patience and pushed on. 'You'll have a couple of hours to explore the area at your leisure before rejoining the coach. At dusk, Paris becomes "The City of Light", dazzling and alluring. You'll discover for yourselves why the magical French capital is deemed the most romantic city in the world.'

Doris sniffed in my ear. 'You make it sound like a love story,' she said wistfully.

'Yes, you do,' Ellen agreed.

'I like your hoop earrings, dear,' Doris complimented, giving one a twirl.

'So do I,' Ellen piped up, fingering the other.

Sod it, I decided, tossing the microphone on the dashboard with a clatter. I'll show off later.

We parked alongside Notre Dame where everyone shuffled off the coach and toddled across the cathedral square in animated groups, dressed for best.

'Hungry, my Paris princess?' Rob asked, blue eyes slanted in amusement.

'Yes.'

I was looking forward to a cosy meal, just the two of us. Yes, the two of us, in the City of Lovers. How romantic is that? Rob stood on the pavement.

'Good. D'you fancy steak and chips?'

'Lovely.'

'Off you get, then.' He raised his arms and swung me down from the coach steps. I giggled as I landed on the cobbles. He circled his arms around me, clamped my backside and pulled me against him. 'I know the perfect place,' he said roguishly, and set off.

Candles, champagne, soft lights and music, I thought. A wave of excitement crashed against my ribs.

A few minutes later, we walked into the restaurant. 'Table for two!' Rob hollered.

The place was heaving. The waiter grunted in acknowledgement and scurried off, head bowed, gesturing for us to follow him. Rob tackled his way through the crowd, dragging me behind him. The waiter showed us to a table the size of a mouse mat. He lifted my chair and one of the legs clattered to the floor.

'*Pas de problème!*' he insisted, winking impishly and, with a mighty thump, he hammered the leg back on. '*Voilà,*' he boomed, bashing the seat against the back of my legs. My knees gave way and I flopped into the chair with a thud.

Rob ordered two steak and chips before taking his blazer off. 'That'll speed things up a bit. No fluffing with menus,' he said cheerily. He appraised the rowdy throng, rubbed his hands together and sat down heavily into his seat. 'Good turn-out!' he said, glancing left and right.

I squirmed. The seat wobbled. Turn-out?

'Rob! It's noisy in here,' I shouted, pitting my voice against the blaring roar coming from a large group of men swarming around the bar.

He nodded reassuringly. 'It'll be fine when the match starts,' he yelled, smiling. 'Best steaks in Paris in here.'

I slitted my eyes against the smoke. Match?

'Er, what match would that be?' I asked.

We were sat almost nose-to-nose. He stretched his neck and kissed me. A globe of red wine, a glass of orange juice and a specimen bottle containing a sorry looking carnation were hastily rattled onto the table.

'France versus Italy,' he informed me, eyes fixed on the television screen in the corner behind me. And that, I swear, was the last thing he said before hustling me out the door two hours later.

He curved his arm around my shoulders and gave me a hug, raising my feet off the pavement.

'Great game. Shame France lost,' he said flippantly.

I dug my elbow into his rib. 'I'd rather have gone out to dinner with Doris and Ellen,' I snapped.

'You don't mean that,' he said, laughing.

'I do!'

'You don't.' He slipped his hand down the back of my jeans and pulled up my knickers, giving me a wedgie.

'Yes I do, actually,' I squealed, slapping his hand.

He pushed me into a shop doorway, unzipped my jeans and gallantly adjusted my knickers. 'You don't,' he said, kissing me hard.

We headed back to the coach. Everyone shuffled back on board, jollied by the bevy, reeking of garlic and raring to go. As we left the city island I pointed out the illuminated magnificence of Notre Dame, and the imposing Hotel de Ville, which was flanked by brightly lit fountains shooting jets of silver-coloured water high into the air.

'Luuvley,' Doris sighed, clutching her handbag to her chest.

Driving north towards Pigalle, I asked Rob to swing left down Rue St Denis.

He rounded on me, eyes like dinner plates. 'We cannot take the passengers there,' he hissed, horrified. 'Not St Denis.'

'Why not?' I gave a nonchalant shrug. 'It *is* of great historical interest. St Denis dates back to the first century, you know. We should go. It is, after all, the ancient Roman road to Rouen.'

'You know full well why we can't go. St Denis is full of prostitutes,' he ploughed on stiffly. 'I can't believe I've agreed to Pigalle, with the strip clubs and sex shops, but St Denis is ten times worse.'

'Oh, Rob. Don't be so stuffy.'

He pointed a finger in warning. 'No. And that's final.'

I flopped petulantly against my seat.

George had obviously been eavesdropping because he said: 'Well, if you're not going to drive me there, I'll walk.'

'We'd like to go,' Doris pleaded.

Alice tutted and sighed heavily. 'Rob, love, don't be frigid,' she said nimbly.

'Frigid, aye right, I wish. Ye annoying baggage,' Duncan, who had been dozing, mumbled.

Alice pounced. 'I didn't say I was frigid! I'm talking about Rob.'

Duncan sat up, and cast Rob a probing glance.

'I'm not frigid,' Rob defended.

'No, he's not,' I agreed loyally.

'Well, I would have been surprised,' Doris added matter-of-factly.

'So would I,' Ellen intoned.

'Come on, Rob,' I pleaded.

George leaned across Rob's shoulder. 'Son, I'm eighty-two. If I'm going to have heart failure I want it to be now, here, tonight.'

Rob's shoulders slumped despairingly. He sighed, dropped down a gear and indicated to turn left. A cheery roar went up as we cumbersomely lumbered around the bend, and turned from Boulevard de Sebastopol into Rue St Denis.

I shuffled excitedly in my seat, eyes wide and searching. Three girls posed in a doorway on the left, dressed like tarts. Well, they would be, I reminded myself, because they are tarts. So, they're dressed for the office, I suppose. One of them beckoned at octogenarian George. I stared at her, unbelieving, and then squinted at George. A shag would kill him, surely?

'No good making a pass at me at my age, love. First of all I'd have to find it, and then I'd have to make it work,' George joked, creamy white whiskers twitching with mirth.

I burst out laughing. 'Make it work,' I echoed and laughed again. Make it work! Ha, hilarious!

Doris nodded knowingly. 'There's medication to help you,' she counselled. 'Watch *Loose Women*, there's a helpline for people like you.'

'I don't need help,' George insisted. 'I need a transplant.'

Doris reached across the aisle and patted his knee. 'It's worth looking into, trust me,' she advised.

My forehead crinkled in thought. I wondered if I really did have the best part of sixty years' shagging to look forward to, or if Doris was taking the piss. Surely she's not still at it?

There was a sharp rat-a-tat-tat on the driver's window. One of the girls was vying for Rob's attention by means of a fairly expressive gesture: she lifted her top and flashed her boobs at him. I gulped; Doris and Ellen hyperventilated with astonished excitement; Alice clapped madly; Duncan roared with laughter, as did everyone sitting behind him; George wheezed and gripped his chest, eyes out on stalks; and Rob, well, Rob just stared straight ahead, wordlessly.

He shot me a menacing glare. I crammed my fist in my mouth to stop me laughing. I could tell by the expression on his face that no smart-arse comments would be welcomed but the coach was in uproar. A fair bit of witty banter was flying around and spirits were soaring, rocketing actually. I was grinning like an idiot myself until I noticed a price list of sorts in a shop window.

'Er, slow down, Rob. Not so fast.' I lifted my bum from my chair to peer closer.

'What's wrong, dear?' Doris asked.

'I'm looking to see how much the girls charge.'

Doris rooted in her handbag for her glasses.

'A fortune! I'm sitting on a fortune!' Alice yelled jubilantly.

Duncan guffawed. 'Yer sitting on a balloon of cellulite.'

'My goodness,' Doris said, giggling. 'It's certainly worth doing, isn't it? And to think all the years my Alistair was alive, I did it for free.'

'Did it for free,' I echoed pensively. 'I'm doing it for free!' I blurted.

Rob crushed the accelerator to the floor, and turned up the volume on the CD player. 'I Love Paris in the Springtime' boomed from the overhead speakers.

'Food for thought, isn't it dear?' Doris clucked.

We left St Denis and climbed the hill towards Pigalle, where I pointed out the landmark red windmill of the Moulin Rouge. The coach then trundled slowly past the numerous sex shops and glitzy clubs.

'Beautiful colours,' Doris said randomly.

'Gorgeous,' Ellen agreed. She leaned forward and pointed over my shoulder at a window display of vibrators. 'What are they, dear?' she asked inquisitively, her little features creased in question.

Rob's face broke into a devilish leer. He wagged his eyebrows in amusement. 'Yes Evie, tell us. What on earth are they?' he asked louder than necessary.

I felt a rush of blood to my cheeks. Duncan sniggered, Alice snorted, and George's head disappeared into the neck of his collar. I could hear pockets of chuckling further down the coach. I flapped my hand vaguely.

'Erm . . . they . . . it's . . . well . . . they're jewellery trees,' I said and bobbed my head in confirmation.

Ellen nodded in understanding. 'Oh, I see. You put your bangles over the top and your rings on the little side claw. I might buy one for myself. A chocolate brown one to match my dressing table doily.'

I squirmed, wide-eyed, and so did George. Alice roared with laughter, tears running down her face. She clutched Duncan's arm and grunted, snorted and guffawed, all the way back to the hotel.

'I think that Alice is a drinker,' Doris confided to Ellen.

At the end of the evening everyone limped happily from the coach, the consensus being that it had been a brilliant evening.

'It went well,' I boasted to Rob.

He marched briskly through the lobby, his hand placed

lightly on my back. 'Mmmm, so it would seem,' he agreed begrudgingly.

A few die-hards were propping up the bar. Doris spotted us and stopped mid-slurp. 'Evie, would you like a tipple?' she spluttered, toasting no one in particular.

I headed towards the bar. 'Yes, please. I'll have a gin and tonic.'

'No thanks,' Rob boomed, spinning me towards the lift.

Chapter Fifteen

Our alarm tring-a-linged at eight o'clock. I snuggled under the quilt, spooning my bum into Rob's belly. 'Morning,' I whispered.

He chuckled into my hair, and enveloped his arms round me. 'Morning,' he said groggily.

I plucked the soft golden hair on his forearm. 'Did you dream?' I asked.

'Yes.'

'What did you dream about?'

He nibbled my shoulder. 'You and breakfast.'

I rolled over to face him. Something was bothering me. Usually a date lasts no longer than four or five hours, a whole night at the most, if you hop in the sack. But this was different. This was our three-day anniversary. No one goes on a date for three whole days. We've practically been living together. OK, I know it's only a hotel room, but even so, this was seriously heady stuff. We've bathed and showered together. He's seen me at my very worst: crying my eyes out and, worse still, drunk as a skunk, and even worse than worse still, without my make-up. We've reached a higher level of intimacy than *just dating*. Bloody hell, we're almost *an item*, considering the seriousness of my commitment throughout this weekend. And to my credit, I haven't run after that gorgeous hotel manager, have I? Snuggling into the crook of Rob's shoulder, I massaged his chest with the heel of my hand. What bothered me was that I knew so little about him. In fact, I knew bugger all about him, except that he's great in bed.

'Can I ask you something?' I ventured.

He pulled the quilt around my shoulders. 'Of course, babe. Ask away.'

'What's your surname?'

'Harrison.'

I sighed, reflectively. Mrs Harrison. That's fine. I almost like it better than Dexter. Yes, Evie Harrison, Lady Harrison . . . he could be knighted. I think there's such a thing as a Coach Driver of the Year Award. Yes, Harrison will do, I decided.

'Do you have any brothers or sisters?'

'No, I'm an only child.'

I made a mental note to watch out for spoiled brat syndrome. 'Do you live alone?'

'Yes.'

'Where?'

'Birmingham.'

Birmingham, fabulous. There's a to-die-for shopping centre there. 'Have you ever had any sexually transmitted diseases?' I continued.

'No I have not!'

OK, I thought, I only asked. 'Can you cook?'

'Yes.'

Brilliant. 'Are you overdrawn?'

'Of course I'm not overdrawn!' he retorted sharply.

What's his problem? There's nothing wrong with being overdrawn. 'Do you feel horny?'

'Yes.' He pounced.

★

We dashed through the lobby with ten minutes to spare before our scheduled Sunday morning departure to Versailles. Fortunately the coach was parked opposite the hotel. Heralded by a few blaring horns, Rob swung the coach around and pulled up outside the main entrance. A merry bunch dutifully waddled on board, armed with bags of boiled sweets, Sunday newspapers, puzzle books, and croissants and rolls they'd pinched from the hotel restaurant. I waved to a couple of tramps sitting in a shop doorway. They swept a gallant bow and saluted their wine bottles theatrically. I really do find the French incredibly friendly.

All settled comfortably, we rumbled past several Sunday morning markets, and drove north out of Paris towards Versailles. It was a lovely day, beautiful actually. I stretched my legs and eyed Rob affectionately. He gave me a sexy wink, I blew him a kiss and then twisted around to peer down the aisle. A few passengers nodded in greeting and I nodded back. The atmosphere was one of peace and tranquillity. I've met friends for life here, I thought. And I'm with my handsome boyfriend and a coach full of jovial cheery tourists, and we were on our way to Versailles. I felt happy and post-sex tingly, and—

Versailles! My God! We're on our way to Versailles! I felt a flutter of panic. The realisation that I knew very little – no, I knew nothing at all – about the chateau or the town hit me like a slap on the face. I'd been so busy swotting up on Paris that I'd forgotten all about Versailles. Suddenly the silence was deafening. Forty-eight people were waiting for me to say something. I looked at Rob. It was all right for him. The coach could more or less drive itself, and big deal, we can all drive, even Lulu. I'm sure I could easily learn to drive a coach. He's got the easy job. I crunched my pen. What could I say? Annoyingly, Doris was humming. Even the brainiest rocket scientist in the world wouldn't be able to concentrate with someone humming in their ear all day. How am I expected to think? I bashed my forehead with the heel of my hand. Think, think! The humming intensified. I felt like clubbing her brains out. All I want is two minutes. Just two minutes to think!

'Tragic, absolutely tragic. Tragic waste,' Ellen said.

Doris stopped humming. 'What is? What's tragic?'

Ellen smacked the pages of her magazine forcefully. 'Rock Hudson was a poofter.'

Doris gasped. 'He was not.'

'He was.'

'He wasn't.'

'Was.'

'Wasn't.'

'Was.'

'Give that magazine to me,' Doris demanded.

'No, buy your own.'

'I bought that one!'

Doris lunged for the magazine. There was a short, violent shuffle of starched petticoats and tweed skirts, before Ellen snapped, 'Have it!'

Aha, I know! We could have a technical fault here on the coach. Happens all the time at concerts. I grabbed the microphone, slunk down into my chair, hugged the window and had a quick shufty above me to make sure I was out of Doris's line of vision. Brilliant, she wasn't watching. Even better, both Ellen and Doris were head to head disputing the Rock-Hudson-was-a-poofter article.

'Good morning,' I said brightly, and was rewarded by a chorus of hearty singsong salutations. 'Today we visit the beautiful Palace of Versailles, and—'

Thwap, thwap, thwap. A horrendous noise reverberated throughout the coach, as I brutally bashed the microphone

146

against the side window. I slunk down further and scribbled noisily on the glass with the heel of my sandal. Screech, screech.

'Oh ... can ... you ... hear ... me?' I punctuated anxiously.

My face slapped against the glass when Rob took a sharp left-hand bend. Two more wallops. Thwap, thwap. I cringed under his probing gaze, but one does what one must. Screech ... screeeeeeech.

'Erm ... testing ... one, two, three,' I babbled to Rob's mounting astonishment.

Thwap, thwap ... screeeech ... thwap ... My knees were burning from kneeling on the step. Two more bashes for good measure, I thought. Thwap, thwap. I placed the microphone on the dashboard and stood to face everyone. I frowned in consternation and shook my head.

'I am so sorry. We appear to have a problem with our sound system.' I sighed elaborately, clutched my throat and choked up a couple of horsy coughs. 'I don't want to shout all the way to Versailles. I'll be hoarse. But I must try.' I took a few deep breaths and a huge painful gulp. 'The chateau of Vers—'

Doris threw the magazine in Ellen's face, bounded from her chair, and wedged her four-foot-eight-inch frame in the centre aisle. 'Of course you can't, dear. You'll make yourself ill.' She tugged on my arm. 'Sit down this instant.' She addressed the rest of the coach. 'She's too conscientious by far, pet lamb that she is.'

That was all it took. Forty-seven people, many kneading their ringing ears, were unanimously in accord that I was indeed a conscientious pet lamb and should on no account shout myself hoarse. So there was nothing else for it but to sit down obediently in my seat and flip through the glossy pages of *Hello!* magazine for the duration of the journey, whilst sucking on a lemon bonbon that Doris had wedged into my mouth.

At Versailles, I set loose the troops, dived for the shops to find a guidebook, beetled up to the chateau and latched on to a group of Americans, who'd hired a private guide. To be honest, I thought the guide rather poor. Still, at least by the end of his tour I knew more about Versailles than I had this morning.

I walked back to where the coach was parked. Rob was sat in a café, reading *The Independent*. I suspect he may be their only reader. I've never seen anyone else buy it.

I punched the newspaper. 'Boo. I'm back,' I said cheerfully, and gave him a big kiss.

He eyed me disapprovingly. 'You could have broken the microphone.'

'Did I?'

He folded his newspaper. 'No,' he admitted flatly.

'Stop moaning then.'

He shrugged. 'Couldn't you just have told everyone you hadn't been to Versailles? Wouldn't that have been easier than kneeling on the step and smashing the microphone against the window? With your skirt around your waist, one shoe on, one shoe off, scratching your heel on the window and leaving a black score on the glass that took me half an hour to wipe off?'

I gave him a placatory smile and sat next to him. 'It's past lunchtime. Order me a glass of wine.'

Later, as we were driving back to Paris, I suggested that every-one should take advantage of the superb facilities available at the hotel. I told them that they should visit the spa, perhaps dine in one of the hotel's three restaurants or take a leisurely evening stroll. The general consensus seemed to be: Let's all meet in the bar.

'You've brought us together, Evie,' Ellen praised. 'I know the difference between a tour guide who cares and one that can't wait to get home. Will you two youngsters be joining us?'

'Oh, I'm not sure. We have paperwork to do,' I lied. I may well have been telling the truth, though. I think I actually did have paperwork to do, but it was gathering dust in Tooting.

Ellen nodded sympathetically. 'You don't stop, do you, dear? There must be ever such a lot for you to do behind the scenes.'

That evening, Rob and I ordered a couple of club sandwiches from Room Service, opened a bottle of wine and dived into bed. We sat propped against the pillows.

'I'm curious,' I said, eyebrows raised.

He studied me over the rim of his glass. 'Curious about what?'

'Well . . .' I paused, slightly hesitant. 'You seem to have an inexhaustible supply of condoms, and I wondered if this, er, this situation, this sleeping-with-the-tour-guide sort of situation . . . well, does it transpire to be the case, more often than not? Or do you buy your condoms as a job lot and throw the box in your suitcase in a Boy-Scouts-be-prepared kind of way?'

'Oh,' Rob chortled, 'well, you're the third guide in eight years so it's not exactly what I'd consider a regular occurrence. And I'm no Boy Scout. I bought them on the ferry,' he admitted.

'On the ferry?' I boomed. 'What exactly made you think to do that?'

He smiled impishly. 'I was hopeful. And optimistic. And horny. And I fancied you like mad.'

I slapped his leg. 'And cheeky,' I said haughtily. 'So whilst I was suffering from delayed shock and under threat of deportation, you were thinking of shagging.'

He grinned. 'Yes, to be honest, I was.'

'Well done,' I congratulated. 'Any left in the box?'

Chapter Sixteen

Monday morning and the hotel lobby looked like Waterloo station, with three groups checking out at the same time. It took me ten seconds to realise I should have advised everyone to settle their bills before going to bed. The Italian and German groups tossed their room keys on the front desk and marched smartly out the door. In contrast, my lot jostled for service, brandishing euros and credit cards and all but lassoing the reception staff to catch their attention.

Outside, Rob was leaning impatiently against the side of the coach, with the luggage flaps raised. 'You should have told everyone to settle their bills last night,' he said.

'Belt up. I know.'

The coach was packed to the gunnels. Where the hell all the extra bags had came from, I had no idea. We lumbered from our parking space, trundled out of Paris, picked up the autoroute and journeyed towards the Channel Tunnel. I breezed through passport control, both leaving France and entering England, explaining that I'd left my passport at the hotel in Paris and that it would be posted on to me. In what seemed like no time at all we'd pulled out of Folkestone and were well on our way to London. I was zealously scribbling away, unsuccessfully attempting to compose a farewell speech. The bin was full of crumpled previous efforts.

'Rob and I . . .' No, that's awful. I sound like the Queen.

'It's time to say farewell . . .' Nope, that's equally bad. The minister at my grandad's funeral sprang to mind. I sucked my pen. This is hard, I mused, forehead knotted. A faint tickle across my cheek broke my concentration.

'What're you doing, dear?'

'I'm writing a farewell speech.'

Doris patted my shoulder affectionately. 'Don't bother. Hellos and goodbyes come from the heart.'

I twisted to face her. 'Do they?'

Her eyes widened. 'They do, and apart from that, you don't have time. We've arrived at Victoria.'

I tossed my latest attempt in the bin, lifted the microphone and stepped up to the elevated passenger section. I felt nervous and apprehensive, shy even, which was absurd, considering I'd been babbling like a clown to these people all weekend. Ninety-six eyes twinkled expectantly. I stood, pink-cheeked and sentrified.

'Here we are, back where we started,' I managed softly. I glanced anxiously at Doris, who was perched on the corner of her seat, with her short legs dangling in the centre aisle. She smiled and nodded encouragingly. 'I'd like to say what a pleasure it's been to meet all of you, and to thank you for making my weekend so enjoyable.'

Ellen, eyes blazing excitedly, threw up her hands in acknowledgement of what she'd known all along.

Alice sighed. 'Ahhhhh, how sweet of you, love.' She gave me a beaming smile. 'Isn't that sweet?' She tugged Duncan's arm. 'Are you deaf? I asked you something,' she challenged, turning on him.

151

Duncan patted her leg. 'Shut up, Alice. Aye, it's sweet. Now let the lass talk.'

I clutched the microphone tensely. 'Rob and I have enjoyed every minute, and we ...' I trailed off, blinking furiously and squiffy-lipped. 'We're going to ... we're going to ... we'll miss, we'll miss ... yooooooooou.'

And with that, I burst into tears. Not discreet sniffles, or a subtle whimper. No, nothing like that. That wouldn't have been good enough. I let rip with gut-wrenching shoulder-shaking sobs. Aided by the microphone, I sounded like a shagging walrus. Mayhem ensued. The two columns of hitherto happy faces buckled in anguished concern. Doris and Ellen shrieked in horror, leaped to standing and threw their arms round me.

'Oomph,' I gasped, straitjacketed.

Alice belly-vaulted over two chairs, elbow-crawling commando-style across the seatbacks. She clutched Ellen's shoulder for support and stretched to pat my head.

'Hu, hu, hu, hu, hu,' I sobbed.

'Oh, love. There, there, there,' Alice wheezed, breathless and horizontally splayed across three seats with Duncan hugging her legs to stop her nose-diving to the floor. She wobbled as Ellen, her leaning post, ferreted in her pocket and produced a hairy Kola Kube, which she forcefully wedged into my mouth.

'You need sugar,' Ellen fretted.

'Rob, stop this bus now!' Doris stormed.

There was a Mexican wave as tissues were hurriedly passed down the centre aisle. Ellen grabbed a bunch from Elaine and, fumbling madly, held one to my nose. 'Blow, dear.'

I did.

Alice wobbled. 'Duncan, I'm going to fall. Catch meeeee!'

Rob pulled over.

I howled on.

With a stiff indulgent sigh, Rob disentangled me from Doris and Ellen and led me, stumbling, from the coach. As soon as my feet hit the pavement I about-turned, burrowed my face in his chest, threw my arms around his neck and let rip afresh.

'Do ye have the keys for the luggage hold, son?' Duncan asked demurely. 'You see to Evie and I'll unload the bags.' He gave my shoulder a compassionate squeeze.

Rob wrestled the coach keys from his pocket, and handed them to Duncan.

'Sshh, come on,' he muttered affectionately, between clenched teeth. The sobs abated briefly when the nose blowing couldn't be put off any longer. One enormous gusty sigh and I was off again. Rob tut-tutted and there-there'd and walloped my back lovingly.

The passengers, after collecting their luggage from Duncan and George, milled around glumly. Like mourners at a funeral, they shuffled up to offer their condolences to Rob, handshaking and back-patting.

Eventually I shuddered to silence, exhausted. I clung to Rob's arm, waving shaky bye-byes with a white hanky.

Alice slipped an address card in my pocket. 'We'll keep in touch,' she said quietly.

'Yes,' I sobbed, 'we must.'

Her arm curved around my neck. 'I know everyone says that,' she whispered in my ear, 'but I mean it. I've had a fantastic weekend and I want to meet on Civvy Street, as they say. Would you like that?'

I felt nippy-nostrilled at her earnestness. 'I'd love it,' I said, and meant it.

She laughed gaily. 'Or, I might just surprise you and turn up when you least expect it.'

'I'd love that too,' I told her, smiling.

Doris stroked my cheek. 'We'll always remember you,' she told me, rheumy-eyed.

'And I you.'

'Till we meet again,' Ellen whispered, sniffing hard.

'Yes,' I sniffed back.

Eventually Rob and I were alone. I foghorned my nose into his monogrammed handkerchief, and handed it back to him.

'I can't bear it. I'll miss them all so much. Is it like this every week? The upset, the heartbreak, and the goodbyes?' I wailed.

'It better not be! Get back on the bus,' he ordered, propelling me towards the edge of the pavement. 'I'm not driving home to Birmingham. I'm knackered so I'm inviting myself to your place. Tooting, isn't it?'

I lowered myself shakily into my seat.

'Here, count this,' he said, slapping something into my hand. It was a fat bundle of money.

'What is it?' I asked, surprised.

'Tips.' He smiled triumphantly.

'What?'

'Tips from the passengers to us,' he chuckled. 'I've had a change of heart. That performance of yours was priceless. If you can pull that off every week, we'll be retiring at thirty-five.'

I gaped at the whopping amount of money lying on my lap, wiped my nose with my sleeve and made a fan with the cash. I beamed excitedly. Gosh, Selfridges, here I come! No, Harrods! Or, what am I thinking, Galeries Lafayette of course.

Head bent, I started flicking through the notes. 'Twenty, thirty, thirty-five, forty, fifty . . .'

'Duncan was helpful,' Rob remarked as he indicated to pull into the line of traffic.

'. . . ninety, one hundred . . .' I frowned. 'Duncan? Duncan who?'

Chapter Seventeen

Having spent five minutes jabbing the doorbell, and what seemed like an agonisingly long time banging on the lounge window, I eventually reached the dreaded conclusion that Lulu wasn't home.

Rob prodded my back. 'You mean to tell me that you made no definite arrangements to collect your keys? Knowing that you were locked out?'

'I thought she'd be in,' I told him defensively. 'She's always in on a Monday.'

'Is that so? Well, not tonight,' he said, as though explaining something very simple to someone very stupid. He leaned against the side wall, arms crossed, watchful. 'So,' he drawled, 'do you by any chance have a Plan B?'

I'll kill Lulu, I thought. Where the hell was she? I chewed my lip in frustration.

'Well?' he challenged.

I rounded on him. 'I'm thinking. Shut up.'

I tapped my finger on the doorframe, and started contemplating a strategy of genius, when, 'Evie, Lulu said to give you these.'

I spun around to see Harry, wearing his blue-and-white-striped pyjamas, and with Lucsie tucked firmly under his arm.

He jiggled my keys at eye level and I whipped them from his outstretched hand.

'Thank you very much, Harry,' I said, to his already departing backside.

I strode purposefully down the lobby and into the flat, leaving Rob to struggle with our bags. I stepped into my bedroom, where the contents of my handbag lay scattered on the bed. I swooped on my mobile lovingly. 'Argh!' I cursed. It was as dead as my great-great-granny. My eyes darted around the room for the charger. I fell to my knees, crawled behind the dressing table and fumbled to plug it in. Reverse crawling, I picked up two pairs of knickers and a furry chocolate cookie and yelped as I bumped into Rob. I clawed up his leg until I was standing and peered at him.

If I didn't know better I'd have thought he was sleepwalking or meditating, but neither was the case. He was just overawed by the mess. I confess it was pretty bad, even by my standards, but in fairness, I'd left in a hurry and Lulu had obviously been in and out all weekend. Lexy had also been round to borrow my Whistles jacket and likely the twins had been playing with my make-up.

I left him in silent reflection, and waltzed to the lounge. He joined me a few moments later, still looking shell-shocked. The light was flashing on the answering machine. Fantastic, messages! I'm contactable again! I stabbed the 'on' button excitedly. Dink, dink, dink. One dink would have sufficed but, as I said, I was excited.

Beep. 'Lulu here! I'm on a training course in Bracknell. The stingy National Health Service has paid for me to stay the night in a rat-infested hotel.' Dropping her voice she rushed on. 'David is here and I don't fancy him, not in the slightest, not at all, and it's not because he owes me two orgasms. Last night he

156

wore a jumper with an animal of some sort on the front. I think it was a raccoon. He looked like an arse . . . I'll have a margarita! . . . We're having a few drinks . . . Of course I want ice. Honestly, Louise is a dummy. Why wouldn't I want ice? . . . Ha! Shagged the driver, did you?' she brayed on.

I lunged at the machine, but Rob was too fast and he wrestled me from behind. 'Not so fast,' he chuckled, pinning my arms to my hips. I gnashed my teeth.

'I suppose it's lucky you didn't go for a job as an astronaut, eh? Ha ha! You couldn't have whipped your knickers off so easily, floating around in an airless capsule, could you? Oh! Sorry about the mess in your room, I had a little raid. I worried for a minute that you'd been kidnapped because your Louis V bag was on the floor and it's been glued to your shoulder since you bought it. Soooooo . . . I've borrowed it! Anyway, see you tomorrow.' And as an afterthought, she added, 'Did you steal my blue shoes? You could have asked!'

Beep. 'Evie, Nikki here. Reconfirming you're working in the bar next Thursday? Dad wants the day off. I need you from lunchtime until eight p.m. I'll see you before then anyway.'

Beep. 'Beloved sister. Call me. Call me the minute you get home. Make it the second you get back. It's urgent.'

I pressed Lexy's speed-dial number. 'It's me,' I announced flatly. 'What's the life or death?'

'You're back. Fantastic! I'm, well, I'm delighted you're home safe. Yes, home and, well, home safe and sound,' Lexy babbled shrilly. 'Not to worry. It's nothing. Must dash.' She rang off.

How odd, I mused. Still, she *is* odd, so perhaps that's explanation enough.

Rob stood behind me, massaging my shoulders and nibbling my ear. 'So, is your flatmate a clairvoyant?' he quizzed.

'Why?'

'If she's not psychic, she was either hiding under our bed in the hotel, and frankly I think I would have noticed, or you've got a mouth the size of the Dartford Tunnel.'

I wriggled free. 'Don't be silly. Everyone gossips. Take the bags into the bedroom and I'll open a bottle of wine. How about a quick drink, a long bath and bed?'

His face lit up. 'Perfect.'

At least the lounge was tidy and there was no washing up in the sink, I thought, as I clattered around the kitchen. I threw open the fridge door in search of a delicious platter of fresh seafood, or similar. No such luck. A flash of gold shone in the vegetable drawer between the cucumber and the rocket. Oh, what's this, then? Jubilantly, I excavated a chilled, lonely bottle of champagne. Must be a thank you from Lulu for lending her my Louis V for a whole weekend, I told myself. I plucked two champagne flutes from the cupboard and tottered down the hallway cradling the ice bucket. Rob lay sexily on the sofa, having removed his shoes, jacket and tie.

'Let me,' he fussed, leaping to help. He placed the ice bucket carefully on the coffee table and looked at the label on the bottle. 'Very nice. What're we celebrating?'

I smiled. 'Our homecoming.'

I snuggled into the sofa and watched as he opened the bottle. Without a shadow of a doubt, he has the nicest bum I've ever seen. It's not too plump or too flat. It's broad, and it looks like, like, a big mango. I squinted and reversed into the armrest, to afford a better vista. Yes, I judged, it's—

'I've asked you three times!'

I jumped. 'Eh, what? Sorry.'

'Why are there eleven angling magazines on the coffee table?' he asked, handing me a glass.

'Oh, I don't know. They must be Lulu's.'

'Does she fish?'.

'Good God, no! Why on earth would she want to do that? Plenty of fish in Sainsbury's if she fancies one.'

He rolled his eyes ceilingwards. 'To show such an avid literary interest, I would have thought her passionate enough about angling to be a fisherman herself. Perhaps she's thinking of taking it up?'

I gave a snort of laughter at the thought of Lulu, lipstick in one hand, fishing rod in the other, being dragged into the river by a fish. 'She buys all sorts of rubbish. Trust me, there's more chance of her taking up witchcraft than fishing.'

He lowered himself slowly next to me and slipped his arm over the back of the sofa. 'It's lovely. Very homely, very, well, very you,' he said softly, appraising the room.

I placed my drink carefully on the table and skated seductively to the window to close the curtains. 'So,' I sighed, gyrating gracefully towards Rob. 'Alone at last.'

He tugged his fingers through his thick blond hair and patted the cushion next to him. 'Come here,' he flirted, lunging towards me.

I stumbled and fell onto his lap.

'Even better,' he said, tightening his arms around me. I stared into his inky blue eyes. He nibbled the tip of my nose. When he spoke, his voice was thick and soft.

'You did a brilliant job,' he said, grinning widely, 'if rather unconventional.'

'Oh, it was nothing,' I boasted, giving a self-deprecating shrug. 'Er, what do you mean, "unconventional"?'

'Well, I'm not referring to you forgetting your passport, getting as drunk as a skunk, being detained on suspicion of shoplifting, taking the passengers to the Red Light District, or the fact that you tell lies whenever the mood strikes,' he admonished. 'Nor am I talking about the incident when you nearly smashed the coach window and broke the microphone.'

I swallowed my irritation. Frankly, there had been times over the course of the weekend when I'd wondered if I couldn't have done a better job of driving the coach myself. OK, I know I'm not overly keen on reversing, but as far as I remember he hadn't reversed anyway.

Rob hoisted me closer, tucking my head firmly under his chin. 'What I'm referring to is, well . . .' He faltered. 'You made friends. You made a point of getting to know everyone. I've never worked with a guide before who bothered to remember passengers' names. And I admit that I'm guilty of that too. There never seemed any point to it. You meet them briefly, do your job and bye-bye. But you, well, you brought them together.'

I smiled and blushed. I was about to tell him what an excellent driver he was when, ding-dong, the doorbell rang. I tore myself from his lap.

'I'll get rid of whoever it is. Won't be a minute, make yourself comfortable,' I said, scoring his jaw with my finger.

'I am comfortable.'

I wiggled my cleavage in his face. 'Use your imagination to make yourself even *more* comfortable,' I rasped lustfully, and gave him a witchy wink.

Odd, I thought, as I walked down the communal hallway. I couldn't see anyone through the glass door panel. I fumbled with the temperamental latch, and with one last tug, the door bounced open. I popped my head around the doorframe, and saw . . . nothing.

'Helllllllloooooooooooooo.'

Unmistakably Lexy's voice. I peered to the right over the garden wall, thinking she might be parking.

'Coooooeeee.'

Ah, there she is, getting out of a black cab. Shit, she's left Graeme again. Whenever she leaves Graeme, she arrives by cab. It's more sensational, more melodramatic, to stagger from a taxi, a now-single mother, child under each arm, pushchair, baby bag and suitcase all stacked crookedly on the pavement as she sobs and burrows around for coins in her handbag. It's all very *Kramer vs Kramer* and usually costs me a fortune in wine and takeaways. I sighed and wished, not for the first time, that I'd been a single child. I'd have loved that.

'Sorry! Back soon!' she yelled from the comfort of the taxi's interior. She flipped up the window, slapped the screen separating her from the driver and the cab throttled off. I hugged the door and leaned forward, watching her speed over the Tooting horizon towards the open landscape of the Wandsworth one-way system.

I shrugged. I couldn't be bothered to work her out. Rob was waiting . . . I felt a pull on the hem of my skirt. My eyes slithered the length of the doorway. *The twins.* I stifled a scream. Lauren, my baby, and Becky, the ghoul, stood side by side, wearing white T-shirts, blue denim dungarees and sparkly pink trainers. Both carried a chocolate brown koala bear backpack, and wheeled a screaming pink Barbie suitcase. I felt sick.

'For you,' Becky said proudly, and handed me a box of Coco Pops. She folded her arms triumphantly. 'We live here,' she announced.

My heart raced. The twins, she's left me with the twins. What have I ever done to her?

Lauren cradled a baby doll, cooing affectionately. The koala bear's head on her backpack was bobbing as she rocked the doll bossily from side to side, and Becky, well not uncharacteristically, Becky was smoking a cheese stick.

'You 'moke?' she asked.

161

'I don't smoke,' I snapped, and jammed the Coco Pops under my arm.

'I do,' she replied. 'Been 'moking for years.'

I punched the door ajar and ushered them inside. The wheels on the Barbie suitcases squeaked as the pair of them trolleyed down the hallway, Lauren rocking her doll and Becky dragging on her cheese stick. I edged into the flat, and with the palm of my hand pushed on the lounge door, forming an arch, to let the kids toddle in.

Splayed beautifully before the fireplace, propped up on one elbow, chin in palm, grinning and naked, lay Rob. A look of terror flashed in his eyes and his chiselled jaw dropped as he grappled to cover himself with one of our new cream cushions. Lauren let out a horrified piercing shriek and threw her arms around my leg, grinding her face into my hip. Becky, in contrast, was propped against the doorframe, arms folded, nodding appraisingly.

'Who he then?' she quizzed, tossing her cheese stick on the carpet and mincing it with her sparkly trainer.

'Evie!' Rob bleated.

I limped to the sofa, as limping was all I could manage with Lauren attached to my leg, and grabbed his clothes. I pitched them across the coffee table at him and then bustled the kids into the bedroom to off-load their luggage.

I stood semi-slumped against the bedroom wall. 'Where's your mum gone?' I asked, terrified of the reply.

'Venna to buy toys,' Becky informed me.

I blanched. Vienna! 'How long for?' I hedged.

'Two years,' Becky announced, mountaineering onto the bed.

My innards contracted with anxiety.

'Two days,' Lauren corrected, the doll now dangling limply from her hand.

Becky perched on her knees like a little gnome and burrowed clasped hands between her thighs. Her eyes evaluated my dressing table. 'Am staying for ever and ever. Happy ever after, if I like it,' she declared brightly.

Rob, now dressed, filled the doorway. I held his eye and nodded invitingly. 'Er, meet my nieces. This is Becky,' I gestured, 'and this is Lauren.'

'Nice. To. Meet. You,' he punctuated, as though they might have suffered a hearing impediment or not understand English.

I waved a hand at Rob. 'This is, this is my . . . my boyfriend,' I introduced.

Lauren glared at him wide-eyed and wobbly lipped.

'Anuffer one?' Becky frowned. 'Dad says you've had hundreds.'

I seethed and hoofed the carpet. 'Is that so? I'm sure he was thinking of someone else,' I snapped curtly.

She eyed me doubtfully.

Rob made a snuffly snorting sound. 'Hundreds,' he echoed.

'Well,' I managed, 'this is nice, just the four of us. Shall we watch telly?' I suggested with a big sigh and a heavy heart.

A few minutes later, Rob and I sat glumly at either end of the sofa with the kids seated between us. Lexy, of course, wasn't answering her phone. Ditto, my brother-in-law. No surprises there. I missiled my mobile onto the armchair, and downed my champagne.

We watched *Parent Trap*. Rob glared at Becky in amazement as she rewound the scene, nine times, where the father's girlfriend has a lizard crawling in her hair, her laughter becoming more and more satanic and voluble each time. Eventually, she slithered from the sofa, slumped to the floor and lay face down, red faced and breathless with mirth. Lauren, on the other hand, was peering in horror from behind a cushion. At the end of the film I stood and exercised an exaggerated yawn, and plodded off to drag the travel cot from the hall cupboard. Rob set it up in the lounge behind the sofa whilst I fought the kids into their pyjamas.

'You seeping with him?' Becky asked nosily, jerking her head towards Rob.

'Yes, I am,' I replied, forcing her arm roughly into her sleep suit.

'Can I seep with you as well?'

'No, you can't,' I shot back. 'You have a comfy bed in here,' I said, lifting her into the travel cot. It was an oblong mesh playpen with a mattress base that my sister had thoughtfully bought me for Christmas last year. The twins snuggled down, head to toe, Lauren cuddling her doll and Becky cradling her vampire.

'Nightie night,' I breathed, and tiptoed from the lounge.

In my bedroom, I threw back the quilt and climbed into bed.

'Your sister's got a bit of a cheek,' Rob said, punching the pillows. 'I mean, she buggers off for two days and leaves her kids. Just like that.' He clicked his fingers.

'Are you wearing your boxers?' I asked numbly.

'No, of course not.'

'Put them on.'

'Why?'

'Just in case.'

'In case of what?'

An hour later we lay in the gloom, four in a row, Becky and Lauren like a couple of dead slugs in the middle, Rob and I perched perilously at either edge of the bed.

'Are they, well ...' He faltered, then rushed on. 'Are they incontinent?'

I smiled tiredly. 'They've been incontinent for most of their lives,' I told him.

He gave a startled gasp.

'But they're not any more.'

He exhaled in relief. 'Right, good. I'll balance here on my belly with my left hand on the floor then, shall I?' he grumbled.

Becky farted.

'Was that you?' Rob asked, knowing perfectly well it wasn't.

Lauren farted.

'You're overexcited. Calm down,' he said.

Rob had set the alarm for six the next morning, claiming that he needed to beat the traffic on the M25. Creeping around the room, he packed his bag, kissed me, and then stole away into the morning dawn, leaving me alone with Lauren and the Child of the Corn. I awoke at ten to find the pair of them hovering above me like a pair of vultures. Becky prised my eyes open with my eyelash curlers. Each wore one of my All Saints tops and full make-up. They had backcombed their hair, which was now stiff with hairspray, and they reeked of my Agent Provocateur perfume.

'She's dead?' Becky stated hollowly.

'She's *not* dead,' Lauren bleated, stroking my brow.

'If she is, am having the make-up bag,' Becky announced excitedly.

I crabbed backwards against the headboard, and wiggled a finger at Becky. 'I am not dead and when I do die, you are *not* having my make-up bag.'

Her chin disappeared into her neck as she shrugged.

'What's your vampire's name?' I asked, nodding at her companion cuddled under her arm.

'Evie, same like you,' she proudly informed me.

'How charming!'

I lumbered out of bed and the girls toddled behind me into

the kitchen. I filled two bowls with Coco Pops and milk and told them to sit on the floor – damage limitation tactics. They snuggled against the fridge, legs in open triangles, playing 'a slurp for you and a slurp for me' with each other. They are, I decided, revolting. I plucked a cloth from the sink and mopped the floor, and for lack of anything else to hand, swished the same cloth over their soppy cheeks. I checked the clock and sighed. I'd only been up twenty minutes. Hands gripping the kitchen worktop, I stared dejectedly out of the window. My mobile beeped. It was a text from Lexy. I fumbled clumsily to open the message.

Back Wednesday afternoon. Thank you so much, you're the best. Graeme and I are having afternoon sex. Surely you don't begrudge me that?

I did.

After breakfast, the twins decided to play dress-up. Lauren pranced around the lounge dressed as Cinderella, tottering dangerously in a pair of my shoes. Her seven Barbies were camped along the sofa. Becky sported a witch's outfit. Her family of wicked trolls floated upside down in a basin of water on the coffee table. She'd said she wanted to wash them, but typically she'd drowned them instead.

I looked at the clock for the hundredth time. Initially, the thought of taking them out without a pushchair, thanks to an oversight on Lexy's part, brought on minor heart palpitations. But a combination of my nerves being shot to bits, a stifling July heat wave and the realisation that I'd actually considered a glass of wine at eleven o'clock forced me out the door.

The three of us cannoned into the pet shop at the end of our road. Amid noisy oohs and aaahs, Becky admired the snakes and Lauren the hamsters.

'Where are they?' I muttered, eyes flashing around the shop. I lurched forward when I spotted what I was looking for.

'Can I have a big black rat peese?' Becky asked.

'No you can't because if Lucsie next door caught it, he would eat it,' I explained

Her eyes shone at the possibility. 'For his lunch?' she asked excitedly. 'Wiff chips?'

I picked up two puppy collars and a duo leash from the shelf. Might as well buy pink to match their T-shirts, I decided. It's never too soon to instil a modicum of good taste. They are, after all, my flesh and blood, I thought loyally.

To the horrified disgust of the ferret-like male shop assistant, I clipped the collars onto the twins' wrists, attached the leash and had a practice tug around the store. It might just work, I thought optimistically, as they tripped behind me. Not ideal, I know, but at least they can't run away and I won't lose them.

Much cheered up, and congratulating myself on my initiative, I ventured towards the High Street, and towed them into the supermarket, where Becky drooled over the lifeless, boggle-eyed fish on the fresh produce counter.

'I like them dead,' she said airily.

She would!

I bought her a couple of trout because she promised she'd play with them for an hour when we got home. Anything for peace and quiet, I decided. We ploughed on to the Found for a Pound shop where I read *OK!* magazine from front to back whilst the kids scoffed greedily at the Pick 'n' Mix counter. This, I thought, is inspired as now I obviously needn't bother to fix them lunch. We plodded to Threshers, where I bought a bottle of gin, replaced Lulu's champagne and the kids each chose a bar of Galaxy chocolate the size of a car roof. Wonderful, I mulled, that's dinner cooked and served. We eventually limped through the door of the flat three hours later.

Lulu was home. All was not well. She was sat on the sofa, twirling her hoop earring, rocking back and forth. A bottle of sparkling Prosecco stood upright in the ice bucket and an empty bottle lay on the floor by her feet. She sniffed loudly and with wide rheumy eyes silently contemplated a spot on the carpet. The kids climbed the armchair and sat squashed, side by side. Lauren, sensing impending doom, looked worriedly between Lulu and me. Becky, also sensing impending doom, squeaked and wriggled excitedly. I propped an elbow against the fireplace and waited, chin in palm, because when Lulu's like this, wait is all you can do. She dresses to suit her mood and judging by her outfit, her mood was manically suicidal. She wore a pair of Arsenal socks – I can't imagine where she found those – and my white dressing gown, which she must've found at the bottom of the wash bin. Banana milkshake decorated the front, there was a coffee stain on the sleeve and a ketchup cloud on the pocket. Her hurricane of blonde hair was tied up with a black fishnet stocking and her mascara and lipstick were smudged. She rocked like a demon, gnawing at her green nail varnish. She ground her fists into her eyes.

'Like it, do you?' she snapped, flinging her arm aimlessly.

I risked a smile. 'Like what?'

Wide-eyed, she addressed the ceiling. 'The chaise longue of course!' she yelled.

I glanced around the room and unless I was mistaken there was no George IV chaise longue, circa 1825, with scrolled foliate decoration in evidence. I raised confused brows. 'Is it in your room? Have you thrown out your bed?' I asked softly.

She jerked her head towards the window. 'It's there!'

She bent down and tugged roughly on her Arsenal socks,

pulling them up over her knees. She plucked her glass from the table and took a large draught of wine. I frowned and cast my eyes towards the ever-familiar dining table in the window alcove.

'There!' she shrieked, raising her glass and toasting the very same alcove.

'Erm,' I hedged. 'Are you . . . I mean, well, how many drinks have you had?'

'Not enough.'

She bounded to standing, lunged towards the window and snatched a small white box from the table. Eyes narrowed and shining with fury, she thrust the box in my chest.

Becky clapped her hands excitedly. 'A rat?' she squealed. 'Call him Ratty.'

Lauren massaged her little knees. 'A budgie,' was her hopeful guess.

I opened the box uneasily. Inside was a beautiful miniature cream chaise longue. I held it up to show the twins. They exchanged a disappointed look, descended the armchair and toddled from the room down the hallway towards the bathroom with the packet of trout we'd bought earlier.

Lulu slammed the door behind them. 'It's for a fucking doll's house!' she stormed. 'I've been mugged off, conned, had-over. It looked huge online, and the seller has disappeared. Well, what a surprise!' She paced the room, swinging her wine bottle. Her hair tornado bobbed and buckled as the fishnet stocking loosened.

'Oh,' I sympathised, sucking my wrist to stop me laughing. 'Surely the dimensions were listed?' I managed between sucks.

She slammed the wine bottle on the coffee table, then grabbed my chin roughly. 'Be honest. Who in their right mind would pay over three hundred quid for a piece of furniture for a doll's house? What kind of fruitcake would do that? Eh, you tell me: what sort of a raving lunatic would buy an antique for a doll's house?' she raged. She slumped by the fireplace, arms by her side, fists clenched.

I could have said, 'you would', but I didn't. I led her to the sofa, sat her down and put my arm around her shoulder.

'How about we treat ourselves to a curry?'

She sniffed dejectedly and fingered the little chaise longue.

'You do buy a load of shite,' I told her.

She sniffed again. 'What shall I do with this?' she lamented, turning it over in her palm.

'Sit your vibrator on it,' I suggested.

She tried for a chuckle. 'It's too small, even for that.'

We huddled together studying the miniature.

'Ah!' she gasped in a flash of inspiration. 'I know. Yes, I know! Shit, of course. Why didn't I think of it before?' She turned to me with bright avid eyes. 'I'll buy an antique doll's house, and collect all the furniture, and take it to that programme, *The Antiques Roadshow*, when they come to Tooting, and I'll be on telly and they'll say, "How much did you pay for this fine collection?" and I'll say, "Oh, about two grand all in." And I'll wave my hand dismissively as if two grand is sod all. And they'll say, "Well, how interesting" and then they'll pause and everyone gathered around me will hold their breath in anticipation, and so will I. And then they'll say, "You made an exceptionally wise purchase, because today, at auction, you could easily expect to achieve over fifteen thousand."' She leaped up from the sofa and grabbed the wine bottle. 'Get a glass. We're celebrating.' The dressing gown fell open. She stood resplendent, naked but for her Arsenal socks. She placed the little chaise longue on top of the television. 'Be careful with this when you're dusting,' she warned.

★

We had a girls' night in. I must have had to wrestle my glass from Becky about ten times. Eventually, Lulu and I climbed inside the travel cot with two plates of curry and the ice bucket, which had gin and tonic propped inside. My brilliant idea, of course. Because of the raised mattress, the kids can climb out of the cot, but they're not tall enough to climb in. Knackered from trying to mountaineer the cot's outer limits, the pair of them lay sprawled on a picnic blanket – also my idea – chomping on naan bread, chicken korma and Galaxy chocolate, while watching the Shopping Channel.

I plopped a couple of ice cubes in our glasses. 'What's with the angling magazines?' I asked as we sat, legs crossed.

'Well, Vic's a marine biologist and I know bugger all about fish.' Lulu relaxed against the cot's mesh wall. 'I want to be able to throw the odd intelligent line into the conversation.'

I nodded in understanding.

'I might buy a fish tank. He's got an Aston Martin, you know, and he's a great shag,' she boasted.

'Oh, this is the guy you went out with last Thursday?'

'Mmm,' she nodded, cramming a fork loaded with curry into her mouth.

'So have you had three nights out, with exquisite dining and fine wines?' I asked.

She shook her head stiffly, and waved her fork aloft. 'Nah,' she said. 'I changed my mind and reduced it to three courses, so I made myself order a dessert on Thursday night, and shagged him on Friday after he'd eaten a bowl of peanuts I put on the table. And he was brilliant. I think I love him.'

She loves them all.

She shuffled closer to me. 'Tell me about your man,' she giggled. 'Your driver.'

So I did, and I left nothing out.

Chapter Eighteen

Lexy ding-donged the doorbell at exactly two-thirty on Wednesday afternoon. I climbed out of the travel cot, where I'd been sipping coffee and daydreaming about Rob, and sprinted to the front door. I threw my arms around her in welcome, and all but threw my legs around her as well, and then I remembered that I wasn't speaking to her. I pushed her back against the doorframe.

'Oooch,' she winced.

'Pick up your kids and go,' I spat venomously.

'Thanks a million for having the twins,' she gushed. She squeezed my arm affectionately, shimmied through the door, and walked past me.

'I never want to see you again!' I shrieked at her marching figure.

'We had a great time, thanks,' she trilled over her shoulder.

I jabbed her in the back. 'Or Graeme. I hate him as much as I hate you.'

She turned and smiled dreamily. 'He enjoyed it too.'

'I could report you to, to, well, to Social Services,' I threatened.

She eyed me reflectively. 'It was fantastic, amazing, and yes, Vienna is beautiful.'

We reached the door of the flat and bustled through simultaneously, hip to hip.

'Don't ask me for anything. No favours, clothes or anything,' I hissed, sidestepping past her.

'You're the best sister in the world,' she praised.

'I hate your guts,' I spat over my shoulder, elbow sprinting down the hallway.

'I bought you a red Mulberry purse and key ring.'

I halted. She bashed into me. I spun around.

'Did you?' I asked.

Her brown eyes shone zealously. She nodded. 'I did. Now give me a hand to get the kids and all my gear together. We'll have a quick coffee and I'll give you your pressie.'

'Oh, OK. I'll put the kettle on then, shall I?' I mustered.

'Were the kids all right?' she asked in a motherly tone.

I flapped my hand. 'Good as gold,' I told her.

Thursday slugged along at an unbelievably slow pace. I missed Rob like mad. I couldn't wait to get to work on Friday and see him again. I exfoliated, plucked, waxed, scrubbed and painted myself to perfection. And just before six o'clock, I leaped into my car and throttled down Garrett Lane and up to Wimbledon, where I pancaked a sales assistant to the wall when she tried to lock me out of Anne Summers. I limboed sideways through the door and spent £150 in five minutes on lots of lovely bras and knickers. My new uniform for my new job, I told myself.

I went to bed early that night, reasoning that asleep I'd miss Rob marginally less than I would if I stayed awake. I also replaced Brad Pitt with Rob in my off-to-sleep shagathon. This was seriously heady stuff. A non-celebrity dream shag had never, hitherto, been allowed. Except for my Viking, of course.

★

My stilettos scraped the kerb as the cab screeched to a halt on Friday morning at Victoria.

'Awright, love?' the driver asked.

I tumbled out and rammed a fistful of notes through his open side window. 'Yes, yes. Keep the change,' I offered generously. I couldn't wait to see Rob. I'd jerked awake twice in the night dreaming about him.

He stood by the coach, shoulders wide, legs slightly apart, strawberry blond hair tousled and fists on hips. He was perfect. I heaved my case along the pavement and trolleyed towards him. Shit, I thought, as I wobbled unsteadily, this case weighs a ton, even with wheels. My heel suddenly wedged itself between two paving stones. I dropped the handle of the case and knelt to rescue my foot. I gazed up at him from my crouched-on-the-pavement position. He waved. I smiled, waved back, struggled to standing and massaged my aching shoulder. Look at him, striking as ever. Well, as striking as the last time I saw him. I limped quickly on, careful to avoid the holes in the pavement.

'Agggg!' A sharp pain shot up my leg when my heel became trapped for the second time. Rob stretched, rested one hand on the side of the coach, winked sexily and blew his fringe from his forehead in a practised sangfroid gesture. I stumbled and stopped short, dropped the handle of my case and whizzed the strap of my handbag up my arm onto my shoulder. Just a minute, I thought. There he is, standing like some bloody Roman Emperor, watching me almost break my bloody leg twice and drag this coffin-sized suitcase behind me.

'Get over here!'

He threw his hands in the air as if surprised that the thought to help me hadn't immediately occurred to him and jogged towards me. 'Sorry, babe. Sorry, I was just looking at you,' he apologised. He bent his head to kiss me.

I jabbed a finger viciously at my case. 'What? Looking at me carry that?' I yelled.

He laughed and spun me around effortlessly. 'I've missed you,' he said. 'Three whole days. I've been a monk,' he promised.

'I've been a nun,' I told him, grinning widely.

He winked. 'Have you now?'

First to arrive at the coach were a group of eight ladies, who I'd guess were in their early to mid seventies. They marched towards me, laden with tapestry bags that were stuffed to the hilt with wool, knitting needles and copies of *Woman*, *Woman's Own* and *Woman's Realm*, which, I have to say, didn't accessorise well with the Louis Vuitton shoes, and matching handbags and suitcases.

'Good morning,' I said, smiling.

'Morning,' they carolled, and steamrolled past in a cloud of Coco Chanel to mount the steps of the coach. The last to charge pivoted on her Louis Vs and rattled off an introduction of sorts.

'Hazel, Kitty, Freya, Meg, Kelly, Amy, Dora.' She smiled and extended her hand. 'And I'm Elise.'

'Right,' I rallied. 'It's your surnames I need,' I informed her, pen frozen over my clipboard.

She bustled over, whipped the pen from my hand and smartly ticked off the names of her gang. I glanced sideways through the coach window. A muddle of cashmere cardigans and Jaeger-clad backsides settled themselves into the front four rows. I decided not to mention seat rotation. I was too scared to move them.

'Is everyone here?' Rob asked when the luggage hold was almost full.

I leaned forward and straightened his already straight tie. 'Yes,' I said, grinning.

'I have a surprise for you,' he teased, circling his thumbs on my hips.

'Oh … what is it?'

He smiled and lightly brushed his lips over mine. 'You'll find out soon enough.'

'Can't wait,' I said sexily.

He must have bought me something. What other kind of surprises are there? I thought excitedly, and floated up the steps of the coach, clutching my clipboard dreamily.

My sales pitch wasn't as harrowing as it had been the previous week. Although I admit to telling a few weeny white lies. If I'm honest, I did blurt out one big whopper: I told everyone that Doris had been robbed.

Once out of London, I waltzed up and down the aisle of the coach, taking excursion bookings. 'Your money or your jewels,' I said, not entirely joking.

When we arrived at the Channel Tunnel terminal in Folkestone, I was perched jubilantly on the edge of my chair, sorting the money into 'them' and 'us' bundles, with the finesse of a Mafia bookkeeper. The restaurant was 'them', and the rest was 'us'. What I need, I thought, is one of those useful little rubber thumbs for counting money. Forty-five out of forty-five for both excursions, I preened triumphantly, wondering if maybe I'd been a highwayman in a previous life. I tossed the cash in my bag, glossed my lips and tugged a comb through my hair. We joined the line of coaches at check-in and lumbered slowly onto the shuttle.

'Fantastic,' I enthused cheerfully to Rob. 'An amazing feat of engineering, don't you think? A tunnel underwater, connecting England and France. Marvellous. Although the ferry, I suppose, has its benefits too,' I felt compelled to add.

He tossed me a look of disapproval. 'Doris was not robbed,' he chided.

'What?' I frowned. I'd forgotten I'd said that.

'You and your lies,' he hissed.

'Oh, shut up. Everyone tells lies.'

'Not as easily as you do. And we came back on the shuttle last week. You didn't seem overly impressed then.'

'I was busy composing my farewell speech.'

He snorted. 'Is that what it was?'

Thirty-five minutes later, we drove off the shuttle, trundled past French Immigration and joined the autoroute to Paris.

Enormous plastic bags crammed with balls of brightly coloured wool blocked the centre aisle as the knitters clicked away feverishly. They were gossiping for gold. I don't know who Agnes is, but I think she ought to join Weight Watchers, be more liberal with her deodorant, visit her hairdresser more often and divorce her husband. She might also consider sticking a bottle of shampoo up her dog's backside and buying a new lounge carpet.

On the A26 autoroute between Calais and Paris a green light on the dashboard flashed intermittently. Frowning, Rob pulled onto the hard shoulder, gave me a shifty quizzical look and jumped off the coach to investigate. The ricocheting of the knitting needles gathered momentum.

After a few minutes, I started feeling jittery and anxious. I flipped the pages of my magazine like a demon. If we broke down, I agonised, we'd be delayed arriving into Paris. If we were late, I panicked, we might not make it to the restaurant and I'd have to refund all the money. I shuddered. I couldn't do it. Giving the money back was unthinkable. I'd cry. I felt twitchy at the thought. I stood and beamed diffidently at the two long rows of inquisitive faces.

'Nothing wrong, I'm sure,' I insisted hollowly.

Forty-five unconvinced faces tried for an air of confident detachment.

'We'll soon be off,' I asserted, fearing the opposite.

I lowered myself back into my seat and drummed my fingers on the armrests. What the hell is he doing? I steamed. I opened my bag and fingered the excursion money. My phone buzzed, heralding a text. It was Rob.

Come out. A problem.

My innards contracted. I shot from my chair, catapulted out the coach door, and quickstepped, as much as a figure-hugging knee-length skirt and a pair of stilettos would allow, around to meet Rob. He was leaning lazily against the side of the coach, arms folded, smirking, with the large flaps to the luggage hold raised.

I rounded on him, fists clenched. 'What's wrong and what the hell are you grinning about? If we're late into Paris, we can't go to the restaurant. We'll have to refund all the money,' I stormed.

He lunged forward, grabbed my wrists, pulled me towards him and planted a forceful kiss on my forehead.

I eyeballed him, exasperated. 'You're time-wasting,' I told him, twisting my wrists ineffectively.

'Look in here,' he said. He spun me around, clutched my skirt waistband and cannoned me inside the luggage hold. He scrambled in behind me, flipped me onto my back and straddled my waist.

'Rob! Stop it!' I giggled and tried to crab backwards. 'Are you mad?'

'No, not mad. Horny,' he replied, cramming something large and soft under my head.

'What're you doing?'

'I'm ravishing you. I can't wait until we get to the hotel,' he said, his fingers working the buckle of his belt. 'I can't wait another ten minutes, never mind another three hours.' Clink. His belt unclipped.

My heart gave an excited pop. 'Here?' I panted, eyeing the neatly stacked rows of suitcases. Whoosh. His zip was down. My eyes boggled, rotated even. 'Someone might see . . .' I started, but then, thinking about it, who? Who would see? And did I really care?

He covered my mouth with his, simultaneously yanking at the hem of my skirt. 'No one will see,' he breathed, still kissing me. 'We're on the side of the autoroute. Do you see anyone lurking around? And I've pressed the central locking on the coach so no one can get off.'

My eyes darted a quick left and right. He was absolutely right. We were definitely the only two people in the luggage compartment, there was no doubt about it. 'No,' I admitted, my skirt now wrapped around my waist, 'I don't see anyone, now that you mention it.' I was wavering. 'But Rob, can't you wait?' I said, half-heartedly.

'No! I can't wait,' he whispered into my neck before burying his chin in his chest and fumbling to fit a condom.

I watched. 'I'll have to wait too, you know,' I tried again, still watching.

'No you don't. You don't have to wait. I won't hear of it,' he insisted magnanimously.

My eyes slid to my pillow. It was the knitters' wool. 'Argh!' I yelled. 'I'm not shagging in front of the knitters' wool!'

'Wool can't talk,' Rob said, laughing. He wriggled down the length of my hips and lay above me, weight on his elbows. My tummy cartwheeled as our eyes locked. He kissed the tip of my nose lightly. When he spoke, his voice was throaty and husky and sexy. 'Shall we?'

My back arched and my arms flew around his neck. I pulled his face towards mine and kissed him hard. He beamed. I peered over his shoulder, where I had a panoramic view of a pert bare bum.

'Evie,' he breathed, trembling with excitement. 'Wrap your legs around my waist. We don't have much time. You'll have to be quick. No time for "left a bit Rob, right a bit Rob, up a bit Rob". Don't want to let myself down on my ladies-first policy.'

'I absolutely insist on your ladies-first policy,' I told him.

Afterwards, he quickly buttoned my blouse before we tumbled from the luggage hold, clutching our shoes.

'Fix your hair, babe. You look more like a scarecrow than a scarecrow does, and close your mouth, your jaw's hanging open.' He took his comb from his back pocket and handed it to me. 'Turn around and I'll straighten your skirt.'

I snatched his comb from his outstretched hand and turned my back on him. 'That was so, well, so improper and highly unprofessional, don't you think? Rob, promise you won't tell anyone.'

'Tell anyone what?'

'That we, well, did it with everyone on board.' I trailed off awkwardly.

He turned me to face him. 'Who would I tell? What do you take me for?' he asked indignantly.

'So you promise you won't tell?'

'Of course I bloody won't. Our sex life is nobody's business but ours.'

'My sentiments exactly,' I said, 'but some men are not so discreet.'

'Well, I'm not one of them,' he insisted, affronted.

I hopped into my shoes as he closed the luggage flaps and, as if walking home from church, he gripped my elbow and sauntered languidly around to the front of the coach. He leaped up the steps two at a time, leaving me nervously tidying my hair, checking my bra was fastened and that the buttons on my blouse were done up. Rob slid in comfortably behind the steering wheel while I scuttled up the steps, my face puce.

'What was the problem?' one of the knitters asked. She jerked her elbow in a practised gesture, causing her ball of wool to unfurl and dance a jig on her lap.

'Oh, just a trip switch on the main door to the luggage hold. It's a safety device to ensure we don't lose baggage when we're moving. I've fixed it,' Rob boasted.

I burrowed around in my bag, looking for my foundation.

'And Evie?' Rob remarked casually, sliding into gear. 'That was your surprise.'

Chapter Nineteen

Checking into the hotel was a far more organised affair than the previous week. I used the microphone on the coach to rattle off the names and room numbers. In no time at all, the task was complete and I was clip-clopping smartly through the lobby en route to the elevator so I could meet Rob in our room.

Rob had stupidly filled the jacuzzi with bubble bath, so we had to spend twenty minutes mopping the floor with towels and spooning armfuls of soap suds from the floor to the sink.

'If ever you need a cleaning job . . .'

'Very funny,' he wheezed, beetling towards the sink for the fourth time.

Naked, I tiptoed past him and settled in the bath, causing an avalanche of bubbles to spill over the edge. He heaved an exasperated sigh, as a river of soap suds swam over his feet and flowed out the bathroom door.

'Leave the floor. Bubbles burst.' I crooked a finger. 'Come here. Get in.'

He did.

Later, Rob shaved and dressed and then shot off to re-fuel the coach. I quickly charged around the room, tugged on my clothes, checked my face, hurriedly brushed my hair and was walking through the lobby with over half an hour to spare before we had to leave for the restaurant.

'Bonjour, *chérie*,' the barman welcomed, as I catwalked through the lounge. He placed two chubby, hairy hands on the bar, leaned forward and delivered a garlicky, watery kiss to each cheek.

'Bonjour,' I grimaced.

'*Voilà!*' he sang cheerfully and slid a large gin and tonic towards me.

Diving rather niftily, I managed to catch the glass before it shot off the bar.

'On zee house,' he breezed.

'Evie, darling girl, join us.'

I turned and frowned, not immediately recognising the tall, glamorous, well-dressed lady floating towards me. 'Elise!' I said. 'You look so different without your knitting.'

She wore a three-quarter-length jade velvet jacket, with billowing Anne Boleyn sleeves, twinned with a pair of matching silk fitted trousers. I ogled at the diamond golf ball perched on her finger. It glittered and sparkled as she patted her silver hair, which she'd fashioned neatly in a stylish chignon. She tottered elegantly towards me on three-inch heels.

'Cheeky madam,' she joked, over the rim of her glass. 'Come here. You look divine, absolutely divine, my darling,' she flattered, fingering the neckline of my black linen mini dress and linking her arm through mine.

I was bustled zealously into the middle of the knitting gang's circle. They were chatting harmoniously as they sipped champagne. I stole a hasty, hopefully unnoticed, calculating glance at their baubles, trinkets and ornaments, which I reckon would have settled the debt of the third world. Not to mention the designer togs. Meg's bejewelled hand plucked the champagne bottle from the ice bucket.

183

'You must,' she trilled, and rammed a full-to-the brim frothy champagne flute into my hand. Too polite to refuse, I swallowed my gin and accepted the drink.

'So, darling,' Elise ventured. 'Our driver is rather dreamy, don't you think? And you would know, wouldn't you?'

Amy, wide-eyed, made a clucking noise and nudged my elbow playfully.

'Yes, yes he is,' I agreed, still semi-hypnotised by all the stylish glittery chic.

'He'll do for now,' Elise said.

'What do you mean, "for now"?'

The glitter ball on her finger shot a kaleidoscope of flashing lights across the bar as she flicked a non-existent speck of dust from her shoulder. 'Darling, at your age, all you want is amazing sex of Olympic proportions, someone to pay for your drinks, pick up the restaurant bills and treat you to the odd weekend away. Oh,' she added, 'and, of course, the occasional pretty birthday trinket.'

Well, I wasn't about to contradict her because she was spot on. She'd more or less characterised the epitome of male perfection. 'So,' I asked, curious, 'what do you look for in a man at your age?'

Elise's voice softened. 'That's an easy one. At my age all you ask is that he be dead,' she said firmly, her eyes wide and re-assuring.

Amy bobbed her head in agreement. 'Essential,' she affirmed, flickering her eyes heavenwards.

I took a larger than intended mouthful of champagne. 'Dead? You like them dead?' I faltered, belching softly. This was a new one to me and I pride myself on being fairly open-minded.

'We're all widows,' Amy explained cheerfully.

'Yes,' Elise attested. 'Marvellous, isn't it?'

I coloured. 'Did they, the husbands, all die together?' I asked. 'Erm, in, in a plane crash or something?'

'Hell no. That would have been lovely but sadly no,' Elise blustered. She cradled her glass in the crook of her arm and held up her hands to count on her fingers. 'I did twenty years, Amy did twenty-three. I can't remember how many years Meg did.' She shook her head apologetically and then pushed on. 'Dora was lucky. She only did ten, but poor Kelly, well, she served over thirty years.'

Amy and Elise sighed in compassionate agreement.

'Dear, poor Kelly,' Amy said. 'Still, that's all behind her. He's gone now.'

Not knowing the form for congratulating someone on the death of their husband and at the same time commiserating over the length of time he'd been alive, all I could think of to say was, 'Dreadful business.'

Elise clutched my hand, and eyed me urgently. 'Yes, dreadful,' she echoed.

Suddenly a throat-catching explosion of Chanel No 5 wafted through the bar. 'Darlings!' Freya sopranoed. 'Late as ever.' She shimmied towards us, arms outstretched in greeting with a very expensive crocodile skin handbag dangling from her wrist. Impressively elegant in a floaty leopard print chiffon wrap, she flamingoed around the table air-kissing cheeks. 'I had a fight with my hair straighteners. Rang my Henry in desperation; he called the French Energy Minister, who apparently confirmed the voltage here in France is compatible, so I gave them a bit of a bash, plugged them in again and, hey presto, success,' she beamed, patting her short white hair, styled à la Meg Ryan.

'Who's Henry?' I had to ask.

'My baby boy,' Freya replied.

'Deputy Prime Minister,' Meg added swiftly.

'Attention all,' Freya trilled. She clapped her hands gleefully. 'Our cruise is confirmed. Seventy glorious days on the open sea. We leave Southampton on November tenth. Our agent just texted me.'

There was a unified whoop of joy, much tinkling of glasses and excited jolly banter as they rattled off the cruise itinerary and started planning pre-cruise shopping trips. By the time we boarded the coach I was as sick as a pig and green with envy that I didn't have a dead husband of my own and, at the same time, I was fretting over how many years I might have to put up with one.

When we arrived at the restaurant I was greeted like a returning war hero. Delia gave me a bone-crushing hug. '*Quarante-cinq personnes. Mon Dieu. Superbe!*' she clucked, ushering our passengers to their seats.

'Don't drink too much,' Rob warned as he walked me to the crew table at the back of the room. 'Remember that you're working. It's not your birthday party,' he nagged, pulling out my chair.

Initially I thought we had the restaurant to ourselves for the evening, but just after eight o'clock, a small English group caterpillared through the door. Rob stood to welcome the guide and driver.

'Evie, this is Helen,' he introduced. 'She works for your agency.' I gave her a welcoming smile, and was rewarded with a lemon-sucking grimace. Her driver, in contrast, was a jovial, chubby, red-faced chap called Ralph who shook my hand eagerly, although with difficulty, as the size and roundness of his belly distanced him substantially from the table. The buttons and buttonholes of his shirt struggled to meet and a couple of red belly hairs protruded from the gaps between one button and the next. I've always wondered why fat men don't just bite the bullet and buy fat clothes.

Helen was cradling a glass of red wine. 'Where have you been?' she asked Rob.

He gestured towards me. 'Evie and I are doing a weekend break.'

She eyed him as a cat does a mouse, and slowly circled her finger around the rim of her glass. 'Oh really?' she replied, one eyebrow lifted. 'I haven't done a weekend break for years. How boring! We've been in Italy all week, stayed in Switzerland last night, two nights here in Paris, then back to London.' She jerked her head towards her group. 'Can't wait to get rid of this lot, older than Moses some of them. Had one die on me in Venice. The bloody paperwork is a nightmare. It's easier if they drop dead as a couple, then you can pack them off in the same direction, rather than putting one in a box and one on a flight home. Do the honours, darling,' she simpered, eyeing the bottle of red wine.

I studied her. What a horrible individual, I thought.

'It's one bloody moan and groan after the other,' Helen continued, perching a pair of lilac-rimmed bifocals on the end of her nose. She buried her head in the menu. 'Nothing changes in here. Serveeeeeeeece *s'il vous plait*,' she shouted, clicking her fingers aloft.

When the waiter arrived, she barked her order, frisbeed the menu at his chest and snaked her arm in her handbag to retrieve her ringing mobile. Rob, deep in discussion with Ralph, absently placed his hand over mine and squeezed it gently. The exchange didn't escape Helen's attention and she gave a cynical snort. For lack of anything better to do, I sat quaffing the wine. By the time Rob had finished his analysis of the European Championships with Ralph, I was half a carafe for the worse. Or for the better, considering the present company.

Rob cradled my hand and kissed my palm. 'Sorry, babe. I know I've been neglecting you but I haven't seen Ralph for a while.'

'S'awright,' I said, exhaling loudly.

Helen's telephone conversation ended with a passionate 'Ciao, ciao dahrling,' and she scanned the room. 'What have we here?' she asked, her gaze resting on the knitters. 'A table of drag queens?'

She really was quite insufferable company. 'Excuse me,' I snapped testily. 'I think I'll go check on my group.' Standing, I pushed my chair against the wall.

Helen drummed her orange talons on the table and raised her eyes heavenwards. 'Why?' she asked frostily. 'You'll only encourage complaints.'

I started walking over to my group's table but Delia ambushed me. She linked her arm through mine and tugged me behind the bar. ''Orrible, no?' she whispered conspiratorially, eyes darting towards Helen. '*Cochon.*'

'Just a bit,' I agreed, plucking a glass of wine from the tray of a passing waiter.

Delia clutched my shoulders and drew me in. Her already wide eyes grew wider. 'Eelen, a time ago, she go with Rob, but not now. Oui oui, she tell me,' she confided, nodding manically. 'She go with him *to bed.*'

I cast a venomous look towards the crew table. Helen and Rob were deep in conversation, head to curly bleached perm. 'You don't say?' I replied distantly, and I admit that I felt the wriggle of a green-eyed worm in my tummy. But then I shook my head judiciously. Everyone has a past and I'm not the jealous type. I've never been jealous. Men can come and go, it's friends who count. Besides, Helen's hair is a mess and she's got no bust so there's absolutely nothing to be jealous about. And she's too skinny, I decided, eyeing what looked like a bone on her hip.

Delia gave me a knowing nod and marched off, balancing a

tray of drinks on her fingertips, dark hair billowing behind her. Not overly enthused at the prospect of rejoining my colleagues, I decided to continue making my way towards the knitters instead. En route I bumped into Arthur, a willowy, nimble, vibrant chap in his early eighties. Arthur had been a bit of a pest for most of the day. Flirting shamelessly, he'd actually chased me down the aisle of the coach when we stopped at the service station. He wiggled a skeletal finger at my chest.

'If I were ten years younger,' he tittered dirtily.

'Ten!?' I blustered. 'Don't you mean fifty-five?'

He guffawed and squeezed my shoulder. 'OK, maybe twenty years younger,' he conceded, beaming broadly. 'Marvellous evening, my dear. Scrumptious cuisine, flavoursome wines, elegant surroundings, faultless service.'

Oh, I thought guiltily, he's actually quite nice, not a lecherous old codger at all. I'd obviously misjudged him. I smiled.

'And as for the muff,' he enthused breathlessly, eyeing the knitters.

My smile buckled.

'Blinding display,' he sneered toothily. He strutted off towards the gents, stopped midstride, doubled back and pinched my backside. I yelped but let him off. I do nothing else for charity, I thought.

Where was I going? Ah yes, the knitters. I searched the crowd. They were over by the door, not too far away and conveniently in the right direction, as we would be leaving soon.

The singer, accordion strapped to his chest, strolled between the tables crooning throatily. He danced backwards when he spotted me and subjected me to a thirty-second serenade. I swooned and swayed in tandem for form's sake. Actually I might learn to play the accordion. I've been meaning to take up a musical instrument, and as far as I can see it's simply a matter of squeezing the box in and out, and it would be brilliant for my pecs.

'Sit down,' Meg shouted, spotting me.

There was a fair bit of scraping and scuffling as we shuffled to fit nine chairs around a table for eight. The knitters were roaring and their table was littered with empty champagne bottles, a positive indication that I would be happy here.

We had a blast. They had me in hysterics from the off. Champagne puts me in such a happy-go-lucky party mood. All I want to do is talk, talk, talk . . . By the time Rob came to tell me it was time to leave, I was exhausted from laughing. The nine of us were cackling helplessly. I was hugging my tummy, as was Meg. Freya was panting and dabbing her eyes with the edge of the tablecloth. Kitty and Amy were howling hysterically. Rob stood at the head of the table smiling with contrived patience.

'What's so funny?' He looked puzzled.

All heads turned towards him and immediately the raucous whoops tripled in volume. My eyes were like watery glass dinner plates. Breathless, I thumped my hand repeatedly on the table. Rob gripped my forearm and levered me to standing. I tottered in a circle, doubled over in mirth, mindful not to spill any of my drink.

'They, they,' I gasped, 'didn't believe me.'

His eyes swept the table.

'But they believe me now,' I panted, nodding with exaggerated purpose.

His brows met then lifted. 'Believe what?'

'That we had a shag on their coats and their bags on the bus.' I burst out laughing again. God, it was hilarious.

Eight faces convulsed as Rob, mortified, clutched my arm and cranked my elbow to ear level. He then spun on his heel and piloted me towards the door.

'Rob, you sexy little devil!' someone shouted, and I thought I was going to burst. Honestly, how funny was that?

'Oh . . . oh . . . too fast. Too fast. Slow down,' I pleaded as we cannoned outside into the street.

He put a finger under my chin and lifted my face. 'The KGB wouldn't have to torture you for information, would they? A couple of drinks and you'd tell them all they wanted to know.'

I frowned, confused. 'KGB,' I stammered. 'I don't even like fried chicken.'

He gave an exasperated sigh. 'Get the group together and meet me on the coach,' he said, gruffly.

On the drive back to the hotel the knitters were the life and soul of the party.

'Shall we have a singsong?' Meg suggested.

Everyone cheered, including me. Why not? I thought.

'Evie,' Rob hissed, 'I don't think a singsong in your condition is a good idea.'

I gave him a sharp look. 'In my condition? What condition would that be?' The cheek of him.

'What shall we sing?' Elise asked.

'Dwiwa,' Freya slurred.

There was a murmur of confused undertones. Elise stabbed aimlessly at her collapsed chignon with her hairpin. 'What?' she asked.

'Dewiwa,' Freya repeated, already swaying from side to side.

'Delilah,' I translated, in a flash of understanding.

'One, twooo, three,' Dora counted.

But no one could remember how the song started. Fortunately, I knew the chorus. 'My, my, my, Delilah, why, why, why, Delilah, my, my . . .'

And everyone joined in. Well, everyone except Rob. And we

roared and roared all the way back to the hotel, which is what you're supposed to do on a coach tour.

I fumbled for the bedside lamp and stumbled out of bed, dying of thirst. I switched on the bathroom light, and looked in the mirror. A seventy-four-year-old troll in full make-up stared back at me. I groped for my cotton wool and make-up remover. A bongo drum beat steadily somewhere close by. I didn't deserve to feel this bad. I hadn't had that much to drink. Rob padded in behind me, flipped up the toilet seat and peed.

'Got enough lights on? It's only three o'clock, d'you realise that?'

'I'm ill,' I croaked, scrubbing my face.

'No way? Do you think you might have the measles or something?' He washed his hands, lifted his toilet bag from the shelf, plopped two tablets in a glass, filled it with water and handed it to me.

'What's this?'

'Solpadeine.'

I peered into the glass of hissing cloudy water. 'How many calories are in it?'

'Why?'

'Well, I'd rather be ill if there's more than two hundred.'

He rested one hand on the wall and loomed healthily above me. 'I wouldn't worry about that, if I were you,' he said, shaking his head. 'I'd take all the help I could get if I looked like you do now.'

I suddenly remembered what Delia had told me about Rob and Helen. I grimaced and swallowed the fizzy liquid. It's of no consequence, I thought. He's with me now and that's all that matters. Previous conquests are irrelevant. It's not as though I don't have a past myself. Bloody hell, I'm no angel and he's entitled to his privacy. I wouldn't dream of mentioning it. I don't want him to think I'm obsessed with him or possessive or jealous. I have my pride. I wouldn't ask him about her if the survival of the human race depended on it. I thumped the glass on the sink and missiled the used cotton wool down the toilet. Truth be known, I didn't really care.

I stabbed him with my bottle of make-up remover. 'Did you shag that g . . . girl Helen?' I yelled, faltering. I had just about managed to say 'girl'. I'd almost said ghoul.

'When? Tonight?' he asked sarcastically.

I pushed past him. He grabbed my shoulders, rugby tackled me onto the bed and pulled the quilt over us.

'Yes,' he admitted. 'I did, about five years ago. We worked in Italy together for a week, we—'

I slapped my palm over his mouth to silence him. 'It's none of my business. It was something Delia said and I was merely curious, but of course you don't have to tell me anything,' I said glibly. 'We both have a past. Of course we do, and frankly I'm not in the slightest bit interested. In fact, I don't even know why I asked.' I flounced onto my side, bashed the pillow and wriggled to the edge of the bed, as far away from him as I could. I whizzed around to face him. 'A week in Italy! A whole week in Italy! You slut!' I shrieked.

He burst out laughing and his strong hands flipped me onto my back. He crawled on top of me and our eyes locked.

'You're squashing me,' I wheezed.

He levered his weight onto his elbows. 'I haven't seen her for three years,' he said innocently. 'Now shall we discuss all the men you've had in the past five years?'

I harrumphed. 'Switch off the light,' I told him.

Chapter Twenty

To my credit, I managed to get up on Saturday morning. I made a big show of simulating good health by singing 'Like a Virgin' whilst drying my hair. But to be honest I felt awful. I blamed the knitters. I am never drinking again. Champagne and I don't get along, and now that I think of it, I hadn't eaten much last night.

I walked down to the lobby and propped myself up against the reception desk. Carla, our guide, swept through the main entrance and breezed towards me, ruffling her shiny black hair with a perfectly manicured hand. She looked stunning in a red linen miniskirt and a white lace camisole top. Her wrists rattled with an assortment of gold bangles, and a gorgeous crystal heart pendant garnished her bronzed cleavage. I felt sick, fat, frumpy and about a hundred and eighty years old next to her.

'Bonjour, ça va?' she trilled.

'Fine thanks,' I lied glumly, and then brightened when I spotted a huge, pulsing yellow-head on her chin. I decided to expel her from the rest of the conversation and address the spot directly for the rest of the day.

The atmosphere on the city tour was subdued to say the least. Carla tried her best, she really did, but all said and done, she was lucky not to have been booed to silence. The lumbering, lurching movements of the coach made everyone, with the exception of Carla and Rob, want to throw up. Elise was a lurid shade of vanilla and Kelly had a sallow green look about her. I poked Arthur in the arm twice to make sure he was still alive. He certainly didn't look it. At the end of the tour we dropped everyone by the Opera House where they ambushed Café de la Paix.

I sat trance-like in my chair.

'The Louvre? That's where you wanted to go this week, wasn't it?' Rob asked, indicating to pull into the line of traffic.

I gripped the armrests and closed my eyes. The sight of cars whizzing past the coach made me feel dizzy.

'Er, well, d'you know what? I'm not fussed, to be honest. It's very, um, very warm today.' I swallowed hard. 'Next week perhaps.' My eyelids were sweating. I blinked slowly, like a drowsy baby.

'No, no. A promise is a promise, and I promised to take you so that's exactly what I'll do,' he insisted. 'We'll leave the coach parked here in Rivoli and walk to the Louvre.'

He slammed on the brakes. My tummy heaved.

'That was lucky,' he said with a triumphant smile, 'finding a parking space so quickly.'

I guzzled from my almost empty two litre bottle of Evian.

'Come on then,' he said, clapping his hands. 'Let's be off.' He was on his feet. I dreaded trying to get onto mine. 'Ups-a-daisy,' he said, clutching my elbow.

'No . . . er, OK, Rob.' I was standing. At least that was a start. He prodded me in the back to speed me off the coach. 'I can walk without a push,' I lamented.

Arm curved firmly around my shoulders, Rob marched purposefully along the Parisian cobbles. 'Beautiful city,' he said, and gave me a bone-crushing hug.

I kept my eyes riveted to the pavement to oversee the complicated procedure of placing one foot in front of the other. I had to simulate a Max Wall march to keep up with him. The heat was bloody unbearable, my hair was soldered to my neck, my feet throbbed and we hadn't even got to the Louvre yet. And I was burping champagne.

'You're quiet, babe.'

Eventually, we arrived at the Louvre. There were thousands of people in there.

'A tour,' Rob announced cheerfully, and dragged me along to follow attractive, sober-looking Japanese curator.

The guide was rambling on. '*Mona Lisa* haang in hur own pwivate room, prwbably most famous pwainting in history of art, bewieved to be young Italian girl name Lisa Gherardini del Giocondo. Bought by Fwench King Fwancois fwom Leonardo da Vinci, has been housed in the Louvre for ovwer two hundwed years.'

Rob's brows quirked. 'How interesting! Did you know that?'

I was semi-dozing, my cheek against the wall.

'Are you OK?' he asked, shaking me. 'Wake up. Let's rush on and hear what else she has to say.' He grabbed my hand and bowled forward, skittling the throng out of his way. 'Best keep up with the guide, we don't want to miss anything,' he said with eager eyes. 'I know how much you enjoy sightseeing and gawping at dusty old paintings. I'm only here for your sake.'

I gazed up at him. 'Am going to be sick,' I said in a weak, gravelly voice.

He folded his arms triumphantly. His forehead fell into creases as he pretended to think hard. 'Do you think it might have been something you ate?'

I clamped my hand to my mouth.

His smile buckled, then collapsed. He scanned the hall for the toilet. 'Don't you dare!' he warned. 'Come on.' He grabbed my hand and lurched toward the toilets, spiriting me through the door with literally seconds to spare. I made it. Just.

Fifteen minutes later we were heading for the exit. I felt brilliant. Well, not *brilliant*, but much better. I was a new person and there was a slight spring in my step.

'I feel fine,' I told Rob brightly.

He gave me a doubtful look.

'I do. I feel much better,' I assured him. 'Peckish even. I fancy a sandwich, do you? It's such a warm day. Shall we find an ice cream bar?' I fumbled in my bag for my lipstick. 'Now that I think of it, that's exactly what I want, a double mint choc chip,' I said, licking my lips.

But the exit was a hundred and seventy-nine miles from the ladies' toilet. And the heat would have blistered the bum off a camel. I hung off Rob's arm. My lungs burned, my mouth was as dry as the Gobi desert, my legs were jellified and my feet were killing me. I hobbled, bent double, into the sun-drenched courtyard of the Louvre.

'I can't walk,' I sobbed. 'New shoes,' I wailed.

'You can.'

'I can't and I won't.' I stumbled and tightened my hold on his arm. 'Look,' I sobbed, and pointed to my feet where two enormous aubergines protruded from my white slingback Prada sandals. I halted, hen-toed and back bowed. 'Carry me,' I pleaded.

'Carry you? Are you having a laugh?'

'You made me come here.'

Rob sighed, exasperated. 'Walk to Concorde and I'll drive the coach around to pick you up,' he said sharply.

'I can't. I can't walk the length of the Tuileries, and I can't take my shoes off because I can't walk on the stones and the grass is too far away,' I bleated, swaying.

He threw his hands up in annoyance. 'I can't get the coach any closer to here than Concorde.'

'Buy me flip-flops.'

'Oh, right. What size and colour?' He feigned a search of the museum courtyard, by making a peaked cap over his eyes with his hand. 'And where from? Do you see a flip-flop shop in the middle of the Louvre?'

I swayed and gripped his belt. 'I'm in agony,' I wailed. 'I'm—' and I stopped mid-wail.

Divine intervention . . .

A tramp was sleeping, slumped against the wall behind us, wearing a comfortable looking pair of leather flip-flops. They were a size ten perhaps, so they'd fit my swollen size four feet perfectly. How opportune.

'Get me those,' I demanded, pointing trampwards.

Rob stretched to his full six feet and two inches. 'You want me,' he spat, incredulous, 'to steal a pair of flip-flops from a drunk down-and-out? I don't think so.'

Still clutching his belt for support, I shook my head. 'No, of course not. Wake him up and offer to buy them.'

His blue eyes were like match flames.

'Or carry me,' I said flatly.

Ten minutes later I flippered a good five paces behind Rob, who was reeling with laughter.

'It's not that funny,' I yelled to the back of his head.

'It is,' he insisted over his shoulder.

'Wait for me.'

'Do I have to?'

'Yes.'

He held his tummy and bent over, breathless, as another wave of hysteria hit him.

'If you don't stop laughing, I'm going on a sex strike.' I

198

waved a finger in warning. 'I'm not shagging you again all weekend.'

He guffawed loudly. 'You, a sex strike? You couldn't do it, any more than you can walk in your white heels.'

'That's what you think,' I sneered. On I trudged, arms swinging to add speed. I even overtook him. 'I most certainly could do it, and make no mistake, I mean what I say. It's a matter of principle.' I flippered sideways up a set of stairs, gripping the railing with both hands. I was bloody knackered. 'I don't make idle threats you know,' I wheezed.

We argued and argued, and he roared and roared all the way back to the hotel, where we had the best sex ever before we had to start getting ready for the evening's Illuminations Tour.

Just before we were due to leave, I sat on the edge of the bed, feet soaking in two ice buckets, TV remote in hand, and flicked through the television channels. Rob padded from the bathroom, towel wrapped around his waist, his chest bare and his face covered in shaving foam.

'Are you going to sit there all night?' he asked, brandishing a lethal looking razor.

'Nope. My feet have shrunk back to a size four,' I said with relief. 'I'm ready. I only have to slip my dress on.'

He grinned. 'Glad to hear it.'

After dropping the group off at Notre Dame so that they could have dinner, Rob and I stumbled across a quaint, bustling Italian restaurant opposite the cathedral square. The waiter swept us along to a table in the window alcove and skittled two menus in front of us. He disappeared and returned thirty seconds later with a bottle of red wine. He barely managed to stand still long enough to take our order before bolting off again, pen swishing madly.

'Can I stay with you in London on Monday and Tuesday?' Rob asked as he poured the wine.

The waiter skidded alongside our table, tossed a basket of bread at us that landed like a flying saucer, eyeballed my cleavage, winked roguishly at Rob and scurried off.

'Of course you can. I'll introduce you to my sister, and Lulu is desperate to meet you.'

'I'll be busy all day Wednesday,' he said, tearing at the bread basket.

'Busy doing what?' I asked.

Two steaming plates of pasta spun and rattled in front of us.

'I'm thinking of buying four new coaches but I want to make sure I've got hire contracts in place to cover the finance before I do. I'll be visiting a couple of tour operators in London on Wednesday, then driving to Birmingham to make a few contacts there.'

My fork froze en route to my mouth. Did he say buying coaches? Buying them? Surely coach drivers don't just pop out and spend hundreds of thousands of pounds on, well, on coaches. I mean, I never did get around to buying my own ad agency.

He ambushed his pasta.

I felt a flicker of excitement. 'Erm, buying coaches?' I hedged, with a nonchalant giggle.

He nodded, driving a forkload of food into his mouth. I sipped my wine and studied him over the rim of my glass.

'I think it's time to expand,' he said with a cautious grin.

Expand could mean put on three stone, I thought. He's just eaten a whole basket of bread.

'Expand what?' I asked.

'My fleet,' he replied, dabbing his mouth with a napkin.

'Fleet?' I squeaked.

'Yes.'

His fleet? Of course. Of course it's his fleet. He is Robert Harrison and surprise, surprise, wake up, Evie. The coach has a big gold Harrison's logo painted on each side. Now we were getting somewhere.

'How much does a coach cost?'

'About three hundred grand.'

My jaw dropped open. 'What?!' I spluttered. 'And you're buying four?'

I swallowed my elation with difficulty. Money, he's got money and so I'll have money because what's his will be mine and what's mine ... well, he can have whatever he likes of mine because I have nothing, now that I think of it. Still, it's the thought that counts. I felt like leaping up and skipping around the table. *I have a rich boyfriend! I have a rich boyfriend!* The pressure's off, my overdraft will be history. In fact, what overdraft? It's not an overdraft at all. It's a *shortfall* due to my allowance (or is it maintenance payment?) being overdue.

'If you don't want that pasta, pass it over here,' he interrupted.

I passed him the plate with the enthusiasm of a table hockey world champion. I'd lost my appetite. He can buy me the Links gold sweetie bracelet and twenty charms. No, no, that's far too tacky. Ten charms will do, and a red Mulberry bag and Jimmy Choos, and all sorts of things. I'll write a list, I decided. He'll want to know what I need. I don't want him wasting his money on a load of rubbish. And he could take me to the Caribbean for Christmas. And pay for hair extensions.

I scowled solicitously to myself. Rein it in, I thought. I'm not with him for his money. Definitely not. Material things mean nothing to me. I'm a people person. I'm a 'for richer or poorer' type of girl. I gulped my wine thirstily. No, I couldn't care less if he were penniless. It doesn't matter a tinker's cuss to me how poor he is. I won't pry. His business affairs don't concern me. He might get the wrong idea and think I'm some sort of gold digger.

'This pasta is delicious. What's up, babe? Don't you feel well?'

'So,' I sighed, tight-lipped, and then rushed on. 'How many coaches do you have? Do you have a business partner? Are all the vehicles on finance? Do you own your office and how successful is your company?' I leaned across the table. 'And how come you've got time to saunter around Paris. Why aren't you at home bossing everyone around as bosses do?'

Rob's shoulders shook as he laughed. 'Ten coaches, soon to be fourteen; no partner; only the new coaches will be on partial finance; office is freehold and I don't do too badly. My parents take care of the admin and I boss everyone around by email and text. Does that answer all your questions?'

I ordered a slab of chocolate cake. I was suddenly starving.

Back on board the coach, we began the Illuminations Tour. When we reached Pigalle, a gorgeous mountain of a doorman semaphored Elise from the pavement outside a strip club. She twittered and dithered and bum-hopped in her chair before boldly jumping to her feet.

'Right, girls. Let's go,' she said decisively.

Seven faces crinkled in silent uncertainty.

'We're invited, darlings,' she added, with a jubilant grin. She flapped her hand towards the seven-foot yeti in a dinner suit leaning against the canopied awnings of the club.

Still no takers.

Elise raised her arm like a traffic cop. 'Rob, stop the coach! Stop!' she boomed.

He pulled over and gave me a questioning look. I shrugged.

'Girls, what's to lose? I've never been to a strip club and it's on my list of things to do before I meet Matthew again,' she proclaimed, flicking her eyes heavenwards. She ferreted in her handbag and whipped out her lipstick.

'Shall I try to negotiate a group rate?' I offered.

She smiled, her bottom lip now slashed bright red. 'Darling,' she said, 'that is so utterly above and beyond the call of duty. Thank you so much.'

Rob snorted disapprovingly.

I got out of the coach and walked towards the club. The incredible hunk's name was Lorenzo. He was from Naples and had lived in Paris for eighteen years. By the end of the negotiations we were best pals. I skipped back on the coach, feeling very pleased with myself.

'Two entry tickets for the price of one,' I boasted proudly. 'There's a Chippendales show in half an hour and your first two drinks are complimentary.'

Elise vaulted from her chair. 'Fabulous!' she beamed.

'Chippendales,' Amy and Kelly chorused lustfully.

All seven knitters leaped to standing.

'Er,' I interrupted. 'The club insists on a minimum of ten people in the group . . .' there was a millisecond of disappointed panic, '. . . so,' I announced on the microphone, 'we're looking for two more volunteers for the topless Chippendale show.'

Arthur bolted from his chair. 'Count me in,' he shouted.

'If it's good enough for them,' chirped a granny from Bristol, sweeping a hand at the knitters, 'then it's good enough for me.' She clutched her shopper to her chest and nudged her astonished husband. 'Cyril, up you get!'

Cyril, not surprisingly, shot out of his seat like ferret up a drainpipe.

Gracie and Sarah, two sisters from Glasgow, stood up in a flurry of neck scarves, handbags and size twenty-two raincoats.

'Aye, we'll go, hen, but we're only goin' tay make up the numbers,' they offered charitably.

'That's nice of you,' I told them.

There followed a bit of an exodus. In fact, there were only seven glum married couples left on board in the end. I ushered everyone who was going into the club, arranged payment and dragged myself back to the coach.

'Rob, I should stay and make sure everyone gets back to the hotel safely. Don't you think?'

'No, I don't. Get on and finish this tour.' Rob jerked his chin towards Lorenzo. 'Offer you an incentive to stay, did he?'

'He offered me a job, actually,' I admitted, thumping down miserably into my chair.

'A job?' he chuckled, turning the ignition. 'I'll keep you busy when we get back to the hotel.'

'Doing what?' I challenged.

'I bought you a jewellery tree when you were in the club, so you might want to tidy the dressing table.' He casts me a saucy grin. 'I'll help of course.'

Chapter Twenty-one

I bounced out of bed on Sunday morning, hangover-free. I felt fabulous. I might stop drinking, I thought. Imagine being able to wave my hand flippantly and say, 'No thanks,' when someone offers me a drink. They'd look at me with respect and admiration and envy and think, How does she do it? And they'd feel inferior, and I'd be about a stone lighter. Yes, I might give it a go. But obviously not until Lulu and I have finished the wine we bought in Tesco, and obviously not now that I've started this new job and am under so much pressure. I glanced at Rob. One strong, toned arm blindly searched my side of the bed. He sat up, tousle-haired and bleary-eyed.

'Come back to bed.'

'Why?'

'My back's cold.'

'In this blistering heat, your back's cold?'

'OK, I fancy a shag,' he admitted.

'Do you ever think of anything else?'

'Like what?' he asked.

I shrugged. I couldn't think of anything else either.

★

I was, if I'm honest, a right show-off on the morning excursion to Versailles. I sounded like David Attenborough.

'Versailles was the residence of the kings of France from 1682 until 1790. The palace, originally commissioned as a small hunting lodge, was lavishly extended over the years by almost every monarch. The beauty of the French classical architecture was enhanced further with the extension of the gardens and the installation of the stunning Latona Basin and fountains. I think it's fair to say that the palace set a trend amongst European royals, with its marble courtyards, luxurious soft furnishings and priceless works of art.'

I leaned over the side of my seat and squinted down the aisle of the coach. Everyone was gawping into the middle distance nodding thoughtfully, obviously enjoying my informative narrative. Everyone except Arthur, that is, who was peering over the top of the seat in front of him and down the cleavage of two buxom ladies, who were busy murdering a packet of sherbet bonbons.

I hastened on. 'With such a distinguished history, I think the best thing to do to fully appreciate your visit is to join one of the guided tours conducted by the palace curators.' I carefully placed the microphone on the cradle.

'Swallow a book?' Rob asked sarcastically.

Driving through the leafy suburb of St Cloud, Rob suddenly indicated and pulled over.

'What's up?' I asked.

'Wait and see,' he replied.

Elise, who was sitting behind me, leaned forward to whisper confidentially. 'Not again, I hope,' she said, making my cheeks flame.

I turned and gave her a reproachful wiggly eyebrow. *As if?*

Rob pressed the button on the dashboard to open the door,

squeezed my knee as he sidled past and took the steps two at a time. I clutched my hands in my lap as I felt a needle of irritation. What was he up to? He can't just pull over at the side of the road with a coach full of passengers whenever the mood strikes. I was about to lean out of the door and tell him so, when he came back, his arms laden with a rustling bouquet of beautiful flowers. I had to collapse my chair and stand up to let him pass. With a bit of an awkward shuffle and a face full of birds of paradise, he gave me a huge hug.

'For you,' he said, bending his head to kiss my forehead. 'Because you're worth it,' he added, beaming at his own wit.

There was a burst of laughter, a huge cheer and a round of applause. Then, much to Rob's amusement, a line of husbands snaked off the bus to do the same. And Arthur, the letch, bought a rose for each of the knitters, which earned him eight kisses. Twenty minutes later, a delighted florist stood beside an empty stall waving us on our way.

When we arrived at Versailles, Rob cleaned the coach and I sauntered around the town. Every second shop sold cakes and pastries so, unless my aim was to balloon to twenty stone, there was pretty much nothing to buy. I strolled back towards the palace and sunbathed on the grass for an hour. Hot, bothered, bored and nosy, I ambled back to the coach and poked around the knitters' handiwork and, I have to be honest, it was a load of rubbish. I'm no expert but surely sleeves aren't meant to be square, and I know that the tension is supposed to be uniform, not stretched and blobby with holes in it. I'm more or less certain that they've only been knitting sober. I was about to shout for Rob to come in and see it, when I spotted the eight of them regally striding through the coach park. I stuffed everything back in the bags and scurried off the coach.

'Darling, what a fantastic experience. Poor Marie Antoinette.

Such a sad tale, she was so misunderstood,' Kelly lamented sincerely.

'Yes, so sad,' I agreed. Who wouldn't agree? She had her bloody head chopped off.

The eight of them settled themselves and whipped out the knitting. I had to say something. Tactfully, of course.

I folded my arms inquisitively. 'So you're all avid knitters, are you?' I asked, casting an eye over the bags of wool in the centre aisle.

Amy laughed. 'No, no, no. Goodness me, dear, we don't have time normally. Kelly got chatting to the vicar at the party after her husband's funeral, and he asked if she could help out with one of his pet projects,' she explained.

She held up an enormous lemon sock, which was dangling forlornly from a chunky needle. I think she should have cast off two days ago, somewhere between Calais and Paris. Either that, or she was knitting a pair of socks for the Statue of Liberty.

She eyed the sock proudly. 'All these lovely bits and pieces will be going in the church's Christmas boxes.'

'That's kind of you,' I remarked, feeling sorry for whoever would be receiving them.

She smiled. 'One does what one can.'

That evening, Rob and I walked from our hotel behind St Lazare to the Champs Elysées, where we had a lovely meal and shared a bottle of wine in a pavement café. We sat on a table for two, holding hands in the wavering light of a table candle. For a while, we didn't speak. We just sipped wine and smiled in romantic silence. I could have stayed there for ever. When we stood to leave, Rob gripped my forearms and drew me to him. I felt his heart beat against my cheek as I snuggled my face to his chest.

'You're beautiful, Evie,' he mouthed into my hair.

'So are you,' I told him.

The following day I tackled the farewell ceremony with a dignified and professional approach. I thanked everyone for choosing to travel with us and told them that they were the friendliest and most interesting group of people I'd ever worked with. And because it went down so well, and because our tips were fabulous (again!), I decided that I would say this every week. Why not?

Chapter Twenty-two

Lulu and Vic, her marine biologist, were leaving the flat to go out for dinner when Rob and I arrived home. Vic is South African. He has thick collar-length white-blond hair, large poppy-out brown eyes framed with bushy white eyebrows and clumped-together white eyelashes. He looks like a seal pup. On the plus side, he has a fab tan and an Aston Martin.

Lulu hijacked me and pulled me into the bathroom. She looked gorgeous in white flared jeans and a pink wraparound top. Her hand fluttered excitedly, tinkling an assortment of silver chains that decorated her impressive cleavage.

'What d'you think?' she asked eagerly, lips curving into a smile. 'You didn't get a good look the first time you met him, did you?' She pouted in the mirror and slashed her lips with some strawberry crush lipstick.

'Nice,' I said woodenly.

She swooped around. 'Nice,' she echoed. 'Is that all you've got to say?'

'He's a bit too, well, a bit too white around the eyes and fringe for me.'

She held her lipstick aloft. 'White around the eyes?' she snapped. 'What is that supposed to mean?'

'Well, a bit too Santafied.'

'Santafied!' she shrieked.

I laughed chummily. 'Yes, as in, you know, Santa?'

She screwed the lid on her lipstick. 'Of course I know who fucking Santa is and he looks nothing like Vic! And let me tell you, he's got a mickey like a garden hose.'

I eyed her doubtfully and plucked the lipstick from her hand. 'What d'you think of Rob?' I asked, beaming into the mirror.

She smoothed her vanilla mane and folded her arms. 'He's awright but he reminds me of Bruce Forsyth,' she retorted.

I gasped, horrified. 'Bruce Forsyth! He looks nothing like him!' I stretched my lips and whizzed a circle with the lipstick.

She bobbed her head. 'Oh yes he does. It's the old man's suit,' she said.

'It's a uniform,' I corrected, slapping the lipstick in her out-stretched hand.

'Sadly it's not a pilot's uniform, is it? He's a coach driver, isn't he?'

'He owns the company, I'll have you know.'

She jabbed my shoulder. 'I'll have you know, Vic has an Oxford degree.'

That was it. The jabbing riled me. 'Vic's a fish doctor! And how hard can that be, eh? It's not as though his patients will ever be able to blab if he messes up, is it? In fact, I saw a few of them on ice in Sainsbury's.'

She whipped open the bathroom door with a flourish. 'You're a spiteful cow,' she hissed over her shoulder. 'I'm going out and staying the night at Vic's. You and Postman Pat can have the place to yourselves.' And with that she flounced from the bathroom, nearly taking the door with her.

Lulu and I have never, *ever*, ever gone after the same man.

★

I called Lexy on Tuesday and told her I was popping over to visit. I didn't mention Rob would be with me. I thought it would be a nice surprise if I just produced him.

'You'll love my sister,' I told him, ringing the doorbell. 'She's a bit on the chatty side though, so you'll have to humour her.'

'If she's anything at all like you, I'm sure I'll like her.' He gripped me around the waist, pulled me towards him and kissed me. 'Will the kids be in?' he asked, chuckling into my forehead.

'No,' I said, secretly thanking Jesus and the twelve disciples. 'They'll be at nursery.'

We stood idly on the doorstep.

'She's taking her time,' he said, and he was absolutely right, she was taking her bloody time.

I stabbed the doorbell and hollered, 'It's me!' through the letterbox. I heard footsteps clattering on the wooden floor. Lexy opened the door, pivoted, hitched her skirt up, and sprinted back down the hallway. I marched after her, leading Rob by the hand. She ran the length of the kitchen, swerved around the table and leaped on top of the base unit beside the sink. She knelt, stooped forward and peered between the wooden slatted blinds.

Rob raised surprised brows.

'I've had the best morning. We're having some of our trees cut down. I've got an army of the horniest men you've ever clapped your peepers on in my garden. Lumberjacks!' she rattled, breathless. 'Even the word "lumberjack" is a turn on. Anyway, feast your eyes. Look at these fabulous naked sweaty torsos. They look good enough to eat.' She licked her lips lustfully and hastened on. 'Check out the big thick leather belts around their waists. And look at the way they hold those massive heavy saws with one hand. D'you call them chainsaws? I think you do. You'd think they were no heavier than an egg whisk. And that guy up there,' she rushed on, jabbing the blinds demonstratively, 'he leaped from that tree to that tree. He looked *amazing*. I want to run up, drag them all into the middle of the garden and shag them all at once. I've had to shut the blinds so they can't see me spying. I've made them four coffees and I've been out three times with jugs of my delicious homemade lemonade. They love it.'

She scooted over and patted the worktop. 'Come and sit up here. You can't see bugger all from down there. Oh my God, one of them is ... look ... Oh, just look at that. His eyes are closed against the sun and he's scratching his flute with the handle of the saw. How can he do that and not fall out of the tree? D'you know what? Graeme could never do that. And he won't be home till six.' She took a deep breath. 'I can't wait that long,' she wailed.

I cleared my throat. 'Lexy, this is Rob.'

'Huh!?' She spun around, lost her balance, scootered off the edge of the unit and landed on the floor like a fallen tree, oddly enough. Rob helped her to her feet.

There was a frozen pause.

She eyed me murderously. 'You didn't mention that you were bringing someone,' she managed through gritted teeth, smoothing down her skirt.

The doorbell rang.

'Excuse me,' she said shrilly, swooping out into the hall. Rob's eyes followed her in dumbfounded amazement.

She tottered back into the kitchen, balancing a silver platter of sandwiches and another one with a mouth-watering whole poached salmon on it. 'I ordered a bit of a snack for the, for the, the workmen,' she said pinkly.

'That was nice of you. I don't remember you doing that for Alf and Eddie when they fitted your bathroom.'

213

She threw me an icy glare. 'So, Rob, nice to meet you,' she said, proffering the sandwich platter. 'Are you hungry?'

She laid the trays on the table and with an elegant tailspin, glided towards the Aga and plucked the kettle from the hob. 'Graeme tried to trim the trees himself at the weekend, but he cut through the wire of the electric saw and got a nasty shock. He flew the length of the garden and ended up in the pond. I thought he was dead. So did the kids. Thankfully he was all right but Becky suggested we bury him anyway.' *This is exactly the kind of situation that reinforces my suspicions about that child.* 'So we thought it best to draft in the professionals to finish the job.' She trailed off, and did a fake do-you-know-what-I-mean laugh. Rob nodded politely and stepped outside onto the patio.

Lexy ambushed me. 'How embarrassing! You could have stopped me. What must he think? He is gorgeous. No wonder you love your job, tell him I—'

He walked back in.

'Rob, milk and sugar?' she asked.

And do you know what? She wasn't planning on sharing the salmon with us. She babbled something about presentation and wanting to serve it whole. She tried to stuff me full of sandwiches instead, and told me that my eyes were bigger than my belly. She pushed me away from the table and stretched herself horizontally across the salmon platter, so I spun her by the hair out into the hall and scooped a chunk from the middle with a teaspoon, which set her off on one of her rants where she brought up every argument we had ever had. Apart from that, we had a pleasant afternoon. She and Rob seemed to hit it off really well.

It was almost five o'clock when Rob and I arrived back at the flat. Lulu was splayed moodily on the sofa, feet on the coffee table, flicking through one of her angling magazines. She lit a Marlboro and popped a Nicorette chewing gum in her mouth. An enormous brown rabbit sat in the armchair. I sank down silently next to her on the sofa. Rob stood by the door staring hypnotically at the rabbit, which was shitting all over the cushion.

'Thought you'd stopped smoking?' I said, deadpan, studying the rabbit.

She plucked her drink from the table and peered at me over the rim of the glass. 'I have, but today has *not* been a good day. I need to de-stress.'

'Is that a rabbit?' I asked, jerking my chin rabbitwards.

She took a heavy drag on her fag. 'It most certainly is,' she confirmed, and blew out a string of perfect smoke rings.

The rabbit bounded off the seat, hopped over to the window, stood up on its hind legs and took a look up and down the road. Lulu lurched towards the table and poured the last of the wine into her glass. The rabbit started nibbling the curtain.

'Is it our rabbit?' I asked, dreading her reply. I hoped not. It was the size of a Yorkshire terrier.

She chewed on the Nicorette gum. 'Until tomorrow it is.'

'Why?'

She tapped ash into the empty wine bottle before taking another powerful drag. There was a beat of silence before she spoke.

'Remember when little Charlotte from next door asked me if I would look after her rabbit while she went on her school trip?'

'Mmmm . . .'

'And I kindly agreed?'

'Mmmm . . .'

She blew another couple of smoke rings. 'I've been looking

after it all weekend but, but,' she faltered, twisting the cord of her dressing gown. 'Well it's dead,' she said quickly.

'Dead?' I echoed, feeling a swoop of alarm. 'Did you kill it?'

She took a sip of wine. 'Kind of,' she admitted.

'What did you do to it?'

She gave the cushion a nervous bash. 'I broke the latch on the hutch. The rabbit must have been watching and cottoned on that it could get out, so it escaped and hopped out the gate, and along came the 155 bus to Clapham, which as you know is usually late, but today, miraculously, it was on time, and so at precisely one p.m. . . .' She trailed off miserably.

My stomach gave an anxious leap, and my hands flew to my mouth in horror. 'Don't tell me,' I said. 'Don't tell me.'

She studied her toenails. 'I've spent the entire afternoon driving the length and breadth of southwest London looking for a bunny because the crappy pet shop at the end of the road sells nothing but vermin.'

'But wasn't Charlotte's rabbit tiny and fluffy and white and cute?'

She sniffed. 'It most certainly was.'

I looked at Thumper in the corner. 'But that thing is gigantic and brown.'

Her eyes flashed. 'Aha, but it's alive,' she said factually. 'And that's the main thing.'

The rabbit bounced past the table, knocked over a candle and boomeranged back onto the leather chair. A strangled throaty chuckle came from behind me. Lulu and I twirled and shot Rob an evil glare.

'D'you mind if I help myself to a beer?' he asked, and beetled out of the room without waiting for an answer.

'Bring in another bottle of wine,' Lulu shouted. 'Sod it,' she said breezily, waving her fag. 'I'll tell Charlotte it put on weight,

216

and lost all its baby fur. She's as thick as two planks. She'll believe me. D'you fancy a Chinese?'

'Evie,' Rob whispered, as we spooned in bed later that evening.
  'What?'
  'Would you say that today was a normal day, in so much as there was nothing abnormal about the behaviour of your friends and family?' he asked.
  'Of course it was normal. What are you implying?' I challenged.
  He tucked my head under his chin and wrapped his arms around me. 'Nothing, babe. Nothing at all,' he insisted, immediately backing off.

On Wednesday morning a chauffeur-driven limousine, sent by the coach builders, arrived to collect Rob. I suppose you're worth a limo when you're writing a cheque for over a million quid.
  I babysat the rabbit all day, whilst Harry hammered and chiselled frantically to replace the latch on the hutch. He huffed, puffed, sweated and popped in and out every two sodding minutes for beer, water, a bit of a snack, a tea break and to watch the lunchtime news. I made a nappy for the rabbit out of Lulu's white cashmere Gucci scarf, which I thought was inspired, and joined an online French language class, which I enjoyed.
  That evening Lulu fretted at the thought of giving the rabbit to Charlotte. She ended up handing it back like a big boar's head on a plate and Charlotte was delighted that her rabbit was all grown up, and had lost its baby fur. In celebration, Lulu and I drank half a litre of gin and gave ourselves a £250 budget each to blow on the Topshop website.
  On Thursday I worked in Bar Thea. Nikki told me to wear

black trousers and a white blouse, which I sexed up with a neon pink bra. I gathered my hair into a ponytail and weaved a biro through the band. I practised whipping the pen out a couple of times, and I've got to say, I looked as though I'd been waitressing for years. Nikki tucked a white apron into my waistband, which fell to just above my ankles, and fastened a gold cravat around my neck. I looked absolutely brilliant. A real pro. I was born to do this.

I stubbed my big toe. I lost my forty-pound cash float. I burnt my finger on a plate of fajitas. I let one table leave without paying. I slapped Costas for skiving to the bookies and leaving me on my own. Nikki slapped me for eating chips from a customer's plate. The chef slapped Nikki for slapping me. I dropped a plate of chilli on Nikki's foot, and pinged open the till drawer as he was walking past, catching him on the balls. I had a cry in the toilet because Nikki shouted at me. I ripped the cord light from the ceiling in the ladies' toilet in temper, but no one knows it was me. I saw my hairdresser Charlene's boyfriend kissing another girl so I phoned her and told her. She came down to the bar and hit him over the head with a plate of fried squid, and Nikki shouted at me for not minding my own business, which, frankly, I find astonishing. It *was* my business. She is *my* hairdresser.

I'm working in the bar again next Thursday.

Chapter Twenty-three

I was surprised and delighted to see Alice at Victoria station on Friday morning. We'd texted each other a couple of times, but she'd never mentioned she was coming on another Paris break. At first glance I didn't recognise her. She wore beige Ugg boots, an ankle-length flouncy aubergine dress with a handkerchief hemline, and a loose belt made of chunky purple glass beads. Her make-up was fabulous. Her cheekbones were subtly high-lighted with a whisper of plum blusher. A flesh coloured lip gloss gave her a sultry plump-lipped pout and charcoal eye shadow with a black kohl liner made her eyes look like smoked glass windows. The overall effect was stylish and trendy in a bohemian kind of way, as opposed to the Miss Moneypenny look she'd sported the first time I'd met her. She tucked her bobbed hair behind her ears and rushed towards me, black wooden bangles clattering on her outstretched arms.

'You look fantastic,' I said in wide-eyed admiration. I fingered the Celtic cross around her neck. 'Have you left Duncan and had a makeover?'

She hugged me. 'No, love. Duncan calls me Rupert Bear when I wear these boots,' she said, stamping her foot and chuck-ling. 'The last time I wore them he spat on his thumb and

219

smudged my mascara and said, "There ye are, that's better. Let's see if we can find ye a wee bow tie, and a checked jacket from somewhere",' she mimicked, contemplating her freshly painted black fingernails. 'He has very firm views on how a woman should dress, the bossy, chauvinistic big eejit that he is.'

I grinned. 'D'you call him a big eejit to his face?' I asked doubtfully.

'Not as often as I call him a big eejit behind his back.'

Alice introduced her friend Shirley, a Morticia Addams clone.

'Is that mythical creature coming with us?' Shirley asked, bobbing her head towards Rob.

Alice looped her arm through Shirley's. 'He is, but that's where the good news ends because he shacks up with her,' she said, eyeing me approvingly.

'But it's my birthday,' Shirley wailed. 'Can't I have him for an hour or so?'

'Nope,' Alice retorted. 'We agreed on a man-free weekend, didn't we? And that's exactly what we're going to have. And Shirl, I'm not drinking. I put on half a stone when Duncan and I went to Paris last time.'

Shirley gave a stiff nod of agreement. 'I was thinking exactly the same. I don't want to pile it on either.'

Later, as we lumbered through the streets of Paris, I marvelled at the enviable, dazzling elegance of French women. With a diet of bread, wine and fags surely they should be overweight, with booze-bloated faces and yellow teeth. And every second one of them has a poodle jammed under her arm so why don't their handbags have fleas and smell of dog shite? A prickle of envy had just started fluttering below my ribcage when my slithering gaze halted on a graceful tall brunette. She was clutching a Chanel bag in the crook of her tanned arm, in which bobbed a furry black head with a pink diamanté collar. Her dog was having a fight with another dog at the traffic lights. I grimaced. What if my poodle growled, yapped and chewed my sleeves? I hated the bloody thing already.

'Evie,' Rob said, penetrating my thoughts. 'We're here. Are you going to pick up the room keys or not?'

Rob was checking his emails in our room. He sat at the dressing table peering studiously at his laptop, bashing away like billy-o. I flicked an eye at my watch. We'd been in the room ten minutes now and he hadn't tried to seduce me. I sat on the bed twisting my pinkie ring and idly toeing the bed-side table. This was a first. The stampede into the hotel room in a flurry of luggage, jackets and briefcases usually preceded a mad frantic rush to get naked. This display of indifference was a bad sign, an ill omen. I felt gloomy, I felt depressed. I flopped back on the bed and lay wide-eyed, staring at the ceiling. So this is it? This is what it's come to. He feels he no longer needs to make the effort. I studied his profile. He had an irritating smirk on his face. He was chuckling at his laptop and setting about the keyboard with the finesse of Neil Sedaka. I bolted upright. Did I say depressed? Hell no, not depressed. What I meant was I was furious, because if he's not shagging me, then who is he shagging? The slut! I'm going to have it out with him.

'There's a present for you in my pocket,' he said, gesturing towards his blazer that was hanging on the bathroom door.

I bounded from the bed and in two determined strides was frisking his pockets. My eyes rounded to saucers when I excavated the velvet Chopard box. I felt a bit shaky and nippy-eyed and excited. My heart raced as I opened the box. Inside was a beautiful white gold heart-shaped diamond pendant. The sight of it brought tears rushing to my ducts. Rob stood in front of me. I flicked my eyes between him and the pendant in the palm of my hand.

'It's our three-week anniversary,' he said, lifting the necklace. 'I know it's not a landmark date, but for me it's a landmark occasion. The occasion being that I've realised I'm only ever really happy when I'm with you.' He slipped his hands under my hairline and fastened the chain. 'And so I bought you Happy Diamonds. That's what they're called,' he added softly.

My tummy did a loop-de-loop as I gazed into his warm blue eyes, overwhelmed at his thoughtfulness. He lowered his face to mine and kissed me while tracing his forefingers down the length of my arms, which sent a tingly electric current down my spine. He is, without a shadow of a doubt, the perfect man. I wouldn't swap him for all the money in the world. He's wonderful.

I strolled into the foyer bar later that evening, swinging my handbag with practised nonchalance. This taking everyone out on a Friday night is a piece of cake, I thought. All I have to do is turn up and enjoy myself, and everyone acts like I'm some sort of celebrated wedding planner. It couldn't be easier.

Alice and Shirley were already in the bar, swaying drunkenly. I eyed them in astonishment. Alice was still wearing her floaty purple number and I realised that they hadn't changed. My eyes slid to their suitcases propped against the wall. They hadn't even checked into their room. I watched Shirley totter around cackling, trying to close the distance between herself and Alice, and grimaced.

Before we left the hotel bar:
    Alice . . . spoke English with a French accent; crawled around the floor of the bar looking for her Celtic cross, which hung down her back as opposed to her front; lost her handbag;

scootered off the edge of the bar chasing a vodka and Coke and cannoned into a floor-to-ceiling wine rack. I don't want to talk about the chaos and the mess she caused; was doing high-kicks and singing 'New York, New York' as we boarded the coach to leave for the restaurant.

Shirley . . . slashed red lipstick from lip to ear, and wouldn't let me fix it; asked the barman if he would rearrange the furniture in the hotel bar to make a dance floor, even though it was only six forty-five; started singing 'I Will Survive' using a Tampax as a microphone.

At the restaurant:

Alice . . . tore the accordion from the neck of the musician and subjected us to a performance which, frankly, I can't begin to describe; could not navigate her way out of a cubicle in the ladies' toilet so I had to clamber over the top of the adjacent cubicle and open the door myself; was sick in Shirley's handbag; boarded a coach full of Japanese tourists at the end of the evening and refused to budge because she was adamant it was our bus. Infuriated beyond endurance, Rob towed her off the coach by her lovely beaded belt; lost her shoes.

Shirley . . . slept like a log.

Rob . . . moaned like mad and blamed me for everything, bellowing that I should have left Alice and Shirley behind in the hotel.

I was . . . as sober as a bloody judge, knackered and fit to kill Alice and Shirley.

Delia . . . confessed to having an affair and asked if she could use me as an alibi. She was going to Salzburg for a couple of days with a German coach driver and had told her husband she was visiting me in London. Would I back her up? What choice did I have? I'm no traitor.

Delia's husband . . . asked for my home telephone number. I gave him Rob's.

In bed at two a.m.:

Phone rings. It was Duncan . . . 'I'm sorry tae wake you lass, but it's an emergency. Alice has been on the phone and she's drunk and lost. As far as I can make out, she's in the hotel next door, but g'tting her to understand that all she has to do is walk a hundred yards is no easy task. Can ye go get her?'

Rob . . . 'Well we've got no choice but to go and get her, have we?'

I was . . . demented, exhausted, still sober and very quickly going off Alice.

Alice and Shirley . . . were splayed, snoring, on the sofa in the lobby of the Holiday Plaza Hotel. Rob, none too gently, clamped each of them by the arm and marched them on tiptoe back to our hotel. I trotted behind, swinging my clipboard. I don't know why I brought it. I mean, what on earth was I thinking? I winced as Alice hollered and screamed for her lawyer until Rob banged her bedroom door shut behind her.

In bed at three a.m.:

Rob rolled towards me . . . 'If that phone rings, *don't* answer it,' he snapped.

On Saturday afternoon Rob and I had just returned to the hotel after the city tour, which not surprisingly Alice and Shirley had missed, when the phone rang.

'Are you the representative from Insignia Tours?' a plummy voice asked.

I felt a ripple of excitement. Maybe I'd won something! 'Yes, yes I am,' I replied eagerly, giving an excited air punch.

'British Embassy here. Unfortunately I have to inform you that one of your clients, Mr Harold Henderson, has been hospitalised. Suspected heart attack. He's in the Hertford British Hospital.'

I eyed Rob frantically as I fought for calm. I felt like I was having a heart attack myself.

'The administration department notified us of his admission. You can take over from here. The case number is eight-nine-three-eight.' I scribbled the number on the notepad on the bedside table. 'Good day to you,' the plummy voice pitched frostily and clicked off.

Take over from here? Take over what? I panicked. I repeated the conversation to Rob, who nodded knowingly.

'A heart attack!' I bellowed, massaging my chest. 'What am I supposed to do about that? I'm a tour guide, not a consultant cardiologist!'

'We'd better go,' Rob said, and rang the front desk to order us a taxi.

Henderson, Harold. Harold Henderson. Shit, who's he? I couldn't for the life of me remember him. I checked my passenger list. His wife's name was Ena. Who is Ena? I tried to visualise everyone on the coach but I'd spent so much time with Alice and Shirley that I hadn't had the opportunity to get to know anyone else. I paced the bedroom. Rob sat calmly picking his teeth with his Visa card. I rounded on him.

'Will you stop doing that? Harold is dying and you're picking your teeth!' I yelled. 'There's a time and a place for everything. Now is not the time to be picking your teeth.'

Harold and Ena needed me. The phone buzzed. I jumped. It was the front desk telling us that our cab driver was waiting in the lobby.

Chapter Twenty-four

I barged through the swing doors of Accident & Emergency like a demon, hair billowing, eyes darting left and right in search of Ena. Rob had to trot to keep up with me. I spotted her immediately. She sat hunched and forlorn on a plastic chair at the end of the corridor next to the coffee machine.

Ena was enormous. I'm not being rude, I'm being truthful. She had brown hair, curled like two big sausage rolls down each side of her round face, rosy apple cheeks and green eyes. She must easily weigh in at about nineteen stone, I thought. And now that I'd seen her, I remembered Harold. He was a tiny man, about a foot shorter than Ena, with a bald head and a fire-engine-red face. I had nicknamed them Little and Extra Large. Oh my God! Little was ill and Extra Large needed me!

Ena smiled wanly when she saw me. I ran to her and fell to my knees between the two Corinthian columns she uses for legs and put my arms around as much of her as I could.

'Leave everything to me,' I heard myself say. Me? Am I serious? 'Leave everything to me,' I repeated assertively, to her two bellies. I took three of her chins in my hands and kissed her forehead. 'Everything is going to be just fine, trust me,' I punctuated, with wide-eyed confidence.

226

I sprung into action. Luckily *Casualty* is one of my favourite programmes. I'll consult with, consult with, well, the consultant, I thought. Yes, that's what I'll do.

'Rob, buy Ena a hot chocolate,' I ordered firmly, and marched through the glass doors to the reception desk.

A gorgeous French doctor with dark brown hair, smouldering hazel eyes, ruby lips and a smattering of designer stubble told me that Harold was going to be fine, absolutely fine. He hadn't had a heart attack at all, he'd just fainted. But according to Ena, this had happened before and so, because of the desert heat (Paris was bloody boiling) and the fact that Harold suffered from high blood pressure, the doctor had thought it a good idea if they kept him in for a couple of days. The doctor linked his white-coated arm through mine and led me, our heads locked in a two-professionals–conferring kind of way, down the corridor to his office and kindly offered me a glass of mineral water. A shadow fell across the room as Rob filled the doorway.

'What are you doing?' he demanded.

Not my idea I might add, but Gregory, the doctor, was removing the cuff from my arm after having checked my blood pressure.

'Oh, I'm coming,' I said smoothly. 'Gregory, er, Doctor,' I squinted so I could read his name badge, 'Doctor Lacroix was saying that I looked rather flushed.'

Rob exhaled noisily and two blond eyebrows met as he frowned. He leaned against the doorframe and folded his arms. 'Perhaps I should hold you under a cold shower and keep you there when we get back to the hotel,' he suggested. 'That's sure to cool you down.'

I found my feet.

★

Rob and I sat side by side in the waiting area, whilst Ena spent a few minutes with Harold. I'd told Rob I couldn't possibly leave Ena and that I would have to stay at the hospital with her for tonight at least.

'You'll have to do the Illuminations Tour on your own,' I told him resolutely. 'Use your headset so that you can narrate and drive at the same time.'

'I can't,' he hissed, 'definitely not.'

'Why not? Other drivers do it.'

'I've done it before,' he slapped his chest in a self-appreciating gesture, 'but I can't do what you do,' he added witheringly.

'What're you talking about? Of course you can.'

He hunched forward, elbows on knees, fingers in a spire, and dropped his voice. 'I can't and I won't. If you're staying here, we'll cancel the evening tour.'

I smacked his knee. 'We are not refunding over a thousand euros,' I insisted sharply. 'You'll do it.'

He turned incredulous eyes on me. 'I won't,' he snapped.

I glanced ruefully at my watch. I realised that a change of tactic might be called for here so I stroked the knee I'd just slapped. 'Rob,' I cajoled, 'it's not the money. You know how much everyone enjoys the tour.'

He sighed. 'I know, but it's you they enjoy. It's your anecdotes, the way you gossip about the Empress Josephine being a shopaholic and Madame Tussauds taking wax impressions of the decapitated heads during the revolution.' He raised his hands demonstratively. 'And all the other stuff no one but you seems to know.' He tossed me an expression of awe. 'Where do you get all your information from?'

I tried not to gloat but I'm actually very good at this tour guiding lark. I've made up some fabulous stories. OK, I've reached the point where I've kind of lost the plot so far as remembering what's true and what I've embroidered, and I couldn't give you Napoleon's date of birth to within a hundred years, but, honestly, no one gives a toss. My stories are romantic and exciting and sometimes racy and raunchy, kind of Mills & Boon with a *Sharpe* twist. Everyone loves them, including me. And if anyone asks me a question that I don't know the answer to, I glare menacingly and say, 'I covered that on the tour,' and accuse them of not listening. They're usually mortified and so they pretend to think hard and then bob their head reflectively and say, 'Oh yes you did, didn't you?'

'I'm fairly well read,' I told Rob dismissively. 'Will you do the tour if I ring Carla and ask her to guide with you?' I asked, patting his hand encouragingly.

He exhaled moodily and punched a paper coffee cup on the chair next to him. 'If I have to,' he sulked.

'You do,' I insisted.

After the evening tour, Rob arrived at the hospital by taxi to give Ena and me a lift back to the hotel. I linked my arm through Ena's as we trudged, exhausted, through the silent hotel lobby.

'This is the first night in thirty-five years that I haven't slept with Harold,' Ena said.

'I'll stay in your room with you if you like,' I offered, 'if you'd rather not be on your own.'

Rob, who was on the other side of Ena, blanched and scanned my face warningly.

'Honestly Ena, if you'd rather I stayed with you, then I will,' I offered again.

Rob gasped and stopped walking – and then had to run to catch up.

Ena squeezed my hand as we waddled towards the elevator.

'No love, you've been fabulous. I enjoyed our meal and chat in the canteen, I almost forgot what we were doing there, and you cheered Harold up. I honestly don't know what I'd have done without you. I couldn't have phoned our boys and dealt with them the way you did. I'm so grateful you've arranged for them to fly out and stay here at the hotel with me. And Harold is delighted with the private room you wangled. He won't want to leave.' She pinched my cheek affectionately. It hurt.

'I'll see you tomorrow,' she said, negotiating her huge frame through the elevator door. 'Harold's in good hands and I'll sleep well on that thought alone,' she added with a faraway look in her eye. I gave her a night-night wave as the elevator door closed.

Rob clutched my elbow. 'That was a close call. What if she'd said yes?' He spirited me down the hallway. 'That,' he repeated, bug-eyed, 'was a very close call.'

Chapter Twenty-five

Alice and Shirley were suitably mortified when I bumped into them in the lobby on Sunday morning, ready to depart on the trip to Versailles.

'So sorry, love,' Alice said. 'I'm fragile even now. Can you believe that?'

I most certainly could.

On Sunday afternoon Rob and I visited Harold, who was much improved. Ena and her two enormous boys were with him. I arranged an extended stay at the hotel for Ena, a twin room for her sons, spoke to the insurance company to reserve flights for them to London and had the medical bills taken care of. On Sunday evening Rob and I ate a light supper and shared a bottle of wine in a café two doors down from the hotel.

'I need my clipboard from the coach,' I told Rob. 'There's an insurance form I have to leave with the hotel to cover Ena's room charges.'

He nodded and scooped the last of the omelette from my plate and tipped it in his mouth.

The coach was quiet, shadowy and kind of ghostly. It was almost midnight and the usual manically busy Paris traffic had trickled to the sporadic whizzing scooter and the odd speeding

Peugeot 206. I folded the insurance papers and tucked them into my handbag.

'All sorted,' I sighed tiredly. 'Let's go.'

Rob stared at me with bright avid eyes. 'Not so fast,' he protested firmly, taking my hand and leading me to the back of the coach.

'Rob, what're you up to? I'm knackered, let's go,' I said, tripping behind him.

'Sit down,' he said softly. He placed a finger over my lips and lowered his voice disarmingly. 'No questions. Be patient.'

I sat down on the back seat, tucked my hands beneath my bottom and looked dazedly down the length of the centre aisle. I watched as his tall, broad frame, barely visible in the gloom, descended the centre steps. He reappeared two minutes later clutching a large quilt. He walked slowly towards me, his lips curved in an ear-splitting smile. He spread the quilt on the floor and clasping my hands in his, he coaxed me to standing.

I felt a surge of blood rush to my face and a flicker of excitement tighten in my chest as I stumbled, smiling, towards him. He slid strong hands beneath my hairline and jutting my chin up roughly with his thumbs, covered my mouth with his. Probing lips attacked mine. Smiling through his kiss, he flexed his fingers in the coils of my hair, cupped my face and gently massaged my neck. I relaxed against him, circling his waist and exploring his jaw with my nose. For a moment we swayed wordlessly.

'Sit down,' he said in a grainy voice, 'on the floor.' He held my hands and slowly, together, eyes locked, we moved to kneel. 'Happy?' he asked.

I nodded in reply. 'And you?'

His already wide smile grew wider. 'Couldn't be happier.'

My stomach did a flippy thing. He lay on his back, pulled me close and palmed my hair in slow gentle strokes. A muted siren sounded in the distance.

'There's a difference between having sex and making love. Sometimes I feel no matter what I do, I can't get close enough to you,' he said, his voice steady but chalky.

'What do you mean?' I whispered.

He stirred a little uncomfortably. 'I can't explain it. I think what I mean is that I'm not content to have just your body.' He tilted my chin to force my gaze to meet his. 'I want your mind and your heart too.' There was a faraway look in his eye, as though he was listening hard to something in the distance. 'And,' he gave me a lopsided grin and reached to trace my lips with his index finger, 'and I will. I'll have it all.'

I curled in closer. The hollow of his throat lay soft against my face. 'Will you now?' I asked, massaging the flat slant of his belly.

I felt him swallow against my cheek. 'Yes,' he said. 'I will.'

Duncan met Alice when we arrived back into London. He looked very smart in a white Ralph Lauren shirt and navy blazer. His broad shoulders and riot of red hair eclipsed the early evening sun as he strode purposefully towards us, hands jammed deep in the pockets of his beige chinos.

'Look at him,' Alice said, looping her arm through mine. 'He looks like the Honey Monster.'

I put on a husky voice. 'Alice, he is gorgeous.'

She gave a proud chuckle.

'For an old man,' I added.

Duncan kissed us and then turned to Alice. 'Ye're a disgrace,' he scolded.

'She is,' I agreed.

His dark intelligent eyes flicked between me and Alice. 'Ye're the town drunk.'

'She's that as well,' I piped up, 'and she's worn her Rupert Bear boots all weekend.'

He tutted and shook his red mane in disapproval. 'Get in the car,' he said to her, nodding his head towards a rather posh looking four by four.

Alice kissed my cheek. 'Keep in touch, love.'

I hugged her. 'Of course I will.'

Rob and I arrived home to a methodical thump thump thump reverberating on the floor. At first I thought Lulu must have the builders in, but to do what?

We stood in the doorway watching Lulu stamp, hop and crash up and down the lounge. She had bought a dance mat. Her eyes were glued to the television and she was flapping her arms while her feet thundered in time to the music. She wore her Arsenal socks with a pair of denim shorts and a T-shirt that said 'I'm hot to trot'. All I can say is that the dance mat should have come with a decent sports bra. We closed the door and left her to it.

'Join . . . me . . . if . . . you . . . like,' she managed. 'Aaaagggggg!' she screamed, falling over the coffee table.

On Thursday Rob went to Birmingham to finalise the finance agreement for his new coaches and I worked in Bar Thea. I pointed out to Nikki that the Broadway was buzzing between three o'clock and dinner time but that the bar was always empty. I suggested that we could grab some of the granny business that was going to the deli opposite if he invested in some hazelnut and vanilla liqueur, a selection of brightly coloured glass coffee cups and a decorative cake display-cabinet. He said, 'sort it'. I also suggested that we should start a happy hour where we offered roast potatoes and a cocktail of the day between five and seven o'clock to catch the office workers on their way to the tube station. He said, 'sort it' to that as well. So I did.

Chapter Twenty-six

Rob and I worked together in Paris every weekend throughout August and September. Fridays and Saturdays were more or less taken up with our scheduled itinerary but we had the afternoon and evening to ourselves every Sunday. We constantly disagreed on how best to spend our spare time. Rob wanted to scoff an enormous lunch, knock back a couple of drinks, hot tail it to the hotel, romp around like a couple of porn stars, have a sleep, watch Sky Sports, pop out for a beer and a sandwich and finish off the evening trying to find something on television worth watching. Well, I don't think so.

We went to Musée d'Orsay where I *loved* the Impressionist exhibition so much that I talked Rob into taking a train to Giverny to visit the former home of Claude Monet. I thought it was fabulous, especially the gardens, but Rob fell in the lily pond, whilst saving me from falling in the lily pond, and that more or less put the kibosh on the rest of the day, as we had to go back to the hotel because he was all wet.

And we visited the Arc de Triomphe where we had our biggest argument ever. Rob agreed to go because I assured him there was a lift. Do you honestly think I'd have gone myself if I'd known I'd have to hoof it up 234 stairs? And would I have worn a pair of high-heeled sandals? I begged two rest stops. I wanted a third stop, but he refused and kept climbing and when my heel got stuck and I fell over, he pulled me to my feet by my elbow without breaking his stride and made me bite my tongue. I cried with exhaustion and dehydration and absolute despair. Eventually we made it to the top and I stopped crying. It was sooooooooo romantic. Rob jammed a tissue on my nose for a blow and pulled his arm tight around my shoulders. We oohed and aaahed at the spectacular view stretching the length of the Champs Elysées, over the Place de la Concorde, to the Louvre.

And we went on an evening dinner cruise on the glass-topped Bateau Mouche. We held hands across the candlelit table and stared wide-eyed at the sights as we glided under the city bridges. The cruise itself was brilliant, but Rob got deli belly. Now, what are the odds on this? I ate eleven oysters and he ate one. I was tickety-boo and he turned green, slumped off his chair and collapsed onto the floor, seized by some form of almost deadly food poisoning, and the maitre d' had to call the paramedics. Still, at least he now knows that oysters don't agree with him.

And we visited the flea market, which I loved but Rob hated because two gypsy kids hit him on the back of the head with a tomato when he wouldn't give them any money.

And we took a trip to Euro Disney, which was a disaster because we lost each other and had no mobile signal. I knuckled down and made the most of the day. I went on lots of rides, watched the Disney parade and spent a fortune in the shops on the twins. But Rob spent three hours waiting for me at the missing persons meeting point, which was full of screaming kids. I said, 'If only you'd had my initiative, you could have enjoyed yourself,' which, let's face it, was the truth, but like a big baby he sulked and wouldn't speak to me all the way back to Paris. We made up later though, because I'd bought a chiffon Arabian belly dancer's outfit and I refused to wear it unless he said 'sorry' five times, kissed my hand and called me Queen.

And we went down the Paris sewers, which were full of gothic tunnels and secret arches. We also took the train to Fontainebleau and went to the top of the Eiffel Tower and spent an afternoon wandering around Sacré Coeur. We toured the Opera House and the Pompidou Centre.

And we walked and walked and walked, and Rob moaned and moaned and moaned, but he admitted that he'd learned more about Paris in two short months than he had in eight years. My French was now fabulous, sometimes I even thought in French. Rob is useless, he doesn't even try. He either points or grunts to signify what he wants, or I do the talking for him.

We spent Monday to Wednesday in cosmopolitan Tooting, and Rob would visit Birmingham every Thursday to make sure the office was running smoothly. This worked well because I was always at Bar Thea on Thursdays.

We'd grown inseparable. Our life together was romantic, passionate and blissfully wonderful. We were so incredibly happy. I can't remember what I did with my time before I met him. It was as though I'd known him all my life and he felt the same. I only had to look at him and a flame of desire would ignite and burn inside me. He made me feel attractive, sexy and constantly lustful. With Rob, I had no inhibitions. I'd do anything for him or anything with him, if you know what I mean.

Last week he told me that he loved me, and I said it back, although at the time I only said it because he said it, but since then I had come to realise that I really did love him. Love isn't the realisation that you've met someone you can live with. It's realising that you've met someone you can't live without. And Rob was perfect. He was charming, funny and clever bought me a red Mulberry shoulder bag and matching suitcase for no reason. And he could cook and iron and he was horny with a big ding-a-ling and he put the bin out.

A chunk of my wardrobe was now taken up with his suits and shirts. Subsequently, beneath the bed was packed to the gunnels. I kicked one of my slippers under there the other day and it boomeranged back out. I must have a spring-clean, but obviously not until next March as you can't have a spring-clean in the autumn. Still I wouldn't be without him.

The country is in a state of national frenzy. England has made it through to the European Championship semi final and they're playing Italy. It's as though the entire populace is on speed.

Londoners are chummily asking fellow Londoners, 'What are your plans for the game?' and smiling simultaneously, which is frankly astonishing because normally we practise a couple of scowls in the mirror every morning to make sure we're frightening and miserable enough to go forth and survive the morning commute. And on the underground citizens are sitting, heads locked, sharing newspapers, sponging every piece of news on the footie they can. And the crime rate has fallen. According to Trevor McDonald, thieves and murderers can't be bothered thieving and murdering when they're in such unparalleled high spirits. Everywhere I look England flags are billowing from lounge and bedroom windows and fluttering on car roofs, and there is fantastic merchandise for sale everywhere. It's in shops, tube stations, pubs, even the dentist is flogging red and white toothbrushes. I bought a spaghetti-strap Union Jack T-shirt, a pair of red and white fluffy moonwalker slippers, and a bra and panties set emblazoned with red lions. The overall effect when I wear the complete ensemble is Black Lace with a WAG twist. I love it.

Rob wants to watch the match at home. I suggested the pub, but he said he wants to make sure he has a good view, so guess what? He bought me a forty-two-inch plasma screen, and installed it above the fireplace. It looks fabulous.

The big day arrived. Rob rocked back and forth on the sofa, hugging himself.

'Come on, boys,' I cheered. 'Here we go, here we go, here we go,' I chanted loudly.

I bum-bounced on the sofa next to Rob and punched the air enthusiastically. Surprisingly, I was looking forward to this. Normally I hate football but this is different. This is living history. This is a once in a lifetime experience and I, for one, was determined to savour every minute and enjoy it.

'Ooops.' I shot to standing. 'Rob, stand up. It's the National Anthem.' I tugged on his arm and he reluctantly lumbered to his feet. I stood tall, clenched fists by my side and chin held high.

'God save our gracious Queen,' I bellowed proudly.

'I downloaded this onto my iPod,' I told him, thrusting back my shoulders.

'Na na na na na,' I chorused because I'd forgotten the words.

Rob chewed his thumbnail, and glared hypnotically at the screen.

I whipped up my Union Jack T-shirt to flash my England bra and wriggled my shorts over my hips to flaunt my England panties. 'I'm flying the flag,' I singsonged.

I studied my England panties and decided I didn't need the shorts. I gripped Rob's forearm for support and wobbling slightly, tugged the shorts off and frisbeed them in his face. 'That's better,' I said, admiring my scantily clad form.

I turned and frowned at Rob. 'You could have bought a scarf

to wear for the match,' I told him curtly. 'Look at me. At least I've made the effort.'

I certainly had made the effort, with my furry moonwalkers, Union Jack top and my lion rampant bra and knicks set. I looked like the team mascot. Rob stared at the plasma screen transfixed, rubbed his thighs violently and slowly sat down so he could resume his rocking and hugging motion.

The game started.

'Picnic time,' I said, flourishing a plate of chocolate pastries. 'I made them myself. I know they look like I bought them, but I didn't. I made them from scratch.' I circled the plate under his nose and then placed it on the coffee table. 'You don't believe me, do you?' I rushed on. 'Right, fine, I'll tell you exactly how I did it and then you'll have to believe me.' I folded my arms reflectively. 'First you lay flat a sheet of puff pastry and smear it with chocolate Nutella, and then you—'

He snatched a pastry from the plate and stuffed it in his mouth. 'A bewieve you,' he chewed, spluttering pastry on the carpet.

I glared. He was revolting. I reached for a pastry, which I nibbled delicately, and studied his profile. I decided not to say anything right now but I was definitely going to bring this up later. I knelt in front of him to pick up the crumbs and he pushed my head down, nearly bashing my nose on the coffee table.

'Careful,' I snapped, slapping his arm. I put the crumbs on the plate and settled beside him, arms folded and legs crossed, in an attentive football spectator's pose. I straightened my leg to admire my moonwalkers. 'These slippers make my feet look bloody enormous, don't they?' I grumbled.

He ignored me.

'Still, they were only a tenner,' I confided.

He ignored me again.

'What's the score?' I asked.

No response was forthcoming.

My pants were rather lean on the fabric side. They were more like a thong actually, which I'm not overly keen on. I slithered my hand under my backside, had a grope and grimaced. It *was* a thong.

I was a bit disappointed because, well, it was just like a normal game and it had only been on three minutes and I was already bored senseless and I couldn't for the life of me imagine how the hell I was supposed to survive ninety minutes of this. I extended my arms and studied my hands. I want a set of acrylic nails, I decided. I've had them before but I couldn't get my contact lenses in or out, so I'd had them taken off. I could try again and persevere, and maybe this time I could try to manage without my contacts. Yes, I hadn't thought of that. Maybe the over-whelming desire for a lovely set of acrylic nails would be an incentive to manage with limited sight. I glanced at Rob, who was sitting trancelike. I waved my hand in front of his face and he didn't blink. I squeezed his knee.

'Back in a minute,' I said.

'Get me a beer!' he boomed, even though I was still sitting next to him.

No bloody please. And no bloody thank you. When I thrust the beer in his chest all I got was a snort. I moonwalked huffily to the bedroom.

I might as well do something useful for the first half, I thought, and savour this living historical event for the second half. I decided to sort out my shoes. I desperately needed cup-board space so I simply had to be ruthless. I counted five pairs of red shoes and wrinkled my nose. Red's not my colour. Three of them I hated so that left two. I tried on one flat dolly pump and one four-inch stiletto. I studied my feet. I wasn't sure about either so I peg-legged into the lounge.

'Rob, which d'you like best?' I asked. I hobbled from the chair, past the plasma screen to the window. Thump, dink, thump, dink, thump, dink.

'Uuuggg,' he grunted.

'Which d'you like?' I repeated, retracing my steps from the window, past the plasma screen to the chair.

'Dunno,' he said absently. 'Go try on the other pair.'

I stomped furiously, my left shoulder four inches higher than my right. Chair, plasma, window, window, plasma, chair, chair, plasma, window. Thump, dink, thump, dink, thump, dink.

I halted in front of him and spread my arms demonstratively. 'Rob, this is not a pair. These are two completely different shoes.'

His gaze dodged past me.

'A matching pair would not have a heel difference of four inches, would they?'

'I like them,' he told the television.

I gave a snort of impatience and limped to the bedroom. He's insufferable. I don't know why I put up with him. I'll keep both, I decided. I worked like a demon and by the time I'd finished I had eighteen pairs of shoes for the charity shop. I put them under the bed for now, and decided to see what was in the fridge to eat. Rob stood in the hallway, arms splayed, palms resting on the wall above his head, watching the football through a narrow slit in the lounge door.

I prodded his shoulder blade. 'What're you doing?' I asked.

'It's nil all and two minutes to half-time,' he said hollowly.

'Why aren't you sitting on the sofa?'

'Too stressful.' He ran a frantic hand through his hair.

'Why is it less stressful standing in the hallway?'

He gripped the back of his head with both hands and rocked on his heels. 'I dunno. It just is.' His forehead thumped mechanically against the door.

'Why?'

'Will you shut up, or I'll club you to death!'

I fired a stinger on his backside with the tea towel I was holding. 'How *dare* you speak to me like that! I won't have it. You're—'

The half-time whistle went.

Rob swooped around. 'OK, brat, I'm all yours.' He hustled me into the bedroom and wrestled me to the bed. I giggled as he straddled me and pinned my arms above my head, lowering his mouth to mine. He sucked my bottom lip, hard.

'Trust me?' It was a question. His tongue explored my neck.

'Of course,' I giggled. 'With my life,' I added loyally.

'Good,' he breathed. He reached into the drawer of the bedside cabinet and tugged out a couple of stockings. 'I'm going to tie you up.'

I shrieked with laughter. He's so creative and inventive, a real prime mover. He always thinks of new things to do. He's the best lover I've ever had. I feigned a pathetic struggle. He nibbled my ears as he tied each wrist to the bedpost, making my heart pump and my cheeks blaze with excitement. He snaked down my hips, blew a raspberry in my belly button and chafed his stubbly chin the length of my thighs to my knees, before tying my ankles to the bottom bedposts. I was starfished to the bed.

I raised my head slightly, as slightly was all I could manage, tossed my hair stiffly, and milled my pelvis into his groin. His eyeballs rotated with pleasure. I chuckled when I saw the effect this had on him. His face lit up with an ear-splitting I-want-you-more-than-anything smile. He can't resist me, I thought. I only have to flash a naked shoulder and Mr Wiggly's doing the hooky kooky. And I admit it, I can't resist him either.

'OK, babe?' he asked, eyes narrowed with lust. He traced a finger slowly up and down my cleavage, making the hairs on my neck prickle and my nostrils flare and sting with the effort of trying to calm my breathing.

'I sure am,' I managed. 'What're you going to do now, big boy?' I drawled sexily. I was, quite honestly, fit to burst. He loomed above me, hands balled in a fist either side of my head. I raised my chin to meet his lips and sniffed wantonly along his jaw and cheek. I was sucking on his ear when suddenly he stood up and playfully slapped my thigh. My heart flipped.

'Well, now ... I'm going to watch the second half of the match, and you're going to stay right here until the final whistle goes,' he informed me firmly.

My eyes flickered in confusion. I blinked hard and opened my mouth. My jaw contracted but no sound came out. I tried for words again, but zilch. Rob jammed a pillow under my head, and laughing eerily like the baddie in a pantomime, kissed my cheek.

I shook my head. 'Er, excuse me?' I stuttered, raising quizzical eyebrows.

'You heard,' he said flatly.

I most certainly had. 'Untie me now you big gobshite or I'll scream and scream and scream!'

I raised my head. He stood at the foot of the bed, between my open legs. He leaned forward and dropped his tone to a sinister whisper. 'I'm going to shut the bedroom and the lounge door and if I can still hear you, babe, then I'm coming back in here to gag you,' he warned, and out he went.

'I hope Italy win a hundred nil,' I bellowed. 'I hate you! You're chucked, do you hear me? Chucked! I'm finishing with

244

you!' And I shouted and shouted and shouted. 'That's it. We *are* finished!' But the telly was blaring and I was exhausted and I must have fallen asleep because when I woke up Rob was on top of me, naked.

'Italy won, two one,' he mumbled through a kiss.

'Whaaaat?' I managed. I'd forgotten about the game.

I was sorry England lost, but at least I didn't have to worry about the stressful business of watching a cup final.

Rob relived the entire match in his sleep. I wanted to kill him, he kicked me twice. Demented with insomnia and exhaustion, I got up at two in the morning and cut his toenails. On the plus side, he left at five to go to Birmingham so I had the bed to myself until I had to start work in the bar at lunchtime.

Chapter Twenty-seven

The bar was heaving every Thursday. Enticing the grannies away from the deli had been easy. On our blackboard outside, I'd advertised that we were giving away free shower caps and with that, a stampede of shopping trolleys and walking sticks ambushed the door. Sadie from the baker's across the road was over the moon because she spent Thursdays ducking the traffic and scurrying over with trays of chocolate caramel shortcake. We ran out of shower caps pretty quickly so we gave away something different every week. The mountain of Lulu's rubbish in our bathroom was steadily shifting. The calamine lotion had gone and so had the boxes of tissues.

'People like added value,' I told Nikki as I frisbeed boxes of paracetamol at customers one Thursday morning.

'They certainly do,' he said, eyeing the little packets of tablets in astonished agreement.

Dot on five o'clock the granny brigade left, steamrolling towards the British Legion where two dinners for the price of one was on offer between five thirty and seven o'clock. This worked well because our roast potatoes and happy cocktail hour was becoming equally successful. By eight, Nikki would be leafing the money in the till and belting out a Greek opera.

But we had a major Human Resources issue on our hands. Nikki may have been thrilled at how busy we were but Costas and the other lazy waiter, Pepi, were furious. There's nothing worse for a lazy person than having to work but, in fairness, they were now overworked. The arguments in the bar and in the kitchen were frequent, voluble, and occasionally physical. Last week, Nikki had held Pepi against the fire exit door and threatened to boil his head like a potato. He was very precise and descriptive, detailing exactly how he would go about it. I was bitterly disappointed when the argument fizzled out because I'm not overly keen on Pepi and had been looking forward to watching him have his head boiled. I'd even got my phone out to take a picture. The upshot of the argument was that Nikki had admitted we couldn't cope so he's now drafted in his mother and two aunts to help in the bar between two o'clock and four-thirty.

Nikki's mother is the most annoying person in the universe. When she's not rushed off her feet eating caramel shortcake, glossing her lips or arguing with her sisters, she's brushing *my* hair. She licks her thumb and smoothes chocolatey spit on my eyebrows and tells me constantly how virile Greek men are, all the while nudging me meaningfully and flicking her eyes at Nikki. She brought in a tape measure once, lassoed me around the hips and told me that I could easily produce a ten-pound baby, as if that was something I should be looking forward to. And she's threatening to teach me how to use a sewing machine. But every now and again she gives Nikki the odd thick ear, which is a right laugh to watch, because he's built like a gladiator and she's built like a piggy bank. OK, I wasn't going to admit this, but I tell tales on him and sometimes I even make up blatant lies just so she'll give him a smack. It's hilarious.

The kitchen staff consists of Nikki's Uncle Spiros, Buffet

Spiros and Washing-up Spiros. Square jawed and handsome, Uncle Spiros is the chef. He's a towering bulk of a man with shoulder-length grey hair that he wears in a ponytail, deep-set charcoal eyes, sweeping black eyelashes, broad shoulders and a proud barrel chest. Buffet Spiros works on the buffet counter (obviously), preparing all the cold salads, desserts and side dishes. He's squat, bald and fat and looks like a sallow-skinned Humpty Dumpty. Washing-up Spiros is short, slim and weedy with a tornado of thick black hair, the pallor of a corpse and unblinking grey eyes. He looks like a caricature of himself.

Uncle Spiros is a wild-eyed psychopath, a raving lunatic with a temper like a scorpion that's stung its own backside. If Costas or Pepi make a mistake on an order, like asking for fries instead of potatoes or requesting a steak well done instead of medium, he missiles whatever comes to hand and he never misses, or he'll bounce their heads against the wall, or sometimes he'll take aim with the air rifle he keeps loaded near the back door.

Fortunately, he adores me. Subsequently I have a rather lucrative sideline underway. I charge Costas and Pepi a fiver to take a meal back to the kitchen. The potentially condemned waiter begs, pleads and stabs the unwanted meal in my chest. I feign disinterest and try to shimmy past until the five pound is paid. The money is usually thrust at me, together with a stamp on my toe or a vicious shaking of my elbow. I slowly hold the given note to the light to make sure it's not fake. This time wasting makes the condemned demented, especially when I refuse to give them change if they only have a tenner.

As soon as I sense the mood is about to morph from furious to murderous, I snatch the meal, beaver into the kitchen, smile and apologise to Uncle Spiros and explain *my* mistake. He listens intently, even though his English is only marginally better than my non-existent Greek. Apparently he just loves the sound of my voice so sometimes I talk a load of rubbish. I slag my sister off or I tell him what a couple of wankers Costas and Pepi are, while I gesture at the chips or I grab a steak from the fridge. He looks at me gooey- and rheumy-eyed, strokes my cheek, holds my hands, presses my knuckles to his lips and envelops me in his arms. Then, *ena*, *thia*, *dria*, one, two, three, we waltz around the kitchen as we wait for the fries or steak or whatever it is he's had to rustle up. Sometimes he'll pop a CD in the player so we have music to dance to. This sends Nikki crashing through the kitchen door, bellowing like a bear, because the kitchen CD player overrides the music in the bar and forces everyone to listen to Uncle Spiros's crappy Greek ballroom dance music. I then take the plate out to the bar, where the no-longer-condemned pounces, snatches the plate and squirrels off to his waiting customer. I do it for the crack, not the money. I see myself as a vigilante because these Greek waiters I'm working with are taking the royal piss out of the female population of London in a way that beggars belief.

Chapter Twenty-eight

Early autumn in Paris was a damn sight more comfortable than summer had been. It wasn't humid and desert-hot for a start, and there were only hundreds of tourist coaches as opposed to thousands. Rob and I were sipping café au lait, al fresco, while Carla walked the group through Notre Dame. We sat heads locked, his laptop between us. I'd drafted a spreadsheet to determine the daily hire rates he would need to charge to cover the finance on his new vehicles.

'Looks good.' He relaxed back in his chair and clasped his hands behind his head. 'Your formula is amazing. It's so easy to understand. You're brilliant.' He leaned back further so that he was almost horizontal. 'Of course, I'd have reached the same conclusion myself but I'd have gone all around the houses to get there.'

'Oh, it's nothing. You know me, slut in the bedroom and chef in the kitchen.'

His blue eyes slanted in amusement. He sat up and hugged me to him, rubbing his chin gently against my cheek. 'You're my life,' he whispered.

My heart squeezed in my chest. 'And you're mine,' I told him.

'The new coaches will be ready next week,' he said matter-of-factly. 'Three of my drivers and I will fly to Brussels to drive them back, and then,' he crossed his fingers, gesturing his hopeful expectations, 'they'll be out on the road within two days of delivery.'

I cupped his face. Our eyes locked silently. 'Fantastic.'

'Get the bill, shall I?' he asked.

I nodded and kissed him.

He stood, straightened his tie, gave me a saucy wink and strolled into the café. I finished my coffee and then picked up my bag and zigzagged between the tables to wait on the pavement for Rob. I hugged the laptop to my chest, raised my face to a cloudless sky and leaned on the pillar at the entrance to the café. Paris is divine, I thought, closing my eyes against the sun, it's so vibrant and bustling, and—

A vicious painful tug on my arm took me completely unawares. Instinctively, I pulled back. A motorbike screeched to a halt. The engine roared and I shrieked in agony as a searing blast from the exhaust scorched my leg. A strong hand clamped my forearm and tore at my bag, dragging me forward in line with the bike. The pillion passenger wrenched at my laptop, and with determined viciousness, smashed my temple with the safety helmet. My head flew back, smacking against the concrete pillar of the café. My vision grew white and my hands and feet felt numb. I collapsed onto all fours. An engine revved and I heard someone scream. A kaleidoscope of coloured shoes and sandals whirred in and out of focus. I rolled onto my back. The last thing I saw was Rob's haunted white face as he knelt over me. I clutched his wrist.

'Babe,' he bleated, and all went black.

I woke to find myself being whizzed through a hospital corridor on a trolley with Rob quick-stepping alongside me, gripping my hand. He looked terrified.

'You'll be fine, babe.' He smoothed the hair away from my face. 'Does it hurt?' he asked anxiously.

'No,' I managed, and it didn't. Shock is obviously a good armour for pain.

Sometime in the night I woke again. My head throbbed at both my temple and the base of my skull, and the pain in my right shoulder and wrist was unbearable. I groaned. There was a rustle of bedclothes and then the comforting sound of Rob's voice. His breath was warm on my cheek.

'I'm here,' he soothed, patting my hand. 'You're going to be fine,' he said in a brittle, broken voice.

A sliver of light from the corridor threw a shadow on his face. He looked drawn and harried, his brow was furrowed and his blue eyes were weary and rheumy. A nurse appeared and gave me an injection.

'My handbag?' I breathed.

His eyes searched mine. 'Safe as the Bank of England.'

'The laptop?'

He cupped my face. 'Ditto. You should have let go.'

I slept.

I spent three days in the hospital. Rob never left my side. He looked liked a caveman, hairy-faced and hungry. I had eleven stitches above my right eye where my brow had made contact with the crash helmet, a broken wrist, a nasty burn on my leg, a dislocated shoulder and eighteen stitches behind my right ear where I'd bounced back against the concrete pillar. I'd been admitted to a very plush private hospital, courtesy of Insignia Tours. Under different circumstances I think I could have enjoyed myself here.

I sat up in bed, studying my reflection in a hand-held mirror. A large strip of white gauze was taped to my temple, yellow iodine spots splattered my cheek and I had a lovely black eye. Another strip of gauze was taped to the base of my skull behind my right ear. I twisted my neck slowly to the left and angled the mirror to the right, and gently tweaked the bandage to see how much of my hair had been shaved. It was a patch the size of a large beer mat. My heart sank. I flicked the mirror to the magnified side, winced at the vision of ugliness and hurled it to the bottom of the bed.

Tina from the London office came to see me. She'd flown into Paris, together with an agency driver, to take over the group.

'You're on full pay for as long as it takes to get back on your feet.' She waved a clipboard in front of my face and wedged a pen in my left hand. 'Sign here.' She tilted her head towards Rob. 'Does that hunk work for us?' she whispered lustfully. 'I never get to meet the drivers. Assume you're boffing him?'

Mum and Dad called. Should they come back from Australia where they were visiting mum's sister, Auntie Ruth? Definitely not. I was adamant. They'd saved for this trip for two years, and they weren't due back until February. And more to the point, Mum is a professional hypochondriac. God only knows what ailments she'd develop if she clapped eyes on me. I just wasn't in the mood.

Lexy and Graeme arrived. Lexy stumbled into the room, arms outstretched, flapping a tissue, and wearing my new All Saints suit.

'You look like something from a Hammer Horror movie,' she sobbed in a strangled tone. 'And look at your head. They've shaved your hair. My bikini line is longer than that.' She chewed the back of her hand anxiously. 'D'you think you could have a hair transplant,' her brows lifted in question, 'like Elton John?'

I sighed. She's the one with the Vulcan fringe, I thought.

Lulu arrived a little while later, crashing through the door as if she were first in the queue at the Harrods sale. She was excited. And wearing my new Hobbs sandals.

'Da da da da . . . I'm hee'aar,' she sang. She spread her arms, curtseyed and tossed her blonde mane over her shoulder. 'Fan-bloody-tastic. Free flights, free hotel, free food,' she breezed. 'Evie, I take back all the negative shite I spat about that company you work for. Hope you don't mind, but I implied I was your partner. I think that might be why they paid for everything.' She tottered to a halt beside my bed, leaned over me, scanned my face and clutched her chest. Her jaw dropped and she burst into tears. She handed me a wilting bunch of roses. 'Cosmetic surgery is always an option,' she sobbed.

Rob, Graeme, Lexy, Lulu and my doctor, who looked like Jack Nicholson in *The Shining*, milled around the room. A lengthy, embarrassing discussion with the doctor ensued, which Lulu interrupted every ten seconds. Finally the doctor managed to string a sentence together. He said that I would mend but that I wouldn't be able to manage on my own for several weeks.

Lexy parroted the doctor. 'You'll mend.' She nodded solemnly, and bent to kiss my forehead.

Lulu stood by the bed stroking my leg. 'I hate seeing you like this,' she fretted.

'Lulu hates seeing you like this,' Lexy felt compelled to repeat, as though English wasn't my first language.

Lulu's gazed lifted and she scanned the room appraisingly. 'Still, this is a nice crib you've got here. It's like a hotel suite,' she added. Something caught her eye and she lurched towards the bedside table. 'Bloody hell,' she said, snatching a white card propped against a lamp.

'Lulu says it's like a hotel suite,' Lexy repeated, patting my good hand.

'A menu and a wine list!' Lulu announced.

Lexy tore her sympathetic eyes from mine and scurried around the bed. 'Getaway, it's not?' She whipped the card from Lulu. 'It is,' she said, eyes out on stalks.

Heads locked, their faces disappeared behind the menu.

'We might as well order a little something,' Lulu said, clucking her tongue.

'The food on the plane was crap,' Lexy grumbled.

Lulu chewed her lips contemplatively. 'Yes, a little starter-taster-kind-of-something.'

'Is there a calorie counter?' Lexy asked.

Lulu pitched her an incredulous look. 'Sod that. We're on our holidays.' And fifteen minutes later, a banquet had arrived.

Rob filled the doorway of the en suite bathroom. He'd taken advantage of the fact that I had visitors to shave, have a long soak in the bath and change. He'd dressed in jeans and a white shirt and stood rubbing his wet hair with a towel. Lulu and Lexy sat either side of me, elbows on the bed, jaws cupped in drumming fingers. They were pissed. Rob's blue eyes flicked between them judiciously.

'D'you get wine in hopispals at home?' Lexy slurred.

Rob buried his face in his towel and shook his head.

'D'you know, I j'ont fink y'do,' Lulu replied. Her brow furrowed in reflective creases. 'Ah yesh yesh shumtimes,' she said, jabbing a finger in certainty.

Graeme, who'd spent the last half hour marching up and down the corridor snarling into his BlackBerry, came back into the room. Lulu and Lexy stared at him, wobbly headed.

'So,' Graeme began assertively. 'We'll take Evie home with us when she's discharged. As the doctor pointed out, she won't be

255

able to cope on her own.' His BlackBerry beeped. 'Excuse me,' he apologised, and shot out of the door bellowing 'Hello, mate,' into his phone.

Lulu's hand shot up. 'S'cuse me but I am a nurse and I am her fwatmate,' she proclaimed loudly. 'She shud come home wiv me.'

I sat motionless. I'd rather be nursed by Doctor Crippen.

Lexy jumped to her feet brandishing a glass of Prosecco. 'I am her shister and I will loof after her,' she insisted.

Rob hung his towel on the end of my bed, ran an irritated hand through his damp hair and stretched to his full height. He stood legs apart, clenched fists on hips, and cleared his throat.

'Obviously with her shoulder strapped and a broken wrist she won't be able to lift anything,' he pointed out sternly.

Lexy sank further into her chair and nodded. Lulu relaxed back, folded her arms with exaggerated precision, and inclined her head knowingly.

'So she'll need her food prepared and cut up for her, and she'll want help dressing and undressing,' he added.

Lexy and Lulu exchanged a silent evaluating glance.

'Bathing on her own is completely out of the question as well,' Rob stated solemnly.

There was a reflective pause.

'And, of course, someone will have to wash her hair.'

Graeme rushed back into the room. 'Sorry sis,' he said, and pressed my foot lightly.

There was a stretch of silence. Lexy peered at Graeme over the rim of her glass. Lulu studied her fingernails.

'I was thinking of moving in with her. Full-time,' Rob announced soundly. 'And I'll stay here until she's discharged.'

Lulu crossed one long leg over the other, grinned stupidly and gave Rob two thumbs up.

'Bwilliant idea.' Lexy wriggled in her seat. 'That's shettled then.'

My shoulder throbbed and a stabbing pain periodically shot from my temple to my eye, with a sharper ache hammering at the back of my head. Red pinwheels appeared before my eyes.

'Rob, I feel sick,' I said groggily.

He hurried around the bed and held a stainless-steel bowl under my chin and tucked an arm firmly behind my back. 'Go on, babe,' he soothed.

Lexy clamped her hand to her mouth, shot to her feet and ran to the open window. Her torso disappeared and her legs pedalled mid-air as she hung out of the casement swallowing huge gulps of air. 'Uugg, dwont be shick. You know what I'm like.'

I retched violently, filling the bowl for the fourth time that day with green slimy bile.

'Better now?' Rob asked when I buried my face in his shoulder.

Lulu flapped her arm aimlessly. 'D'you know, vomit dushn't boffer me,' she said in a dismissive tone. 'I shee it all the time.' She shifted to the edge of her chair and sat tall.

Rob teased a glass of water between my lips.

Graeme rubbed his hands firmly together. 'So, well, we'll be off. Got to get back home for the kids. We've left them with my mum, she's babysitting at our house. They drive her mad! Becky attached the tablecloth to the hem of Mum's skirt with the sewing machine the last time Mum had them.' He winced. 'Terrible mess.'

Lulu and Lexy swooped like a couple of landing swans, theatrically kissing the uninjured half of my face.

'We've got open flight tickets but I'd like to push on and get back tonight,' Graeme said, pumping Rob's hand and thumping him on the arm blokeishly. 'I can see that you have everything under control here.'

Rob gave a nod of understanding. 'Hopefully I'll be taking Evie home on Wednesday,' he replied, returning the wallop.

'I'll pwick you up from the nairport,' Lulu offered, tottering perilously.

Lexy stamped her foot, losing her balance. 'I'll pwick her up. I am her shister.'

Lulu jabbed a finger in Lexy's face. 'No you won't, I will. I'm her fwatmate.'

'No, I will.'

Lulu pounded her chest with a clenched fist. 'I will.'

Graeme ushered the pair of them towards the door.

'We'll all pwick you up,' Lexy shouted, twisting to peer over Graeme's shoulder. 'We'll cum togeffer. That'll be nice.'

The door closed behind them.

I slept restlessly that night, and woke with a pounding headache. Rob lay awkwardly in a makeshift bed beside the window. His lean, toned back rose as he snored softly, filling the room with the sound of rhythmic breathing. I sat up and swung my legs over the side of the bed and wobbled to standing, then padded along the wall to the bathroom. I ran the taps and sat glumly on the edge of the bath, staring at the rushing water. A shadow fell across my face. Rob, wearing a pair of boxers and a broad smile, padded into the bathroom and knelt before me. He laid his cheek on the crown of my head.

'I'll tie your hair up. The doctor said not to wash it for a couple of days.'

'What?' I gave my hair a tug. 'It's like rats' tails. I have to wash it.'

He shook his head grimly. 'Rats' tails will have to do.'

Rob slowly helped me into the tub. What a vision of elegance I must have been, languishing in soapsuds. For lack of anything else to hand, Rob tied my hair up with one of his dirty socks. I knew it was dirty because I could smell it. I was terrified to rest my right leg in the water because of the burn on my calf, so I balanced on my left buttock and dangled my right leg over the side of the bath. My right shoulder was strapped to my chest and my wrist was in a cast, and both had to be kept dry, so my right elbow (with determined engineering) followed my right leg over the edge. And as if I didn't look ridiculous enough, a strip of gauze the size of a sanitary towel was stuck to my forehead and another to the back of my head.

'Relax, babe,' Rob said, teasing his arm behind my back. 'I've put your Jo Malone bubbly in the water so you should enjoy this.'

I sighed. I doubted it.

I quickly realised that I felt a zillion times better whenever the nurse gave me one of what I called her happy tablets. I suspect they were a fairly senior member of the morphine dynasty. They gave me a woozy, cheery feeling. They made me dream when I wasn't asleep and I could kind of choose and control my dream. They were fabulous. And I admit that I acted up now and again to get one.

Right now, I was skipping through meadows that were awash with summer flowers. My Viking appeared carrying a Topshop bag, and I was slim, very slim. I wore a floaty *Strictly Come Dancing* number and my hair had miraculously grown down to my waist. I was admiring my reflection in a stream when a voice rudely interrupted me, which annoyed me at first, but as I continued eavesdropping I immediately realised that I had to dump the dream and concentrate on listening.

'I'm well aware of that,' an agitated voice said sharply.

There was a pause.

'As soon as I can!'

Another pause.

'I know, I know,' the agitated voice added in hushed, rushed tones. 'Listen! No one is more anxious than I am to get this sorted but as I've explained, it just won't happen within the next week or so . . . you don't have to remind me what's at stake.'

I prised my eyes open. Rob stood, back bowed, looking out of the window. The muscles on his broad shoulders flexed as he fidgeted with the shutters. He was on the phone.

'I know,' he snapped. He looked over his shoulder, caught my eye and smiled wanly. 'I'll call you back,' his voice trailed off awkwardly. 'Yes, soon.' He flipped his phone shut and tucked it in his trouser pocket. 'Sleepyhead,' he said, walking towards my bed.

'What was that about?' I asked.

His blue eyes narrowed to triangles as he forced a smile. He traced his index finger along my cheek and across my lips. 'Nothing,' he said and kissed the tip of my nose.

I leaned on my good elbow.

He gave me a nonchalant stare.

'Rob, it was *not* nothing!'

A muscle in his jaw twitched suspiciously. 'It wasn't important. Are you hungry, babe?'

Suddenly I remembered. 'The coaches. You're supposed to be in Belgium.'

He shook his head. 'Look at you. How can I?'

'Rob, I'm not dying. I've got a banging head and am fairly uncomfortable, and yes, I need help, but you know I'll manage. Those four coaches are costing you ten grand a month. Go over there and bring them back. You've got to get them working.'

He thumped down wearily into the chair beside my bed and massaged his temple with the heel of his hand. He sighed.

'Go, Rob. You must,' I insisted.

He shook his head forlornly. 'No way. No way am I leaving you like this.'

'How will you make the payments if the coaches aren't on the road?'

'I'm trying to sort something out, I'm looking—'

'Go!'

'No.'

'Yes! Arguing with you is giving me a headache,' I snapped.

After much deliberation it was decided. We would fly to London together; Lexy would pick me up at the airport and Rob would catch a connecting flight to Brussels. He'd be gone for a week and, for my sins, I'd be moving in with Lexy, Graeme and the twins until he came back. Lulu had booked a three-week holiday to South Africa with Vic, the Santa clone. She said that my accident had come as a terrible shock, and that she badly needed a break, a holiday, time to convalesce. Ever the thoughtful best friend, she'd arranged for Harry from next door to look after me, if needs be. Well, hello!!!!!!

PARIS

Chapter Twenty-nine

The arrivals hall at Heathrow Airport was packed.

'Right, I've got our bags. Come on,' Rob said, heaving my case from the conveyor belt. I looped my arm through his and trudged alongside him as we trolleyed slowly through Customs.

I felt a swoop of despair when I saw my welcome committee. Graeme had a rush on at work so Lexy, arguing that she couldn't possibly find the airport on her own, had called Nikki and asked him to drive her, which he'd kindly agreed to do. But why the hell Nikki's mother was waiting with an enormous green first aid box wedged under her arm, I didn't know. Her chin and lips twitched and her chocolate eyes swam with unshed tears when she spotted me. She chanted in Greek, thrust the first aid box at Nikki and with outstretched arms stumbled towards me.

'Evie!' she shrieked, scaring us all. She swayed, eyes closed, and locked her arms around my waist. For form's sake, I swayed with her and patted her lacquered beehive with my left hand. 'Ggggg . . . hhhhhh,' she chanted, on and on and on.

Lexy stood behind her. She wore a tight fitted pink blouse with a ruffled low neckline, hipster jeans and pink stilettos. She looked fabulous. I was dead jealous. Rob had made me wear shorts because of the bandage on my leg, flip-flops for comfort and one of his shirts, as none of my own clothes covered the dressing on my shoulder. He'd packed my make-up in my suitcase and refused to dig it out, telling me that I looked better without it when I knew for a fact that I looked like a four-day-old corpse. Lexy ferreted in her handbag for a tissue.

'You look like a four-day-old corpse,' she sniffed, dabbing at her eyes. 'Your poor face. It's, well, it's . . . you look like the Roadrunner, all bug-eyed and haunted,' she felt obliged to say.

Nikki effortlessly lifted my suitcase from Rob's trolley. Oddly, they'd never met. They exchanged a brief gesture of introduction before Rob turned and tactfully disentangled me from Nikki's mum's embrace. He cupped my face. I blinked madly. I didn't want him to leave me, not for a whole week.

'I'm a phone call away, you know that, babe, and you'll be fine.'

I cuddled him with my good arm. We'd been together three months and we hadn't spent more than two nights apart.

'And as soon as you're better, I'll take you on holiday.'

I didn't want a holiday. I wanted him to stay with me. He traced his thumbs the length of my cheeks.

'We'll go wherever you want. Anywhere, I don't care. The Far East,' he kissed me, 'the Caribbean,' he kissed me again, 'or Australia. Wherever!' he soothed.

I sniffed and tried to muster a smile but I couldn't because (a) I was miserable, (b) Rob was squashing my cheeks together, making my lips pucker and (c) I was dressed like one of the Walton brothers.

'And I'll buy you a present in Brussels.'

I cheered up a little.

'What kind of present?' I asked.

His chest heaved and rumbled as he chuckled. 'Wait and see.'

My welcome committee tactfully studied the arrivals board as Rob and I said goodbye properly.

'One week. It's no time at all, and we'll speak every day,' he said. His tone dropped a few decibels. 'And you're with your sister,' he consoled lamely. He stole a sideways glance at Lexy, who was sifting the rails of scarves in Tie Rack like a demon. 'So I know you'll be in good hands,' he added, with a stiff smile.

One last lingering, breathless kiss and then he was gone.

Nikki carried my suitcase, despite the fact that it had wheels, and placed his other hand gently on my back. 'Come, Evie. The car is on level one so not too far to walk.'

I nodded solemnly. Lexy sashay-mamboed around Nikki and skipped in line beside me.

'I've told the kids not to bother you but they tried on their nurses' outfits last night,' she sighed. 'Becky burst her teddy with a fork doing an operation and Lauren asked if she could bring her friends around to see your bandages. Graeme had to have a serious talk with Becky because she told her teacher you would visit the nursery to show all the kids your bald patch, and,' she gave a stiff, embarrassed cough, 'Becky wants to sleep with you. Of course I told her it was absolutely out of the question but she's very disappointed, and frankly we don't trust her, so, for your protection, I'm having a lock put on the door of the spare room.' She patted my good shoulder. 'And I've recorded *The X Factor* omnibus and bought you two sherry trifles and a home spa kit from Boots.' She slipped her hand in mine. 'You're going to be fine.'

I doubted it. An apparition of Becky in a nurse's uniform sent a shiver down my spine. I sighed desolately. And I hate sherry trifle. And I didn't give a flying toss about *The X Factor* omnibus.

Now, I can't really remember what was said in the car on the journey from the airport so I don't know how this came about, and I was too tired to care or protest and Nikki's mother is not to be argued with. And Becky is terrifying and Lexy to be fair has her hands full as it is, and Nikki is not to be argued with either. OK, he is, but not when you're in pain, uncomfortable and tearful. But somehow it was unanimously agreed that I would move into Nikki's flat above the bar, and Nikki, his mum and auntie would look after me. We dropped Lexy at Hampton. I edged back against the seat rest as her upper body shot through the front passenger window.

'I'm not sure about this but we'll see how it goes.' She patted my knee and dropped her tone to a whisper. 'I feel, well, bullied. I wanted you here and I've changed the bed and everything.' She rolled her eyes. 'What am I supposed to do with two sherry trifles? I'll ring you later,' and hugging her Hermès bag, she turned smartly and clattered down her garden path.

Chapter Thirty

Nikki's flat is very much what you would expect from a single, handsome, male slut bag. It's minimalistic, with honey coloured parquet flooring, white walls, Victorian casement windows that are dressed with electronically controlled velvet curtains, and spongy chocolate leather sofas. Large, brightly coloured contemporary canvas prints of scantily dressed women adorn the walls, and an assortment of dead animal rugs are scattered randomly. A king, king, king-size bed, which Nikki told me he'd bought from the Marriott Hotel, dominates the bedroom.

My suitcase, minus my rescued make-up bag, was whisked to a secret location in North London where everything would be washed, pressed and returned. I was stripped and bathed by Nikki's mum and auntie and dressed in a pair of Nikki's pyjamas, which I suspect his mum had bought him, and settled comfortably in Nikki's enormous bed. I snuggled back contentedly and was enjoying the onset of a happy tablet journey when Uncle Spiros came upstairs from the bar to visit.

His formidable frame, dressed in his chef's whites, commandeered the doorway. I gave him a dopey-headed, morphine-y grin. His thick black eyebrows drew together as he strode slowly towards my bed. He bent over me. Dark eyes stabbed searchingly into mine. I slunk back into the pillow. When viewed from a distance of six inches he's a terrifying sight. His hand trembled as he held my chin and his charcoal eyes narrowed menacingly. I lost the trail of my morphine-y dream. He straightened, balled fists on his hips.

'Nicholas!' he bellowed to the ceiling. There was a mad clatter of footsteps on the wooden floor. Nikki, his mum and auntie cannoned into the room.

All hell broke loose.

Uncle Spiros roared like a lion, his barrel chest expanded, the blood rushed to his cheeks and his eyes glistened and blackened with rage. Nikki's mum and auntie huddled together and nudged each other forward to brave the wrath of Goliath, which in the end proved too much for the auntie. She burst into tears, knelt by my bed and gently gathered me in her arms. She was distraught, well, only for a second or two, because suddenly a demonic glazed look flickered in her eyes. She sniffed, patted her beehive, snatched the clock from the bedside table and, trembling bravely, hurled the clock at Uncle Spiros, catching him on the shoulder. We all gasped. The clock bounced off his collarbone and hit the floor. The alarm went off, Nikki pulverised it with his foot. Uncle Spiros crashed a ham bone fist against the doorframe. We all gasped again. Nikki's mum and auntie eyed each other fretfully. And although I hadn't thought it possible, the bellowing grew louder. Auntie lost her nerve and squashed herself behind me.

I was a bit annoyed about all of this. I'd been looking forward to tripping on my happy tablet. This was an ill-timed interruption. Under normal circumstances I'd enjoy a fight like this but I'd totally lost the plot here and didn't even know what they were arguing about.

Nikki shuffled from foot to foot. He appeared shamefaced, embarrassed. Uncle Spiros jabbed his finger in Nikki's chest and rattled off a thunderous tirade. Suddenly Nikki's mood completely changed. His chest expanded and a crimson stain travelled up his neck and burned his cheeks. He picked up an aerosol of deodorant and threw it at the wall. Uncle Spiros smashed his fist into his palm repeatedly and boomed on and on. I wish I spoke Greek.

Suddenly the palm bashing stopped. There was an uncertain silence. Nikki and his mum flanked me, the auntie still hid behind my back. Uncle Spiros stood menacingly at the foot of the bed, his enormous shadow dwarfing us all. For a cliff-hanging three or four seconds, there was a frozen calm. The four of them exchanged shifty, meaningful glances. I joined in with a few shifty glances of my own. There followed a fair bit of spontaneous nodding and 'nay, nay, nay' which means 'yes, yes, yes'. Uncle Spiros seemed appeased. He'd obviously got his own way. I suspect he always does. Eyebrows raised, he inclined his head curtly at each of them in turn, there were a few more 'nay nay nays' all around, and then he thundered out of the room.

The door slammed.

The auntie slumped against my back. Nikki's mum staggered backwards and sank into an armchair, clutching her heaving chest.

'What was all that about?' I asked Nikki groggily.

'Uncle Spiros is moving his mother into the spare room. He thinks you should have a chaperone and not be alone with me in the evenings, so I'm on the sofa.'

'Right.' I nodded numbly. His mother, I thought. He's no spring chicken, so is he digging her up before he brings her round? I wondered.

'I'm tired, Nikki.'

He sighed. 'I can see that. Are you comfortable?' he asked.

'Mmmm,' I nodded, 'but I need to sleep.'

He checked his watch. 'Rest now and I'll wake you for dinner.'

'He ees a pig,' Nikki's mum said, stabbing a finger at the bedroom door, her cheeks flushed with valour. 'I take your keys for cleaning your house,' she said, already rooting through my handbag. 'He Spiros, my brother,' she spat indignantly, 'ees too big for his pants.'

I think she meant boots.

I missed dinner and slept all through the night. The Viking and I went to see Girls Aloud at the Royal Albert Hall. Lulu had two big never-ending spots on her chin, like those joke candles that you blow out and they keep re-lighting. She squeezed and squeezed, they popped and popped, but no matter what she did, they kept coming back. My credit card bill arrived and it was only £1.09. The only item on it was a packet of soap powder. And a Harrods cosmetics gift basket was delivered to me by mistake, which I quickly stuffed under my bed.

I gasped with fright when a tiny, black-clad, shrivelled, toothless figure shook me awake. At first I thought it was the ghost of Christmas past but then I noticed that it held a tray furnished with orange juice, coffee and toast. Clever thing that I am, I deduced that it must be morning and that this must be the chaperone, and I was right. I had four missed calls from Rob, and a text.

Luv u miss u need u R x x x

I called him. Everything his end was fine. He would be in Belgium for a few more days and then he and his colleagues would be driving the new vehicles to Birmingham before he made his way back to London. He'd be back as soon as he could. I actually think soon might be sooner than he'd planned because when I told him I was staying at Nikki's, he sounded positively miffed, surprised and not overly enthused. His exact words were 'And how the fuck did that come about?' I couldn't answer that because I had no idea how it came about, but here I am, and I've got to say that the service isn't bad at all.

Nikki's mum and auntie arrived soon after I woke. Within seconds the kettle was on and the bath was running. They stood, beehive hairdos soldered, contemplating the hospital notes that accompanied the many jars of pills, tubes of cream, packets of gauze, bottles of ointments and rolls and boxes of bandages. But the notes were in French.

'Ees no matter,' the auntie said, flipping open her mobile phone. 'I seemply phone a friend.' By the time the bath was ready, a Greek district nurse had arrived. Greek, honestly.

It's a good job I'm not shy. Four of them attended the removal of the pyjamas and the lowering into the bath ceremony. Yes, Sophia, Uncle Spiros's mother, joined us. She confiscated the cream and gauze in favour of a glass jar, which looked and smelled as though it contained eighty years' worth of the wax from her ears. The other three objected forcefully but after a tantrum from Sophia, it was unanimously agreed that the ear wax would stay.

Sophia knelt on the floor, took the bandage from my leg, which she hung decoratively over the edge of the bath, smeared it with ear wax and carefully lowered my leg into the water. It didn't hurt as much as I'd feared. She then removed the gauze from my temple and from the back of my head and applied her yellow sticky mixture. The other three exchanged untranslatable glances but were, I think, too scared to object. Maria (Nikki's mum. We were now on first-name terms) had brought me underwear and a dressing gown from my flat but she insisted that my nightwear was unsuitable and so had very thoughtfully brought me a couple of her size twenty flannelette floaty nightdresses. I tactfully declined them in favour of Nikki's pyjamas, which were suddenly very appealing, comfortable and stylish, and I happened to know came in a pack of four. I groaned inwardly when Maria boasted that she'd tidied the mess beneath my bed and put everything back in the wardrobe. Honestly. How long and hard had I worked to sort that lot out?

I have a routine. Maria and Auntie Lola arrive at nine o'clock. I take a bath and eat breakfast. Auntie Lola leaves. I then nervously stand guard while Nikki's mother rifles through Nikki's wardrobes and drawers, reading his letters, opening his bills, frisking the contents of his pockets and generally sticking her nosy face where it's obviously not welcome. But I've got to give her her due. She works with the finesse of an FBI Special Agent. I've never seen anyone move so fast. She wears herself out.

'Nikki, he must *never* know,' she insisted, breathless.

She sank onto the sofa. The yellow chiffon scarf covering her beehive quivered as, head bent, she flicked nimbly through a bundle of Nikki's bank statements.

'Ever, *ever*,' she said forcefully, jotting down a series of numbers on a notepad. Her eyes grew wide and she looked at me owlishly. 'Never,' she repeated.

'Never,' I echoed.

She waved a finger in warning.

'I won't tell,' I hurriedly assured her.

Her eyes flashed. '*Never*,' she parroted.

'Never,' I said, sick with panic. She was taking her time with the bank statements. If Nikki walked in, he'd kill us both.

Reassured, she shuffled off the sofa and dropped to her knees, her upper body disappearing back into the cupboard.

'Ah ah, ees here, ees here.' Her big bottom wobbled as she reversed out with a box file marked 'Dad's Papers'. She'd found what she'd been looking for. She struggled to standing with her precious find clutched protectively to her forty-four-inch D-cups. She placed her hand on my head as though bestowing a blessing. 'On pain of death,' she nodded gravely, 'ee's never to know.'

I felt a bolt of indignation. 'I won't tell,' I snapped. How many times did I have to say it?

Her hand still rested on my head. She was waiting.

I sighed and held my cast to my chest in a gesture of sincerity. 'Pain of death,' I promised, with an inscrutable air.

She smiled.

I followed her into the kitchen, where she splayed her chubby body on the worktop and held a letter over a steaming kettle.

'You're a good geerl. I trust you,' she said with fondness.

She'd leave at lunchtime, filofax bulging, and then Lexy would pop around. We'd sit in the lounge as Sophia and two of her friends, who I strongly suspect may be immortal, commandeered the kitchen. When Lexy shot off to pick the kids up from nursery, I'd phone Rob and then have a sleep. In the evening, Nikki and I ate dinner together. We fought like cat and dog for the first couple of nights because he wouldn't let me drink wine.

'You're on medication,' was his reason.

'Medication!' I yelled mutinously, sending shooting pains from my temple to the base of my skull. 'Smackheads puff on crack and weed, swallow blues and pump shitloads of stuff inside them, and they still manage a couple of bevies.'

He was unyielding.

On the third night he wouldn't eat with me at all because Sophia had coated my hair with olive oil. Apparently it's the best conditioner in the whole wide world. And with detailed explicit instruction from me, she'd covered me in fake tan as well.

'You smell like a pair of trainers,' Nikki shouted. 'Get out of this kitchen and back to bed,' he snapped, showing me the door. 'I'll bring a tray in for you.'

By midweek, I'm pleased to say, I felt much better. Sophia's yellow sticky ointment proved to be marvellous. My black eye was now pale yellow, the stitches on my temple were starting to dissolve and the wound on my leg had crusted. My wrist would be in a cast for five more weeks at least but I could live with that, and my shoulder, though still painful, was now relatively flexible. The only thing getting me down was a constant pain in the back of my head and the mess of my hair. Texting was awkward because of the cast on my wrist, so I spent my day lying on the sofa talking to Rob, sipping Shiraz from a coffee mug. Daytime drinking was strictly forbidden. If Nikki popped up and caught me, I'd be dog food.

Sophia proved to be a crap chaperone. She was tipsy and in bed by six o'clock every night, which was, according to Nikki, a godsend. He and I spent a couple of non-fighting evenings at home together, which I enjoyed. He's a bright guy, and funny and handsome, and he smells nice. But he's bossy and chauvinistic and a spoiled brat. It's his way, or no way. We played Scrabble one night and the game ended in a fight. I wouldn't let him have 'krisps' and we had the same argument with 'krane', 'kream' and 'krying'. I eyed him scornfully.

'You can't spell, Nik,' I informed him, removing his letters from the board.

Maddened, he drummed his fingers on the table.

I tossed him an amused glance. 'You can't,' I repeated.

'OK, let's play in Greek and see how you get on,' he spat, sending the Scrabble board into orbit. I leaned back in my seat, crossed my arms and glared at his retreating figure.

Two minutes later, as I was tidying up the game, he was back. With a beaming smile, he handed me a glass of champagne. I'm beginning to think the Greeks are a nation of raving schizo heads, but obviously the nicest raving schizo heads you could ever wish to meet. We fell asleep together, watching telly on the comfy leather sofa with the empty champagne bottle between us. The following morning Sophia stabbed us awake with a knitting needle. Nikki had to bribe her with a hundred quid hush money and a china teapot that she had her eye on, so she wouldn't tell Uncle Spiros we'd slept together. As if.

The muscles on his forearms and neck rippled as he counted out the notes. 'This is extortion,' he protested.

Her black eyes, slitted in amusement, were barely visible, hidden in the folds of her wrinkled cheeks. 'No. Es blackmail,' she corrected.

I was pretty damned impressed because the word 'blackmail' implies that she'll be back for more. I wish I could keep a secret long enough to blackmail someone.

By day six I was climbing the walls with boredom and considering rifling through Nikki's personal papers myself. I rang down to the bar and asked Nikki to go over to my flat and pick up some clothes for me. I wanted to get dressed and go out for a walk.

'No,' he said flatly.

'But Nikki, it's not far. It'll take you two minutes.'

'I know where it is.'

'I'm bored,' I pleaded.

'You're not bored, you're resting. You're *not* going out! You can place the wines and spirits order if you're bored. You know the suppliers and how much stock we use. The order forms are on my desktop. And Evie, contact the refrigeration maintenance people, the ice machine is playing up. Oh! And the fire extinguishers need a service and the cleaning fluid for the lager pump is running low. And find out where the hell the window cleaner has disappeared to, and could you order more coffee and pay the butcher's invoice? Work out how much we owe him and leave a cheque for me to sign.'

So much for me resting, I thought blithely.

'Oh, one more thing. The Cardnet machine is refusing to accept Amex. Can you give them a ring?' He paused. 'How are you feeling?'

'Fine.'

Rob called and said he'd be back tomorrow. I was so excited. A whole day early!

'That's good,' Nikki said distractedly, when I told him.

I was perched on the edge of the bath watching Nikki shave. He'd just come back from the gym. He goes every morning between six and seven and gets home just before nine. He was still wearing his black trackie bottoms and black T-shirt. His ponytail, which he normally wears at the nape of his neck, was tied higher. He lathered his neck, handed me the razor and stood, hands on the sink, bowed forward.

'You sure, Nik? With my left hand?' I laughed.

'Of course I'm sure. If you cut me, I'll kill you,' he joked.

I steadied myself against him with my cast and carefully shaved the back of his neck.

'Rob would never let me do this,' I said.

'He doesn't know what he's missing then, does he?'

I chuckled. 'I think he'd prefer Sweeney Todd. Don't laugh, Nik. Your body shakes when you laugh.'

In the restricted confines of the bathroom he seemed much taller and bigger and, well, different. He seemed more feral.

'Thanks, Nik,' I said meekly.

'Thanks for what?'

'Letting me stay here. I know how busy the bar is and yet you've found time to pop up and see me at least three times a day. And your mum and auntie have been great and, well, everything.'

He took the razor from my hand, quickly rinsed it under the tap and handed it back to me. 'It's in my own best interests to get you on your feet again.' He caught my eye in the mirror. 'Since you started in the bar my profits have gone up by a third.'

'Really?' I was astounded.

'Yes, really.'

'How come?'

'How come? Your High Teas idea for a start.' He chuckled. 'The Happy Hour.' He chuckled again. 'You changed the house wines. The new stock costs twenty per cent less than the old stuff. Oh! And you've saved me a fortune on graphics by designing all the menus and flyers yourself.'

I rinsed his neck and dabbed it dry with the hand towel.

'And my dad owes you one,' he said loftily. 'Big time.'

I giggled. 'Your dad? What have I ever done for him?'

'Because my mum's busy and out of his way every afternoon.' He lifted the soap from the dish and scrubbed his face vigorously. 'He hasn't been able to watch television when she's home because she's set a tripod telescope up in the lounge.' He splashed water on his face. 'She's targeting the Community Centre.' His face disappeared into the hand towel. 'She suspects her two sisters are going to Weight Watchers without her.'

We both cracked up laughing.

'She'll die with her nose jammed in someone else's door,' he said.

We threw our heads back and roared and roared.

'Or someone's cupboards, drawers, wardrobes or pockets,' I wheezed, wiping my eyes.

He doubled up laughing and buried his head in his hands. 'Don't,' he guffawed, slapping his hand repeatedly on the sink. 'Someone else's cupboards, drawers, pockets,' he echoed.

'Yes,' I whooped, bobbing my head. I was doubled up myself now.

He faltered. 'Did, did she, did she go through my things?'

'Mmmmmm,' I managed, waving my hand weakly. My tummy was aching.

He whipped the towel onto the rail, and raised my chin with his index finger. His black eyes, narrowed with rage, held mine. I stopped laughing. He hadn't moved at all but, honest to God, he seemed closer. I shrank back, suddenly aware of the need for a serious bit of backpedalling.

'Did she?' he bellowed.

My heart squeezed with terror.

His hand clamped my jaw. 'She did, didn't she?' he roared.

'Er, d'you know what? I'm not entirely sure,' I babbled, nervously. 'I was tired and as high as a kite most of the time, and well ... Ah yes, I remember now.' I threw my hands up in wonder that the recollection hadn't come to me sooner. 'It was a dream. No, she didn't, of course she didn't. Ah no, yes, it was ... I dreamt it. I remember now.'

'She did, didn't she?' he yelled, marching from the bathroom. I hastened after him. 'Nikki, no, of course not. I've told you.'

He frisked his jacket, which was hanging on the back of the kitchen chair, for his mobile. 'I've warned her before. I had to take my spare keys off her because of her meddling.'

My heart pumped. I broke into a sweaty panic. 'Nikki, are you calling me a liar?' I heard myself shout, lurching towards him to arrest his phone.

It took an hour of cursing and swearing, then pleading and begging, and eventually weeping and wailing, before Nikki promised not to say a word to his mother. It all seems rather vague now but I think at one point I was actually on my knees, crawling around the kitchen, clinging to his leg in desperation. The minute he left for work, I took to my bed with a migraine, exhaustion, heart palpitations and rocketing blood pressure.

Chapter Thirty-one

Rob's back! He bought me a white gold charm bracelet, and I love it, and I love him.

'Babe,' he said in a broken voice, 'you have *no* idea how much I've missed you.' He pulled me onto his lap and circled my waist. 'And to see you looking so much better. It's unbelievable.' He nibbled my ear. 'How's your shoulder?'

'Not too bad.'

'And your wrist?'

'It doesn't hurt that much for a broken bone. It's just awkward.'

He teased my hair and winced at the nasty ragged gash behind my ear. 'This'll take time,' he said in a strangled tone.

I brushed my fingers over the rough stitching on the wound and in contrast the smooth, soft velvet patch of skin where my hair had been shorn. Unexpectedly, tears threatened.

'Don't, don't cry.' He held my hand, pressing his thumb on my palm. 'You'll be fine. I'm back, and I'm going to spoil you and wait on you hand and foot.'

'Well,' I began, 'funny you should say you'd spoil me, because I have a proposal,' I told him, cranking up a smile.

'You do?' he asked.

'Yes.'

'What is it?'

'Actually, I've been mulling over the logistics of this proposal for most of the week.'

'You have?' he asked, intrigued.

I nodded and grinned. 'Yes, I have.'

'Are you going to tell me what it is?'

I slid from his lap and knelt on the floor between his legs. He smoothed the hair from my face, gently laid my cast on his knee, and looped his fingertips through mine. He eyed me expectantly. 'Go on then,' he encouraged, 'what's your proposal?'

My fingers whispered over my now burning cheeks. 'First,' I said pinkly, addressing the ceiling, 'I thought I'd lie down next to you.'

He scanned my face. 'Where?'

'On my bed.'

He nodded. 'Then what?' he asked flatly.

'Then I'll lean across you and start to kiss you.' I chewed my lips. 'And . . . I'll . . . unbutton . . . your . . . shirt.'

'With your good hand?' he interrupted.

'Yes,' I confirmed, 'with my good hand.'

'And then what?'

I pouted. 'I'll unbuckle your belt, and slowly . . . lower your zip . . . and slide my hand inside your boxers.' I paused. 'Just the way you like it.'

'With your good hand?' he repeated annoyingly.

'Yes,' I snapped. 'With. My. Good. Hand,' I punctuated.

'Mmm, I just wondered. And then what?'

I rubbed his thigh. 'Then I'll hold you like you showed me.' I traced my finger lightly up and down his groin. 'You know, the way I hold you lightly but firmly, in the palm of my hand? The way I can, you know, *hold you*, better than anyone you've ever known.' I said, eyes widening in emphasis.

He quirked one eyebrow and nodded curtly. 'Then what?' he asked deadpan.

'I'll straddle you and lean forward and kiss you a bit more and push your shirt over your shoulders and run my tongue along your collarbone.'

Ah, I'd got him going. There was a burnished vibrant glow about him. His lips trembled and his nostrils flared. Lust and want were written all over his face. His eyes narrowed to indigo half-moons. I felt feverish and shameless and wanton. I licked my lips and batted my eyelashes.

'Then what?' he asked.

'Then I'll wriggle down *really* hard on your . . . hips.'

There was a perplexed pause. He frowned. 'What should I be doing while you're doing all this?' he asked.

He was starting to piss me off now because he bloody well knew what he should be doing.

I jumped to my feet. 'You might want to join in.'

'No,' he said. 'I'm not joining in.'

I stamped my foot. 'You're not joining in! What do you mean you're not joining in?'

'I'm not.'

'Well, if you're not joining in, you can pull your own porker.' I spun and strode smartly from the lounge. 'The proposal's off!'

Rob found me in the kitchen, pouring a glass of wine.

'Can I have a glass?' he asked softly.

'Get it yourself,' I snapped, edging my back on him.

Two strong arms entrapped me. 'Thought you'd missed me,' he whispered, kissing my neck.

'Thought you'd missed me,' I hissed, wriggling ineffectively to free myself.

'Evie,' he sighed, locking his arms tighter, 'let's visit the doctor, ask him to take a look at your shoulder, get your stitches taken out and we'll take it from there.'

I exhaled heavily. 'I miss . . . *us*!' I admitted.

'So do I, but just think of the fun we'll have catching up.' He turned me to face him. 'Give me a kiss,' he said.

Chapter Thirty-two

'Lazy old crones,' I grumbled, referring to the receptionists at the doctor's surgery. I'd nearly fractured a finger bashing the hell out of the phone while I tried to book a doctor's appointment. No one was answering the phone. I kept dialling and re-dialling.

'Tooting Surgery, how can I help you?'

'Ah, yes, good morning to you,' I said warmly.

Six days later, my stitches were out. My wrist was on the mend. My shoulder was taking its time, but on the whole it was healing pretty well, and according to the doctor there was no reason at all why I couldn't partake in what he called 'sexually related activities'.

'See, I told you so,' I spat venomously at Rob.

The doctor scratched his head meditatively, trying to figure out how to issue a prescription via cyberspace with the aid of his computer. His transparent bony finger hovered over the key-board. Exasperated, I rolled my eyes heavenwards. He peered at his PC and sipped his tea pensively.

'Can I help you with that?' I asked hollowly. I was so desperate to get home, get naked and get laid.

'You might be able to,' he admitted.

I orbited from my seat. Click, click, click. The prescription printed out.

'Mmmm, how did you do that?' the doctor asked.

'Consult your manual,' I told him, grabbing my bag and simultaneously pulling Rob out of his chair.

We had a three-day shagathon. I ended up with stomach cramps and a curly perm. And Rob complained of a groin strain. On the fourth day, our peace was shattered when Lulu came home from South Africa.

She had an *amazing* tan and her blonde hair was streaked with gold and silver highlights but I wasn't jealous because she'd put on about ten pounds. Metres and metres of brightly coloured animal print fabric were laid out all over the lounge. It was blinding.

'Ankle-length tight skirts look fantastic with matching turbans and bra tops. I knew we'd struggle to find them in London so I bought the fabric. All we need to do is find an ethnic South African dressmaker.' Lulu danced around the lounge, bowing low over each bale of cloth, whipping out an extra expanse here and there. 'The turbans might be a bit of a fashion no-no in downtown Tooting, so perhaps we should replace them with thick hairbands.' She gave me a backward cursory glance. 'You look brilliant by the way. The last time I saw you, you looked like a raccoon.' She lit a fag. 'I don't feel guilty about smoking any more. Even toddlers and monkeys smoke in Africa. And hey, Vic loves me.' She burst out laughing. 'Imagine, how cool is that, so I've decided not to buy a fish tank. Fish are minging and let's face it, if he loves me already, there's no need to try to impress, is there?' She waved her fag randomly. 'Is there?'

★

The following day I was lying on the sofa watching *Jerry Springer* when, 'Get in here,' Rob bellowed. 'Now!'

I felt a worm of apprehension wriggle up the length of my spine. He never shouts. I hauled myself from the sofa and lumbered into the bedroom. Rob stood, fists on hips, à la Clint Eastwood, scowling at the contents of my bedside cabinet, which lay fanned out over the bed, namely hate mail from the bank and the other annoying critters that were after my cash.

I smiled stiffly. 'Ah, yes. I know about that lot. I'll deal with it. I've had more pressing issues to attend to, and I—'

'More pressing issues!' He strode towards me. 'Do you inhabit a different earth plane to the rest of us? Because unless I'm mistaken, it looks to me like you haven't opened a letter or a bill or a statement since January. You don't have a private secretary, do you? You know, someone taking care of your finances for you?'

I peered around his shoulder. There seemed to be more correspondence than I remembered receiving.

'Say something,' he snapped.

I jumped. My mind throttled around in search of an excuse. 'There's *no* excuse.'

I flinched.

In two purposeful strides, he was by the bed. 'It's October, you haven't opened your mail for ten months.'

Had it really been that long? Rob gathered all the letters together and then frisbeed them, one at a time, back onto the bed. He raged on and on.

'Irresponsible . . . immature . . . face the facts . . .'

I didn't appreciate his tone. He smashed his fist on my dressing table, causing my perfumes to rattle and skittle.

'This is outrageous!'

My mouth was devoid of saliva and I could literally hear the blood pumping in my ears and coursing around my head. How dare he speak to me like this? He knows I'm convalescing. I'm still on medication and I hardly have the strength to push the Henry hoover. I'm not myself, and I won't be anytime soon. I'm constantly tearful and my hair's a mess, and—

'How much do you owe?' he bellowed.

My heart was going like a bongo drum and not just because he was shouting. I really didn't want to know how much I owed. If I wanted to know how much I owed, I would have opened the bills, wouldn't I? I read somewhere that the Empress Josephine only ever admitted to half of her debts because she feared the wrath of Napoleon. I was beginning to see her point. I'd have halved my debts myself, if I'd known how much they were.

'How much?'

I risked a smile.

'What are you laughing at? This is no laughing matter,' he shrieked, wearing a no-laughing-matter expression.

My face buckled. 'I'm not absolutely certain. I—'

'Let's find out then, shall we?' he snapped. 'Open them now.'

Good arm outstretched, I limped towards the bed. As it turned out, I didn't have to open any of the letters because Rob swept them all up, sank down on the bed and bellowed, 'I'll do it!' My jaw twitched nervously. There was an insufferable stretched silence, but for the tearing and scrunching of paper.

Suddenly he jumped to his feet. 'Don't you *dare* move. Stay right where you are,' he barked, waving a finger in warning.

I'd no intention of moving, my legs were jellified. I shrank back against the wall. He disappeared, returning twenty seconds later brandishing a calculator. His fringe flopped over his eyes as he bashed the calculator frenziedly, scribbling notes on the front of each envelope, stopping once or twice to give me a fearsome glare.

Eventually he spoke. 'Sit down!'

I slithered the length of the wall and landed on the floor.

'Next to me,' he punched the bed, 'right here.'

I walked slowly to the bed and sat beside him. I was exhausted. I could feel flu symptoms coming on, which was odd because I'd been on top form when I'd been watching *Jerry Springer*.

'Now,' he paused, 'we're going to discuss this calmly and in an adult manner.'

I gave a curt nod. That sounded good to me.

'On the plus side, your mortgage, mobile phone, gas and electricity are paid to date.' He rubbed his forehead in consternation. 'They're covered by direct debits.'

I folded my arms triumphantly. Well I knew that. I gave a self-appreciating head wobble.

He leaned forward, elbows on his knees, hands in a spire. 'But, you're £9,940 overdrawn,' he pointed out acidly.

My innards lurched.

He drew a measured breath and then seemed to forget that he'd suggested we discuss this calmly, and in an adult manner.

'And you owe £3,500 to store cards and £3,000 to Visa,' he boomed. He pounded his fist repeatedly into an open palm. 'That's a total of sixteen grand!'

I felt a surge of anger. Who did he think he was talking to? My finances are my business. I'm behaving like a doormat, a punch bag. I shot up from the bed.

'Actually my affairs are *my* affairs,' I snapped, indignant, arms straight, fists clenched.

'Sit down!' he yelled. 'I am not finished!'

I sat down. I just loathe confrontation. I felt sick and embarrassed, and I don't know why but I felt guilty. And worried. Sixteen grand . . . I can't even remember what I had bought.

Rob hammered on. 'Your salary is paid directly into your bank, and that, together with the rent Lulu pays into your account, covers your direct debits, with a little left over.'

I twisted my hair into a pointy knife and brushed my cheek.

'But you shouldn't be overdrawn. You've earned over ten grand in cash over the last few months, touring. And you've got your job at the bar.'

I contemplated my toenails.

'Where is it?' he punctuated frostily. 'Where's the cash?'

I exhaled. This was persecution at its worst.

'Where is it?' he repeated menacingly.

'I have it,' I managed.

'Where?'

'It's, it's in a box, a box, in, in my wardrobe.'

'You've got ten grand in a box in your wardrobe. Who d'you think you are, Fagin? Get it,' he demanded.

I gave a couple of surprised blinks. 'You want *my* money?' I bleated.

'I do.'

I glared at him defiantly. 'Why?'

'To pay off your overdraft.'

'But then I won't have any money because the bank will take it all,' I explained.

'Your overdraft is expensive. Give me the money.'

'I don't want to give it to you. I like knowing I have it and—'

'You don't have it if you owe it!' he shouted, standing up.

I pressed my fingers on my temples. I had to think. I know exactly what I owe now, what does he take me for? But there's not enough to pay everyone so I was going to sit down and decide who to share it with first. I definitely don't want to fall out with Topshop, so needs must they be a priority—

'Well?' he snapped.

'It's none of your business,' I shot back in a flash of bravery.

'Oh, it is. It's very much *my* business. While we're together, everything about you is *my* business. Now get the money. The bank closes in half an hour!'

I jumped to my feet. My lips twitched with rage. The cheek of him. I was *not* giving him my hard-earned cash just so he could give it to the bank. My cards are all up to their limit, what am I supposed to live on? Do I meddle in his affairs? Rob glared at me expectantly. I had an overwhelming urge to slap him but I couldn't reach his face without my heels. I scanned the room for my shoes.

'Get it or I'll empty your wardrobe and find it myself.'

I swallowed hard and glared. He was *not* speaking to me like this.

'Give me the money to pay your overdraft and I'll cover the rest,' he said brusquely.

Give him the money? I will not. My money . . . wait, what did he say? The rest? As in, the appendix to the overdraft rest? I stuck my finger in my ear and gave it a wiggle to make sure there wasn't a tube ticket wedged down there. You know, something that may have distorted my hearing.

'The, erm, the rest?' I ventured.

He gave a lopsided nod.

He is going to pay the rest, I whispered inwardly. Debt free! Debt free! Debt free! I felt like doing a fairy dance around the bed, or a morris dance! Yes, that's more like it, leaping big skips and hops with a bit of arm waving and stick bashing.

'You can't pay it, can you, because you don't have it?' he said, as he sat dissecting my bank statements.

I felt happy and floaty and excited. Imagine the shopping trip I can have with my store cards paid off. I'll buy some Crème de la Mer. I've always thought a hundred pounds for a jar of moisturiser is a bit of a piss take, but it's not a lot really, is it? In fact, it's bugger all when you've got a budget of £6,500. I'll buy Lulu and Lexy one each. Might as well, I don't want to be labelled a skinflint. And I'll get hair extensions. Not yet obviously, because I'm still partially bald, but when my hair grows back I'll be the first in the queue. And I'll request an increase to the credit limit on my Visa card. Did I say request? Will I hell request, I'll demand one. I'll be a fully paid-up account holder. I'm sorely tempted to tell Karen Millen to piss off, because they were the first to put a stop on my store account, but then I'd be shooting myself in the foot, wouldn't I? So I'll give them a second chance and—

'Give me your cards.'

'Excuse me?' I squeaked.

'The cards,' Rob repeated. Head bent, he flipped through the statements with the expertise of a Mafia bookkeeper. 'Karen Millen, Selfridges, Topshop, Monsoon, and let's not forget Visa,' he said sagely.

My forehead puckered and my bottom lip trembled. I'd just experienced the happiest five seconds of my entire life and now here he was, taking away everything that I had to look forward to.

'I'm not settling these accounts for you just so you can beetle around London, running them all up again.'

'But . . .' I croaked drily.

'No buts. There's nothing in any of these shops that you can't live without.'

'But, Rob, things come up and you never know—'

He clicked his fingers impatiently. 'The cards.'

He lifted my bag from the hook on the back of the door and handed it to me. 'The cards,' he parroted.

And then I thought, he's absolutely right. He's hit the nail on the head, as the saying goes. There is absolutely nothing in any of those shops that I can't live without. With a clean slate, I could take my valued custom elsewhere. Anywhere, actually. I'd rather have All Saints, Fenwick's and Harrods accounts. On dreamy autopilot I handed him the cards. And I'll apply for a Goldfish card to keep Topshop, Karen Millen and Monsoon in the loop.

Rob smiled and I grinned back. He gripped my shoulders and pulled me towards him.

'My nan used to say, "never a borrower or a lender be".'

I nodded. I'm not a lender, I thought. I'm a spender.

When we returned from the bank an hour later, I defrosted two tuna pasta bakes. I feigned interest in the racing and the football and I even watched a baseball game, and as a testament to my devotion, I gave Rob a pedicure.

All my store card statements now have big black stamps on them. And my overdraft is paid but the shoe box in my wardrobe is empty. I don't mind though, because now I can use my bank debit card whenever I like. Whipping it out used to be stressful because I was never sure when the axe would fall, never sure when I'd hit the dreaded ten grand jackpot. But not any more. The overdraft facility is still in place, the girl in the bank slipped me a secret note. That's what I call service. I'm the luckiest girl alive. How perfect is my boyfriend?

Chapter Thirty-three

Rob had to go away again. One of his new coaches was chartered for an eight-day European tour and no one else was available to drive it. I was distraught.

He put his arms around me and clutched my backside, pulling me close. 'You know it's the last thing I want, but I've been here in London for two weeks and three of my drivers are due time off. When you're back on your feet, I'll make sure we're scheduled to work together. Insignia charter all their coaches from me. I'll roster myself for every tour you take. We'll never be apart.'

I gave a little shrug. 'A week's nothing. I'll be fine,' I said halfheartedly. 'I'm just used to having you around and I love it.'

He cupped my face and kissed my forehead. 'Babe, a week's an eternity in my view. I'll phone every day.'

Rob left early on Sunday morning. I slobbed around the flat, reading magazines and eating Jaffa Cakes. I considered doing some dusting but it was a sunny day so I thought, no point because everything will look smeary instead of dusty so sod it. I almost hoovered but the floor was strewn with the contents of the ironing basket, which Lulu had fired around the lounge when she was looking for her white Joseph dress, so I thought, sod that as well. I sprawled on the sofa, unwashed and unshaven, watching the MTV channel for four hours. I was nodding off when my mobile buzzed. I nearly slumped to the floor with fright. It was a text from Rob.

Arrived Limburg, luv u. Miss u. Hate this. R x x x x

I sniffed and blew my phone a kiss. I missed him like mad. I dragged myself from the sofa and ambled down the hallway. I trailed my finger meditatively along the wall and sighed as a vision of his handsome face popped into my head. I smiled at the memory of his sexy smile.

I stood in the kitchen stirring a cup of hot chocolate. I read the message again and again, and then once more out loud, and sighed, rolling my eyes heavenwards at the animalistic grunting noises of Lulu and Vic, boffing away like a couple of stoats in her bedroom, which was next door to the kitchen. I chewed my lip in annoyance. There was a moment's silence. I breathed a sigh of relief but then the ritual banging of the headboard started again. An Apache war cry went up. I gnashed my teeth and circled the spoon in my cup. The chopping board crashed from the kitchen wall onto the worktop. I watched it spin.

'Rock me, rock me!' Lulu yelled.

The slut. It was sickening. She was sickening. She knew I was in and she knew that being in, I'd likely be listening. And it was only six o'clock, not even bedtime. And on a Sunday too. It's indecent. She's indecent. she has no respect. I texted Rob.

Miss u. Luv u. Want u home x x x x

'Aaaaaggg, aaaggg,' howled and air-tunnelled through the flat.

I squeezed my eyes shut. This was not acceptable behaviour, not on the Sabbath.

I texted Lulu.

Your mum's here. She wants u.

I added a little brandy to my hot chocolate and stirred it reflectively. I missed Rob. Really really missed him. I cocked an ear to the wall. There was a dull thud followed by a high-pitched yelp. I smiled triumphantly. The sounds coming through the wall were very different now. Banging of drawers, thumping feet, hushed rushed tones. A door slammed.

I lurched for my hot chocolate and shot out of the kitchen. Lulu flippered from her bedroom and we had a head-on collision in the hallway. Her long blonde hair was matted in a tornado arrangement. Her cheeks were flushed, her mascara smudged and her lips swollen from snogging. She wore a pair of both manicure and pedicure muffs.

Minnie Mouse sprang to mind.

'You look resplendent,' I said, sipping my brandy-laced hot chocolate.

Her dressing gown fell open and she fumbled to tie the belt.

'Eeee yuuuck!' I shrieked, bowing my elbow across my eyes at the sight of her cha cha. 'Put that away or get a gardener in,' I told her.

'Where is she?' Lulu hissed, peering past me. 'Say we're having a spa night. I was supposed to drive to Kent for lunch today.' She karate kicked her bedroom door closed.

'Vic's hiding,' she confided, 'in the wardrobe.' Her eyes scanned the hallway. 'Have you stuck her in the lounge?'

'It wasn't her,' I said flatly.

Her eyes rounded to full moons. 'What d'you mean, *not her?*' she spat scornfully.

'It looked like her through the glass door panel, but it wasn't. It was someone for Dr Who upstairs.'

Her eyes grew wider still. 'Well, would you mind awfully getting your facts right next time,' she snapped icily, pivoting on her foot muff.

'Would you like to watch the *Antiques Roadshow* with me?' I asked her bedroom door, as it slammed in my face.

With forced enthusiasm, I kept myself busy. It was a struggle because I didn't feel like doing anything or going anywhere. I wanted to do the best job I could of missing Rob but I thought if I kept myself occupied, time would soldier on, as opposed to limp by.

So I had lunch with Alice and Shirley. I got home at four o'clock in the morning and I was so hung over that I had to take to my bed for twenty-four hours. Lulu was an angel and left the washing-up bowl beside my bed in case I wanted to throw up. And she brought cod, chicken pie, curry sauce and chips home for tea.

And I met Tina from the office for dinner in town. We didn't eat because we forgot. We honestly meant to, we'd even asked for a menu. We zigzagged from the bar at midnight, fell asleep on the train on the way back to her place and woke up a hundred miles away in Brighton. Luckily Tina's gran is in a residential home outside Hove, so we staggered into a taxi and set off to surprise her. There was an unfortunate case of mistaken identity. A nurse greeted us with a grim-faced expression that Tina and I tried to match and she ushered us silently to a room at the end of a plushly carpeted, dimly lit corridor. The nurse bobbed her be-hatted head and reversed from the room. We hugged our handbags and thanked her. The nurse smiled and clicked the door closed with exaggerated care. It took Tina and me three seconds to spot the open-topped *occupied* coffin and let rip with off-the-Richter-scale screams that came close to waking the entire populace of the South Coast of England. A white-jacketed SWAT team burst through the door to find us huddled behind a curtain.

And I babysat for my sister. Her neighbour's dog barked for three solid hours. I swear to God, I'd have traded my Chopard pendant for a loaded catapult. In a sudden flash of genius, I wrapped eight toffee Quality Streets in a slice of roast beef and slipped it under the fence. It worked. The thing's jaws literally soldered together.

And I went to my hairdresser Charlene's birthday party at Nikki's bar. I don't understand how I got so pissed. I didn't drink much although I did try tequila for the first time. Nikki had to tow me home at eleven o'clock. I'm not speaking to him because he said I was an embarrassment, which I can assure you, I was not. There were three other girls dancing Latino and pretending to shag Ricky Martin. I wasn't the only one.

PARIS

Chapter Thirty-four

Lulu kicked the lounge door open. I was lying on the sofa reading an article on the miracle of Botox.

'Does Rob think you're dead?' she asked caustically.

'Why?'

'More weeds have arrived.'

I sat up and gave her a sanctimonious smile. Dead indeed. Weeds, she says.

She tossed the bouquet at me jealously and marched down the hallway, simultaneously pulling her tunic over her head. I gathered the scented bunch of blooms in my arms. It's the third bouquet he's sent since he left. I appraised the room, which was awash with a fusion of colour. He's so romantic and thoughtful and perfect. I rang to thank him. I felt a ripple of excitement at the mere thought of speaking to him.

'Hello?' A vaguely familiar voice tinkled down the line. A vaguely familiar *female* voice.

I pitched a swift glance at the caller display to make sure I'd rung Rob's mobile. I had.

'Is Rob there?' I asked in a tone that was trying for calm. A woman, a woman, was answering his phone.

'He's in the shower.'

Electric sparks of panic darted in my ribcage. 'The shower?' I squeaked, innards churning. I swept my tongue over dry lips.

'Who's calling?' the voice asked flatly.

Right, I thought, don't overreact. There's a simple explanation as to why a woman on the end of this phone knows Rob is in the shower. He's working with a tour guide. Of course he is, why hadn't that thought occurred to me? The relationship is obviously professional. I breathed in and out, and in and out, and in—

'It's Evie.' I exhaled. 'Who are you?' I shrieked, demented.

'It's Helen. We have met,' she replied conversationally. 'We met briefly in Paris. I'll tell him you rang. We're pushed for time. We're hosting a Tyrolean evening in the hotel bar but I'm sure he'll ring you back at some point,' she said, and rang off.

I felt nauseous, shaky and panicky. My hands flew to my mouth. I rocked back and forth on the sofa. He's in the shower. In *her* shower, in *her* room. No, no, never. I shook my head so hard that my cheeks wobbled. Maybe he left his phone somewhere and she found it, and took it to her room. That doesn't mean he's in her room. He will be in *his* room, and she knows he's having a shower because she rang his room to return his phone. And he told her he was in the shower and he would collect his phone later. I heaved a monumental sigh. Thank God for that. I knew it, I knew it all along. I could have driven myself mad over nothing. What a cheeky bitch for cutting me short. I leaped up from the sofa and paced the room. I trust Rob, I do. I trust him with my life. How could I have doubted him, even for a millisecond? I felt immediately guilty. We're soul mates, and soul mates trust each other irrefutably. And I do trust him, a million per cent.

I lurched towards the computer and logged on to the Insignia Tours website. I checked the tours by departure date, found their itinerary and scrolled down to see where they were staying on day five. I saw that they were staying in the Hilton in Salzburg so I opened the hotel's website and scribbled down the phone number. I dashed into my bedroom, crawled under the bed to retrieve our landline handset and called the hotel. I asked to be connected with Mr Harrison, the driver of the Insignia group. No reply from his room. The operator came back on the line and I asked to be put through to the room of the Insignia tour guide. Helen answered. I hit the redial button on my mobile and I heard Rob's phone ring out *in her room*. I clutched my heart as fear swept through me like a fire. I rang off.

'Lulu!'

I sprinted down the hallway and cannoned into Lulu's room. I stood numbly against the wall, phone dangling limply in my hand. I opened my mouth mutely and snapped it shut again.

'What?' she quizzed, looking up from the task of toenail painting.

Tears poured down my cheeks. She stood and put the nail varnish on the dressing table. Her bottom lip trembled as she walked towards me, arms outstretched. My tummy growled with terror.

'Who, who is it? Who's dead?'

I shook my head miserably.

She cupped her cheeks, and started to cry. 'Tell me.' She grabbed my forearms, searching my eyes anxiously. 'Tell me.'

'No one,' I managed in a strangled tone.

'Well, what? What's wrong?' she sniffed, swiping her eyes with the heel of her hand. 'You're scaring me!' she shrieked, surprising us both.

I startled. 'Rob, he—'

'He what?' she interjected swiftly.

I tried for air. 'He's, he's . . .' I warbled.

Her eyes widened. 'He's what?' she asked, bobbing her head in short sharp jerky movements.

I started to shake. 'He's sharing a room with the girl he's working with,' I blurted.

She frowned and stumbled backwards. We looked at each other for a moment. Her lips risked a smile.

'Evie,' she said thickly, breaking the silence, 'you scared the hell out of me. I thought someone was dead.' She threw her hands up. 'There's probably a shortage of rooms or something. You're not suggesting the guy's up to anything, are you? He adores you, he spends every waking minute with you, he coughed up for all your store cards, he looks at you like he's starving and you're a pork chop, he—'

'Stop!' I shrieked. 'Stop, I know it, I just know it, I know her. She answered her bedroom phone, I called his mobile and his phone rang in her room. There is no reason or excuse for them to be sharing. It's not high season, the hotel wouldn't be over-sold. And if it was, well, she's a horrid cow so she'd have the hotel manager bump someone else. She wouldn't allow a room from her group to be jacked.' I clenched my fists and shivered as my skin goose-pimpled.

Lulu studied me anxiously.

I felt my insides shrink. The saliva in my mouth turned to bile. I bolted from her room and ran into the bathroom, where I fell to my knees in front of the toilet, and vomited. Lulu scurried in my wake and rubbed my back.

'You're wrong. He's a good guy, he idolises you.'

She helped me to my feet, handed me a tissue and led me to the lounge where we sat on the sofa, backs bowed, heads together, fingers entwined. She smiled at me comfortingly.

'Evie, he's a gem. There's a reasonable explanation,' she assured. 'Call him back.'

My shoulders collapsed in a helpless shrug.

'Call him,' she said forcefully.

'No, I can't.' Fresh tears threatened. 'I just can't.'

There was a hesitant silence.

'Oh, for fuck's sake, I'll do it,' she snapped, never one for phrasing anything delicately. 'This is pointless. It's just to put your mind at rest.' She snatched my phone from my lap and hit redial. 'I'm telling you now, that guy is dependable, loyal and, I'm positive, faithful,' she said with a smirk of confidence. 'I'm a good judge of character. My instincts have never let me down yet.'

Helen answered. Lulu's lips puckered in a surprised 'o'. Her brow crinkled. I chewed my thumbnail. She asked to speak with Rob as a matter of urgency, and Helen kindly padded into the bathroom, turned off the shower and told him he had a call.

Lulu orbited from the sofa.

'You two-timing gobshite!' she shrieked, pacing the room. 'I've never liked you. I knew it, knew it, just knew it. Your eyes are too close together,' she ranted venomously, eyes shining with madness. 'You don't know what you've lost. You men are all the same,' she yelled. 'I hope you get a floppy mickey.'

I sank onto the sofa. My eyelids flickered madly, it was more of a twitch than a flicker, I couldn't control it. I looked miserably around the room. Our familiar lounge seemed different, surreal. My heart pumped erratically. Lulu was crazed. She tugged on the curtain as she fired insults down the phone. Her language was terrible, positively foul.

Eventually she exhausted her gamut of name-calling. Red-faced, she threw my phone on the sofa and limped towards me, twirling her earring manically. She looked wretched. She slowly sat down next to me, edging a caring arm around my shoulders.

'You're better off without him,' she said in a gritty tone. 'The guy was a show-off.'

301

The tears trickled slowly at first and then progressed into a torrential tidal wave. Lulu cuddled me fiercely, staring into the middle distance.

'Shh, shh. I don't know what to say.'

Pins and needles ran down the length of my arms. I stood up unsteadily. 'I can't forgive him, Lulu. Never, never,' I said in a trembly voice. I hugged myself.

She looked up at me, eyes wide with indignation. 'And why the fuck should you?' She stood and clutched my shoulders.

'I'll get us a stiffy.' She slapped her hand over her mouth. 'Oh, oh, sorry. I mean, oh God, I can't believe I mentioned stiffies. Oh God, I did it again. I'm sorry, I'm so sorry. I'll get us a large gin. I'll be right back, you wait here,' she said, reversing and bowing reverentially from the room.

'What shall I do?' I bleated, four gins later.

Lulu took a hefty draught from her glass and adopted an air of sobriety. 'Shag one of his friends to get your own back.' She tossed her glass randomly. 'Actually there's lots of things we could do. We could circulate his phone number online as a rent-boy and . . .' She scrunched her face, thinking hard. 'I'll look into it. There's bound to be a revenge helpline. There's probably a whole load of women-scorned websites. Stands to reason because there are millions of two-timing gobshites out there.'

I peered over the rim of my glass. 'I can't take it in. I thought we were happy, I thought everything was perfect,' I lamented. 'He was the one constantly professing undying love,' I added miserably.

She bobbed her head in silent understanding.

'He always said—'

My mobile rang. I jumped and so did Lulu. We scrambled

simultaneously for the phone. I won. Heads together, we looked at the caller display. It was Rob.

'Don't answer it!' she yelled, snatching the phone from my trembling hand. 'Wait until tomorrow. You're upset and tearful and in shock. Don't speak to him until you've got your wits about you, and you're at your nastiest best.' She nodded encouragingly. 'Never negotiate from a position of weakness,' she advised in her ward sister voice.

'Negotiate?'

'You know what I mean,' she said, gripping the phone possessively. 'You're not yourself.'

'You're right,' I agreed. But I felt a stab of longing as I looked at his name flashing red. I snatched the phone.

Lulu fought me for it. We wrestled to the floor. She pulled my hair and I pulled hers. She straddled my waist and pressed her cleavage to my face. I grunted with the effort of trying to move her.

The phone stopped ringing. We glared at each other, nose to nose. It rang again. The phone was in her hand, which was conveniently beside my ear. I grabbed it and quickly pressed 'receive'.

'Bastard!' I shrieked before she tackled the phone off me.

Chapter Thirty-five

I slept with Lulu that night. She made me leave my phone in the lounge. I dreamt of Rob and Helen. Of course, in my dream Helen was somewhat beautified. Her permed bleached hair was now straight and silky, her coarse suntanned skin had acquired a healthy peaches and cream glow, and her boyish size eight figure had morphed into a perfect Mel B cleavage and a curvy J-Lo bum.

I tossed and turned in fretful torment. Eventually I accepted that I wasn't going to sleep and crawled out of bed at five-thirty. Lulu lay on her back, one arm across her chest and the other on the pillow circling her head. She snored softly, periodically pushing her Zorro eye mask up the length of her nose. I tiptoed from the room. The last thing I wanted was to wake her, she'd been brilliant. She'd listened to me cry, sob, rant and rave until well after midnight, and she had to be at work at nine. I closed the bedroom door behind me and crept down the hallway to the lounge.

I had eight missed calls from Rob and six texts:

Plse pick up. x
Call me. x
Call me plse. x

Give me 2 mins. x
Talk to me. x
Hve got cover am flying back. X

I sprinted down the hallway to Lulu's room. I pulled her
Zorro mask and it sprung back with a twang. Her arms flailed
aimlessly.

'Aaaaaaahhhhh!' she screamed.

I leaped on the bed. 'He's flying back. What shall I do?' I
wailed.

She bolted to sitting.

'He's flying back,' I repeated, straddling her.

She whipped her mask off with a flourish, suddenly awake.
'Right, OK. Find my fags, I need a fag to think, and put the
kettle on and get Lexy over here.'

My eyes widened in horror. 'I can't ring Lexy at five-thirty
in the morning.'

'Why not?' she asked, reaching for her lighter. 'D'you
remember when she was pregnant? Huh, do you? She called us
in the middle of the night, at least twice a week, for seven
months to moan about her indigestion. This is payback.'

I rang Lexy.

'Is the great auntie dead?' Lexy asked groggily. 'I'll be honest,
I thought we were going to have to hire an assassin. She must
be at least a hundred and thirty.'

'No, she's not dead.'

'Who is then?'

My voice trembled. 'Rob's shagging around,' I managed,
before wailing like a baby.

I heard the clatter of her alarm clock on the wooden bedroom floor. 'I'm on my way,' she said urgently.

★

305

We settled in the lounge. Lulu and I were huddled on the sofa and Lexy, who'd brought us all Starbucks vanilla lattes, sat in the armchair eyeing me guardedly. I started to cry. Again.

'Don't,' Lulu whispered.

'I can't face him, I don't want excuses. There is *no* excuse.'

Lexy shook her head. 'No, you're right, there isn't, because you've been dead good. You haven't boffed anyone at all since you met him.' She peered over the rim of her cup. 'The very least he could do was not boff anyone else either.'

Lulu nodded vigorously in agreement.

'But everything was perfect,' I sobbed. 'He was perfect. This is so out of character.'

Lexy's eyebrow quirked up. 'Ah,' she said, shaking her head, 'no one is perfect.' She held a finger aloft. 'We'll write two lists, detailing his good points and his bad points, and you'll soon discover that he was *far* from perfect. This is an essential part of the healing process, I saw it on *Trisha*,' she counselled. She took two swift sips of latte, ferreted in her Gucci bag and excavated a notepad and pen. 'OK, shoot with his good points,' she ordered, brandishing her biro.

I sighed, suffering a fresh wave of misery.

'He coughed up for all her store cards,' Lulu said, perplexed.

'Mmm, yes he did,' Lexy conceded, and scribbled 'generous' under the 'Good Points' heading.

'He's handsome,' I offered forlornly.

'Mmm,' Lexy nodded wide-eyed. 'He *was* handsome, not *is* handsome,' she said deadpan.

'He has an amazing body,' I added, reminiscing.

'He *had* an amazing body,' Lexy corrected again.

'Great in the sack . . .' I trailed off

'That doesn't count because Lulu and I haven't had him, and we need to agree on all points,' Lexy informed us.

'Yes, but I heard them shagging sometimes, and he did sound good,' Lulu added.

'Still doesn't count.' Lexy was steadfast. 'Because I never heard them.'

'He can cook,' Lulu chirped brightly. 'And he tidied the flat and washed the bath, and if I couldn't be arsed to wash the bath after I used it, he'd wash it before he got in and again when he got out.'

I rounded on her. 'Has he been cleaning your scummy leg shavings?'

'Sometimes,' she admitted, sipping her coffee.

My eyes narrowed in disgust and I turned from Lulu to Lexy. 'He's romantic and buys me nice presents,' I said.

Lulu clapped her hands as though she were about to announce a happy event, wedding, engagement or something similar. 'He's minted,' she added brightly. 'And he bought our big show-off telly.'

Lexy raised the flat of her hand. 'Enough, we're not starting a fan club,' she snapped. 'The good points list is long enough. Let's start on the bad points.'

Lulu's eyes blazed with fury. 'That's easy. He's a faithless two-timing bastard,' she spat.

Lexy scratched 'scum' across the page. 'Fabulous start. You don't get much better than that from a bad points angle.' She straightened and crossed her legs triumphantly. 'What else?' she asked.

There was an eerie hush.

We sipped our coffees in silent contemplation. My attention drifted to the window. The 220 bus to Shepherd's Bush pulled up. I counted ten people getting off and eight people getting on. Lexy sat, pen frozen over her notepad. Lulu hooked her wrist in front of her face and checked her watch. I couldn't think of any bad points, obviously they couldn't either.

We shuffled restlessly.

'Did he fart in bed?' Lulu asked buoyantly.

'Never,' I denied.

She slunk back and gave a disbelieving snort.

'Did he fart, ever, anywhere?' Lexy asked with a hopeful edge to her voice.

'No,' I said, resting my chin in my hands.

They exchanged doubtful glances.

Lexy leaned forward and scanned my face. 'Did he,' she began tentatively, 'did he ever . . .' She stalled.

'Ever what?' I shot back.

'Come first,' she blurted out.

I gasped. 'Never,' I refuted, horrified that she'd suggest I'd put up with such a thing.

Lulu gave a reverential thumbs up.

Lexy stifled a yawn, fingered her Vulcan fringe and tucked her pen behind her ear. She tossed her notepad on the floor, flopped back into the armchair and spread her legs wide. Lulu studied her split ends. I checked out my moonwalker slippers. The clock ticked on. Lulu lit a fag, tilted back her head and blew a couple of perfectly formed smoke rings. Another bus pulled up outside the window and we all watched.

There was a lengthy stillness.

'For fuck's sake! Think, there must have been something you didn't like about him,' Lulu snapped, waving her fag.

Something tweaked my mind. 'Well,' I swallowed, 'there was one thing.'

Lexy scrambled to the floor for her pad and whipped her pen from behind her ear.

'What?' they carolled.

'He has, he has . . .'

'Has what?' Lexy asked.

'He has ...'

'Has what?' Lulu yelled.

'Ginger pubes,' I announced.

A fountain of coffee sprayed from Lexy's mouth.

'Ginger pubes,' Lulu yowled. 'Did you laugh every time he got his monster out?' she asked, shoulders shaking with mirth.

Lexy dabbed at her mouth with a cushion. 'You kept that quiet,' she admonished, chuckling.

'But, but,' Lulu stuttered, jabbing an inquisitive finger, 'he has blond hair.'

I nodded. 'His hair is *strawberry* blond. Travelling south, it's a sort of burnt gold and then it becomes more and more, well, more and more strawberry,' I explained.

Lulu clapped her hands, her face flushed with delight. 'That's it, that's what you have to remember. He's a faithless two-timing bastard with a carrot muff,' she said brightly. 'This is a very positive negative outlook! Very promising! I'm starting to go off him already.'

'Me too,' Princess Vulcan chipped in. 'I had no idea. I would *never* have guessed!'

'What shall I do when he comes around?' I sniffed. 'We haven't resolved anything.'

'You'll tell him to bugger off,' they clamoured.

Lulu had to go to work so Lexy stayed to babysit me. We watched *John Tucker Must Die*. Lexy snarled and growled all through the film and I sniffed into a cushion.

'Big-headed shite,' she scoffed, jerking her chin at the television.

She left at three o'clock to pick the kids up from nursery. This suited me fine because I was looking forward to some private bawling-my-eyes-out time.

★

309

Rob's key rattled in the lock at four-thirty. I was sat on the sofa, rubbing my cast up and down my thigh. I had a thumping headache and I felt nauseous, dry-mouthed and light-headed. When he appeared in the doorway of the lounge, as devastatingly handsome as ever, my instinct was to leap up and throw my arms around him. But I couldn't because my backside was welded to the sofa and my legs were jellified. He dumped his holdall and in three purposeful strides he was standing in front of me. I hugged myself and blinked madly. I knew I would cry but I wanted to hold out for as long as I could. He knelt between my legs, put his arms around me and cradled my head in the crook of his neck. He smelled of his leather jacket, Dolce & Gabbana and himself.

'Don't,' I warned, and pushed him from me.

He looked at me remorsefully. And so he should. The stupid fucker, he'd spoiled everything. The tension was overwhelming. His face was drained of colour, he looked like he'd seen a ghost. Given the choice, I suppose he'd rather have seen a ghost than been caught shagging someone else.

His eyes scanned my face, assessing my mood. 'I'm sorry,' he said, risking an apologetic smile.

I raised my left hand and delivered the hardest crack across his jaw that I could manage.

He flinched.

'So you should be,' I spat, eyeing him murderously.

He reached for my now stinging hand and circled my palm with his thumb.

'Don't,' I snapped again, and thumped his arm with my cast.

He stared beseechingly, unshed tears swimming in his eyes.

My heart squeezed then raced. I dropped my gaze to my lap and inhaled deeply. 'Why?' I breathed.

His voice quivered. 'I don't know,' he said in a broken voice.

'I don't know. I was drunk and stupid, and . . . and I'm so sorry because I'm scared, Evie. I'm sorry and I'm scared because I need you.'

His words hit me like a punch in the face. I think I'd been hoping for something along the lines of 'this has all been a terrible misunderstanding'.

'She means nothing to me. It was nothing, nothing at all,' he mumbled.

'Nothing at all. Nothing!' I shrieked. 'You showered in her room! You're not telling me that's all that happened, are you?'

He stiffened in rigid embarrassment.

'Are you?' I yelled. 'Tell me, tell me what happened. And don't kneel in front of me, you're too close.' I gestured at the armchair in the corner. 'Get over there.'

He stood up gingerly and lumbered to the armchair. I tugged my fingers through my hair in nervous jerky movements.

'Well?' I demanded. Where was this bravado coming from? Inwardly, I was growling with fear, dread, panic and anxiety.

'She, she called and asked me to go to her room because her window was jammed. She asked me to lever it open.' He massaged a nervous palm on his chest. 'And so I did.' He looked at me, blinking like a tired toddler.

A fresh wave of misery coursed through me and my nostrils stung with the effort of suppressing tears. I stared at him.

'I'd had a good few beers with a couple of Austrian drivers in the bar because we had all parked up for the night.'

I gave a snort of condemnation. 'Go on,' I pounced.

'I used her bathroom and when I came out she was, she was naked.'

'Naked!' I shrieked, and shot up from the sofa. 'And so you thought to yourself, I'll have some of that. I'll have a bit of a rattle on that bag of bones, I'll tug my fingers through that

311

bleached curly perm and snog the face off that naked piece of cheap totty!' My face blazed.

He stared morosely at his expensive black leather boots. 'I didn't kiss her,' he said defensively. 'I didn't.'

'You didn't kiss her,' I echoed.

'Nope, I didn't,' he boasted. 'Not once.'

'Am I supposed to be glad to hear that?'

He shuffled forward in his chair. 'You I kiss, you I can't kiss enough. I want to hold you and touch you. I want to please you and I love knowing I can excite you. With her, it was just sex, just once, with no kissing, no loving, and no—'

I raised my hand. I'd heard enough. 'No kissing, no loving, but tell me, were there no *orgasms*, because that's what I really want to know!' I raved, fists clenched. 'And Rob, ask me if I'd rather you kissed someone else or shagged them.'

His face collapsed in shame.

'Go on, ask me,' I challenged.

He moved to stand.

'Sit down!' I screamed. I was so much more in control if he didn't loom a whole foot above me.

'Evie, it was all down to drink, drink and stupidity. Maybe, I think, well, I wouldn't be surprised if someone had spiked my drink because I can't remember exactly what happened and—'

'Shut up. You don't need anything in your drink to give you a hard-on. If Helen or anyone else had put anything in your drink it must have dulled your eyesight and fried your brain for you to fancy her in the first place. But the hard-on you got all by yourself.'

His face crumbled. 'I'm so sorry. It was stupid, I was stupid. I swear to you, it'll never happen again. I'll never do anything like that again. I haven't been able to think straight since last night, I'm paralysed with fear at the thought of losing you. Tell me what to do and I'll do it, anything. What can I do to put things right?' His brow wrinkled in anguish and his face clouded.

I might have looked calm and composed but I was terrified of giving in to him and terrified of not giving in to him.

He inched to the edge of the armchair. 'Evie, please babe.'

'Don't call me that.'

He flinched.

I rocked on my heels and hugged myself. I felt a swell of something I didn't recognise. Grief? Hopelessness? Whatever it was, I'd never experienced it before. It was like an ache, a terrible ache in the hollow of my chest.

'Go,' I snapped, eyeing the door.

He stood and with arms outstretched, walked towards me. I backed away.

'Don't, please don't shut me out. I love you. We'll get through this. It was just one stupid mistake,' he said, half-pleading, half-injured.

'Go,' I repeated shakily.

His finger whispered gently on the back of my hand. My heart squeezed with desire, despair, longing and fury at his touch.

'Babe, please,' he pleaded. His breath was warm on my forehead. His eyelids dropped, causing a shadow to fall across his cheekbone, and—

'Well, hulllloooo,' Lulu stormed.

Neither of us had heard her come in.

She relaxed against the lounge door, watchful. She wore her nurse's tunic and uniform trousers and her leather medical bag swung from her arm. She sneered at Rob.

'Sooooooooooo, ginger bollocks returns,' she said, swinging her blonde hair in a circle. She pendulumed her medical bag at eye level with exaggerated zeal. 'Shall I take a look in here to see if I have a spare vial of penicillin,' she offered.

'Rob was just leaving,' I said authoritatively, my innards churning.

She folded her arms with a dramatic body-swaying movement. 'So soon?' she asked. 'Why not stay a while and tell us all about your European shagathon?'

Rob ignored her. His eyes burned my face.

'Out,' I told her, pointing towards the hallway.

She pouted and stood firm.

'Lulu, give us a couple of minutes,' I asked with pleading eyes.

Lips pressed together, she pivoted huffily from the lounge.

Rob held my gaze. The hairs on the back of his hand shone as he reached for my cheek. It seemed like an hour before he spoke but it couldn't have been more than a minute or two.

'Evie, I know I've messed up but I'll make it up to you. I'd do anything to turn the clock back.'

Two fat salty tears flooded my eyes. I wiped them with the back of my hand as they plopped onto my cheeks. 'Go,' I breathed.

'Yes, go,' Lulu repeated, returning to the lounge with two glasses of wine. She elbowed herself between Rob and me, handed me a glass and linked her arm through mine. 'Tell me,' she said, addressing his groin directly, 'what IQ does your mickey have?'

He slid me a look of despair, turned around and picked up his holdall.

I felt a chill grip my chest. 'Leave your key, Rob,' I said quietly.

He stopped short, dug his hand into his pocket and tossed his key onto the coffee table.

'The trouble with cocks is they have no conscience,' Lulu bellowed to his departing figure. 'They rely on brains for guidance,' she yelled as the door closed behind him.

She hugged me fondly. 'D'you fancy a curry?' she asked.

Chapter Thirty-six

I simply could not imagine my life without Rob in it. I know we'd only been together four months, but in that time we'd become soul mates. He was my best friend, my colleague, my confidant and my lover. I moped around the flat, dividing my time between my bed and the sofa. The days limped slowly by, suffocating me. My mood swung between the twin forces of rage and anguish. Rage because I was angry with him for spoiling our ideal existence, and anguish because I couldn't accept that someone I loved and trusted would hurt me so badly.

Every so often a flood of hysteria would crash against my ribs at the thought of never cuddling up to him again, or tweaking my fingers through the soft hair on his chest, or relaxing in the bath together. My heart would race with panic at the thought of him sharing his life with someone else, and I'd swallow down the bile that seemed ever present and wonder for the thousandth time what had been going through his head, how he could do this to us. The agony caused by his betrayal was physical. I was disorientated, unnerved, nauseous and tearful.

I told Rob not to contact me. I didn't want to see or speak to him. It's the only way I could see me getting through this.

When you've given someone the key to your heart, they can come and go as they please unless you put some distance between you. Otherwise, there's a window of opportunity that is permanently open for them to walk through and destroy any semblance of self-respect you've managed to hold on to. Rob had left me heartbroken, he was *not* crushing my self-esteem as well. I ignored all his calls and deleted his texts, un-read.

Thirteen days floated past in a fog of tears, Pinot Grigio, Merlot and Gilbey's, but now, I have a routine of sorts. I wake at about four o'clock and stare at the ceiling. Lulu bursts in at seven-thirty, whooshes the curtains open and leaves a cup of coffee on the bedside table, which I never bother to drink. I don't eat breakfast. In fact, now that I think of it I haven't bothered much with lunch or dinner either. My crying time is between eight-thirty, when Lulu leaves for work, and eleven-thirty, when Lexy arrives to babysit me, and again from three o'clock, when Lexy leaves to pick the kids up from nursery, and five o'clock, when Lulu arrives home. This works well because I'm absolutely knackered by then and don't think I could manage to put in any more daytime crying hours. However, I do manage to fit in a fair bit of overnight crying.

I'm taking this depression business quite seriously. I slob around in just my dressing gown all day. No pyjamas, no underwear and no make-up. I don't answer the phone or the door, I don't read my texts or listen to music. I have a bath but I wear a shower cap because I can't be bothered to wash my hair, so I look a right mess, which is depressing. And I'm reading a book on domestic violence, which is also very depressing. So far this week, I've watched *Sophie's Choice*, *Stepmom* and *Beaches*, which were all extremely depressing and left my eyes red, stinging and puffy. Not that my eyes weren't red, stinging and puffy anyway because they're constantly red, stinging and puffy. I look like the devil. And I squeezed two spots, which weren't ready, but I squeezed them anyway so now I have two giant maggot embryos pulsating on my chin, which is depressing. And I've taken to fingering the bald patch at the back of my head, which depressed me before I was depressed about anything else. The trouble is, Rob is everywhere. I see and smell his ghost all over the flat. I miss him so much, and that depresses me, but I tell myself that the Rob I miss is the pre-European-shagathon Rob, not the faithless slug that came back two weeks ago.

And you might think me ungrateful, because Lulu has been brilliant, but I wish she'd go on holiday, or work overtime, or stay at Vic's because she's driving me mad. She talks to me constantly and I have to drag myself out of my own head to answer her. I kind of like being inside my own head because most of the time I'm shagging Rob. And I'm usually at a good bit when she interrupts and it spoils everything, and she speaks to me as though I'm a stone-deaf ninety-four-year-old, slowly and in a monotone.

'Hulllooo.'

I sighed. My tormentor was home. She loomed over my horizontal form, as I lay splayed on the sofa. I grimaced. She looked more excited and animated than usual so I buried my face in a cushion. This was her I-have-an-idea-to-cheer-you-up face that I've grown to dread.

She snatched my cushion and frisbeed it onto the armchair. Her wide brown eyes blinked kindly. 'Evie, I bought you some tights today. It's November now and it's starting to get cold.' She shivered and rubbed her arms in illustration of the word 'cold'. 'Would you like to try them on?' She jiggled the tights proudly in front of my face. 'And maybe before you try them on, you might consider pushing the boat out and pulling on a pair of knickers,' she suggested in a *Watch with Mother* voice.

'I'm not going anywhere,' I replied flatly. 'I don't need knickers, or tights.'

She smoothed the hair from my face indulgently. 'Right, OK, no rush,' she said tight-lipped. 'In your own time.' She knelt beside the sofa, tipped the contents of her carrier bag on the floor and gasped in mock surprise. 'What have we here?' she asked, giving me a feigned puzzled look. 'Ah, a bottle of shampoo and, yes, a pair of high-leg briefs, deodorant and a bar of soap.'

I flicked an uninterested eye from the television to her cache of toiletries.

'Now, I'm going to leave this little lot here, and when you feel ready, I think you should consider perhaps having a bit of a spa day.' She stroked my brow. 'Will you do that for Lulu?' she asked.

I shrugged non-committally.

'Fine, that's a start,' she said, with a tiny glimmer of impatience.

She cooked chilli for dinner, which I couldn't eat, and brought me a blanket that I didn't want, but thoughtfully, she opened a bottle of wine, and then annoyingly turned down the volume on the television.

'Evie,' she sighed. 'It's time.' She was sat on the armchair, deleting my unread text messages from Rob.

'Time for what?'

She tossed the phone over her shoulder and picked up her wine glass. Sipping her drink, she studied my face. 'Dare I say it?' she hedged over the rim of her glass. 'But it's time to exorcise Rob from the flat,' she announced, with a sorrowful tilt of the head.

I nodded. I'd been thinking exactly the same thing myself.

'Everything must go, and I mean *everything*.' She perched on the edge of the chair and crossed one long leg over the other.

I sniffed and buried my nose in my glass.

'Look, I know how upsetting this is, so if you want to go out for a couple of hours, I'll do it, but going out will necessitate getting dressed,' she advised ruefully.

I didn't want to get dressed and I didn't want to go out. I couldn't possibly go out, not in my condition. 'There's not that much. A couple of suits and shirts in the wardrobe, about three pairs of shoes, his shaving stuff and iPod. That's it, I think.'

She wagged a contrite finger. 'Evie, everything.'

'That is everything.'

She placed her glass on the table and lit a fag. 'His dressing gown. You're not thinking of keeping it, are you?' she asked, slitting her eyes against the smoke.

I flapped my hand weakly. 'Oh no, no, I forgot. His dressing gown, of course,' I agreed.

She topped up our glasses.

'And the Mulberry suitcase and handbag,' I said, 'send them back to him.'

'What?' She thumped the wine bottle on the table. 'No, everything means everything except the Mulberry suitcase and handbag,' she backpedalled.

I gave a sullen shrug. 'Send back the Chopard pendant and the charm bracelet as well. I won't wear them again.'

Her eyes boggled. She fingered her flaming cheeks. 'Won't you? You won't wear them again?' she stuttered. 'No, no, we won't send them back. They're also in the "everything except them" category,' she insisted forcefully. 'We'll find a use for them, I'm sure.'

'Well, I'm *definitely* telling him to stick his plasma screen.'

She bolted from the chair, backed up against the wall and spread her arms defensively in front of the television. 'I can't live without the plasma.'

'But if I keep all those things then I won't have exorcised the flat,' I pointed out. 'Will I?'

Her eyes were wild and dark. 'What I meant,' she throttled into reverse, 'was that we need to exorcise the things he left in your wardrobe.'

So we did. We cleared the lot, boxed it up and put it in Lulu's car for her to take to the post office. And she insisted on sleeping with me, which I could have done without because I'd miss out on my overnight crying, but I suspect that was why she wanted to sleep with me.

The following day, I missed my early morning cry as well because Nikki came around. I'd just got out of the bath, where for the first time in two weeks I'd washed my hair. We stood in the kitchen waiting for the coffee percolator to stop spluttering.

'How are you?' he asked timidly. He leaned against the sink, chin on chest, beefy forearms folded.

'I'm fine,' I lied, reaching into the cupboard for coffee cups.

'The man's mad,' he said, his expression stern.

I shrugged wordlessly.

'When does your cast come off?'

'Next Tuesday or Wednesday, I think.'

'I expect you back at work on Thursday,' he said in an officious tone.

I shook my head. 'I'm not sure, Nikki.'

He reached out and held my chin between his forefinger and thumb. His shrewd eyes searched mine. He tugged me towards him. 'You can work the bar instead of the tables, working the bar will be easier on your wrist.'

I faltered. 'Nik, I don't know if I can,' I mumbled weakly. 'I mean, if I want to. . .' I trailed off.

A slow lonely tear trickled down the length of my cheek. Strong fingers gripped my shoulders. I reached out, snaked my arms around his waist and pressed my forehead on his chest. Nikki stroked my hair and swayed with me, whispering softly in

Greek. I cried inconsolably. I'd been crying on a fairly regular basis, but not like this. I literally broke my heart. I gulped for air, fuelling my lungs to bolster the shoulder-racking sobs that made my whole body tremble. Eventually the tears dried up. He raised my chin with the tip of his finger and gave me a thin smile. I snuggled into the nape of his neck and concentrated on the laborious task of regulating my breathing.

'Evie, the loss is his,' he said stonily.

'D'you still want that coffee?' I managed in a broken whisper.

'I do, and I meant what I said. I want you back in the bar next Thursday. You're not hiding in this flat, d'you hear me? Especially after that performance,' he chided, blotting my eyes with the tea towel.

'Milk and sugar?' I sniffed.

'Yes please,' he replied, ruffling my clean wet hair. 'And a smile.'

'So,' I bemoaned to the doctor, 'I need help. I can't sleep or eat, and no matter how much I drink I can't get pissed.' I sighed. 'I think, well, I think I need counselling,' I admitted, sweeping a martyred hand across my brow. 'I'll start at the beginning, shall I?'

'. . . shagged him nine hours after I met him. To tell you the truth I'd have shagged him after twenty minutes. And before you start flipping through your drawer for one of your chlamydia information leaflets, I'll have you know I'm not usually like that . . .'

'. . . She's got a curly perm . . .'

'. . . He paid my credit card bills and although that has nothing to do with how much I loved him, I have to admit that I think I loved him more because of it . . .'

'. . . He moaned about my spending but you tell me, how am I supposed to look this good without spending money?' I wailed, pointing to my Hobbs jacket . . .

'. . . My fantasy is that someone will kidnap my flatmate. I have *never* in my life had a fantasy that wasn't sexually related. Could this be the onset of some form of mental illness? . . .'

'. . . He's in my head every waking moment except when I'm

deliberating over which raving fundamentalist group I'd like to snatch Lulu . . .'

'. . . I know you can be addicted to gambling, drugs, booze, the horses and even the internet, but can you be addicted to a person? Because I think I am . . .'

'. . . Are you listening? Shouldn't you be saying something?'

I'd been prostrate on the couch in the doctor's surgery for over an hour. I slid my bended elbow from my forehead, prised one eye open and raised my head. The old dolt had fallen asleep! I exhaled and toed his chair.

'What do you suggest?' I asked. 'Could you prescribe a week in a spa-cum-rehabilitation centre?'

He stifled a yawn and beetle-marched his chair from the couch to his desk. Now that I think about it, I've never seen the lazy critter stand. He conducts every examination, including a smear test, with his backside soldered to his chair. I struggled from the couch and sank onto the plastic seat beside his desk. His printer hummed.

'Take one tablet as and when you feel you need it,' he said, handing me a prescription.

I slapped my hand over my mouth. 'Is it Valium?' I said worriedly. The two-timing bastard had turned me into a manically depressed junkie.

'No, it's a mild sleeping pill,' he replied.

I shuffled from his office back into the surgery waiting room, which resembled Stansted Airport after the cancellation of two easyJet flights. It was mobbed. I hugged the wall on the way out. Everyone, including two ugly babies, glared at me murderously. I couldn't get out of there and back home quick enough.

'You're dressed!' Lulu said, giving me a round of applause. 'Well done, well done!' She beamed delightedly.

I beamed back.

She gave a startled gasp and dropped her handbag. It clattered onto the coffee table. Arms outstretched, she limped towards me. Her brown eyes narrowed and darkened and the smile slid from her face.

My stomach gave a little lurch. 'What's wrong?' I fretted. She looked suddenly pale.

She took a step closer. 'You, you're wearing your Diesel jeans,' she mumbled.

I hadn't noticed but she was right, and not only did I have them on, but they were quite roomy.

'Have you been dieting?' she asked frostily.

'No,' I replied, smoothing my palms over my now slender hips.

She gave the waistband of my jeans a vicious tug. 'Liar,' she shrieked. 'You have!'

'I have not,' I shot back.

'If you haven't been dieting, where the hell has your arse gone? We promised we'd always diet together and you've gone and done it behind my back!'

'It's all the upset and stress and worry and misery and heartache.'

'And dieting!' she yelled, stabbing an accusing finger at my shrunken backside. 'I can't start tonight because Vic and I are going out for dinner, but I'm definitely dieting from tomorrow,' she snapped, marching from the lounge and slamming the door.

I would ring Lexy. I knew she'd be thrilled to hear from me, to know that I was up and dressed and that I'd been out. I opened the lounge window with a flourish and breathed in the sharp fresh air. Suddenly the world seemed bright and sunny. A dog peed noisily against our wheelie bin, there was a violent elbow-jostling stampede for a seat on the 155 bus to Clapham and two kids outside the newsagent's were belting the bejesus out of each other. It was all so expressively home and comforting and familiar. I'd been gone too long. I flipped my phone open with a twist of the wrist.

Lexy picked up on the first ring.

'It's me. I'm thinking of popping over and—'

'Actually,' she cut me short, and then cleared her throat, 'to be honest, I'd hoped you wouldn't call tonight.'

'What? Why not?' I asked, affronted.

'We're going to the Bushy Park Firework Display.'

'Oh,' I said. 'I might come. I enjoyed it last year and I haven't been out since, well, since you know.'

'You might have enjoyed coming with us but we didn't enjoy taking you.'

Not enjoy taking me? I'm her flesh and blood, I thought.

'I helped with the kids. I bought them ice creams and candy floss,' I reminded her.

'You were the *only* spectator out of a crowd of seven hundred to watch the entire display wearing a pair of ski goggles as a safety precaution. When we got back to the car and took the twins out of the pushchair, we found the pair of them were wearing swimming goggles,' she sighed. 'Graeme wanted to kill you. It was embarrassing.'

'Well,' I defended, 'I'd read an article and—'

'You can come if you promise not to wear your goggles or—'

My landline rang.

'I'll call you back,' I said, lurching for the handset and cutting her off.

It was Alice. 'Love, Duncan and I are in the area. Is it a good time to visit?'

'Er, yes.'

'Fabulous. See you shortly.'

In the area? They live in Epping, which is over an hour's drive away, I mused. Still, it would be nice to see them. I dived in the bath, and for the first time in weeks, I applied make-up, straightened my hair and frisked my wardrobe.

Twenty minutes later, the doorbell rang. Alice enveloped me in a cloud of Chanel Allure. She seemed animated, jittery and kind of high. She billowed through the lobby and into the lounge in a long flappy black dress and a sequinned floaty scarf. I wondered if she'd been drinking.

'I can't believe it. Such a nice boy and he adored you, I know that for a fact, it was written all over his face. He couldn't keep his hands off you, and who could blame him. Look at you, you've the face of an angel. But . . .' Her voice trailed off as she turned and swiped a finger along the side of the television checking for dust. She found loads. Her face crumbled. 'But, well, let's go out for a nice meal and a few drinks and see if we can make some sense of all this,' she said, wiping her dusty finger on her leg.

I sent Lexy a text.

I have a better offer, hope it rains!

We went to the bar and Nikki showed Duncan, Alice and me into the window alcove.

'Champagne on the house,' Nikki said excitedly. 'If you can come here to eat and drink, then you can come here to work.' He folded my hands in his and kissed my knuckles. 'You look fantastic.'

'He's right, lass. Yer a vision of beauty,' Duncan complimented, settling his huge form into the seat opposite mine.

Alice drummed her crimson nails on the table. 'Evie, love, we've . . .' She glanced at Duncan, who flashed her a cross look and waved a fork in warning. Her brow fell into irritated creases. 'Erm,' she muttered, lurching forward for the menu, 'what do you recommend, love?'

'Alice.'

She spun around. 'Yes, love?'

'Is something wrong?'

'No, love,' she insisted, zooming her sleeves up her arms.

Two bottles of champagne later and, 'Evie, we've heard from Rob,' Alice announced sharply. Flushed with excitement, she eyed me feverishly. My heart squeezed as it always does whenever I thought of Rob.

Duncan leaned forward, resting his chin in clenched fists. 'Lass, this is no our business, and I told her we shouldny get involved, but—'

Alice cut him off. 'Rob is so sorry, so very very sorry, and heartbroken.' She shook her head mournfully. 'He's devastated. He wants you back more than anything in the world. He called to ask if you'd confided in me. Well, there was no point denying I knew everything, was there? I'm not saying what he's done is right, on the contrary, but Evie, maybe you could just talk to him. Listen to what he has to say, things are not always—'

Duncan interjected. 'Yes, lass, perhaps a few words.'

Alice bobbed her head and squeezed my knee.

'And ye never know, things are often not as bad as they may seem,' Duncan added, his intelligent eyes flicking between Alice and me.

'And just what is that supposed to mean?' Alice snapped, taking Duncan by surprise. 'Are you telling me that being unfaithful is not as bad as it may seem?' She tossed the contents of her glass down her throat with practised ease, slammed her

328

glass on the table and sprang to her feet. 'Because if you are,' she pointed to the door, 'you can—'

'Sit down now,' Duncan ordered.

I teased her into her chair by her scarf.

Duncan held up his hands defensively. 'Alice, 'twas you that said it first.'

She folded her arms and contemplated the floor tiles. There was an awkward silence. I suddenly felt very lonely and sad.

'The meal was lovely,' Duncan said, patting my hand. 'I've no room for dessert, which is a good sign.'

Nikki appeared with another bottle of champagne. 'Can I join you?' he asked.

Alice brightened. 'Yes, please do,' she said, flapping a hand at the empty chair next to Duncan.

She hugged my arm. I cranked up a smile but she didn't smile back. Her jaw hung open and her eyes grew wide and dark. She sank her nails into my forearm and stared owlishly somewhere above my head. She slid off my arm as I followed her line of vision.

Rob stood behind me.

My stomach flipped. He looked handsome, tall, and striking. I gripped the edge of my seat and looked at him dazedly. My heartbeat went into overdrive. I had an overwhelming urge to bolt from my chair, pull his face towards mine and kiss him.

Alice studied me. Duncan studied the salt and pepper pots. Nikki folded his meaty forearms, leaned forward, snorted and studied Rob.

'Can we talk?' Rob asked softly. 'Outside,' he gestured towards the door, 'please?'

I didn't say anything.

'You won't return my calls or reply to my texts. I thought if I stood any chance at all of communicating with you, it would have to be in person.' He pressed his palm on my shoulder. 'Give me a few minutes.'

Alice made an excited bleating noise. Duncan gave an embarrassed harrumph. Nikki grunted.

A surge of panic squeezed in my chest. I swallowed and made a concerted effort to keep my head tilted back and my eyes raised, otherwise I'd be eyeballing his crotch.

'Actually, no, I think we've said it all,' I managed, finding my voice.

Alice eyed me beseechingly and jerked her chin towards the door.

Rob bent his blond head to mine and took hold of my elbow. I felt scared and excited and breathless. I closed my eyes to savour the warmth of his breath on my neck and the sweep of his jaw against my forehead. I wanted to bury my face in the curve of his shoulder and for him to press his mouth in my hair and—

'Outside, you owe me that much,' Rob said.

I blinked. Owe him? Did he say that I *owed* him? He shags a skinny ghoul with a curly perm, breaks my heart and I *owe* him? My chest contracted.

'Out,' he hissed.

'I owe you bugger all,' I told him.

'Evie, you don't mean that, you're upset.' His strong hands gripped my forearms.

'Leave me alone,' I yelled. 'A curly perm!' This was fast becoming my war cry.

Duncan shook his head and buried his face in his hands.

My heels scraped the tiled floor as Rob pulled me from behind the table. 'And no tits. You chose a curly perm and no tits over me!'

'Stop it, and keep your voice down,' Rob chided. 'Out.'

'And lilac glasses and orange lipstick.' I was on a roll. 'Does she think it's Halloween every night?'

He sighed, exasperated, and grunted with the effort of tugging me towards the door.

'Don't you have any taste at all?'

'Evie, ssssh. We'll discuss this outside,' he snapped.

I fought him off and gripped the back of Alice's chair. I was going nowhere.

'Ola!' Uncle Spiros bellowed.

The entire restaurant lapsed into silence.

Uncle Spiros stood with his air rifle aimed between Rob's eyes.

My heart stopped. I held my hands high in a 'don't shoot' gesture. Uncle Spiros jerked the rifle back against his shoulder. His black eyes held Rob's startled gaze. I lurched forward, and splayed myself protectively in front of Rob.

'Don't,' I muttered, terrified. 'Don't shoot him.'

My eyes slid a frantic right and left. Nikki was casually cleaning his fingernails with a fork. Alice and Duncan glared on hypnotically, and four terrified raccoons sat on the adjacent table.

Uncle Spiros smiled at Rob. He was enjoying himself. My heart raced and a pulse in my neck was throbbing like billy-o. I had to defuse this situation.

Rob pressed my shoulders, crushing my back against his chest. 'Outside now,' he hissed into the folds of my hair.

Again, just like that, I thought, he said outside now, and with another hiss.

'Now,' he repeated forcefully, body shuffling us to the right.

He's repeated now again, I thought, and he's pulling me.

'Move it,' he snapped into my ear, sinking his fingers into my collarbone.

He's snapping move it, I thought after, after . . .

331

An overwhelming surge of adrenalin-fuelled anger gripped me like a demon. I lunged forward and gripped the rifle butt with both hands. Uncle Spiros wrestled the barrel ceilingwards. I had to have it, I had to.

'Why should you get to shoot him? I want to shoot him!' I shrieked. Why hadn't I thought of it before? I could have invited him over and blown his brains out weeks ago, but I hadn't been myself, had I?

I fought with strength and determination. I was a woman scorned, we're capable of anything. A woman's best weapon is poison, I know that, but in its absence a rifle will do. I gave Uncle Spiros a sharp kick in the shin. He just would not let go. It's not as though I wouldn't give him the bloody rifle back when I was finished with it. Nikki vaulted over the table, grabbed me around the waist and lifted me back towards our table. Duncan bolted from his chair and linked his arm through Rob's, and Rob, who in fairness has never worked with Greeks or, I suspect, been shot by a chef or an ex-girlfriend, let Duncan lead him out into the street.

Imprisoned by a ham bone forearm, I air-cycled.

'Evie, be still and calm down,' Nikki said.

'Put me down,' I hollered. 'I am calm.'

Alice lifted her glass and toasted. 'I was only trying to help,' she said, to no one in particular. 'I told him not to arrive until we were on the coffee.' She threw Uncle Spiros an admiring glance. 'Is that a real gun?'

Not surprisingly, the restaurant quickly emptied in a flurry of hats, coats and umbrellas. Rob had gone, Duncan rejoined us, Uncle Spiros was back in the kitchen, and Nikki was calming a queue of people waiting to settle their bills at the bar. I cradled my champagne glass.

'I'm sorry, love,' Alice said feebly.

I shrugged. 'Don't be.'

'Aye, let her be sorry, for it's no often it happens,' Duncan urged.

'I thought it would be nice,' she said humbly.

I nodded. 'Maybe another time,' I suggested.

'Yes,' she said, and folded her arms resolutely. 'Another time.'

Duncan stood up. 'Aye well, next time will ye let Evie arrange it herself, Alice. I'm stepping outside for a cigar. I need it.'

Alice waved her hand. 'When you strike the match, d'you think you could blow yourself up? You condescending big eejit.'

My mobile buzzed. It was a text from Rob.

I saw the look in your eyes. There's still something there.
R xxx

Alice peered over my shoulder, eyes shining with optimism. 'That's nice,' she gushed.

I deleted the text. 'Big-headed bastard,' I said.

Her smile deflated like a burst balloon as she refilled her glass.

Chapter Thirty-eight

My cast came off on Wednesday and I was back at work in the bar on Thursday. For two weeks I worked daily eight-hour shifts. I have to admit that the unpredictable manically erratic Greek temperament suited me perfectly because my behaviour could only have been described as unpredictable and manically erratic. Costas and Pepi made the most of it. On my doleful 'missing Rob to death' days, I'd dreamscape and sleepwalk around, doing anything they told me. They'd set me to work waiting their tables whilst they skived to the bookies, chatted up totty, or knelt, hunched behind the bar, over a miniature portable television, worshipping the Racing Channel. But on one of my 'what do I need a man for' days, the pair of them gave me a *wide* berth.

Today was a 'missing Rob to death' day.

I sat numbly and filled sixty-four salt and pepper pots, after which Costas led me by the elbow to the gantry, jammed an aerosol of glass cleaner and a J cloth in my hand and gestured to the seventy bottles of red wines, ports and liqueurs and told me to clean them. He flashed Pepi a sideways glance of triumph, perched himself on a stool and spread his *Sporting Life* out on the bar. Pepi did a few Greek-style high kicks, yelled 'Ooopa', tucked his *Racing Post* under his arm, gave Costas a jaunty backwards wave and headed out of the door. I looked at my watch. It was twelve o'clock so there was another hour before the bar would fill up.

'Evie, when you feenished the bottles, you fold the napkins,' Costas ordered, his head bent over his newspaper.

I shrugged indifferently as I lined the brandies on the bar.

You see, I wanted to hate Rob's guts, but I couldn't. In fact, I missed him like mad. I wanted him back soooooooooooo badly. I knew that all I had to do was pick up the phone, just pick up the phone, and I could be cuddled up to him tonight, in bed, legs wrapped around legs, my bum squashed into the hollow of his belly. I'd be on the verge of ringing him when, like a blowtorch in the face, an apparition of Helen would appear. My stomach would literally twist with rage because now, in my mind's eye, Helen's perm was a hurricane of paprika-coloured corkscrews, her lipstick was screaming tangerine and her glasses were dark purple. In short, she was a horror and I'd wonder for the millionth time what the fuck had been going through Rob's head.

'Evie!' Costas shouted. 'Feenish the bottles quickly and do the napkins.'

I put the glass cleaner and cloth on a table and peered at myself judgementally in the mirror behind the bar. The weight I'd lost suited me and my hair didn't look too bad. I wore it in a ponytail tied below my right ear and unless you stood directly behind me, you'd never know I had a bikini line hairdo at the back of my head.

'Evie, the napkins.'

I took the band from my hair and shook it loose. It fell halfway down my back. Charlene said I should be able to have hair extensions by mid December, so only two more weeks to go.

'Evie,' Costas boomed in a voice that tried for authority.

I edged a line down the centre of my head with the tip of my biro and separated my hair into two equal bunches. Mmmm, I thought, that looks nice. I spun on my heel, pinged the till open and whipped a couple of elastic bands from the neatly stacked bundles of notes. I pouted sexily, wrapped the bands around my hair and stood back to admire myself from a different perspective. Very *St Trinian's*. I dug my lipstick from my pocket.

'The napkins.'

OK, Rob was a great catch but he wasn't Brad Pitt.

'Evie.'

I closed my eyes and shook my head in exasperation. The hairs on the back of my neck lifted and my nostrils flared with suppressed rage. I turned from the mirror, chest heaving with fury, and launched myself up and over the bar, grabbing Costas by his gold cravat.

'Will you shut up?' I yelled in his face.

I snapped the cravat, unravelling the knot, and used its length to lift myself from the floor, and with determined strength I pulled on the strip of gold silk. Costas's eyes bulged and his tongue drooped from his mouth. His breath felt warm on my cheeks. I let my head hang loosely to the side and mimicked him.

'I am doing my hair,' I told him.

His fingers grappled to loosen the cravat.

'And I can't do my hair with you bleating in my ear hole.'

He gave a jerky nod in silent understanding and slumped forward. One hand tugged on the cravat and the other did a palm-slapping countdown on the bar.

'So shut up, stoat head.' I explored his nose with mine. 'Is that clear?'

His throat rattled in agreement.

336

'Evie, if you kill him you'll serve his tables as well as your own!' Nikki bellowed from the kitchen door. 'I'll make sure you do.'

I let go of the cravat. Costas swayed and toppled off his stool. I stood on tiptoe and peered over the bar to check his slumped form was still breathing. It was.

Pepi cannoned through the door. He almost fainted with fright when he spotted Nikki. He knew he was done for. My day was getting better and better.

Nikki thundered towards him. 'Where have you been? You do *not* leave this bar during a shift without my permission.'

Pepi, doe-eyed, scanned the bar for a fairy godmother.

'Oh, I can answer that. He's been to place a bet,' I tell-taled. 'Look, he has the *Racing Post* tucked under his arm.'

Pepi dropped his newspaper. He'd have eaten it, if he'd had time.

Blood flooded Nikki's face. He reeled forward, grabbed Pepi by the throat and yo-yo'd his head against the wooden slatted window blinds.

'He goes every day,' I shouted over Pepi's screams. 'They both do. Sometimes they go together,' I yelled informatively, wiggling my finger.

Between Costas snorkelling in the ice bucket and Pepi bouncing against the window, all hell broke loose, but it was *hilarious* because Nikki can hammer the living daylights out of the pair of them at the same time, and still pull a pint.

Chapter Thirty-nine

Lulu was lying on the sofa, propped up on one elbow with her long blonde hair fanned behind her. She lit a cigarette.

'Don't bother looking in the bathroom for your sleeping pills. I've flushed them down the toilet,' she said, blowing a fine line of smoke.

I flounced into the armchair. I was knackered. 'Why did you do that?'

She stabbed a defiant finger. 'I'll tell you why,' she spat mutinously. 'Because I want someone to talk to after eight o'clock at night, that's why. Either forgive him and put an end to your misery, or get out there and shag someone else, or turn lezzo! But whatever you decide to do, do it quickly because I'm not sitting back and watching you cry and snore your life away.' She flapped a hand towards the lounge door and her voice softened. 'Casanova's sent another explosion of flowers. They're in the bath.'

I gazed at the coffee table. She'd put her miniature chaise longue to good use as a holder for the TV remote. And I noticed that her dance mat was rolled and jammed in the doorway, now an effective draught excluder.

'Evie, look at me.'

I did.

She smiled. 'Juliet got over Romeo,' she tutored.

I kicked off my dolly pumps, tucked my legs beneath my bum and snuggled into the armchair. 'No she didn't, Juliet killed herself.'

She sat up and swung her legs over the edge of the sofa. 'Did Romeo shag around, then? I can't remember. Is that why she killed herself?'

'No.' I shook my head. 'She had problems with the in-laws.'

She wore a look of mingled concern and irritation. 'Mothers-in-law.' She waved her ciggie aloft. 'D'you know what? I am *not* marrying a guy if his mother lives on the same continent. There are too many jokes and too much bad press about mothers-in-law being a proven marriage kibosh missile.'

I shrugged. My eyes landed on an enormous cream leather-bound book on the floor beside her. '*Wellbeing: a Permanent Lifestyle*,' I read, lopsided.

'Ah, yes,' she said, following my line of vision, 'there's going to be a few changes in this house.' She picked the book up and hugged it. 'For a start, I'm buying a bread maker and a packet of lentils and some Indian spices.' She massaged the book's cover. 'And every time you fancy a glass of wine, you have to ask yourself if you *really* want it. Ask yourself, do you *really* need it?' She glared at me, wide-eyed.

I nodded. 'Fine, I will.'

Her gaze lingered.

I stared back.

There was a contemplative silence.

'Seriously, look at you,' she said, her tone grave. 'You're a size ten for the first time since Noah filled the Ark, and you're minted in so much as you're not skint because you're debt free, and that,' she added triumphantly, 'is cause for celebration. So how about a glass of wine?'

'Do you *really* want it? I mean, do you *really* need it?' I asked.

'Want what?'

'A glass of wine.'

She leaped up from the sofa and threw the book on the coffee table. 'Of course I bloody do,' she said, already heading for the door. 'Oh, by the way, Tina from Insignia called. She wants you to ring her back.'

I flicked idly through *Wellbeing: a Permanent Lifestyle* and then rang Tina. I wasn't sure about going back to touring because (a) I didn't want to run the risk of finding myself working with Rob and (b) I didn't want to work with any other driver but Rob.

'Evie, your sick note has expired,' Tina said.

I sighed.

'Well?' she snapped.

I hadn't spoken to her since our night out so I told her *everything*.

'. . . Helen of Barnet, blah blah blah . . .'

'. . . walked in on her naked, skinny slut . . .'

'. . . sleeping tablets . . .'

'. . . air rifle . . .'

'Right,' Tina boomed assertively when I'd finished. 'Revenge is what's needed here.'

'I can't be bothered. I'd rather forget him.'

'I'm not talking about him. I'm talking about her.'

'What d'you mean?'

I could hear her bashing away at her computer keyboard. 'Our worst programme by far is our four-night Isle of Wight package. I'm pulling up the tour itinerary now. Let me see . . . Pick up in Aldershot, Camberley, Alton, Basingstoke and Winchester. She'll be knackered and travel sick before she's got a full complement. The ferry from Portsmouth to the Isle of

Wight takes fifty minutes, during which at least half of the passengers empty the contents of their stomach over each other's feet. I think the ferries on that route are second-hand Russian warships,' she said gleefully. 'Let me check out the accommodation.' She clucked her tongue. 'Aha! The hotel needs refurbishing. It looks awful, I don't know why we use it. Candlewick bedspreads, red and yellow seventies carpets, et cetera et cetera. This is looking better by the minute. The resident entertainer is a Larry Grayson lookalike with an orange fake tan and a toupée. Oh, and he mimes! The weather in winter is guaranteed to make her perm even frizzier than it already is, if that's possible.' She sucked her teeth. 'Perfect, there's bingo every night.'

Click, click, click. I heard her fingers dancing over her keyboard. 'What're you doing?' I asked.

'I'm cancelling the bingo caller. She might as well do that while she's there.'

I smiled. 'She'd like that,' I said sweetly.

'That's agreed, then. Helen of Barnet will now be known as Helen of the Isle of Wight,' Tina said.

I laughed, glad that she was my friend and not my enemy.

'Two little ducks,' she whooped.

Click, click, click.

'What're you doing now?'

'I'm contracting her for the next seven consecutive weeks,' she said. 'She won't be bumping into Rob for a while.'

'She might refuse to go,' I pointed out.

'She can't refuse. We pay her a retainer, even if we have no work for her. She's been with us for years. So, if you don't want to work with Rob, you could escort a fly tour.'

I frowned. I didn't know what a fly tour was. 'What do you mean?' I hedged.

'Not all of our clients want to travel long-haul by coach. So we have tours that fly from the UK to Europe, and they hook up with resort-based coach operators.' I could hear her fingers flying over the keyboard again. 'OK, a brilliant tour is available. It leaves next Friday to the South of France for two nights. It's a corporate event, eighteen businessmen to a sales conference in Nice. The client is Jackson Enterprises.'

'I've never done any corporate work,' I admitted.

'Well, you'd never done any tourist work either, had you, you lying trollop, but you soon picked it up. This is the perfect trip to get you back in the swing of things. A few days away with a bunch of guys on a jolly in the sun. You'll love it.'

I wasn't so sure. 'But—'

'No buts,' she interrupted swiftly.

I exhaled. I might as well be depressed in the South of France, I thought. It can't be any different to being depressed in Tooting.

'Well, OK, if you think . . .'

'I do. I'll stick the documentation in the post. And leave Helen of the Isle of Wight to me. And chin up! Rob's only a man. If I could teach my Anne Summers rabbit to mow the lawn and earn a hundred grand a year, I'd marry it.'

Chapter Forty

John Jackson is, according to Tina, Mr God.

'If the Queen had Jackson's money she'd burn her own. He's our key corporate client, the margins on his events are enormous. His account represents a third of our turnover so don't mess up. If you do, don't come back, drown yourself in the Med instead,' she'd advised flatly. 'He's terrifying, an absolute ogre, he eats his enemies.' She had growled and gnashed her teeth in illustration. 'But corporate pays three times the daily rate you'd normally earn because there are no excursions to supplement your salary. I'm going to be honest with you,' her voice had dropped to a whisper, 'when he phones, my teeth rattle, my heart races, my tummy flips, and I can recommend doing business with him as a cure for constipation. He's *terrifying*. Even our MD, who's a certified evil warlock, is scared of him. But you'll be fine because you're not really aware of what's going on around you at the moment. That's why I thought this would be perfect for you.'

Sitting at Heathrow Airport, I certainly was aware of what was going on around me. I was suffering nervous contractions. Meeting my group had been both formal and intimidating, a bit too grown up for my liking with a lot of stiff nods and sore handshakes. When John Jackson introduced himself he'd squished my new Accessorize ring into my pinkie finger. I'd wanted to cry.

OK, I can do this, I thought. It's only a matter of honing in on my organisational skills. Sitting tall, my neck swivelled like a submarine's periscope. I eyed the rabble of noisy kids, toupéed Pierce Brosnans, peroxide blondes and my eighteen lounge-suited businessmen crowding the seating area at the departure gate.

I picked up my *Financial Times* with a flourish. Cleverly, I'd hidden a copy of *OK!* magazine in the centrefold. I laid the lacklustre Companies & Markets section across my lap, and spread the uninspiring Executive Appointments pages neatly on top of my empty briefcase. I had a quick shufty round to see if anyone seemed impressed by my choice of reading material. A girl opposite me stared at my lap with impressed green eyes. It was exactly the effect I'd expected.

A deep thick voice penetrated my thoughts.

'You read the *FT*, do you?'

I gasped. It was Ogre Jackson.

I did a big phoney of-course-I-do laugh, unsure exactly what FT stood for. I mean, ET was an ugly little bug-eyed alien, this guy could be trying to catch me out.

'Do you mind if I join you? I'd like to run through a few minor details relating to the weekend,' he said softly. Surprisingly, his smile was broad and gracious. At the very least, I'd expected an explosion of scorching flames to shoot out of his mouth and blister my eyelashes off.

I gave the chair next to mine a terrified, welcoming nod. Run through minor details, I fretted. They'd better be *really* minor, minor enough for me to understand.

John Jackson was about sixty years old, with short dove-grey hair, a sun-kissed complexion, charcoal eyes framed with thick

344

black eyelashes, and rose coloured lips that curved and parted to display a row of dazzling white teeth. He flipped up the tail of his jacket, leaned back into the chair and crossed one leg over the other.

I startled when my *OK!* magazine slid to the floor. He bent to pick it up.

'Oh, that's not mine,' I insisted to his strong broad back.

He slid me an amused grin and chuckled, a deep infectious rumble.

'I must have picked it up by mistake,' I lied.

'You might as well read it, now that you have it,' he said, handing me the magazine and smiling suspiciously. Relaxing his chin on his chest, his fingers worked to straighten his tiepin. His charcoal eyes flicked to my empty briefcase. 'You might want to write this down.'

Well, it wasn't completely empty. I had a packet of Tampax and a box of Jaffa Cakes in it. I'd bought the briefcase to enhance my corporate image.

'Absolutely,' I enthused and rummaged in my handbag for a pen. I couldn't find one so I settled for an eye shadow stick.

He gave my crystal-blue eye shadow a puzzled stare. 'Do you have a writing pad?' he asked.

'Ah yes,' I confirmed. After another quick exploration of my handbag, I pulled out October's unopened bank statement and gave a please-continue hand flap.

He cleared his throat. 'This evening, I need a meeting room for twelve, laid out conference-style. Water, decaf coffee, no mints, thank you. Projector, flip chart, podium . . .' and he rattled on and on and on.

His list of wants and needs was bloody never-ending. At times I thought he was speaking some foreign language, but I managed to write it all down, ruining two shadow sticks in the process. When the overhead PA system crackled to life and announced that our flight was ready to board, I nearly fainted with relief. I looked back at my notes. I'd have to Google a couple of words. What exactly is a podium?

When we landed in Nice, I shot off the plane, weaved to the front of the queue at passport control and dashed through Customs to look for our coach driver. I felt sick with nerves. What if he wasn't there? A row of mafia godfather clones stood in the Arrivals hall with welcome name cards perched on barrel bellies. I stiletto-shimmied down the line of short fat men in search of a sign for Insignia Tours, but nada. I took a deep breath, and scanned the terminal.

'Shit,' I cursed and whizzed the strap of my bag up my arm. 'No driver.'

There was a soft tap on my shoulder. I swooped around. A dark-haired, chisel-jawed handsome bloke with emerald eyes and six o'clock stubble, wearing denim shorts, a lemon polo shirt and a pair of flip-flops, grinned at me.

'Yes?' I said.

He adjusted his watchstrap. '*Vous êtes la guide de Insignia Tours?*' he asked in a smooth voice, tilting his head in enquiry.

I gave a brisk nod.

He extended his hand. 'Alain, *votre chauffeur*,' he introduced.

Alain was about twenty-eight, with a broad chest and strong tanned arms that were covered with a smattering of soft dark hairs. He was a contender for top marks on the testosterone barometer if ever I saw one. He still held my hand, or I still held his. I noticed his palm was slightly calloused. I felt a tickle in my tummy when he smiled.

'*Je m'excuse mais je ne parle pas Anglais.*'

I nodded, my throat too dry to speak. So he didn't speak

346

English. I didn't give a toss if he warbled, chirped, quacked or brayed.

'*Suivez-moi*,' he said softly.

Follow him? Absolutely. Anywhere.

He placed his hand on the small of my back and started to lead me towards the exit. I was halfway through the terminal building when suddenly I realised something was missing. I'd almost forgotten about Mr Jackson and the group! I tore myself away from Alain and dashed back to the row of gangster clones, where eleven of my eighteen clients shuffled around in a circle gawping moronically at the ceiling.

Once I had everyone, we glided through the terminal in a flotilla of posh looking laptop carriers and Louis Vuitton suitcases. I'd taken to walking faster than usual. You can't very well dawdle along if you're swinging a briefcase, can you? You have to look important and like you have to be somewhere quickly, like a meeting or something.

Alain was relaxing against the coach with the luggage flaps raised. He pushed his sunglasses to the top of his head and closed his eyes against the sun. He jumped when John catapulted his suitcase into the luggage hold. Five minutes later, fully loaded, we were driving a little too fast along the palm-tree-lined Promenade des Anglais, flanked on one side by the glittering turquoise Mediterranean, which was sprinkled with billowing sail boats, and on the other side by tall cream balconied baroque mansions. It was *so* lovely. I stole a glance at Alain. He was plugged into his iPod, jerking his head from side to side in time to the music and periodically punching the air and cursing at other drivers. I suddenly thought of Rob who was quite the opposite, with his smart navy blazer and tie and his *pas devant les clients* attitude. We lumbered cumbersomely down a narrow cobbled road that was edged with vanilla stone-terraced shops and apartments garlanded with blue awnings and window boxes spilling over with clusters of red and pink geraniums and indigo lobelia. I wriggled excitedly in the crew seat.

'It's beautiful,' I muttered unconsciously.

'It certainly is,' John agreed from his lofty position behind me.

The hotel was fabulous. Two huge marble pillars heralded the entrance to an enormous Romanesque lobby that was dominated by a blond stone fountain, which cascaded into an oval mosaic pond. I clip-clopped to the reception area and walked past several expensive looking shops with walnut-panelled exteriors and dazzling window displays stuffed with jewellery, handbags and shoes.

I was about to throw back my head and scream for a porter, which is what I have to do in Paris, when a uniformed concierge materialised like a genie beside me. He knew my name. I eyed him suspiciously. He held my elbow between forefinger and thumb and steered me towards a walnut desk flanked by two black urns overflowing with white scented flowers. I gazed at him blankly.

'Ze rooms are ready, Mees Dexter. All ze keys are here,' he said.

And hey bloody presto, the electronic keys, each with a name card attached, were lined up in alphabetical order. I *loved* this hotel.

John strode into the lobby, followed by his seventeen hangers-on who had to jog to keep up with him.

'Evie,' he addressed me smartly, 'I want the meeting room ready at seven o'clock and as you know, tonight we eat independently.'

I bobbed my head.

He swooped off and so did everyone else.

So far so good.

Chapter Forty-one

'I'm telling you there are no meeting rooms available!' I yelled down the phone. I was demented. So was Tina, she'd forgotten to book one. I crunched my plastic biro to bits and marched up and down the tiled lobby.

'I've got tickets for the Sugababes at the O2 tonight. I can't go with this hanging over my head, can I?' Tina wailed. 'Do something pleeeeeeeeeeeease!'

My stomach cramped and my head was spinning. I felt feverish. I massaged my chest and struggled for calm. 'Do what exactly? I can't just pull a meeting room out my handbag, can I?'

I felt tearful.

Tina sniffed.

There was a frantic silence.

The uniformed genie floated past and something tweaked my brain. I had a sudden flash of inspiration. All I needed to do was shift the problem onto someone else . . .

'I'll call you back,' I told Tina, flicking my phone shut.

I walloped the genie with my clipboard, clutched his arm, flattened him against the wall and explained my predicament. He gave my cleavage his undivided attention. When I told him the client was Mr Jackson, his eyes travelled to my face and he began to hyperventilate. I was delighted, fear was a great motivator. His cavalier moustache twitched with terror.

'Pierre!' the genie roared, and another genie appeared.

And I promise you, Spartacus never worked as hard as we had to, to transform the dining room of the penthouse suite into a meeting room, laid conference style with water, decaf coffee, no mints, projector, flip chart and podium. I hugged the genies, who dismissed my thanks with a congenial nod.

I texted Tina.

Sorted. x

She replied:

Luv u. x

I was knackered. I'd have one drink, escort the clients into the meeting room and then I could go to bed. I slumped, exhausted, into a seat in the piano lounge with one foot propped on the table. I almost toppled over reaching to pluck my gin and tonic from the waiter's tray. My phone rang and I saw that it was Alain. We'd exchanged numbers earlier when he'd explained he might not always be able to park outside the hotel and that he may need to call to tell me where to find him. Resort drivers, according to Tina, preferred to go home rather than stay in the hotel.

'*Bonjour chérie,*' he greeted cheerfully.

I felt a little ripple of excitement. He sounded so jovial and manly and French.

'Come out tonight,' he invited in French. 'Let me show you Nice.'

I sighed. 'I'm tired.'

'Tired? *Chérie*, you are too young and alive to be tired, and too beautiful to be in a hotel room alone.'

I jerked my chin up. Yes, damn it, young, alive and beautiful. How right he was. I quickly signalled for another gin and tonic.

'What time?' I heard myself say.

'I'll pick you up at eight,' he replied.

Fifteen minutes later, I stood like a sentry at the entrance to the penthouse suite and welcomed my group, who were now wearing a new uniform of chinos and long-sleeved pastel shirts.

'Thank you, Evie,' John said briskly. 'Have a pleasant evening,' he added, flapping his hand in a dismissive motion.

It took all of my self-control not to click my heels and salute.

My room was *amazing*. The walls were hung with ivory silk, threaded with a subtle cerise vein. Cream and gold voile curtains dressed the two floor-to-ceiling casement windows, in between which nestled a cherry chintz sofa scattered with pale gold cushions. A king-size bed topped with a cream chiffon canopy occupied centre stage.

I sank down on the bed and glanced around. Someone had unpacked for me, how cool is that? My make-up and perfume lined the Marie Antoinette dressing table, my briefcase lay on the desk and the open wardrobe door displayed my clothes hanging neatly inside. I kicked off my stilettos and moseyed into the bathroom. It was huge with salmon-coloured marble flooring and matching wall tiles. A white porcelain free-standing bathtub with gold balled feet crouched below a large oval window. I curved my hand over a velvety dressing gown draped on a tiered gold-plated towel rail. My lip quivered. Rob would have loved it, the two-timing bastard. Tears welled. I picked up the dressing gown, buried my face in the hood and sobbed.

Right, pull yourself together, I told myself. I sniffed and began applying my lipstick. This is *not* a date so there's no need to panic or go too over the top with my wardrobe. I bolted from the room and shot down to the lobby and bought a pair of gold Tiffany hoop earrings from the jeweller's. They were only £430 which is bugger all because I'll still have £9,570 of my ten grand overdraft left at my disposal.

I decided on my long-sleeved knee-length black Versace halterneck dress and a pair of rather lofty black jewel-encrusted sandals. OK, they're a bit *too* lofty, and I can't really walk in them, but I'm only planning to stay out for an hour or so, and most of that will be sitting down so this is the perfect opportunity to wear them. They cost £380. I bought them at the airport, they were cheer-myself-up shoes, so medicinal really and much better for me than valium. But now that I think of it, that brings my bank balance down to £9,190. There's also the £350 worth of stuff I ordered from the Next Catalogue, but I haven't received that yet and I might end up sending it all back, so obviously that doesn't count. Even if I do keep it, it still won't count because I don't have to pay it all off at once.

I wound a gold braid around my now trademark ear-hugging ponytail and had a little twirl in the mirror. Perfect, I thought, as I blotted my lipstick with a tissue. I tossed my room key in my handbag, tugged a gold pashmina around my arms and made my way to the lobby. I was working tomorrow so I decided that I wouldn't drink much. Alain had said that we were meeting a few of his friends, so I may well end up sitting like a lemon once the conversation gets flowing. To be polite, I'll perhaps have one or two sips of what everyone else is drinking and then make my excuses.

Alain was waiting in the lobby when I stepped out of the elevator. He looked as though he'd just walked out of a soap powder advert. He also looked like Colin Farrell. He wore a white long-sleeved shirt, cream knee-length shorts and a pair of beige leather moccasins. I waved a jaunty bye-bye to the two genies and let Alain shepherd me through the hotel lobby, out the door and into the warm evening air. My jaw dropped when he gestured towards a motorbike. Eyes darting between my hemline and the bike, I suggested that maybe I should change into jeans.

He jammed a crash helmet on my head. 'No problem,' he insisted, hoisting my Versace dress to knicker level.

He half lifted me onto the bike, climbed in front and pulled my arms around his waist. I was glad I'd decided on my high-heel sandals because from gusset to toe, my legs looked a mile long. I'd just spotted an annoying new blob of cellulite when, heigh ho Tonto, we took off.

It was *so* exhilarating. The cobbled road whizzed beneath us as Alain weaved and zigzagged past zooming Renaults, honking Fiats and sleek limos. He swooped and beep-beeped around the square of the Old Town, where crowded café tables spilled onto the pavements, and he raced past the pink stucco marketplace, where we wobbled and shuddered when Alain waved to some friends without dropping his speed. It felt nice to have my arms around him, and OK, it felt nice to have my legs around him as well.

Alain dismounted with exercised ease. I slumped onto my tummy, clutched the handlebars, and high-kneed my right leg off the bike, landing on the pavement with a thud. I was still per-suading my dress down over my backside when Alain, cradling my shoulder, ushered me through the door of the bar. As we meandered between packed tables of cheery diners, he tugged me closer.

'*Mes amis,*' he said, pointing to the far corner where a raucous rabble of waving arms and beaming smiles beckoned.

Three handsome guys and two pretty girls shuffled around a table to make space for us, gabbling greetings in high-speed French. I bobbed my head to each in turn as Alain introduced me and, clutching my handbag to my chest, I sank into a chair and tried to fluff a bit of life into my helmet-damaged ponytail. Alain deliberated over the wine list, massaging his dark stubble with his forefinger and thumb.

'What would you like, *chérie*?' he asked.

I beamed at the girls' peachy-coloured cocktails.

He patted my hand. 'Bellini it is,' he said.

I tried to join in the conversation by pitching in the odd reluctant mumble but I was worried that I wouldn't be able to keep up. My French isn't bad at all, but I usually chat one-to-one, which is much easier than following crossfire banter, and I didn't want to make a pillock of myself. I took a hesitant sip of my drink. I'd stay no more than an hour.

But the drinks were delicious and it turns out that I'm a rather talented bilingual conversationalist. It was all so atmospheric and I got totally caught up in the waving of hands, guzzling of champagne, gobbling of olives and smoking of fags. Yes, chubby brown smelly fags. Everyone else was smoking so why not? I thought.

Alain hugged me to him. The soft but spiky stubble of his chin brushed my forehead. He raised the flat of his hand to my mouth and teased a cigarette between my lips. His warm dark eyes held mine. I pursed my lips, inhaled and pouted as I slowly blew out a thin line of smoke, just like one of those glamorous 1940s Hollywood film stars. A fleeting image of me splayed over a grand piano wearing a gold sequinned evening dress popped into my head. Another image of me shagging Alain also popped into my head. My elbow slid off the table. I felt pissed and dizzy and jolly. I marvelled that I knew how to smoke, I must be a natural. I just picked it up, no gagging or choking. There just seems no end to the things I can do. I wondered what other hidden talents I might have.

Alain grinned sexily. 'One more, *chérie*,' he offered.

I took another long drag on the cigarette. Alain chuckled and kissed my cheek. My tummy gave a joyful little lurch. He smelled so clean and fresh, soapy and spicy. His nearness and dark good looks were, frankly, making me feel quite horny. My attention drifted boozily to my sandals. They really are gorgeous. There must be lots of places where I can sit down all night. I could join the library or maybe enrol in an evening class of some sort, like flower arranging perhaps.

I jumped when one of the guys slammed a bottle of Calvados on the table and slid a shot glass to each of us. I felt trashed as it was and I wasn't planning on getting into the stickies as well.

'No no, no thank you,' I insisted, raising the flat of my hand. 'Not for me.'

Alain short-circuited my refusal by cramming his fag back in my mouth and leaving it there. With an OK-you've-persuaded-me shrug, I slitted my eyes against the smoke and accepted a brandy. Before I knew it I was on my second.

I stumbled to my feet, looming like the leaning Tower of Pisa over Alain's bowed back.

'Cheers,' I boomed, toasting the ceiling, and hobbled off in a determined zigzag to the toilets.

I swayed in front of the mirror and looked at my watch. I couldn't see the hands. I'll stop drinking now, I decided determinedly, because I know for a fact that my watch has hands, so obviously I'm too pissed to see them. I'll order a Diet Coke. I descended the perilous two steps outside the ladies' toilet with meticulous care and crisscrossed back through the throng.

Alain held my hand and teased me into my seat and beckoning the waiter, he ordered a round of pina coladas, which happens to be my favourite cocktail in the whole world.

Chapter forty-two

I prised one eye open. I was in a strange bed in a room I'd never seen before. I breathed. A flurry of nausea hit my throat and my head throbbed. My eyes slid a slow left and right. Cherry chintz sofa, open floor-to-ceiling windows, billowing voile curtains. I remember now, this was my room! My mouth was dry and my tongue swollen and furry, like yuk furry. I swung my legs out of bed, staggered to the bathroom and peered in the mirror. I looked like a gremlin, puffy-cheeked and bug-eyed. And still fully clothed. I dropped my chin on my chest and looked at my watch.

'Sod it!'

I ripped my dress over my head, marched my knickers down and climbed into the shower. I had exactly twenty minutes to wash, get dressed and be on parade downstairs, ready to escort JJ & Co to the Acropolis Convention Centre for their sales conference.

Stumbling into the already dimly lit elevator, I jammed my sunglasses on my face. I was practising breathing in and out, and getting the hang of it when, 'Good morning, Evie. Are you well?' John Jackson asked.

His gaze lingered expectantly. I flipped open my clipboard file and ran my finger down, well, ran my finger down nothing. The file was empty because I'd left my paperwork on the coach but he couldn't see that. As clever as he thinks he is, he doesn't have two alien antennae protruding from his head with an eyeball bouncing on each. I flipped my file shut and hugged it to my chest.

'Yes thank you,' I said in newsreader tones, and added, 'And you, are you well?'

He leafed through a wad of spreadsheets, looking very dapper in a navy blue pinstripe suit and a red silk tie. 'Very well,' he replied.

I stood with my nose in the crack of the door, ready to beetle off the second we hit lobby level.

As my lounge-suited group trooped onto the coach, I pulled Alain to one side.

'I'm dying,' I confessed. 'I can't remember leaving the bar. Did I come back to the hotel on your motorbike?'

He clutched my elbow and bent his head to whisper, 'I brought you back in a taxi, my bike is still at the bar.' His lips curved and he winked saucily. 'Me and the two concierges put you to bed.'

I cringed and skittled past him onto the coach. I sank into my seat, my cheeks aflame. Slapping my knee playfully, Alain squeezed past me and took the driving seat. I dared a sideways glance as we lurched into the melee of the rush-hour traffic, recoiling in shame when he blew me a kiss. I must have been absolutely legless if putting me to bed was a three-man job. This called for some serious explanation.

'Alain, I'm sorry. I don't usually drink Calvados and I had a couple of gins before I left the hotel and champagne doesn't mix with anything,' I babbled.

He chuckled. '*Chérie*, you were nervous. I don't know why, but you were. And so, I gave you something to help you *relax*.'

I bristled. 'You what? You gave me something?'

He grinned mischievously.

'What exactly did you give me?' I asked, confused.

'Marijuana. We smoked it, *chérie*,' he replied, beaming.

I felt a queasiness in my stomach. I was so angry, furious actually.

'Alain,' I snapped in hushed tones, 'you shouldn't have done that. You shouldn't have given me, well, drugs.'

He looked nonplussed. 'Why not? If you had been hungry, I would have ordered you a steak,' he told me with a nonchalant shrug.

'It's not the same thing,' I retorted sharply.

He flapped a hand in a don't-be-silly gesture and pulled into the Convention Centre car park.

'Would you like to spend the day in Cannes, *chérie*?' he asked brightly, scanning the bays for a parking space.

I sighed. As if my hangovers weren't wicked enough, I now had to deal with being stoned as well.

John, who was sitting directly behind me, snapped his briefcase shut with such force that I felt a blast of air in my ear. He was on his feet to leave the coach before we'd even come to a standstill. He stepped down from the elevated passenger section and stood on my right flank.

'Evie,' his voice reverberated.

I looked up. Sitting with my neck tilted made my head swim. I clutched my knees protectively, and held his gaze.

'Yes,' I managed.

'I see no reason why you shouldn't attend today's conference.'

I recoiled in panic. I had plans, namely sobering up, detoxing, drying out and going back to bed.

'Erm, won't I be in the way? I mean, I don't know anything about, er,' I consulted my paperwork, 'er, about Innovative Film Makers,' I said, trying to keep the desperation from my voice.

Alain pushed the button and the door purred open. I stood. John loomed soberly beside me.

'It won't hurt you to learn,' he replied flatly, descending the steps, with me clumping slowly behind.

'OK, *chérie*, we'll take a taxi to pick up the bike, and can be in Cannes within the hour,' Alain said.

I was still cross with him. I pulled a stiff regretful face. 'I have to attend the conference.'

He pinched my cheek and gave a perturbed sigh. 'Oh well, I'll be picking you up later so maybe we can go out tonight,' he said, massaging my shoulders.

'Evie!' John bellowed.

Flashing Alain a non-committal smile, I hastened towards the Convention Centre. How was I expected to survive this? I was ill and should be in bed. This is sheer purgatory. I can't think of anything I'd like less. I'd rather be executed or go up a dress size, than sit in a conference all day. I limped up the steps of the Acropolis, clinging to the railings for support. I felt nippy-eyed and wobbly lipped. I was so disappointed. I'd been looking forward to getting back into bed since the minute I'd got out of it.

At the top of the stairs a tidal wave of business-suited men and women sluiced me through a set of enormous glass doors. The place was heaving. I pressed my forehead and palms against a cool marble pillar and shut my eyes. I am not drinking for at least a week, no, make that a fortnight. And what must the genies think of me?

'Evie.'

I turned.

'You'll need these,' John said, slapping a silver name badge and a delegate pack in my hand.

'Right, OK. Thank you,' I managed.

He gave me a penetrating look. 'There's an hour before the conference begins. Have a wander, there are many aspects of the film industry that you may find interesting.'

I doubted it.

'I'm sure I will. I'm looking forward to it,' I lied.

'I'll see you inside,' he said, and turned on his heel and marched off to annoy the hell out of some other poor unsuspecting soul.

OK, I just need to find a seat and a drink. A conference is no different from a trip to the cinema so I'll sit at the back and have a sleep. In fact, I often take the twins to the cinema for that very reason. I buy them a tenner's worth of tooth-rotting rubbish to keep them quiet, and a million-calorie milkshake which has the same effect on them as three gins have on me. Then I tie the three of us together with the toggles from their anoraks to put the kibosh on any breaks for freedom. I've had some of the best sleeps of my life at the cinema.

I pitched the delegate pack in a bin and swept a cursory glance around and brightened slightly. Throngs of people milled inside what looked like a huge white vaulted cathedral. I mounted the steps to the main vestibule area and was pleasantly surprised to see what appeared to be a colourful tented indoor market. I spotted John who was hemmed in by three black-suited, shiny-haired Japanese men each vying for his attention. I gave him an isn't-this-amazing look when he caught me staring, and marched purposefully towards the market.

And guess what? I had such a good time I almost forgot about my hangover. It wasn't an indoor market at all, the tents were exhibition booths. Everyone wanted to give me freebies.

A couple of girls on the Fuji stand gave me a laptop bag, a sweatshirt and a fancy desktop dartboard. I know I don't have a desk but I could scratch off the logo and give the dartboard to Graeme for Christmas. I moseyed on and was immediately hijacked by a chap wearing a black T-shirt with Kodak printed boldly across his chest. He gave me a baseball cap, a dozen golf balls, a penknife, a leather handbag diary, an ashtray, a lovely big yellow teddy bear with a black eye patch and a set of coloured pencils. I now had a teddy bear and three heavy bags to carry. I was struggling but I didn't want to put any of the stuff back, so I wedged the teddy bear under my arm and looped the handles of the two heaviest bags in the cradle of my elbow and waddled on.

The throng drifted slowly towards two enormous glass doors at the rear of the building. Assuming I wouldn't be the only one desperate for a sleep, I elbowed forward to grab a seat at the back but would you believe it, it was assigned seating. I was placed at the front surrounded by my group, with John sitting directly behind me. He eyed my bags and teddy bear. He gave me a stiff grin and then buried his face in a large leather-bound folder. I sank into my chair and cast a glance around the room. The bloody place was packed.

The lights faded. There was a unified attentive hush. Three gigantic HD screens flanking the stage lit up with 'A World of Film', and then the picture shattered into about a thousand little digital cameras. A squat, barrel-chested man with a tornado of white hair wearing a crushed linen suit strode onto the stage amid riotous applause. I clapped once, lamely. He stood, hands clasped above his head, until order was restored. After about two minutes I wanted to kill him. He droned on and on and on . . .

'Environmental health imaging . . .'

'Harmonious third world relationships . . .'

'Pre-determine the needs of film makers . . .'

'Philosophical approach to innovative technological advancement . . .'

'Post production global support . . .'

'Restore and preserve Middle Eastern outlets . . .'

'Lobby Government ministers to award much needed tax concessions . . .'

'Embrace the digital revolution . . .'

I peeked under the teddy bear's eye patch to make sure he had two eyes. He did. I stifled a yawn and leafed through the handbag diary. It wasn't bad at all for a freebie. I rustled the sweatshirt from the bag and dangled it in front of me. I wasn't sure if it would fit so I might give it to Dad for Christmas. I contemplated my penknife. I've never had a penknife, why would I? It was actually a nifty little tool, there was even a nail file. I could practically give myself a professional manicure with it. I made sure all the coloured pencils were sharp. I might pop back to the Fuji stand and ask for another box, then I could give the twins one each. Becky isn't one for sharing, you see. I checked the room. Not the best light, but I might as well file my nails now. The chap on my left fidgeted annoyingly. I gave a snort of displeasure. The guy on my right started jiggling the change in his pocket. How was I supposed to concentrate?

'Mr John Jackson!' boomed and reverberated throughout the room.

A round of applause made me jump.

'. . . For unprecedented donations to charitable causes!' the troll on the stage bellowed.

My elbow missed the armrest and the penknife slashed my finger. I let out an almighty ear-splitting shriek. A cornfield-sized yellow spotlight searched the room and then homed in on John who was simultaneously wrapping a monogrammed handkerchief around my hand while giving a royal wave of acknowledgement to the clapping throng who'd taken to their feet in unified esteem. John's dove-grey head bent over my shoulder, and my face, boggle-eyed like a rabbit about to buy it on the motorway, loomed enormously on the three gigantic HD screens. I made myself crank up a smile, instead of cry, which was what I actually wanted to do because my finger was throbbing.

'Let's get you out of here,' John said indulgently, levering me by the wrist from my chair.

He confiscated my penknife, quick-stepped me to the first aid room and quickly shot back into the conference. A nurse administered antiseptic and a bandage, gave me a little something for my hangover and let me have an hour of sleep on her comfy bed. At my request, she also arranged for my bags and teddy bear to be picked up from the conference room and delivered to the main reception desk.

After I left the first aid room, I walked back into the white vaulted cathedral. It had been totally transformed and it looked amazing. Cream tented linen banners crowned with spotlights billowed from ceiling to floor. Every so often the lighting altered and the banners subtly changed colour, swamping the vestibule with a kaleidoscope of beautiful pastel shades. Delegates milled in a steady, chattering trickle from the conference suite where two rows of white-jacketed waiters lined up with trays of champagne. Free champagne? I might as well have one, I thought. It could be years before such an opportunity comes my way again.

A throng of people huddled around three huge oval tables, which were laden with a buffet of medieval banquet proportions. Each table was decorated with scattered rose petals and an elaborate ice sculpture in the shape of a movie camera. I was suddenly starving. I held my glass aloft and headed for the buffet. I was on my third butterfly prawn when John jostled alongside me.

'How's your finger, Evie?'

'Fine, yes fine, I didn't expect such a sharp blade, I—'

'You should not have been given that knife,' he interrupted, 'it's a Swiss Army blade, a multi-tool, not a toy.'

'I see. Put like that, I'm lucky not to have hurt myself.'

'Quite,' he agreed, plucking two glasses of champagne from a passing waiter.

'So, did you learn anything?' he asked in an easy tone, handing me a glass. His charcoal eyes sparkled.

'Oh yes, I did, it was very interesting,' I said, promising myself to pay attention for at least half of the afternoon session.

I ended up sleeping like a log until one of John's guys woke me up with an elbow in the ribs.

Alain jogged towards me as I gingerly descended the Convention Centre steps.

'*Chérie*, you were right, I realise it was wrong to give you marijuana. I apologise,' he said, relieving me of my bags.

To be honest, I'd already forgotten all about that. I'm forgiving by nature and not one to bear a grudge for long. Except with Rob of course, who I intend to despise and ignore until my ninety-second birthday. I gave a noble shrug.

'It's OK,' I assured him, 'forget it.'

'So, I'm forgiven?'

'Yes.' I smiled.

He looped his arm around my waist and planted a kiss on my forehead. 'Dinner tonight?' he suggested lazily.

My tummy loop-de-looped and a heated lust bubble burst in my lady bits region. My surprised eyes travelled bashfully from his handsome face to my shoes. I worried the words 'female hard-on' might have bobbed in my eyes like a slot machine roller.

'Mmmm,' I replied, rocking my teddy bear.

'Evie, there you are,' John interrupted in his usual authoritative tone.

I swooped around guiltily.

'You'll join us for dinner tonight,' he said commandingly. It wasn't a question.

'Yes, er, that would be nice,' I managed, gnashing my teeth. This guy was fast becoming a nuisance.

'Good,' he said matter-of-factly, and added, 'reserve one oval table in the hotel conservatory, eight o'clock sharp.'

I gave a tight nod.

'Thank you,' he said, mounting the steps of the coach.

I sat in the crew seat. Alain was studying the road and I was studying him. I'd wolf down dinner and meet Alain afterwards, I decided. I imagined what he'd look like naked, and I've got to say he looked pretty amazing. The muscles in his forearms rippled as he turned the wheel of the coach. He obviously liked me and my ego could do with a boost. I loved his Colin Farrell stubble and he was a great laugh. Well, at least I think he's a great laugh because I remember laughing a lot last night, and OK, I can't remember at this exact moment in time what I was laughing at, but I'm not an eejit that laughs at nothing so obviously he was entertaining. He likes a drink so we have lots in common, and of course he'd be handy to know should I decide to take up spiffing weed on a full-time basis. And he's got great legs.

Alain and I stood, partially shaded, beneath the canopied hotel entrance. A ray of sunshine penetrated the awnings, freckling the crown of his dark head. He held my shoulders.

'What time will you finish eating?' he asked. He lowered his head and swept his nose along my forehead.

'I'm not sure,' I half whispered.

He cupped and raised my face and softly nibbled my lips. My chest tightened. He slid his hands beneath my hair, and gently circled his thumbs on my neck. I felt weak with pleasure. He could have lifted me by my ears and swung me in a circle, and I'd have enjoyed it.

'*Chérie*, call me when you are finished. I will come for you ... anytime.'

I nodded, still in a pouting kissing position. 'I will,' I breathed.

Chapter forty-three

I was wearing a white backless dress, which fitted me perfectly, and as this was going to be a sitting down evening (and hopefully lying down), I wore my killer heel sandals. Walking through the lobby, I shot an irritated glance at an old dolt sitting in the corner plucking a harp to death, and made my way to the conservatory restaurant. The restaurant was a bright breezy area with palm trees, enormous terracotta pots spilling over with purple and lilac flowers and white cane furniture. The patio doors were flung open and the warm evening air carried the scent of the landscaped garden. The group were relaxing around the bar, wearing mufti shorts and polo shirts. I wondered if they hit the phones to check what everyone else was wearing before they left their rooms. John waved a welcoming hand when he saw me in the doorway.

I daydreamed through three courses. Alain is handsome and sexy and obviously fancies me, I thought. I like him, I like him a lot, and I'm single after all. *So* I'll meet him and see how things go, and if I feel like it, I'll sleep with him. I'm no nun and he's French, and French men are supposed to be really ridey, all Frenchmen say so and they can't all be lying. Yes, I'm definitely going to do it.

I shivered at the thought of taking my clothes off. I wasn't sure I wanted to because, well, he wasn't Rob. I actually felt slightly sick, sick at the thought of getting naked in front of another man. But, I thought acidly, Rob hadn't wasted any time whipping his shreddies off, the faithless slug. I swallowed a large draught of wine. Oh, for God's sake, I admonished myself. Get naked and get laid. Why am I making such a trumpet-blowing affair out of having a shag? I threw the remains of my glass down my throat. If Rob can sleep with someone else, then so can I. So that's that, tonight's the night.

I circled the rim of my empty wine glass pensively. But perhaps I should be more philosophical and ask myself if this is a revenge shag, or ... Oh, listen to me! What's a revenge shag? You'd think I was an assassin or something. I've been reading too many of those crappy magazines that Lulu brings home from the surgery. I'll do it. What's wrong with me? He looks like bloody Colin Farrell.

John rattled his fork on a glass and, with the flat of his hands on the table, stood up.

'OK team, you know why we're here. I've spent close to three million on research. I think it's safe to say we've sold to the industry but that's as a consequence of the product itself. It has nothing to do with you, my sales team.' There was a collective tight-lipped wince. 'I want this product launched to the global marketplace. You've had three months to formulate a game plan.' He slid a shrewd eye left and right. 'I want it.'

The guys looked pale and drained. No, they looked anaemic and terrified. There was an agitated stir among them as they fired each other nervous looks.

John swept his fork around the table. 'After coffee,' he said, and sat down slowly.

I stole a sideways glance at John, who was sat beside me, as he reached for the brandy. He seemed morbidly amused at the reaction to his speech. I lurched towards the wine bottle.

'So,' I ventured, 'you've spent three million. Is it an anti-ageing product? Or a slimming aid?'

I wish I hadn't bloody asked. John produced a thick swatch of what looked like brightly coloured tracing paper, explaining in complicated detail that they were samples of a revolutionary gel filter. Apparently sheets of gel are clipped to spotlights to enhance, change and neutralise the colour of the background when filming. I flipped through the swatch. The colours were beautiful. I counted nine shades of blue. I danced a sheet of the swatch around my glass and studied the wine as its colour slid from navy to indigo to sapphire.

'Nice, isn't it?' I said to no one in particular, so I shouldn't have been very surprised when no one replied.

I stopped gel dancing. I was suddenly aware of a silent and expectant awkwardness. Seventeen pairs of eyes studied the centrepiece floral arrangement. John sat ramrod straight. A muscle pulsed in his neck. There was a fair bit of spoon massaging and exaggerated napkin folding around the table. John's charcoal eyes darted left and right.

'Well?' he snapped.

I blinked and jumped.

Steve, one of the group, was sitting opposite and cleared his throat. All heads swivelled like a family of meerkats.

'John,' Steve hedged apprehensively, 'as brilliant as this gel filter is, and you know we're all incredibly proud of it, the simple truth is, it's not a multipurpose product. It has nowhere to sit outside of the media industry.' He shook his head regretfully and slid a knowing smile around the table, but there were no knowing smiles sliding back.

John stared into the middle distance. 'So,' his eyes searched the room, 'what have you come up with?' he repeated, completely dismissing what Steve had just boldly pointed out.

Steve's chin disappeared into his neck as he slunk into his chair.

John slammed a ham fist on the table.

I spilled my wine.

'Three million!' he yelled, scaring us all. 'We will sit here all night if necessary, until one of you comes up with something.'

I looked at my watch. I'm quite good at doing nothing, on account of the fact that I've spent hours and hours in the last couple of months doing exactly that. Also, my head wasn't on the block here and John doesn't shout anywhere near as loud as Nikki does, which is a minor plus. I snaked my hand around my plate and reached for a chocolate truffle.

John gripped the edge of the table, leaned forward and glowered at each of his guys murderously. 'I'm waiting for an answer,' he warned in a low no-nonsense tone.

I popped another chocolate in my mouth and checked my watch for the second time. Two minutes had passed since I'd last looked, which is bugger all if we're going to be here all night. I danced the purple filter around my glass. I suppose I could just sit and gorge on the chocolates but then, I fretted, I want to meet Alain. My sex life depended very much on me getting out of here. I sipped my drink, ate another truffle and pendulumed the green gel filter in front of the wine bottle.

'Erm,' I cleared my throat, 'does the gel stick to glass?'

Steve gave a snort of laughter. 'And what use would the spotlight be afterwards if it did?' he asked.

'I'm not thinking of spotlights, I'm thinking of windows.'

John leaned back and massaged the tablecloth absently. 'Go on, Evie,' he encouraged, tilting his head in enquiry.

I'd been thinking and before I knew it I was talking and now ...

'Evie, go on.'

I took a sip of wine. 'Well, stained glass is expensive. Very few people would consider having a stained glass window indoors. If you manufactured a compatible adhesive, you could design all sorts of DIY stained glass window kits, like flowers, landscapes or even religious scenes, and,' I ventured in a weak voice, 'I, I, um, well, I just thought . . .' I trailed off and clamped my lips together, feeling suddenly stupid.

John squeezed his bottom lip between his forefinger and thumb. 'Does the gel stick to glass?' he punctuated stiffly to the ceiling.

There was an uncertain silence.

'Does it?' he asked the ceiling again.

'It should do,' one of the guys confirmed quietly.

There was a flurry of nervous bum shuffling.

John rapped his fingers on the table. 'Will someone explain to me why I pay you lot a hundred grand a year, when none of you know what a stained glass window is?'

I blanched.

His eyes scanned the room. 'Get out of my sight!'

They all beetled off. I tried to follow but John lurched forward, grabbed my wrist and pulled me back. He made me draw windows on napkins until two o'clock in the morning. I was exhausted. I also had three missed calls from Alain. I texted him to apologise and to tell him that I'd only just finished dinner. As I punched at my phone I experienced a stab of something. It wasn't fear or apprehension. It was a kind of panicky loneliness, and I knew that being with Alain wouldn't take the loneliness away. I was also overcome by a horrible nauseousness but that had nothing to do with Rob. It was because I'd eaten a whole plate of truffles. I felt a rush of pure misery and bitterness and rage and everything except lust and so, yellow belly that I am, after I had sent the text, I switched off my phone.

★

371

Alain arrived at the hotel at noon to drive us to the airport. He tossed the luggage into the coach carelessly.

'*Chérie*, come back to Nice, visit me,' he pleaded urgently. 'Or I can visit you?'

'Erm, yes, that would be lovely. I'm busy until Christmas but you could visit me in London in January,' I heard myself offer.

He circled my waist and spun me around.

'January it is,' he affirmed solidly. 'I would like to get to know you better.'

The bloody flight was delayed two hours. I sat in the departures area brutalising a copy of *Elle* magazine. Nothing pisses me off more than delayed flights.

'Do you mind if I join you?' John asked.

I flapped a hand at the empty chair next to mine. 'By all means,' I said.

'A bottle of Chablis,' he announced, placing an ice bucket on the table.

I held my hands up. 'No more drawing on napkins or talking about windows?' I warned.

His warm eyes crinkled with mirth. 'I promise,' he said, smiling.

I toasted my glass haphazardly as we started on our second bottle, after I'd sponged most of the first one. 'Are you married?' I asked, flopping one leg aimlessly over the other.

'Yes,' he said with a reflective nod.

'Are you faithful to your wife?'

He looked taken aback. 'Yes,' he retorted staunchly, as liars often do.

On the flight, I sat next to John. I was now on the gin.

'And he shagged her . . .' Snivel.

'Curly perm, orange lipstick . . .' Sob.

'And I did everything for him . . .' Snuffle.

'Not had sex for nearly two months. I took my belly bar out once and in two days the hole closed up.' I glanced at my crotch worriedly. 'You don't think, do you . . .' Blubber, blubber.

'Flatmate goes at it like a steam train and I'm so jealous, and she has no respect, she knows I'm in . . .' Howl.

'And I had the chance to shag Alain but you and your stupid gel filters put the lid on that . . .' Sniff, sniff, sniff.

John handed our empty glasses to the stewardess. 'Evie, give me your card.'

'What card? Cards? He took all my credit and store cards, the bastard!' I wailed. 'And he took all my money and left me with a *paid* overdraft, and he . . .'

I was on a roll now. I sniffed and wiped my nose with the back of my hand.

'Your business card,' John interrupted.

I plucked his fancy pen from his breast pocket and scribbled my name, address and number on the airline sick bag.

'Here,' I said, and thrust it at him.

He stabbed at his BlackBerry. 'One of my chauffeurs will meet you at Heathrow and drive you home. I'll see you to the car personally. And Evie, Alain was not for you. A gentleman does not ply a lady with alcohol and drugs, and—'

'How did you know that?'

He eyed me shrewdly. 'My French is as good as your own.'

I sniffed.

Chapter Forty-four

I was pottering around my bedroom at home. I'd been on the phone to Tina for twenty minutes.

'Be honest, you did, didn't you? You slept with him?' she said.

I sighed, exasperated. 'No. For the tenth time, I didn't,' I told her, affronted.

'You did,' she said, sure of herself.

'I didn't.'

She chuckled. 'You can tell me. I'll take it to the grave.'

I eyed my phone doubtfully.

'So why would John Jackson's PA call this office and book you for Dublin in February and Marrakech in April next year, and invite you and a guest, who'd better be me, to a black tie piss-up at the Dorchester next week?'

'I have no idea.'

'He's got a helicopter and a jet and a private island and—'

'And a wife,' I snapped.

'You will take me, won't you? I kept my promise. Helen's drafted to the Isle of Wight until the end of January. She'll look like Edward Scissorhands' granny by Christmas, what with the wind and that perm of hers.'

'Of course I'll take you.'

I stared at my bum in the mirror and saw that I had a new dimple on each cheek. I'll check the Champneys website, and perhaps treat myself to a spa weekend. I can afford it, and—

'Evie,' Tina said, her tone suddenly serious.

'What?'

'Rob's been ringing me.'

She had my attention now.

'He wants to know how you are, where you are, what you're up to.' She faltered. 'I've got to say I'm kind of melting towards him. Why don't you give him a call?'

My tummy cramped the way it always did when Rob's name was mentioned.

'I've got nothing to say to him,' I retorted indifferently. 'Nothing.'

She sighed. 'Fair enough. I tried,' she said glumly, then rushed on. 'Whilst I've got you on the phone, Insignia take over a hotel in Aviemore in the Scottish Highlands for four days at New Year. D'you fancy working? It's a bit of a blast with bagpipes and men in skirts.'

I gave my bum dimple an agitated tap. 'Sure, I'm spending Christmas with Lexy. I'll have fallen out with her by New Year's Eve,' I told her, not entirely joking.

'Fabulous, I'll sign you up for it. Right, next Friday, the Dorchester, seven o'clock, meet in the lobby. It's the Jackson Corporation Christmas Party. I'm glad you invited me because I've already broadcast to the building that I'm going. Even our MD is jealous. Oh, and I've bought a dress.'

'I'll be there,' I said, realising that I was actually looking forward to going out for the first time in months.

It was a cold but sunny December day. I felt a huge swell of happiness as I ducked the traffic while crossing the road to Tooting

Broadway tube station. I was going shopping, not I–don't–know–what–I–need–until–I–see–it shopping because I had put that frivolous, irresponsible attitude to spending behind me. I was going Christmas shopping. I'd made a list. I was going to be fastidiously disciplined and buy only what I needed. I was heading for Knightsbridge because if you couldn't buy it in Knightsbridge then it didn't exist. And I had over eight grand in the bank, so money was no object.

In Harrods, I had a St Tropez tan treatment. Frankly, I wonder why it hadn't occurred to me to have one before because I've been looking positively anaemic lately. I bought a black faux fur hip-length jacket, a matching Cossack hat and a pair of black knee-high boots with fur on the inside as well as the outside because I'm going to arctic Scotland. As I'd already spent over a grand, I also got a pair of ski gloves at forty per cent off and two fur hairbands for the price of one. I'll look *fantastic* on the slopes, assuming I go on the slopes, but slopes apart, I don't want to freeze.

I opened a Harrods Store Account because it would have been reckless not to as they have a points-mean-prizes system. To make sure that it worked, I bought a red Vera Wang evening dress to wear to John Jackson's bash, which was an essential purchase. I can't go looking like a tavern wench from *Oliver Twist*, can I? I also treated myself to a stunning blue Louis Vuitton Monogram Vernis Alma MM bag, which was my one *tiny* extravagance. I don't want to talk about how much it cost because I feel a bit sick when I think about it, but then I don't smoke, do I? And I save a fortune by not smoking.

I lurched off the top of the escalator, jackknifing back to read a poster that was promoting their in-store hairdresser. For one day only, and today just happens to be the day, I could have a full set of hair extensions for £650 instead of £750. There is a God! Perhaps he's a hairdresser. I elbowed my way through the irritating melee of Christmas shoppers and within twenty minutes I was sitting comfortably, sipping a frothy latte and leafing through a hair colour chart while chatting to my consultant.

My extensions are *amazing*. I don't want to boast, but I've now got Cheryl Cole hair. It's a glossy chocolate colour with a discreet whisper of auburn, and it bounces down way past my bra strap. Worth every penny and every minute of the four hours I spent in the hairdresser's. Bye-bye bald patch.

I sprinted through ladies' fashions, seesawing my head like some show-off model in a shampoo advert. I only had half an hour left to do my Christmas shopping. I cannoned around the store, racing up and down escalators and stopping every now and then to admire myself in a mirror or display-cabinet or shiny elevator door or in anything where the tiniest glimmer of my hair was evident. Eventually I stood panting and breathless in the Customer Services department, ticking things off my list: Crème de la Mer and a £50 voucher for both Lexy and Lulu; a rather posh free-standing cash register for each of the twins; a golf bag, shirt and tie for Graeme; aftershave for Nikki; and a deluxe hamper was on its way to Australia for Mum and Dad. Obviously I couldn't be expected to hoof it on the tube with my shopping, so the whole shebang is being delivered next week. Wrapped.

Lulu oohed and aaahed when she saw my hair, and when I walked into the bar, Nikki whistled. So did Costas and Pepi, which surprised me because I've reduced my shifts to three days a week so they haven't been speaking to me. Even though the Christmas rush was unrelenting, Nikki didn't seem to mind. He's drafted in a few more lunatic family members to help spread the shifts across the working week and give us all a bit of breathing space.

Chapter forty-five

I don't know where the time has gone. Unbelievably, it's already the night of John Jackson's bash and there are only six days until Christmas.

I caught sight of myself in the mirror in the lobby of the Dorchester Hotel. My hair was wavy, moussed and tousled with ruby crystal hair gems dotted randomly. I was wearing red lipstick, black kohl eyeliner, false eyelashes and charcoal eye shadow that gave my blue eyes a glow-in-the-dark effect. My red Vera Wang dress looked stunning, swirling gracefully around my ankles. I tightened my grip on my jewelled clutch bag and searched the lobby for Tina.

There was an urgent grip on my arm. 'I can't believe it, I can't believe we're here,' Tina said excitedly, spinning me around. 'You look fantastic.'

'So do you,' I complimented, and she did.

Her long platinum hair framed her heart-shaped face, and her large brown eyes, which were underscored with lilac glitter, flashed with anticipation. She wore a lavender sheath dress and a pair of multi-storey gold sandals.

'Can you walk in those?' I asked, eyeing her feet doubtfully.

She made a lemon-sucking face. 'Good God, no,' she admitted, gripping my arm for balance. 'Amazing, aren't they?'

I peered at her seamless bum. 'Are you wearing a thong?'

'No.' She smoothed her hand over her hip. 'I'm going commando.' She tugged me along the floor. 'Let's go to the ballroom. I cannot tell you how much I've been looking forward to this. John Jackson's seriously minted, but it's not him I'm after. I'd never shag anyone over fifty-five, they could die on you.' She shook her head and shuddered. 'I want one of those hundred grand a year salesmen you told me about.'

The ballroom was enormous, with gigantic glittering chandeliers and a polished wooden floor. The walls were festooned with silver and white tinfoily stuff, and on every table stood a tall slim vase, spilling over with sprayed silver flowers. A twinkling twenty-foot Christmas tree towered in one corner of the room and a huge oval buffet table, garlanded with holly and ivy, dominated the other. The room was buzzing, and although we were on time, it looked like we were the last to arrive. Tina stood wide-eyed and open-jawed. She plucked two glasses of champagne from the tray of a passing waiter.

'Get your own,' she said to my outstretched hand. 'These are for me.' She searched the room, sipping pensively. 'And Evie, don't get hammered and expect me to take you home, and don't leave me on my own because I don't know anyone, do I? And don't eat, because this dress is too tight as it is so obviously I can't eat, and—'

John Jackson bent his dove-grey head to kiss my cheek. 'Evie, it's a delight to see you,' he said in that deep grainy voice of his.

I introduced Tina, who stared reverentially.

He gave her a welcoming nod and led us both slowly by the arm towards the bar. 'There is someone I'd like you to meet,' he whispered conspiratorially. 'And Evie, it seems that your stained

379

glass windows might be a *go*. My accounts department will contact you after Christmas. I owe you a designer's consultancy fee.'

I felt a flutter of pride. Me, a designer!

He tilted his head in enquiry. 'I had my secretary call your office. You will come to Dublin and Marrakech next year, won't you?'

'Yes, of course.'

'Good girl.' He clicked his fingers aloft. 'Charles!' he shouted to a Savile Row jacket.

A tall thirty-something man with blond hair, warm blue eyes and a soft curved smile disentangled himself from three almost identical Jane Norman dresses and walked towards us.

'Evie,' John said loudly, 'I'd like to introduce you to my godson, Charles. I'm sure you two will get along famously.'

And we did. Charles was a tad stiff and formal and serious, but he was also friendly, gentlemanly and witty. We didn't get to chat for long though because the three Jane Normans crashed between Tina and me to take him back after about fifteen minutes. The party was in full swing by that point. The band played a rendition of Beatles tracks to a packed, gyrating dance floor. Streamers and party poppers littered the decimated buffet table and the champagne top-up service was now a do-it-yourself free for all, with bottles scattered all over the place.

'I can't believe *that's* John Jackson,' Tina said, toasting John's back incredulously. 'He's gorgeous. I expected a squat ugly little troll.'

I gave John an assessing glance. He is a very attractive man, I thought, and I'm sure that the Ivana Trump lookalike hanging off his arm, who I'm also sure is *not* his wife, would agree.

'This is amazing. I don't want the night to end,' Tina said dreamily. 'I'll get us a bottle of champagne of our own,' she said, lurching off to the bar.

★

Ten minutes later, 'I've got to go,' Tina said quickly, scrambling on the floor by my feet for her bag.

I frowned. 'Why?' I asked.

'I'm, I'm ill.' She clutched her tummy.

'Ill?'

'Yes.'

'I'll come with you,' I offered.

'No no, don't,' she insisted, hastily.

I looked around the room. 'Why would I want to stay here on my own?'

Tina blushed. 'Yes, you must, must stay. It would be rude, rude to leave,' she retorted, eyes wide and reassuring.

A light went on in my head. 'You've met someone, haven't you?' I hissed. 'And you're dumping me?'

'Admit it, you'd do the same if you weren't clinically depressed.' With that, she pivoted, hoisted her lilac sheath and penguined off across the dance floor.

I tossed my already swishy hair. I was just deciding what to do next, when ...

'All alone?'

I turned and looked straight into Charles's kind blue eyes. 'It would seem so,' I replied.

'Have you eaten?' he asked. His gaze lingered expectantly.

'No, actually I haven't,' I told him.

'Can I take you for a late supper?'

I slid a hungry glance at the emaciated buffet table. 'Yes, that would be lovely.'

He laughed and curled his arm around my shoulder. 'Shall we go?'

Chapter Forty-six

Charles took me to the Theo Randall restaurant in the Inter-continental Hotel. It was soooooo posh.

The maitre d' appeared from behind a plant. I suspect he'd been hiding, waiting.

'Your usual, m'lord?' he asked Charles austerely, as if address-ing a life or death situation.

Did he say m'lord, as in, my lord? Surely not.

'Yes, thank you,' Charles replied, giving him a hearty hand-shake. 'Good man,' he added.

I cruised behind the maitre d' and Charles cruised behind me. The maitre d' halted abruptly, clicked his heels and his arm shot out as he gestured towards an alcove table. I half expected him to shout 'tada!' I gave my Vera Wang a theatrical kicky swish and swooped into my seat.

'Champagne please, Alistair,' Charles said to the maitre d', who glided off in an invisible-broomstick-wedged-up-his-arse kind of way.

'This is very nice,' I said gravely, matching the maitre d's tone.

'Evie, if you'd rather go somewhere else, please say.'

Over my dead body, I thought. Who else do I know who is likely to bring me here? I gave a pop-eyed smile. 'Charles,'

I gushed, flapping a hand randomly, 'this is perfect, just perfect.'

The champagne arrived. We drank it, laughed, ordered another bottle and drank that too. We took the piss out of 'Uncle John', ate steak and fancy potatoes, and the maitre d' called Charles m'lord again. I roared, slapped the table a couple of times and told him I was a duchess. When he asked me what my full title was, I said I was the Duchess of Tooting, formerly the Duchess of Wandsworth, but that I'd divorced the Duke and we had divided our estate so I only had the Tooting end of Wandsworth left. I doubled over laughing because I was pissed and there's nothing better than my own jokes when I'm hammered. Charles howled as well and I asked him why the maitre d' called him m'lord, and I shrieked when he told me, straight faced, that his full name was Charles Edward Harold Frederick Harry William, Lord Brockhurst. He asked me what was so funny about that and I stopped laughing because, through the haze of champagne, it suddenly struck me that he wasn't joking.

'Evie, I don't want to sound presumptuous, but would you like to come back to my place for coffee?'

A lord! My seat rattled off the wall as I bent to pick up my bag, and three seconds later I was on my toes.

'Love to,' I said, bag clamped possessively to my chest and suddenly sober, well soberish. 'I thought you'd never ask.'

His place just happened to be a penthouse apartment on the Embankment, with a smart looking flunkey manning the security desk. A granite-topped table with an enormous crystal vase full of birds of paradise and scented lilies stood proudly beside his front door. I had a fleeting grim apparition of our two wheelie bins.

'Open,' he said to a voice-sensitive wall-mounted entry system. And, hey presto, no fighting with a bent key for him.

Hand on the small of my back, he steered me through the marble-floored hallway. Dark green walls lined with ornate mounted paintings of ugly, poker-faced seventeenth- and eighteenth-century bleary-eyed ghouls adorned the walls.

'My ancestors,' Charles said proudly, sweeping an arm at the canvases. 'Can you see the likeness?' he asked, profiling himself against the wall.

If I could, I thought, I wouldn't be here, lord or no lord.

'Yes,' I enthused. 'It's the bone structure.'

He nodded, delighted. 'Yes, you're right,' he agreed, appraising a horsey old crone in a green top hat.

He led me into the lounge. Pictures of more grim-looking critters, together with about ten paintings of the same scruffy hairy greyhound, cluttered mahogany-panelled walls. The curtains were a rich Edwardian red and Persian rugs, also in red, were strewn across a highly polished wooden floor. Two enormous russet leather sofas sat either side of a low-level dark wood coffee table that was littered with leather-bound antique books, an array of dust-collecting crystal ornaments and about twenty copies of the *Financial Times*.

'Champagne?' he asked.

I nodded numbly. I'd have to have a car boot sale if I moved in here, I thought.

I adjusted my spaghetti straps, which had slipped from my shoulders, and walked to the window. I gasped. The view was magnificent. To the right stood the London Eye, motionless and imposing. Buses and taxis zoomed like buzzing fireflies across Westminster Bridge and a lone slim barge sliced the dark, still water of the Thames. To the right loomed the impressive illuminated dome of St Paul's Cathedral, silhouetted against a navy sky sprinkled with stars. It was all so serene and calming. I jumped when my phone buzzed.

I think I'm in love. Teen xx

Charles and I relaxed on the sofa and he felt it appropriate to tell me exactly how the land lay, which I suppose was pretty decent of him. He was a thirty-four-year-old merchant banker and had two children, aged two and five, who lived with their mother on his estate in Bedfordshire. He and his wife had been separated for eight months. Apparently she has a chemical dependency and, he suspects, a girlfriend.

He's nice, and I know nice is not handsome or horny or charismatic, but that's honestly how I'd describe him. I felt no ripple of excitement, no tummy flutters, no hot flushes, no flicker in the groin and no bouncing lust bubble. He placed his hand over mine. It wasn't a proper man's hand, I noted. It wasn't a strong hand, like Rob's, or a sturdy hand covered with a smattering of dark hair, like Alain's. It was a soft hand with long slim fingers, like, well, like ET.

'Let's get you home, shall we,' he said lightly.

Did he say get me home? Here I am dolled up to the nines and he's not even going to try it on? OK, fair enough, I don't fancy him but it still would've been nice to be appreciated, to be made to feel attractive and wanted. And it would have been damned nice to have had the opportunity to turn him down. Had I just been dumped? I stood up quickly.

Charles looked at me sadly. 'You've been preoccupied, Evie,' he said with a sigh. 'All evening.'

'Have I?' I asked, feeling suddenly guilty.

He nodded. 'Yes, I've asked you three times if you'd like another drink.'

I glanced wearily around his opulent lounge. 'I'm sorry, Charles,' I shook my head. 'I'm tired, that's all.'

Getting home meant a ride in a plush custom-built Bentley that was piloted by a chauffeur called Martin. It was marvellous. I got a second wind and I even went as far as to hold Charles's hand. I could buy him a pair of thick black leather gloves in the Harrods sale, I mused. Yes, that might make his hands look better. And I could buy him a jacket with shoulder pads, he's a bit on the thin side, and I could suggest he joins a gym, and look into cosmetic surgery for men . . .

Chapter forty-seven

'I've looked him up on the net. Lord Brockhurst is the thirty-ninth richest man in the whole country and you're talking about lust bubbles not bursting!' Lulu shrieked. She slumped onto the sofa, and threw an exasperated elbow across her eyes. 'You're not being fair, he's got a country pad. I've always wanted an excuse to buy a pair of wellies and the twins could have had a pony each. You might have ended up in *OK!* or *Hello!* magazine and if you married him, you'd be a lady.' She lit a cigarette. 'Evie,' she sighed forlornly, slitting her eyes against the smoke. 'Are you expecting a roll of the drums to herald the removal of your knickers? Tell me, are you? Trust me, once you pass the starting line it really doesn't matter who you're shagging.'

There was a beat of silence.

'You,' she said, leaping to her feet and pointing her fag accusingly, 'are wasting your life away.' She wiped her brow with the back of her hand and paced the lounge.

'He has hands like ET,' I said flatly.

She rounded on me. 'So what? So bloody what? In fact, who cares if he *is* ET, he's minted and titled.' She flopped heavily into the armchair.

We stared at each other testily.

'Well, can I have him?' she asked, twirling a strand of long blonde hair pensively.

'You've got Vic,' I snapped, indignant.

'Can I have him?' she yelled.

'Have him if you want him!' I yelled back.

She waved her fag aloft. 'Do you have his number?'

'I do, but I thought you loved Vic?'

'I do love Vic, but he's in South Africa for Christmas.'

'So what?'

She jumped to her feet. Again. 'How am I supposed to love him if he's not even here?'

Bar Thea was packed. I'd worked three shifts this week. I was knackered and I wasn't talking to Nikki. Tonight should have been my night off but Nikki had been calling me all day. I knew he'd wanted me to work so, cleverly, I hadn't answered my phone. At six o'clock the doorbell had rung and I'd peered between the lounge curtains in case it was him. I'd been surprised to see an adorable looking white-haired old lady so I'd answered the door. Nikki had leaped out from behind the wall, lassoed me around the neck with his meaty big arm, paid the deceitful old crone a tenner for her trouble, and threatened to drag me across the Broadway in my pyjamas if I didn't get dressed and come over to help him. So here I am.

We had a table of twelve girls. They were hammered and loud and getting on my nerves. If they'd pay their bill and leave, I could go home. I ambled into the now dark and empty kitchen where my phone was on charge. I had a missed call from Charles, it was the third time he'd rung. I felt guilty. I slid down the wall and sat on the tiled floor. I'd been avoiding him and I knew it wasn't fair so I decided to call him back.

He picked up on the first ring and I poured my heart out. I

told him how much I'd loved Rob, how he'd hurt me and that I was finding it difficult to move on. I thanked him for a lovely evening and told him that I would love to see him again socially, but it was only fair he knew how I felt. He explained that although he was separated from his wife, for the sake of the children they would be spending Christmas together at his estate as a family, so why didn't we catch up in January. That sounded good to me. I didn't mention Lulu, I wouldn't wish her on the Devil himself, but oddly Charles did. They'd met briefly the night of John's party. She'd opened the door when her flash car antenna had picked up the Bentley's signal.

'Send my best to your delightful flatmate,' he said.

The table of twelve had thinned out by the time I came out of the kitchen. There were only four die-hards left. Nikki stood by the till, cashing up. He jerked his head towards the door.

'Evie, you go, I'll finish here.' His eyes flashed mischievously. 'And thanks for coming in.' He walked towards me, carrying my coat, and threw it across my shoulders. He tugged me towards him. 'I eavesdropped on your phone call.' Chocolate eyes held mine. 'You need a holiday.'

I nodded. 'I do,' I agreed.

'I'm going to Greece in January with my mum and dad for a family wedding. Come with us.' He tucked a loose strand of hair behind my ear. 'My mum would love you to come.' His face broke into a smile. 'And so would I.'

There was a stretched silence. He was still tugging on my lapels while his chin explored my forehead.

'OK, I will,' I said assertively, surprising us both. 'Why not?'

'Brilliant,' he beamed. 'We'll book flights after New Year.' He buttoned my coat and then turned me towards the door. 'OK, off you go.'

Crossing the road, I realised I'd left my phone and charger in the kitchen and so I doubled back to the bar. Three girls were swaying to standing, toasting each other boozily. It was with a certain amount of inevitability that I watched one lurch towards her friend and go flying over the table. The other two girls shrieked with laughter. I sidestepped past them and, arm outstretched, slapped the flat of my hand on the kitchen door.

I felt a bolt of shock. My heart raced and my jaw dropped. I froze, transfixed, and stared at the sight of Nikki's bare bum as he thrust back and forth between a pair of legs that were hanging like a couple of dead ferrets over the edge of the buffet counter. The swing door rattled behind me. Nikki's head spun around, our eyes locked, my face burned and his bum halted.

'Erm, sorry,' I flustered, yanking my charger from the wall and throttling backwards.

I woke Lulu up when I got home and told her what had happened. She tweaked her Zorro mask and sniggered sleepily. 'Hopefully that'll get your starter motor working,' she said.

I twanged her mask.

'Is Nikki's arse the same colour as the rest of him?' she bellowed as I closed her bedroom door.

The following day, as I loaded Christmas presents into the car ready to go to Lexy's, Nikki sidled up beside me.

'Evie, I'm, well I'm . . .' He trailed off.

I smacked gloved hands together, enjoying his discomfort. 'You're what?' I asked. 'Horny, tired or, no don't tell me, you're itchy?'

He sighed. 'Sorry,' he said. 'I'm sorry, I am really sorry,' he offered miserably.

I smiled at his downcast eyes.

He reached over and pushed Graeme's golf bag further into the boot of the car. 'She, well, she . . .' he stuttered, shamefaced.

'Nik, forget it. It's your bar and your kitchen,' I said with feigned politeness, 'and your ... your bare bum,' I managed, before bending double and laughing hysterically.

He jammed his hands deep in the pockets of his navy mohair donkey jacket. 'Shut up, it's not funny,' he snapped. 'Apologising doesn't come easy for me.'

'It's not a Greek man thing to do, is it, Nik?'

His mouth twitched as he suppressed a smile.

I leaned against the car, arms folded. 'Will you be seeing her again?'

He gave me an incredulous stare. 'I've no idea,' he replied blankly, as though I'd just asked him to explain the evolution of man.

'I was going to pop over to the bar anyway. You've saved me a walk,' I said.

He ran his fingers through his hair.

'To give you your Christmas present,' I told him.

'You bought *me* a present?' he asked, surprised.

'I did,' I said, jiggling a Harrods bag.

'But I didn't get you anything.'

'It's Christmas Eve, you've still got time,' I joked.

He took the bag from my outstretched hand. 'What is it?'

'Aftershave. It cost me forty-five quid.'

His broad shoulders shook as he chuckled. 'When I asked you what it was, I didn't expect you to actually tell me.'

I gave a nonchalant shrug. 'You shouldn't have asked then, should you?'

'When do you get back from your sister's?'

'I'm coming back on the twenty-eighth and I go to Scotland on the twenty-ninth.'

He gave me a sorrowful smile. 'I won't see you until after New Year. I go skiing on the twenty-sixth.'

There was a moment's silence.

'Come here,' he said, hugging me to him. 'When I get back, I'll take you shopping. You can choose your own present,' he whispered into my hair.

'It's a date,' I said, 'we'll go to the Sales.'

'Where's Lulu for Christmas?' he asked, pulling back.

'Her mum's.'

He opened the driver's door. 'Are you still up for the Big Greek Wedding?' he asked.

'Definitely. And Nik,' I said in a warning tone, 'I'm telling your mum.'

'Telling her what?'

'That you were shagging on the buffet table in the kitchen and that I've seen your bum,' I said, sliding into the driving seat.

His eyes grew wide. 'You dare!'

Chapter forty-eight

I tiptoed into the twins' bedroom by the amber glow of a ceramic teddy bear lamp, to give them a good night kiss. Lauren was asleep. She looked so innocent and tranquil. Her cute button nose twitched as she snored softly.

'Am awake,' Becky grumbled, twisting beneath the quilt.

I bent my head to hers. 'If Santa finds you awake he won't leave presents,' I whispered, so as not to wake Lauren.

'I know.' She burrowed her little hand beneath the pillow. 'Have this,' she said, arm outstretched.

'What is it?' I asked.

She shook her blonde head robustly. 'I don't like,' she said, slapping three mushy, half-eaten chocolates in my palm.

'I'll throw them out then, shall I?'

'You can eat them,' she offered, generously.

The twins woke up at five o'clock on Christmas day. OK, I thought grimly, this is obviously what you do with kids. You get up at sparrow's fart and run around shouting, 'He's been, he's been' because that's what everyone else in the house was doing. So I joined in even though I was knackered, which was a mistake because I stayed knackered all day.

Just before lunch, Graeme tripped down the last two stairs, landing on a scooter Becky had left in the hallway. He nosedived towards the front door, wobbled off the scooter, slid on an apple core and smashed his head on the hat stand. Complaining of dizziness, he staggered into the downstairs toilet and vomited and then, in sympathy, Lexy vomited as well, which kind of dampened my appetite. But there was worse to come. Graeme's mother had bought the kids a karaoke machine *each*. I am never speaking to her again. What a wicked spiteful thing to do. I couldn't bring myself to talk to her when she rang to wish us a Merry Christmas.

'Tell her I hate her!' I yelled, with my head under the cushion where I'd been writhing in torment for what seemed like for ever. No one in our family can sing and as if that's not bad enough, the twins can't read either so they were making up their own words. It was hell on earth.

After lunch, I lay on the sofa with my Christmas hat on, whilst Becky sold me the contents of my handbag. She rang everything through on her Harrods checkout machine, which I have to confess was perhaps not my wisest purchase. I eyed her murderously. We'd been at it since six o'clock and it was now eight-thirty. The cash register flashed and beeped as she swiped the plastic credit card on the key pad.

'What time does your shop close?' I asked, with a sigh of impatience.

'I'm open all night,' she told me. 'I'm a corner shop.' She chewed her bottom lip. 'You owe me ten pounds for the make-up.'

'But it's *my* make-up,' I pointed out.

'But it's *my* shop,' she replied tartly, fists on hips.

'I'm not paying a tenner for my own make-up.' My empty wine glass dangled limply from my hand. 'Can you pass me the remote control,' I asked, jerking my head towards the coffee table, 'and the Milk Tray?'

'Will you pay me?'

'No.'

She chewed the sleeve of her Barbie dressing gown thoughtfully. 'Why should I?' she asked.

'Because I'll buy you rubbish presents for your birthday if you don't,' I threatened.

'OK,' she agreed.

I felt a disproportionate rush of excitement when Lexy finally shouted, 'Bedtime, girlies,' but it was short-lived because when I eventually crawled up to bed myself, the twins were in it. And they were awake.

'We've waited for you, we'll cuddle,' Becky suggested. 'You can be the middle one.'

'Thanks,' I said, trying for enthusiasm and crawling between them.

Lauren snuggled into the crook of my neck, with a curled up fist clutching the strap of my top. Becky placed her tiny hand on my cheek and burrowed her nose in my ear. I hugged them to me, gently stroking their velvety hair and kissing them. They smelled of talcum powder and shampoo. I darted a glance at the clock. Midnight, what a day. Still, it had been a family day and that's what life is all about, family. I felt a little tickle travel the length of my calf and scratched it with my toe. When the twins are asleep, I adore them. It's when they're awake that they annoy the living daylights out of me, but here in bed it's nice. More than nice, it's cosy and comfortable.

'Nanty, can you move over because my gerbils have jumped out of my pyjama pocket,' Becky said.

They're good kids really, I thought. I felt a prick and a scratch on my thigh.

'What?' I shrieked in a delayed flash of genius. 'You mean there are two gerbils in the bed?'

I threw back the quilt, scrambled over Lauren and landed on the floor with a thud. It took Lexy and me half an hour, with the hindrance of the twins, to find the gerbils and put them back in their cage. Graeme feigned sleep. The bedroom looked liked a SWAT team of ten had just left after a warrant search.

On Boxing Day, I slept until noon. It wasn't so much that the twins let me sleep, it was more a case of them not being able to wake me up. I was blissfully unconscious.

'They've been as good as gold,' my sister said, handing me a cup of coffee. 'They've been playing quietly on the bed beside you.'

Consequently I had three gummy bears and a strawberry lolly stuck and matted in my hair extensions. There was also a wash-off tattoo of a butterfly on my forehead.

Lexy made a turkey stew for dinner which turned out to be a bit of a disaster. Apparently, while rifling in the greenhouse she'd mistaken daffodil bulbs for shallots and damn well nearly poisoned us all. Luckily it was only Graeme who tasted the stew, so he was the only one with the galloping trots, which did little to improve his mood as he still had an ice pack attached to the lump on his forehead.

On the twenty-seventh I didn't bother to shower or dress because no one else did. The house looked like a Beirut bomb site, with the lounge being the epicentre of the strike. For lack of anything else to do, I was pissed by eight o'clock and in danger of becoming unhinged.

'Is this a one-channel telly?' I yelled, toasting my gin haphazardly. 'Because unless I'm mistaken, football has been on since I got here three days ago.'

Graeme gave me a jaded glance. Christmas had hit him hard. 'It's the Chelsea Channel,' he said flatly.

I was about to tell him what I thought of the bloody Chelsea Channel when he groaned, clutched his tummy, leaped to his feet and shot out the lounge door. I tied my dressing gown belt and, glass in hand, staggered into the kitchen. The twins lay on top of the kitchen table fiddling studiously with the knobs on their karaoke machines. I felt a surge of self-gratification because I knew the batteries were hidden in the bread bin behind the cream crackers.

'Don't cook,' I said to Lexy, cramming a handful of Thai Sweet Chilli Sensations in my mouth, 'because our food taster is green and lucky to be alive and we'd have to chance it ourselves and I'm not *that* hungry.'

She stood at the Aga, empty sherry glass balanced in folded arms.

'It's been fantastic having you here. We've had a great time, haven't we?' she said dreamily.

For a minute, I was silenced. I couldn't decide whether she was taking the piss or not.

Her already wide grin widened.

'Yes,' I heard myself say.

I arrived home in the early evening on the twenty-eighth to prepare for my trip to Scotland. As I kicked my overnight bag into the bedroom I felt my spirits lift. I had a huge smile on my face. I'm home, and believe me that's a lot to smile about. I needed a recovery drink. I walked briskly down the hallway to the kitchen, swinging my elbows. I even managed a whistle. I wouldn't visit my sister again until February, I decided. I'd be over the shock of Christmas by then.

I burst into the kitchen. My jaw dropped, blood flooded my

cheeks and I felt a dart of breathlessness because there, to my horrified astonishment, wearing naught but a pair of boxers and a mortified half-smile, stood Charles.

'What are you doing here?' I asked, sounding stupid. It was obvious what he was doing here.

He looked like a startled doe.

'Hulloooooo.' Lulu's penetrating yodel made us both jump. She breezed into the kitchen, giving me a welcoming hug and a couple of air kisses. 'Darling, you're home,' she gushed, clutching my bewildered shoulders. 'I thought you were coming back tomorrow.'

Darling?

She wore a floor-length Agent Provocateur pink silk dressing gown and a pair of furry black mules. She slid an arm around Charles's waist, laid her head on his shoulder and placed her palm on his chest. She kicked a leg through the folds of her dressing gown and toed Charles's shin with a furry mule.

'No, I'm going to Scotland tomorrow,' I managed, lurching forward to bury my head in the fridge so that I could find the wine.

'We're going out for dinner. Would you like to join us?' Lulu asked in a Marilyn Monroe-esque pouty voice.

'Er no, I've got to pack.' I poured myself a glass of wine. 'I'll leave you to it,' I said, addressing Charles.

'Yes, yes,' Charles replied with a stiff cough.

I scurried down the hallway, shut myself in my bedroom and texted Lulu.

Me: What u doin?

Lulu: You said I cud have him!

Me: You can but what about Vic?

Lulu: Told u he's in Africa!

Me: D'you like Charles?
Lulu: His car is a better ride than him.
Me: Is that a no?
Lulu: I cud always have affairs.

Chapter forty-nine

I peered out of the window as the plane descended towards Inverness Airport. Snowy mountains, fir trees and houses came into view. Fluffy mounds of fresh white snow lined the runway and an enormous snowman, about twenty feet in height, stood commandingly beside the entrance to the arrivals hall.

Seized by a rush of excitement, I clutched my Cossack hat to my chest. It was sooooo Christmassy and Wonderlandish. And then I felt a lick of loneliness because I was on my own. I looked out at the whirl of falling snow. I'd make the most of it, I determined. I'm going to be with over three hundred people, I'll hardly be on my own at all.

The cab from the airport swooped and honked around hairpin bends through a leafy snow-covered forest. In a spurt of eagerness, I stuck my head out of the window to better appreciate the stunning views and crisp Highland air. My hair whipped around my head, slapping me hard across the face and making my nostrils sting and my eyes water, and when I accidentally breathed in, I suffered some sort of deadly burning throat and chest seizure. I dived back inside the cab. It was arctic! Sniffing and massaging my red nose, I wondered how many Scottish people died from sticking their heads out of car windows every year.

The cab crunched onto a snow-covered horseshoe drive, where the sandstone-turreted facade of the Highlander Hotel loomed like a fairytale castle against a blue cloudless sky. Cleverly, I asked the driver how much I owed him before I stepped out of the car. I didn't want to have to breathe outside so soon after the last time.

I wobbled through the tartan-carpeted vestibule, dragging my suitcase behind me. There was a roaring fire in a Jacobean fireplace that was flanked by two pewter wall sconces, and a mismatch of numerous comfortable looking chairs and chesterfield sofas. Dark wood occasional tables laden with board games and leather-bound books were scattered randomly, and a selection of gigantic decapitated animal heads and gilded paintings of Highland scenes adorned the walls.

It turns out that we have three hundred guests and there are only seven members of staff so, in short, it's potential bedlam. I'm responsible for the Young Highlander Yellow Brigade, which is comprised of twenty-six kids. There are four Brigades, totalling a hundred and five children altogether. The concept is that we operate two itineraries in tandem, an adults' programme and a children's schedule, and rarely do the twain meet. It's the perfect weekend break for parents who can't stand the sight of their own kids. This evening the adults will be enjoying a formal gourmet meal in the Bruce Dining Room, whilst we'll be taking the kids to the cinema in Aviemore. I sighed. What joy.

I was wearing my black faux fur jacket and Cossack hat, jeans and my new fur boots. I was also wearing a ridiculous neon yellow body bib, but here in the lobby of the Highlander Hotel, I didn't look that ridiculous. In fact, I looked quite normal, because my twenty-five kids were also wearing neon yellow bibs. And another thirty kids were wearing neon orange bibs, and outside where two double-decker coaches were preparing for the off, there were forty more kids wearing glow-in-the-dark green and pink bibs.

I swallowed a couple of Panadols without a drink, feeling a prickle of fear. What if I lose one of the kids? I worried. I must have head counted twenty-five about a hundred times and we haven't even left the hotel yet. I'm waiting on one last boy but no one has appeared to deliver him into my care yet. I don't mind, the fewer the better in my view.

I'm going to have to calm myself down, my nerves are shot to bits. A little fiend called Tommy, who's about eleven, had blasted another boy on the leg with a catapult full of coffee beans earlier. Impulsively, I had snatched the catapult and fired him a stinger on the arm at point blank range, just to let him see how he liked it, and now I was worried because there are all sorts of laws and stuff these days. I don't want to be deported to Thailand to do a stint in the Bangkok Hilton. He could have a Thai granny who might sue me for child abuse and insist that I do my time in her country, you never know! On the plus side, the incident had a calming effect on the rest of the kids. They're lined up mutely, against the wall, waiting for the first bus to pull out so that we can board the second.

I caught sight of myself in the glass door. I jammed my clipboard under my arm and tweaked my fur-trimmed Cossack hat to eyebrow level and gave my Rapunzel locks a loving tug. I took a step back and had a twirl. I love this fur jacket, and the hair extensions trailing down my back look fabulous. I gave my head a swish. I had bought a flesh-coloured lipstick, which isn't really me, but I'd thought it would complete my Julie-Christie-in-*Doctor-Zhivago* look. I felt an irritating hand yank on my arm. I teased it off. That said, I do like the fleshtone look.

I sighed as there was another tug on my arm. 'Stand in line, we are waiting for our bus. How many times do I need to say it?' I yelled, authoritatively. I peered closer at my reflection and rubbed a blob of lipstick off my teeth.

'You're looking good, Evie,' a familiar voice rumbled.

The speaker was unmistakable. I swivelled around so fast I felt a whiplash snap.

Rob.

I couldn't breathe. I managed to swallow and blink, but not breathe. He tilted his head and smiled. I felt a leap of exhilaration, a swell of happiness and a huge surge of, well, of crotch-exploding lust. I broke into a sweat. My mind raced. He's here? What are the chances of us coming face-to-face in a hotel lobby in the middle of the Scottish Highlands? A zillion to one, no, easily more than that. My God, I'm so pleased to see him, so, so pleased. And then I felt a rush of bitterness and anger.

'You're looking *really* good,' he said, with an appraising nod.

I may be looking good but he's looking *gorgeous*. His hair was tousled and tweaked with wax, he had a smattering of six o'clock stubble, his blue eyes were shining wickedly and his pink lips were curved into a lazy smile. He was wearing jeans, a big black puffa jacket and suede gloves, and a black fur trimmed hat with floppy ear pieces was casually tucked in the crook of his arm.

Suddenly I realised that it was my turn to speak but I couldn't think of anything to say. Not a single word, nothing. I breathed in and out, in and out.

He scanned my face.

A coil of fury unfurled inside me. The faithless bastard, I swiftly reminded myself. I felt a whoosh of panic because suddenly my mind shrieked that he could be here with someone! What if he has a new squeeze? I darted a glance behind him but there was no one in tow. I couldn't bear to see him with someone else, but then, why should I care?

And then I realised twenty-five inquisitive little faces were upturned expectantly.

'What the hell are you doing here?' I hissed, adjusting my already perfectly placed Cossack hat in a short sharp jerky movement.

'I'm celebrating New Year like everyone else,' he replied nonchalantly. 'If that's all right with you?' he added, with a challenging glare.

I swept a dismissive hand. 'Well, enjoy yourself,' I said blithely, and turned my back on him. 'I'll see you around no doubt. I'm going out now.'

'So am I, I'm going to the cinema,' he drawled.

I pivoted. 'The cinema!' I squeaked, in a voice that was trying for indifference.

To my astonishment, he tugged a neon yellow bib over his head. It was too small for him and it dangled around his neck like a nun's collar.

'Yes,' he said brightly, 'the cinema.'

I flicked the bottom of his yellow bib. 'Why are you wearing that?'

'I have to. I think it's to make sure you don't lose me.'

'Lose you!'

He took a step back and held up the flat of his gloved hands. 'Calm down. I'm not implying you will lose me. It's likely that you won't. I trust you.' He slid a lazy glance at the door. 'I think that's our bus.'

I grabbed his arm and dragged him out of earshot of our twenty-five eavesdroppers. 'What are you playing at?'

In one swift motion he clutched my shoulders, pulled me towards him and bent his head to mine. His warm breath on my cheek made my spine tingle and my innards melt.

'What am I playing at?' he parroted.

I crossed my legs in defiance.

'Evie, for the next four days I am a fully paid-up Yellow Brigade Young Highlander and you are going to look after me because the brochure says you will. I suggest you start by helping me on the bus and taking me to the cinema.'

My brain couldn't quite take this in. 'You're not on my list,' I spat, jabbing my clipboard.

'I'll think you'll find I am,' he shot back. He whipped my clipboard from my hand, tugged his glove off with his teeth and ran a finger down the list of names. 'Aha,' he announced triumphantly, 'Master Andrew Harrison. It's my middle name.'

'You're too old to be in the kids' club,' I snapped.

'I'm not.'

'You are.'

'I'm not.'

'You are!'

'I'm not. There is *no* age limit. The brochure states children must be "dry and out of nappies" but it *does not* stipulate an age band.'

I glared at him in stunned silence. I haven't read the brochure.

'To the bus,' he said, gripping my elbow and marching me towards the door.

Chapter Fifty

We went to see *The Lion, the Witch and the Wardrobe*. I sat on the aisle seat, two little girls and a boy sat between Rob and me, and the rest of the group were in the row at the front. He's booked himself on my tour, I thought, chewing my glove like a hungry gremlin. What's he playing at? Not a text in a month that I could have the pleasure of deleting, and now he turns up in the middle of the Highlands just like that, looking stunning and smelling even better than he looks. I'd noticed because I'd sniffed him. I gave my hair a tossy swish. Still, who cares?

'Here,' Sally, one of the other escorts, said, dumping a box in my lap.

I peered at it blankly. 'What is it?'

'Ice creams for the kids,' she said.

I fired and frisbeed them out. If I shouted 'catch' once, I shouted it twenty-six times.

'Evie,' Rob whispered in the shadows.

I continued watching the film, feigning deafness.

'Evie,' he repeated, reaching across three kids to pinch my ear.

'What?' I snapped.

'I'd prefer a strawberry cone. Could you go to the shop in the lobby and change this?' he asked, brandishing a mint Cornetto.

I tried for calm. 'No,' I breathed.

He wore a mocking smile. 'But I don't like mint ice cream and the brochure said there was a selection.'

I cleared my throat. 'The shop is closed during the film,' I lied in an authoritative tone.

'I'll swap you,' one of the little girls sitting between us offered sweetly. 'I've only had four licks, I haven't bitten mine yet,' she assured him, sticking a gooey choc ice under his nose.

'Problem solved. One of your friends will swap with you,' I said with a smirk. 'And it's only been licked four times,' I felt compelled to add. His smile buckled.

I didn't watch the film. I spent two hours counting to twenty-six and stealing lustful glances at Rob. On our return to the hotel a cyclone of snow raged and swirled around the coach. We lumbered and lurched at a snail's pace behind an enormous orange snow plough that had wheels the size of the London Eye. I had a sudden vision of us lost and stranded on the mountain, reduced to cannibalism, with the last to die found frozen, wide-eyed and vampire-mouthed fifty years from now. Why do people come here? Why am I here? Why didn't I stay in London?

Eventually we pulled up outside the hotel. I counted to twenty-six for the hundredth time and flapped around, lining my kids up against the reception desk. I stood sentrified with my clipboard, scoring names off with a flourish as the parents, bedecked in evening dress, arrived to squirrel them off. Mary Poppins couldn't have done a better job.

Very slowly, Rob walked towards me. I swallowed nervously.

'No one is collecting me,' he said smiling.

'You don't say?' I retorted.

He stood close. My nostrils twitched for a whiff of his aftershave.

'Can I buy you a drink?' he asked, toeing the tartan carpet with a Timberland boot.

'No thank you.' I strode off briskly in the direction of the elevator.

'Evie!' he shouted.

I spun around. 'What?'

He stuck out his chest. 'Can you unbutton my coat and take me to the toilet?'

I whipped my Cossack hat from my head, jammed it under my arm, about turned, and marched off.

I'd been in bed for two hours, writhing in torment. I couldn't sleep or concentrate, I could barely breathe. He's here in *this* hotel, in a bed. Which bed? I had to know which bed! I lurched towards the lamp, switched it on, threw back the quilt and tumbled to the floor. I grabbed my clipboard and frenziedly tossed my paperwork all over the carpet searching for the room list. My eyes scanned the column of names. Room 424. So, I quickly calculated, drawing a map of the hotel with my finger on the rug, he's two floors above me and three doors to the left. 'Two floors and three doors,' I whisper. Shit, that's not far. I looked at the bedside clock, it was midnight. I'd call Lulu. She's remained impartial, sort of. Well no, she hasn't, not even sort of, but still, sometimes she does offer sound advice. She picked up on the second ring, and broke into song.

'Should auld acquaintance be forgot and never brought to mind, should . . .'

I crunched my teeth. 'It's not New Year's Eve yet,' I bellowed.

'Huuuuu. Whaaaa. When ish it then?' she slurred.

'The day after tomorrow,' I snapped, exasperated. 'Listen, are you listening? I want to tell you something important and I need to know if you're sober enough to understand.'

'Coursh I am. Turn the mushic down!' she yelled, to God knows who. I heard her high heels rap quickly on a wooden floor, and then a door slammed. 'Am outshide,' she said with a sigh of exertion. 'Whaas up?'

'Rob's here,' I said, excitedly.

'Where . . . are . . . you?' she asked very slowly.

'In Scotland, of course.'

'You're confushing me.'

A bubble of air burst in my windpipe and with it my previously in check, mixed-up thoughts and emotions all tumbled out. It was completely irrelevant that I was talking to the brain-dead town drunk.

'He's followed me here. He's booked himself on this trip, he looks amazing and horny and shit I want him. I want him sooooo much but Lulu, I've lasted almost two months and I do have other options. I have things to look forward to like going on holiday with Nikki, and maybe visiting Alain, and I have trips lined up with John Jackson and I'm a size ten. And could I ever trust him? His job comes with a double bed included and that's not going to change, and—'

'Evie,' Lulu interrupted, 'the guy's a fanny magnet. You eiffer want to stick to him or you dwon't,' she advised, solemnly.

'Right,' I said, understanding completely.

Chapter Fifty-one

I didn't sleep a wink all night, but I wasn't tired. I was hyper, in a light floaty stoned kind of way. I got up at six o'clock. I was scheduled to take the kids tobogganing at nine, so there were only three short hours to get ready.

In the shower, I exfoliated like a mad thing. By the time I'd finished I didn't have a single molecule of dead, flaky or dry skin on my body. I shampooed my hair twice and then soaked it in conditioner. Usually I can't be bothered to wait the customary twenty minutes for the Concentrated Hair Care Kit to work but today I waited, and used the time to pluck my eyebrows and repaint my nails. No need to worry about waxing, that's something I never slack on. I'd have my bits waxed to face a firing squad.

I hurriedly spread all my make-up on the dressing table, but I couldn't decide on shades or tones until I knew what I was wearing so I threw my suitcase open and nearly cried in despair. Do you have any idea how hard it is to look glamorous in sub-zero temperatures? I wish I hadn't been so frugal in Harrods. Everything I had was thermal and sensible and frumpy. I decided on my favourite La Senza black lace underwear, thermal tights, leggings and a figure-hugging black cashmere jumper that I'd stolen from Lulu. The second I pulled the jumper over my head, I started to writhe, pant and thrash around in panic. I couldn't breathe. It was so tight at the neck, it was claustrophobic. I quickly whipped it off and decided on a flattering baby pink cashmere hip-length jersey instead, also stolen from Lulu.

I dried and curled my hair and immediately hated it. I dampened it, dried it again and straightened it. I gave my eyelashes three generous coats of mascara and underscored with an Urban Decay charcoal glitter liner. Pouting in the mirror, I applied my lipstick with precision. I was looking my best, my very best. Slim, tousle haired and attractive. Let him see what he's missing, and then my mind yells, eager and desperate and available! I quickly whipped off my clothes and changed out of my sexy black La Senza underwear in favour of a previously lilac set, which had turned grey in the wash, that's been lying in my suitcase for about three years. Lexy maintains that the best contraceptive a girl can have is a pair of old drawers. Immediately, I felt virtuous and chaste because I know these knickers won't be coming off in front of anyone other than a mortician. I'll show him, I thought, gobshite that he is.

I strode through the lobby, hat and gloves in hand, clipboard under my arm, hair swishing, and gathered the kids together. I'm getting quite good at this, in a Supernanny kind of way, but I still couldn't help wonder why people have kids. I felt a tap on my arm.

'Sleep well?' Rob asked, bending to kiss my cheek.

My tummy flipped at his touch but I kept my voice light and easy. 'I watched *Dirty Dancing* on the Movie Channel then slept like a log, thank you,' I told him. 'And you?'

'Oh, I watched a bit of porn,' he said, deadpan, and sauntered past me, sinking into a chair by the fireplace.

I clamped my lips together and rapped my fountain pen on my clipboard. Porn indeed, like I care. He crossed one leg over the other and shook open his newspaper.

I leaned so far across the front desk that my feet left the floor. I glanced over my shoulder swiftly. Rob was splayed and relaxed, grinning like an eejit into the *Telegraph*, yellow neon bib positioned decoratively around his shoulders.

'I want parental control on the Movie Channel in room four-two-four,' I whispered to the receptionist commandingly.

She tapped her pen on my arm. 'Aye, right, but are ye sure, because de ye know if I block it ye canna watch so much as a certified fifteen?' she pointed out, eyebrows raised.

My fist clenched tightly around my Cossack hat. 'I'm positive. That's exactly what I want,' I assured her.

That's the end of the porn, I thought triumphantly.

At the toboggan run, I swallowed a lump of panic. Counting twenty-five yellow bibs was, quite honestly, impossible. The kids beetled up and down the slope like an army of ants. Why am I here? I asked myself again. I hugged a tree as a harsh wind slapped me and thought about texting Tina to tell her that I hated her. After all, she talked me into this, but texting would have meant taking my gloves off, which was out of the question. My face was crimson with the cold, my nose was running, my lips had gone all numb and blubbery and I'd only got off the bus ten minutes ago. If we stayed here for the scheduled three hours, I'd die of hypothermia, it was a medical certainty. I sniffed. Thank God for my cosy fur jacket and my beautiful hat.

A strong hand gripped my shoulder. 'Come down with me,' Rob said, smiling boyishly.

'What?' I snapped, in horrified disgust. 'I most certainly will not.'

He dangled a blue plastic toboggan in my face. 'Come on, come down with me.'

I thought he'd said, go down on me.

I rallied. 'I don't think so,' I replied, blubbery lipped. 'It's not really my scene.'

He tore me from the tree and curved a strong arm around my shoulders. 'You can't stand there all morning,' he said, marching me uphill.

'I am not doing this,' I insisted, bent against the wind.

At the top, he slapped the toboggan on the ground.

'I'm working,' I reminded him. 'I'm not here to play games.'

He straddled the toboggan. 'Sit on it,' he ordered.

'I will not,' I snapped.

He grabbed my shoulders and pulled me in front of him. 'Sit,' he repeated, kicking my feet out from under me.

'No!' I yelled, landing on the toboggan with a thud.

'If I were you, I'd draw my knees to my chin and hug my shins, otherwise you might fall off,' he said, curving himself behind me. He wedged his chin in the crook of my neck and pulled on the ropes. 'Ready?' he asked, giving us a mighty push with his foot.

It was amazing. I can't explain it, you have to try it for yourself. My chest expanded with excitement as we whipped past trees and bounced over lumps and bumps. I squealed at the thrill of it. Rob held me tight, laughing in my ear, driving us downhill in an exaggerated wide-angled zigzag.

'Evie, you're too stiff, lean with me,' he said, his voice warm on my face.

And I did. Our shoulders scraped the snow as we twisted from left to right. I felt an instant affinity with those nutters who drop from helicopters onto mountain tops and whiz over cliffs on a snowboard the size of a tea tray. With a bit of practice, I

413

could be one of them. I certainly have the balance. All too soon, we tail spun and skidded to a halt at the bottom of the slope in a huge spray of snow. I felt breathless and wobbly-kneed. My heart raced with exhilaration and I breathed a huge pleasure-soaked sigh. Rob stood up and offered me his gloved hand.

'Did you enjoy it?' he asked, hauling me to my feet.

'No,' I said, smacking snow from my sleeves.

He tweaked my hat over my eyes. 'Shall we try it once more?'

I shrugged. 'If you like,' I offered, slapping his hand off my hat.

We were the last group to leave. I was enjoying myself so much that I kept the kids on the slopes for an hour longer than the itinerary specified. Most of them were delighted but a few, who were frozen and knackered, moaned that they wanted to go back to the hotel. I gave them twenty quid and stuck them in the café at the top of the slopes where they gorged on hot chocolate and ice cream Mars bars. It was past one o'clock before we rejoined the coach for the drive back to the hotel.

We were late for the Make a Crown Competition. Two girls started crying. Although they'd enjoyed the extra time on the toboggans, they selfishly wanted to enter the crown-making competition as well. As luck would have it, there was a craft shop in town so I stopped the bus and bought two crowns. The devious witches were beside themselves with excitement because their chances of winning the competition were now pretty high. Judging was scheduled to take place at the New Year's Eve Gala Dinner, so we would all be rooting for them. The other kids were sworn to secrecy by my new friend Tommy and his catapult.

'Drink before lunch?' Rob asked when the kids had cleared the lobby.

'No thanks,' I said. 'I don't have time. I have a meeting in the library about tomorrow's clay pigeon shoot. I really don't know why you came. You're wasting your time if you thought I'd be spending any time with you,' I added, and walked off. I stole a backward glance and saw him sigh and sink into a chair. Tommy's mop of red hair sank down beside him.

I touched up my make-up in the ladies' toilet. I was determined to look my very best every waking moment. Fortunately this Julie Christie look is relatively low maintenance. It's the fur jacket and the gorgeous hat that does it. I sighed. How am I going to be able to resist him for three whole days? I thought grimly. An unbidden vision of a paprika curly perm popped into my head. I felt a slap of anger and shivered with disgust. Sod him, he's no more handsome than Alain. I tossed my lipstick in my bag and checked my watch. I was due on bouncy castle duty in the playzone for a couple of hours. Surely he wouldn't turn up for that.

He did.

A remote control for my ears would have been handy, as the noise was deafening. The playzone was a hall the size of a football pitch housing three bouncy castles, a ball pond, a climbing frame and a couple of pool tables. I sat glumly in a red plastic chair, elbows on knees, chin in hands. Rob sat next to me. He nodded towards the pool table.

'Fancy a game?'

I shrugged. 'Not really.'

'Shall we play for money?' he asked. 'Make it more interesting.'

'If you want.'

He shot up, rubbing his hands together briskly. 'OK, twenty pounds,' he said. 'That's the bet.'

I stood and smoothed my pink sweater over my leggings.

'Fine, you pay me twenty pounds if I win, and if I lose you don't have to pay me anything,' I said.

His face clouded. 'But what's the advantage for me?'

I folded my arms. 'I've just said you don't have to pay if I lose. Were you not listening?'

'But,' he ventured, 'what can I win?'

He was taking this far too seriously.

'Look,' I snapped, 'either you want to play or you don't!'

'Yes I do, I do want to play,' he said enthusiastically.

I cheated.

He still won.

I sulked.

'See you around sometime,' he said, and to my astonishment, he threw his jacket casually over his shoulder and sauntered through the playzone swing doors. Charming, I thought, is that the extent of his devotion and pursuit?

I bulleted around my room with only fifteen minutes to dress and get down for dinner. My phone rang. It was Sally, the head coordinator.

'Can you babysit tonight?' she asked.

'Why me?'

'Because the guest insists on a girl, so obviously none of our guys can do it, and you're the only one of the girls not down for the bingo.'

I sighed. 'Well I'll have to then, won't I?'

'Sorry,' she said, not sounding sorry at all. 'Room three hundred. They want you there at nine o'clock.'

'Fine,' I replied, discomfited, although I couldn't put my finger on why. After all, I had nothing else planned.

She wasn't finished. 'Tell me to mind my own business if you like, but—'

'Mind your own business,' I interrupted.

'Who is the Brad Pitt lookalike following you all over the place?'

'Brad Pitt lookalike . . .' I tailed away dreamily. I freeze-framed Rob's face in my mind's eye, vis à vis Brad, and yes, there was a definite likeness. Now that I think of it, they could be twins. I've thought that before.

'Just a friend,' I told her proudly, suddenly grinning.

'I wouldn't kick him out of bed,' she said in a fake husky voice. 'See you later.'

My face buckled.

You wouldn't have to kick him out of bed, I thought grimly, if you worked with him in Austria and stayed at the Hilton Salzburg, the two-timing shite.

I walked into the dining room. Rob sat in the corner, on a table for one, smiling into the wine list. His smile widened when the waiter deposited a doorstep-sized Aberdeen Angus fillet steak in front of him. Inspired, I rushed over to him.

'Is that a medium rare fillet with roast potatoes, cauliflower cheese, green beans and parsnips, and a side order of peppercorn sauce?' I asked.

'Yes,' he said, knife and fork hovering mid air.

I whipped the plate from the table and held it aloft. 'You,' I reminded him, 'are on the kids' menu, and as such your evening meal selection comprises of chicken nuggets, fish whales, Mr Tiddly sausages with mash or a hoppie hotdog.'

He dropped his cutlery, leaned back in his chair and nodded as though thinking hard. I jabbed the plate in the chest of a passing waiter and told his surprised face to get rid of it.

'So what's it to be?' I asked, folding my arms triumphantly.

He clenched his hands on the edge of the table, staring at me wordlessly.

'I can see you need time to decide. The choices are quite mouth-watering, aren't they?' I enthused. 'I'll leave you to it. I'm going out on a date, a dinner date.'

He lurched forward and grabbed my hand. 'Who with?' he interrupted.

'None of your business,' I shot back.

'Going anywhere nice?' he asked in a tone I didn't recognise.

I pulled my hand free from his. 'As I said, it's none of your business.' I spun on my heel.

'Enjoy yourself,' he snapped to my marching figure.

That'll show him, I thought, greedy big gomeril that he is.

I ordered a sandwich from room service. I could hardly go back down to the dining room after boasting I was going out for dinner, could I? I changed into my Kermit pyjamas and pulled on a hoodie over them. I scrubbed off my make-up, tweaked out my contact lenses and fished around in my suitcase for my slippers. I tied my hair in a ponytail, put on my reading glasses and plucked my book from the bedside table. Closing the door behind me, I set off to babysit.

I slid my glasses up my nose, did a quick left and right of the silent corridor and rapped on the door of Room 300.

'Aaaagggg! What do you think you're doing?' I shrieked as Rob grabbed hold of my wrists and dragged me through the doorway.

Chapter fifty-two

I fell to my knees. Rob kicked the door closed, pulled me up and threw me onto the bed. Crawling, he straddled my thighs and pinned my arms above my head.

'This is abduction,' I yelled, thrashing. 'Let go of me!'

'No, I won't.'

'Let me up!'

His eyes narrowed. 'No.'

I fought like a fiend. 'I am leaving this room,' I yelled.

'No, you're not. You're not going anywhere.' Breathing hard, he pulled my arms down by my sides.

'You can't make me stay,' I screeched.

He shifted his thighs and pinned my elbows. 'Oh I can, I *can* make you stay. I'll sit on top of you like this all night if I have to.' He smoothed the hair from my face. 'We need to talk,' he said commandingly, brows furrowed.

I crooked my neck and managed to raise my shoulders from the bed. 'Talk,' I snapped. 'Is this your idea of a cosy chat?'

'You left me no choice. If I'd invited you to my room, you wouldn't have come.'

'What do you want to talk about?' I hissed.

'That's better,' he said, with a smile.

419

I flopped back and studied the ceiling.

'You must have good eyesight to see through those thick glasses, Evie. You look like the snake in *The Jungle Book*. When I saw you at the door, I nearly pushed you back instead of dragging you in. I'd forgotten about those,' he joked, and gave a shoulder-shaking chuckle.

'Just get to the point. Say what you have to say and let me go.'

He whispered his fingers over the scar behind my ear.

I tossed my head from side to side. 'Don't touch me.'

'Your hair's beautiful. These are obviously the hair extensions you chanted about in your sleep in the hospital.'

I flicked him a surprised look. This was news to me. Chanting in my sleep?

He bent forward. 'The scar above your eye is no more than a thread now.' His finger traced my eyebrow and travelled the length of my jaw. I reddened under his penetrating gaze.

There was an electric hush.

'Evie,' he breathed.

He stared at me, unblinking. A muscle in the corner of his mouth quivered. Clearing his throat, he placed a trembling hand on my cheek. Instinctively, I turned slowly to nestle in the curve of his palm. I felt a rush of blood flood my face and a tremor of excitement squeeze in my chest. He cupped my face and leaned forward to kiss my forehead. I swallowed a golf-ball-sized lump as his lips brushed my hair. Massaging my shoulders, he traced his thumbs along the swell of my collarbone. Our eyes locked.

'Touch me,' he said softly.

'What with? You're sitting on my arms,' I reminded him.

His pink lips parted in amusement. 'If I let you up, will you behave yourself?'

I didn't answer.

He wriggled down my hips. Gripping my wrists with biting

fingers, he pressed my palms flat to his chest and closed his eyes as my fingertips touched his nipples.

'Touch me,' he exhaled.

'I am,' I croaked, dry-mouthed.

God, I'd missed him.

'My skin, I want to feel your touch on my skin,' he whispered, raising my hands to work the buttons of his shirt.

I couldn't stop myself.

His chest swelled as he breathed. I worked my palms across his hard chest and down the slant of his flat belly. He bent forward and pressed himself hard against me. Finding my mouth, he ran his tongue along the edge of my teeth. He buried his face in the folds of my neck and bit down hard on my shoulder. My back arched, my chest rose and my hips jerked towards him. He raised himself on his elbows and gazed at me levelly. Flicking his hand inside the waistband of my pyjamas, he pressed his thumb in the nook of my hipbone. I thought I would melt.

'I can't stop now,' he said, covering my mouth with his.

I circled his neck and pulled him towards me. 'I don't want you to stop,' I whispered through his kiss.

And I didn't.

Afterwards, he pressed his forehead to mine. Eyes closed, he lay still until his breathing calmed. He raised himself onto the heels of his hands and searched my face.

'I don't know what it is we've always had between us.' He inhaled deeply. 'It's like an invisible cord or something, but what I do know is that it's still there.'

He rolled over to lie on his back and gathered me to him. I nestled my head in the curve of his shoulder and played lazily with the soft golden hair on his chest. He caught my hand and squeezed it tight, then lifted a lock of my hair to his lips and grinned.

'Whose room is this?' I asked, curious.

'Technically, it's my mum and dad's,' he replied casually.

'What?' I shot up and fired a frantic look around, half expecting a buxom white-haired battleaxe in an oatmeal suit to ask me what I thought I was doing having a good old ride in her bed.

He pulled me back. 'They're not actually here. I wasn't allowed to travel as an unaccompanied minor so I had to reserve a couple of adult places.'

'So you paid for fictitious parents?'

'Yes.'

I was quiet for a minute, and then said, 'Why didn't you book one child and one adult place, and just pay for one room?'

'Because I didn't want a twin, and I know doubles are allocated to couples.'

I cast an appraising look around the room. 'But this isn't a standard double. This looks like a suite.'

'It is a suite,' he sighed.

'So why do you need a single, a double and a suite?'

He gave a tired smile. 'Is this conversation going somewhere, like does it matter?'

'I want to know so yes, it matters.'

'OK, the single room is of no use to me *but* I needed the child's place on the Highlander programme so I still have it but I haven't actually been in it. I checked into the double room and stayed there last night but the bed is as wide as my shoulders. The movie channel doesn't work either. I wanted to watch *American Pie* this afternoon and it was unavailable for viewing. I phoned the front desk, who insisted there was nothing they could do, I don't know what that's all about. And when Tommy suggested I book you to babysit, he pointed out that you might not come if you knew my room number so I reserved the suite as a decoy.' He gave a resigned shrug. 'I've ended up with rooms coming out of my arse.'

'Tommy?'

'Bright kid. Shall we open a bottle of champagne?' he asked.

'Yes,' I replied absently, as I tried to count how much he'd spent to come here.

I woke in the night to find Rob sitting naked in a chair beside the bed, staring. A shard of moonlight danced on his face.

'What's wrong?' I asked, rubbing the sleep from my eyes.

He pulled the chair closer to the bed. 'Evie,' he said softly, 'it's just . . .'

I raised myself up on the pillow. 'It's just what?' I asked, studying his handsome features.

He reached out and touched my cheek. 'I was watching you,' he said in a soft voice.

'Watching me?'

He nodded slowly. 'Yes, I was watching you sleep. I thought I would never get the chance to watch you sleep again.' His eyes held mine. 'At some point in the night, I would always watch you sleep.'

This threw me. 'Did you?' I asked lightly.

He bobbed his head.

I wasn't used to seeing the vulnerable side of him and I didn't know if I liked it. His eyes swam with unshed tears and I felt an overwhelming surge of affection towards him. I pulled back the quilt.

'Well, do you think you could get in here, make wild passionate love to me and then watch whilst I sleep the sleep of the sexually fulfilled?'

His face broke into a wide smile. 'Don't know. I'm knackered and we've already done it three times.'

I shot him a cynical look.

'Oh, all right then, if I have to,' he shot back, leaping into bed with the finesse of an Olympic sprinter.

Chapter fifty-three

A Fun Swim supervised by qualified swimming instructors was scheduled for the kids, so I was rostered on to the adult programme to host the clay pigeon shoot. I left Rob asleep and dashed back to my room to dress. I was in the lobby promptly at nine o'clock to meet the driver taking us to the shooting range.

I shouldn't have slept with him, but a shag is only a shag. It doesn't necessarily follow that I'll do it again, I reasoned. And it'll remind him what a tit he was to look elsewhere, and—

'All right?' Rob asked, giving me a hearty thump on the back. I stumbled forward.

I turned around slowly. He was grinning like an idiot and tugging his Sherlock Holmes hat over his ears.

'Am fine,' I said brightly.

'I'm looking forward to this,' he said, shuffling from one foot to the other.

He stamped a Timberland boot forward, bent his knees, raised an imaginary rifle to ear level, and shouted, 'Bang, bang, bang!'

I stifled a yawn. 'Shouldn't you be in the Fun Swim?' I asked. 'With your friends?'

'Nope, I'm taking my dad's place on the shoot.' He crouched

low and aimed at an already dead stag hanging on the wall, and pulled the trigger. 'Bang!'

'Rob,' I said, folding my arms purposefully.

He walked slowly towards me. 'Yes, my sweet?'

'Erm, about last night . . .'

He lowered his behatted head to my beautiful Harrods hairband, narrowed his eyes and gave me a sultry smile. 'Evie, it was fantas—'

I held up a silencing hand. 'It was a hundred pounds,' I interrupted.

'Excuse me?'

'You booked me to babysit, and I did. I babysat from nine o'clock in the evening until seven o'clock this morning, so ten hours in total.'

The pout slackened into an open-mouthed eye popper. 'You want *me* to pay *you*?' he asked affronted. 'For last night?'

'Yes, I do. I want a hundred quid.'

He stared at me, his arms folded. 'Fine. If you want money, you can have it,' he spat acidly.

'Of course I want money. I'm not babysitting for free. Business is business, and that's all it was.'

Flint-blue eyes flashed. There was a beat of silence.

'So, can I have it?' I asked.

'Now?'

I gave an insistent nod. 'Yes, now.'

'You want me to pay you now?'

'Yes I do. You should really have paid me before I left.'

He flipped the edge of his puffa jacket and jammed a hand in his back pocket. 'Will two fifties do?' he asked, slapping a couple of notes into my outstretched hand.

'Perfect,' I assured him. 'And Rob, if you book a babysitter for tonight, it won't be me because it's not my turn.'

'Is that so?'

'Yes it is.' I said, stuffing the money in my bag.

I walked outside to head-count my group onto the minibus. Last night was great, but it doesn't necessarily mean I'll be repeating it anytime soon, I confirmed to myself. In fact, I definitely won't be.

I was quite looking forward to this shooting event. I had a clear vision in my mind of an ancient castle, you know, Balmoral or similar, with elegant waitresses edging deftly between antique sofas and tables, serving canapés and hot toddies. Guests were relaxing in winged velvet chairs, with open rifles slung lazily over their arms, waiting for their turn to saunter onto the flag-stone terrace and pop a few clays. I adjusted my silver faux-fur hairband and smacked my gloved hands together excitedly. I couldn't wait, I might even have a few pops myself.

Twenty minutes later the coach turned off the main road and edged between two snow-covered crags, climbing a narrow, steep tree-lined slope. I gave a whoop and clutched my heart in awe at a waterfall cascading about forty feet down a rocky gorge. Sparkling with rainbows, it roared and frothed as the cold water plunged into a pond of melted silver. The landscape was so beautiful, serene and peaceful. Gosh, I thought, I love the dazzling brightness of the snow, it makes everything much prettier, so much so it's worth freezing for. I actually wish it snowed more often in London. I checked my lipstick in my hand mirror and tweaked my hairband. I would probably end up spending most of the time chatting to the staff indoors whilst the men were shooting, so there was no real need for my hat.

I gripped the edge of my seat as the coach rumbled in jerky movements over a bumpy stone bridge that arched across a frozen brook.

426

'Right ye are, we've arrived,' the driver announced, pointing to a dilapidated Second World War bomb shelter.

I eyed the igloo-shaped grey stone building doubtfully.

'Er, are you positive?' I asked, leafing through my notes for details about the venue. 'Ah, found it ... Queen's Lodge Gun Club,' I told him loud and clear. 'So obviously this can't be it,' I said with a knowing snort of confidence.

He bobbed his red curly head insistently. 'Aye, this is it, sure, yees are expected,' he said, jerking his chin towards a couple of rudely dressed dwarf tinkers waving so hard it's a wonder they didn't fall flat.

'Right, well, thank you,' I rallied, rising from my seat. OK, I thought, a bit grim on the outside but probably palatial on the inside.

We got off the bus and stumbled in a uniform line through a tangle of snow-covered nettles to a gravelly path. We tripped and lurched over slippery ice-coated stones and broken rocks to the crumbling steps of the Queen's Lodge, a chalet style affair that was situated behind the igloo, with a flagstone floor and a beamed ceiling. Tartan banners and tapestries hung between narrow leaded-light windows. A too-fat-and-too-lazy-to-walk Labrador slept in front of a crackling fire, and another couple of fat lazy Labradors lay comfortably on two leather chesterfield sofas. There was a lot of back-slapping and joviality as the tinkers distributed rifles. Rob beamed, he was beside himself with joy. All tooled up, we fought our way through matted ice-covered branches to a clearing where another couple of tinkers stood guard over what I intelligently deduced was the clays ejaculator, or whatever you call it.

It was my job to keep the scores. Every time someone shot, I had to bite off my glove and mark their points on a score card, but it was freezing, so I'd stopped doing that about twenty minutes ago when two of my fingers had turned blue. I wouldn't take my gloves off in these temperatures, not even for a tickle of Justin Timberlake's goolies, so I cleverly filled in all the score cards when no one was looking and decided on a winner. One of the tinkers kept shouting out names and scores, so for form's sake, I raised my pen and bobbed my head eagerly, like I was bidding for something in an auction that I was determined not to go home without.

It's snowing and no one else except me seemed to mind, but then they're all men so that's not surprising. I had to bend my head to breathe because I didn't want to sniff a blizzard up my nose. My hair extensions were snowstorm-soaked, my mascara had dissolved and I was marching between two trees to stop rigor mortis setting in. White puffs of snow blew up with every step I took, and a bunch of ice cubes had formed and stuck to each of my furry boots. Thick, heavy accumulating flakes were gathering on my head like a big meringue.

I wrapped my fur jacket tightly around me and peered towards the men, but I couldn't see through the swirling cyclone of snow. I scraped ice from my eyebrows and, head bent, continued marching. My rat's tail of a hairband slipped over my eyes. Struggling blindly to push it up, I tripped over a log and landed flat on my face. I wanted to die. I was half dead anyway. There was no reason to live in these temperatures, why would anyone want to? I let my shoulders flop and my head sagged into the snow. Siberian Gulag camps, Cairngorms of Scotland, you tell me what the difference is? Because I can't see it. I started to cry. Rob came over to pick me up but I wouldn't let him. There was no point getting up because it was no warmer than lying down. He flipped me over onto my back.

'Leavemealoneleavemealone,' I wailed. I thrashed like an upside-down crab.

'Come on, up you get,' he coaxed, gently levering my shoulders.

I slapped him and slapped him and slapped him. 'All you care about is your shooting.'

He raised cynical brows. 'Now you know that's not true,' he said in a compelling tone.

'Yesitisyesitisyesitis.'

He gave an indulgent sigh. 'Let me help you.'

'No, leave me, leave me, leave me!'

We had a glove slapping fight.

He grabbed my lapels. 'Get up now,' he bellowed, and pulled me with such force that my head disappeared inside my jacket. 'You'll freeze.'

'I'm frozen already!'

He hoisted me on his shoulder like an old carpet, marched through the deep snow towards the Lodge and put me down inside the door.

'Have a hot drink. I'll be back at the end of the shoot,' he said, whipping the score cards from my jacket pocket.

I waddled towards the fire, kicked one of the dogs from the sofa and splayed myself starfish style across four cushions. Rob woke me an hour later when it was time to leave.

There was a charged hush on the mini bus as I sat rocking back and forth mutely.

Back at the hotel, we relaxed in the bath and Rob cradled me to him. He breathed heavily and his chest rumbled as he chuckled.

'What are you laughing at?' I asked, sleepily enveloped in strong arms and scented warm water.

'You.'

'Why?'

'Sixteen men had to scramble for one sofa because you were horizontal and snoring on the other one.'

'I don't care,' I said.

'I know you don't, that's what I'm laughing at. I had to throw the score cards in the fire and tell everyone they blew out of your hand. Some of those guys were very passionate about shooting. And competitive. But if you had to cheat, you could at least have made me the winner.'

We spent the afternoon in bed. He rolled on top of me, resting his elbows either side of my head.

'Shall we stay in tonight?' he asked.

'Are you joking? It's New Year's Eve and we're in Scotland. No one does it better.'

He gave me a kiss. 'Fair enough, but I don't want a late one,' he said, bending his head and nibbling my lips. 'I have a surprise for you.'

I grinned up at him. 'What is it?'

'Close your eyes,' he whispered.

'Why?'

'Close your eyes or you're not having the surprise.'

He jumped off the bed. I heard the rustle of paper and the tearing of foil and a wicked chuckle. And a strange humming sound. Seconds later, he was on top and inside me.

'Oh my God, oh my God,' I panted.

I thrashed my head from side to side as a series of pulsing throbs caused every nerve in my lower body to contract. Spasm after spasm of heat exploded in my thighs and belly. Rob's breath was hot in my ear, he tucked his arm behind my neck and held me tight. I wrapped my legs around his back.

'Rob,' I gasped. 'What's that?'

He smoothed back my hair and held my startled gaze. 'Happy?' he asked with a grunt of triumph.

Happy? His mickey was suddenly remote controlled and he asks if I'm happy. I was fit to burst with pleasure. I'd had the happiest Happy Hour anyone had ever had.

Afterwards Rob held himself above me, breathing slowly, eyes bright with satisfaction, sweat glistening on his heaving chest. He exhaled, rolled over and sank back on the pillow. I licked my lips, closed my eyes and swept the back of my hand across my wet brow. He pulled me to him, curling a strong arm and a toned thigh around me. I shook my head stiffly. There was a buzzing in my ear. Actually, it was a hum and it wasn't in my ear, it was coming from under the quilt. Rob lay on his side, eyes closed, grinning like a clown, his nose exploring my jaw.

'What's that noise?' I asked, still breathless.

'This,' he said, pulling the quilt back with a flourish. He worked his fingers at his crotch and then handed me a little rubber ring with a rectangular vibrating tube attached.

I stared at it in wonder. The ring danced on my palm. 'What is it?' I asked.

'A vibrating ring.'

'Where did you get it?'

'Boots.'

'How long does it last?'

'Don't know.'

'Why don't you know?'

He shrugged.

'Well, how long do you think it lasts?'

'Twenty minutes, I think.'

'How much was it?'

'Don't know. They were on a three for two offer.'

'How many did you buy?'

'One.'

I slapped him.

'You bought one, and they were on a three for two. No one buys one of anything that's on a three for two. We've probably only got about fifteen minutes' buzzing time left and we're miles away from the nearest Boots,' I shrieked, running a frantic hand through my damp hair. 'And what are we supposed to do when we're all buzzed out?'

'Evie, be fair, I do pretty well without it,' he boasted with a wicked smile.

'Rob, stick a mercury engine on the back of a plastic canoe and tell me that it doesn't make a difference. Don't flatter yourself.'

I wrapped the ring around the third finger of my left hand, and trembling slightly because I was still suffering from post-coital exertion, I raised my hand before my eyes and stared at it hypnotically. How come I'd never heard of these? Some ancient relic of an actor that you've never heard of drops dead, and it makes the news, but when something that can practically transform a man's mickey into an oblong cartwheel is invented, there's not a mention.

'Like it?' he asked.

'S'awright, I suppose,' I said.

Chapter Fifty-four

The Balmoral Suite looked amazing. Glitterballs threw a kaleidoscope of silver lights around the room. The walls were adorned with paintings, gilt mirrors and illuminated wall sconces. Each circular table was dressed in tartan with a large crystal candelabra centrepiece. Waiters edged slowly between the tables, placing party poppers and cone hats on each setting. On stage, behind the polished dance floor, two DJs were belting the bejasus out of each other, in contrast to the four-piece band who were enthusiastically doing a one, two, three sound check.

My hair was loose, moussed and ruffled. I was wearing my red Vera Wang dress and a pair of gold sandals. A gold glitter shadow, false eyelashes with an underscore of kohl, and red lipstick gave me a Cleopatra look. I glanced at my watch. Half an hour and the room would start filling up. I swished out of the ballroom, clipboard in hand, ready to direct the guests to their allocated tables.

The lobby was heaving. Tall straight-backed men in full Highland regalia, sipping scotch from crystal glasses, chatted with well dressed, willowy looking women, who swayed with practised ease between kids dive bombing around their feet. A rabble

433

of teenagers, snowboards tucked under their arms, stamped snow onto the tartan carpet, and a squad of dinner jacket clad men lounged around the fireplace in animated conversation.

'Hi.'

I turned around.

Rob's thick blond hair, teased and waxed, whispered against the collar of a white tuxedo shirt. He wore an impeccably cut black Argyll jacket with matching waistcoat fashioned with silver buttons, and a gorgeous red tartan kilt with two leather straps on the waist and one on the hip. Oatmeal-coloured socks covered his thick toned calves and a sporran hanging loosely from his waist completed the ensemble. I was gob-smacked.

'Mmm,' I mumbled, dry-mouthed and quite speechless.

He appraised me slowly, lingering longer than necessary on my cleavage. His gaze returned unhurriedly to my flushed face.

'Not bad,' he complimented with a sardonic smile. 'You don't look too bad at all. Shall we have a drink? You've got half an hour to spare before you're on parade.'

He placed a firm hand on my back and piloted me through the lobby melee. The crisp pleats of his kilt swished and swooshed as he walked. I dropped back a step to stare, wondering if he was wearing anything under his kilt. Apparently men don't.

'No I'm not,' he said, pink lips curving into a smile. He took my hand and tucked it into the crook of his arm.

'Not what?' I asked.

'Wearing anything under my kilt,' he said casually.

'Well,' I snapped affronted, 'I wasn't even thinking about that.'

'Don't tell lies.'

'I'm *not* lying.'

434

'That's another lie.'

A wicked crimson stain ran up the length of my neck and cheeks. 'What, er, what made you think to wear a kilt?'

'Alice said you wouldn't be able to resist me.'

My head swivelled. 'Alice?'

'Yes, my friend Alice. She loaned me this,' he boasted, smoothing a hand over his hip. 'It was Duncan's about a hundred years ago, but apparently they don't age.'

'Really?'

And for a minute, I stopped walking.

He turned around. 'Come on, do you want a drink or not?'

I had to jog to catch up. He had the nicest bum in the whole wide world, and to think it was out in public without pants.

'Wine or gin?' he asked, his elbow resting casually on the bar.

'So you've got a bare bum?' I asked.

'Yes. Wine or gin?' he repeated.

'Is your bum cold?'

'There's a draught, I'll admit. Wine or gin?'

'Is your bum itchy from the woollen kilt?'

He rolled his eyes. 'Can I have a pint of Fosters and a gin and tonic?' he asked the barman.

Rob sat with me and the other Insignia staff members on the crew table. I didn't have to ask how he'd managed to wangle a seat because Sally dribbled through the three courses. Dinner was fabulous. Slabs of roast beef the size of a car roof, roast potatoes and a selection of crunchy vegetables, finished off with strawberry cheesecake, and washed down with copious amounts of scrummy Shiraz. Delicious.

The hotel manager took to the stage. He expanded his beer barrel chest and ran a nervous hand through his hair. His microphone crackled to life, followed by a collective tinkle of forks on glasses.

'And so here we aw are,' he announced. 'Another Hogmanay, seems tay me we only just celebrated the last one.'

There was a communal rumble of agreement.

'And what a fine crowd ye aw make sitting there in yer finery. Before the party gets under way we have a few announcements tay make, the first one bein' the winners of the Make a Crown Competition, so would all our entrants please take to the dance floor, and stand together with their Insignia hostess.'

And you'd have thought I'd been called to receive an Oscar. I stood, kick tossed the hem of my Vera Wang, sidestepped a couple of tables and sashayed to the dance floor where Jenna and Gabrielle, the two little girls from my group, joined me. Each gripped my hand nervously, both wore their crowns. I felt something slimy move around my belly and I realised that I was nervous. I desperately wanted them to win, they'd worked so hard, and I'd helped, and their crowns were miles better than all the others.

'A fabulous display, yees have aw done an amazin job,' the manager boomed. 'Now we'd like aw you children tay form a circle and do a lap of honour on the dance floor tay let us aw get a fine look at these works of art.'

The seventeen entrants paraded proudly around the dance floor, encouraged by the deafening applause of the three-hundred-strong crowd. Halfway through their third lap, the manager rapped on the microphone and held up his hand.

'Fine, now that we've aw had a look, I'd like you children tay rejoin yer hostess.'

There was a frantic scurrying as the kids broke the circle. Jenna, Gabrielle and I stood rigid, holding hands in a white-knuckled clench. I was beside myself with nerves. I could hear the blood pounding in my ears, my heart raced and I needed a wee. The manager warbled on but I was too excited to listen.

He opened an envelope that contained the names of the winners.

'And it's a tie between two yellow Highlanders, Jenna and Gabrielle!'

'Oh my God, my God, we've done it,' I said excitedly. 'We won, we won!'

Their delighted adorable faces beamed up at me, hands positioning the crowns on their angelic heads. I was sooooooo proud of them and of what they'd achieved. We sailed towards the stage in a flotilla of party frocks. I was almost breathless with excitement. I felt like, well, like I imagined a mother would feel after years of coughing up for school fees, when finally a university degree is achieved. My nostrils twitched with emotion as the manager handed them each a huge wrapped gift. I clapped and clapped and clapped, and so did everyone else. It was amazing.

'You cheated,' Rob whispered as I smoothed my dress over my bum and edged back into my chair.

I shot him a look of contempt. 'Shut up, Goldilocks.'

He eyed me shrewdly. 'Get me a pint of lager or I'll tell.'

'You wouldn't.'

'I would,' he insisted and moved to stand.

'OK, OK, Carling or Fosters?' I offered.

Rob took my hand and led me to the dance floor. 'We've never danced together,' he whispered, lips brushing my forehead.

He placed a hand firmly on my back and twirled me around the room to the accompaniment of the ceilidh band. As he bent his head to mine and kissed me, my heart floated. I squeezed my eyes shut and told myself to make a memory, to freeze frame this moment, to never forget. Suddenly we were torn apart, and he disappeared into the crowd of laughing dancing strangers and for the next hour and a half we were tutored and bossed into learning Scottish reels, the Dashing White Sergeant and the Military

Two Step. I danced with an eighty-nine-year-old ex-sailor, a nine-year-old boy who tripped me up and sent me flying into a dessert trolley, and a woman who told me she loses a stone every time her husband goes to prison. Apparently even a six-month stretch does the trick.

At eleven o'clock an announcement was made to say that the bar would be closing in half an hour. I felt sick with fright. Close, the bar would close? Before midnight? I scanned the room for the manager. I had to lynch someone, before someone lynched me. What was going on? I clutched the arm of a speeding waitress who told me that the bar would close for an hour to allow the staff to celebrate New Year and then it would reopen until the last soul collapsed, so in theory it stays open all night. I felt my innards relax. That settled, I tottered off to buy myself a bottle of champagne. Why not? Happy New Year to me!

Rob swooped from behind and lifted me off my feet. 'I've mished you,' he said boozily.

I eyed him judiciously. 'Are you by any chance a little on the tiddly side?'

He shook his head. 'No,' he said, his mouth twitching suspiciously.

He put his arms round me and smiled warmly. He smelled of Dolce & Gabbana and scotch.

'Evie, I—'

'And the countdown begins! Ten, nine, eight, seven, six, five, four, three, two, one! Happy New Year!'

The dance floor burst into a melee of cheering, jumping, clapping party animals. The lighting switched from subdued to crazy laser, the band belted out 'Auld Lang Syne' and silver and gold tickertape fluttered from the ceiling. And Rob disappeared again.

I found him an hour later, asleep in a chair in the lobby. I was sorely tempted to leave him but he's always looked after me when I've been plastered. I woke him, helped him up and zig-zagged him to the lift. God knows how, but I got him to his room and positioned him flat out on the bed. My feet were killing me, my shoulder ached and my back hurt.

'Happy New Year,' I said to his snoring form and went to my own room. Oddly enough, despite the kilt, I was able to resist him in his present state.

Chapter fifty-five

It was noon on New Year's Day and the lobby resembled the decks of the *Mary Celeste*. A lone receptionist was slumped across the front desk stirring a glass of something medicinal and fizzy. I was dressed as a Japanese geisha, in a pale blue silk number. My face was coated with white panstick, my lipstick was a screaming crimson and my hair was piled high in a bird's nest arrangement, with a couple of chopsticks angled strategically.

The receptionist blinked uninterested and bleary eyes at me and snorted in greeting.

'Where is everyone?' I asked her.

'Bed,' she managed.

I tapped on my watch. 'It's noon, the Fancy Dress Brunch should have started at eleven o'clock,' I said, eyebrows raised soberly.

'Aye, well the bar shut at seven this mornin'.'

'Give the whole hotel a wake-up call,' I said, eyes flashing around the empty lobby. 'If I can get up, then so can everyone else.' I held her rheumy gaze and adjusted my rib-crushing bodice. 'Wake-up calls are computer generated, it's a matter of flicking a few switches. Could you please do it?' I urged.

She bobbed her head and slunk off lazily.

By two o'clock, the conservatory was almost full. We had Little Red Riding Hood, Alice in Wonderland, Tinkerbell, the Queen of Hearts, nurses, doctors, vicars and tarts, milkmaids, Batman and Robin, a pantomime reindeer and at least a dozen Marilyn Monroes. My feet were killing me. I lurched forward and clutched the decorated arched trellis entrance. I was exhausted from the effort of nodding in greeting, smiling and saying, 'goodmorninghappynewyear, goodmorninghappynewyear, goodmorninghappynewyear'. Two more hours and I could go back to bed, I thought. I wasn't hungover. My drinking time had been cut short by dancing and chatting for a good part of the party but I was tired and irritable. It was now blatantly obvious to me that the reason geishas were so happy to strip off was because their clothes were so bloody uncomfortable.

As there were no more Young Highlander activities scheduled, I said my goodbyes to the kids in my group, who whooped and danced around, heralding me 'the best old person ever'. Bless them.

When the Insignia lazy arses who had managed a lie-in and wangled the Quiz Night shift finally showed their faces, I disappeared into a corner in the lobby behind the library section where I could get a network signal. I had eight texts.

Lulu: Happy New Year, Vic and I back together. xxxxxx
(Not that Vic knew they'd ever been apart.)
Nikki: Family wedding in Greece cancelled, talk wen u back.
Happy New Year. x
Tina: Happy New Year! Helen in love with Larry Grayson
and moving to the Isle of Wight. Hilarious xxxxx
Charles: Happy New Year. Lunch sometime? Sorry for . . .
you know. x
Alain: Bonne Annee cherie x x x x x x x x x x x x

Lexy: Can u babysit on the third? Have put on half a stone, how much have you put on? Happy NY.

Mum: Gaqw mdw wdap jmtd wmt. Zz

(Predictive for Happy New Year, she's a technology dinosaur.)

Alice: Happy New Year, you lucky devil. xx

(Don't know what she's talking about.)

I felt a kiss whisper down the back of my neck. Rob gripped my shoulders and gave a hefty sigh.

'I'm sorry, I can't remember the last time I was drunk.' He scrunched his face in thought. 'I blame the whisky.'

He looked amazing. Electric sparks danced in my tummy. He gave me a lopsided grin, stood back and held his arms wide.

'Like it?' he asked

He was, *undoubtedly*, the horniest pirate I'd ever seen. He wore a white long-sleeved linen shirt, a leather waistcoat, a pair of low-slung cord breeches and knee-length black leather boots. A buccaneer's sword hung loosely from a thick leather belt, fastened with a silver skull and crossbones buckle. A red bandana and a gold hoop earring completed the look.

'It's OK, I suppose,' I said, swallowing a lump of desire-soaked lust.

'I asked the fancy dress shop to kit me out as a marauding Viking but, to be honest, if he'd had a head to match the fur coat, I could've doubled as King Kong. And there was no way I was wearing a tin skull cap with horns. You might want to reconsider that fantasy of yours, the reality wouldn't appeal to you. Let's get something to eat before I faint,' he said, fingering the hilt of his sword.

We sat in the hotel lobby, the geisha and the pirate feasting on mushroom omelette and Diet Coke.

442

'D'you know, I don't think I've ever slept so late. I only got up an hour ago,' he told me, popping the last mouthful of omelette into his mouth. He threw his napkin on his empty plate, sank into his chair and twirled his earring unconsciously.

'Huh really,' I replied distractedly. I gripped the edge of the chair. I was having trouble breathing. The Diet Coke had morphed me from a size ten into a size fourteen.

'I first woke up about elevenish and I couldn't remember where I was,' he continued.

Beads of sweat broke out on my forehead. Rob's face swam in and out of focus.

'My head was spinning,' he grumbled.

I squeezed the armrest and started to pant.

'And I felt sick.' He peered at my face. 'Are you all right?' he asked.

The bodice was cutting into me like a knife.

'This dress,' I gasped, 'too, too tight.' I staggered to standing and exhaled. I felt dizzy and light-headed.

'Get it off! Your face is puce,' he said, clutching my arm.

He quick-stepped me through the lobby as fast as a hemline with the circumference of a tennis racket would allow.

'In here,' he ordered, grabbing my beehive hairdo and spinning me 360 degrees through a door marked 'Laundry'.

'Where's the zip?' he asked.

Gasping, I smacked my bum demonstratively. He frisked my back for the zip and whizzed it down. My belly, hips and backside all celebrated their simultaneous release. I'd barely taken a breath when, nibbling my collarbone, Rob shimmied me flat against the wall and pressed his body hard against my back.

'Now that we've got the zip down, you might as well step out of the dress,' he suggested.

I angled a startled glance over my shoulder. 'Er, I'm not so sure. This is a public place,' I wheezed, chest still heaving.

He twirled me to face him and slid his eyes in a circle. 'Don't see anyone here, do you? Take the dress off. I'll help,' he offered, inching the blue silk fabric up over my hips.

'No,' I shot back, my down belows a-tremble.

His eyes widened expectantly. 'Off,' he ordered.

'Definitely not,' I persisted, feeling a leap of exhilaration squirm in my tummy.

He whipped the dress over my head and lassoed it behind him.

I caved in. 'Oh, all right then.'

Oh my God, I thought, how sexy and risk-taking and cold. I shivered as I was now wearing only high heels, bra and knickers. My arms circled Rob's neck. His eyes narrowed and darkened and his lips curved into a grin. I flushed in the gloom. The laundry was large and chilly and menacingly quiet, with the exception of the sporadic humming of the overhead air conditioning unit. He covered my mouth with his and kissed me hard, and with the flat of his palms he forced my shoulders against the wall.

'Will the white stuff on your face rub off on me?' he asked, cupping my jaw.

'Probably,' I mumbled through his kiss. 'Do you care?'

'Nah,' he said, volleying us on top of a trolley of towels. I quickly grabbed his shoulders as the trolley hurtled across the tiled floor, crashing to a halt against a floor-to-ceiling washing machine. He straddled me and his frantic fingers worked the buckle of his belt. My heart pumped with excitement.

'Keep the breeches on,' I said, tugging a towel around my shivering shoulders.

'What?'

'Keep them on,' I repeated, staying his hand.

'OK, OK,' he agreed and leaped from the trolley, bending double to pull off his boots.

'No, no, keep the boots on. I like the boots,' I said.

His brow wrinkled into impatient creases. He pushed back his shoulders and tugged on his waistcoat.

'Keep that on too. I like the waistcoat, I like it all. Keep everything on, even the sword,' I said thickly. 'Well, you might want to take your earring out, but the boots and all the rest,' I eyed him hungrily, 'I like it, I mean I *really* like it.'

He straightened. 'I'm not keeping the sword on. It has a sharp blade, it's not an egg whisk, you know.'

'OK fine, you can take the sword off, and Rob . . .'

His bandana slid down his forehead, covering his eyes. 'What now?' he yelled as the sword clattered to the floor.

'Talk dirty,' I said witchily.

And he did, really dirty.

After we'd finished, we lay snuggled under two heavy velvet curtains on a bed of towels.

'Do you know what this reminds me of?' I asked dreamily.

'What?'

'It reminds me of the scene in *Titanic* where Kate Winslet slaps a sweaty hand on the steamed-up window after she's had a shag in the car. We never did that, did we? We never had a shag on the car deck.'

'We can soon put that right,' Rob said conversationally. 'When we get back, we'll take the car to Paris. Everything will be exactly like it was before. OK,' he admitted, 'perhaps the cross-Channel ferry isn't the *Titanic*, but a car deck is a car deck.'

I felt something uncomfortable release inside of me. It was a feeling of foreboding, I think. We'd had a fantastic couple of days, but this weekend hadn't been real life. Real life meant him constantly gallivanting across Europe. Having a fantastic time under those circumstances would be harder, stressful, and perhaps even impossible. A flicker of doubt must have shown in my eyes.

'It will, won't it?' Rob asked, giving my cheek a reassuring squeeze.

'Kind of,' I replied, with a chord of hesitation. 'Perhaps it won't be *exactly* as it was before.'

His gaze flickered. 'What do you mean? Of course it'll be the same as before, better even.' He raised himself on one elbow. 'The two months I spent without you made me realise how important you are to me. I was a mess. I've practically stalked Alice since that night in the restaurant. She's been brilliant, I wouldn't have coped if she hadn't kept me up to date on how you were and what you were up to.'

I felt a spasm of irritation and made a mental note to call Alice the first chance I got, nosy traitor that she is.

'I don't trust you,' I said woefully.

He gripped my chin with his index finger and thumb and caught my evading glance. 'You *can* trust me. I'd give my life for you. I will *never* let you down again.'

'I thought you'd never let me down before.' I trailed off miserably, and flipped onto my back. I couldn't look at him. He moved to lean above me, his eyes soft and beseeching.

'Let me prove it to you.'

I chewed my lip and studied the ceiling, choosing my words carefully. 'I was broken-hearted but I got by and I managed to get on with my life. I gave you too much of myself, so somewhere along the line I decided that I wouldn't do that again. Let's date now and again and see how things go, but keep our lives separate in so much as it's OK to, well, to see other people. That way I don't have to carry the burden of mistrust because you can do what you like but,' I sighed, 'so can I.'

He stared at me through narrowed eyes, a muscle in the

corner of his mouth pulsing rhythmically. I realised that as composed as he seemed outwardly, he was holding a percolating temper in check. Suddenly he leaped up from our bed of towels.

'Get dressed,' he snapped. 'Now.'

In my room, Rob stood with his arms folded, leaning against the wall, his expression unreadable.

'We fly back to London tomorrow,' I said, scrubbing my face vigorously with cotton wool and cleanser. 'So how about we meet up on—'

'We don't fly back tomorrow,' he interrupted stiffly.

'We do,' I told him, and I must confess that I couldn't wait. These sub-zero temperatures were deadly.

He paced the room, sword rattling against his thigh. 'We don't because I've—'

'We do,' I short-circuited.

He rounded on me. 'We don't. I changed the flights so that we could stay one more night.'

'Why?' I shrieked.

'Because I thought it would be nice,' he bellowed.

'Nice?' I yelled. 'What is nice about a place where you have to wear every stitch of clothing you possess, together with a body harness and a guy line, just to post a sodding letter?' I jabbed a finger in his face. 'Why would I want to prolong the agonies of living like an Eskimo?'

He raised a commanding hand. 'Calm down.'

'Iamcalm!' I shrieked. 'I just want to go home.'

He gave a nostril-flaring sigh. 'Well, you can't because when I changed our flights the girl on the phone was delighted. Apparently our flight was heavily oversold so you won't get the seats back. So here we are, and here we stay.' He looped his thumbs in his belt, and stood tall, shoulders broad, legs apart. 'Tomorrow we'll pick up a car, have a look around, and see how we get on. And if you still feel the same, namely that you don't want me in the same way that I want you, then we'll fly back to London and you'll never hear from me again.' His eyes clouded over. 'I want you full-time, all or nothing, no dating rubbish. You're either mine or you're not. The thought of you with someone else makes my blood boil. I can't live like that.' He bent his blond head to mine. 'Think about it.'

I opened my mouth but no sound came out.

His eyes blazed. 'You need your space. Meet me in the lobby at nine o'clock tomorrow morning,' he said, and strode from the room.

I went to bed at ten, got up at eleven, drank every gin and brandy miniature in the mini-bar, flopped back into bed and lay, staring at the ceiling, demented with indecision. I thought of Alain with his Latin good looks. Handsome as he was, he hadn't had the tutu-trembling effect on me that Rob has. But then, I pondered tentatively, perhaps if I went to Nice and slept with Alain I could compare. Once should do the trick. I sighed and grimaced as an electric current of uneasiness burned inside me. Would that be fair on Alain? Of course it would, he'd get a shag out of it.

I went rigid with fear. What if Rob met someone else, whilst I was in Nice? The saliva in my mouth evaporated and a surge of nausea swam up and down my windpipe. I could *not* let that happen. I thought of Rob's intoxicating beauty and of, well, of the vibrating ring. My down belows started jiving. My emotions wavered between ecstasy and fury. Sod him, he's a slut, I'm a size ten, I'll find someone else. I clutched a pillow to my chest. Three-thirty flashed in neon green on the bedside clock. I threw back the quilt, shambled from bed, put on my hat and jacket, opened the window and scrolled through my mobile looking for Alice's number. Standing on tiptoes, I managed to get a decent signal.

Floodlights mirrored the white of the frosty Highland landscape, which was backdropped by an indigo sky dotted with twinkling stars. It was so beautiful and peaceful. I shivered. And bloody freezing. Alice picked up on the second ring.

'Alice, it's Evie.'

'Love, how are you? Happy New Year! I was hoping you'd call. I said to Duncan this afternoon, "I hope Evie rings." Didn't I, Duncan?' she prattled, accompanied by a grunt from Duncan. 'He's asleep,' she said.

'I don't know what to do, Alice.'

'What about?'

'About Rob.'

She sighed. 'Evie, that boy,' there was a beat of silence, 'that boy is besotted—'

'But—' I interrupted.

'I know, I know—' she counterattacked.

'So,' I quipped, 'I can't.'

'Evie, listen to me. You *know* he loves you. Do you really want to deny yourself the opportunity of a lifetime of happiness because of one silly mistake on his part? A mistake, I assure you, which is very much regretted and will *never* be repeated. Everyone deserves a second chance. Let him prove himself. Start again, put the past behind you and look to the future,' she advised soothingly.

'Let him prove himself,' I echoed in a whisper.

There was a charged hush. I sniffed and rubbed my pink nose.

'Would you forgive Duncan if he cheated on you?' I asked.

She gasped. 'Would I hell, I'd castrate him.'

I didn't sleep a bloody wink all night.

Chapter Fifty-six

I waddled through the lobby the following morning. I absolutely loathed my new black boots. They made me look short, squat and dumpy, and because of the thick fur trim, I was forced to walk with my legs at least a foot apart, in a cowboy swaggering motion. As if that wasn't bad enough, throbbing pains in my calves were tormenting the hell out of me, and sometimes I would bite my tongue when I plodded down the stairs. I never have any of these problems with heels, I grumbled to myself, but here, in the Arctic, one wears what one must. And as for my faux fur jacket, I hated that as well. My boobs looked like a pair of bull's bollocks.

Rob loomed over the reception desk, arms outstretched, hands either side of a large road map. I sided with him and he reached out and smoothed a hand gently down my cheek.

'Sleep well?' he asked, eyes shining.

'Like a log. I slept in,' I said with a grimace.

A road map? Hang on a minute, if he's reading a map then he doesn't know where he's going.

'Er, Rob . . .'

He bowed an arm around my neck and pulled me towards him, planting a kiss on my forehead. 'Give me a minute, babe,' he said distractedly. 'I'm working out the route.'

I thumped a troubled elbow on the map. 'Route! You're working out the route!' I retorted in horrified alarm. 'I'm in no mood to get lost. I've never understood those selfish eejits who go exploring where no one else will ever want to go. What's the point of exploring a thousand square miles of ice, possibly dying in the process and forcing other people to put their lives at risk to rescue you? And,' I continued, the pitch of my voice rising, 'no one gives a toss what you discover when you're out there.'

He smiled reassuringly. 'We're only driving an hour and a half down the road to Fort William, not climbing Kilimanjaro,' he replied, waving a sheet of paper in my face. 'Look, I've written it down. Turn left onto the B9152, branch off onto the A9, pick up the A86 at the T-junction and then turn left onto the A82. Trust me?'

I wasn't convinced.

He placed a guiding hand on my furry back, steered me through the lobby and out the front door. As per usual, a cycloning blizzard raged. I trudged through the car park using Rob as a body shield, one gloved hand clutching the back of his jacket, the other holding my hat in place. I peered around his beefy arm at our hired car. It looked like a prehistoric mammoth. I battled a wall of swirling snow, mountaineered the passenger seat and pulled the door closed.

'I'm bloody boiling,' I moaned, twisting red-faced in my seat. I swept a palm across my forehead. 'The heater is like a furnace. Sweat is dripping off me, are you trying to fry me?'

He gave me a sideways glance, and smiled. 'Take your jacket off,' he suggested smoothly, 'and your boots.'

I propped my feet on the dashboard and evil-eyed the furry monster boots. Rob chuckled. 'What are you laughing at?' I asked him.

'They're not you, are they?' he asked. 'The boots, I mean. I bet you think they make you look short, squat and dumpy, and I wouldn't be surprised if you had throbbing pains in your calves. You always wear heels.'

'They're fine, actually, comfortable and warm,' I told him.

He eyed the overhead road sign, indicated, and steered the car smoothly onto the main road. 'Have you eaten?'

'No, have you?'

'Of course I have.'

Of course he had. The greedy big lummox would be chewing a burger waiting his turn on the gallows.

'Are you hungry? Would you like to stop before Fort William?'

'No thanks, I'm fine.'

'OK, if you're sure,' he said, piloting the steering wheel with one finger. I tried to drive like that once. I'd ended up in a ditch and lost a wheel trim and my wing mirror.

I must admit that I found the Highland countryside beautiful with its craggy snow-covered uplands, sweeping hills and breathtaking views, so much so that I'd quite like to come back in the summer, when I could dress like, well, dress like me. I sank into my seat and watched the snow-capped forest speed by. Unexpectedly, I experienced a deep feeling of calm and tranquillity.

I looked at Rob. His long lashes shadowed the curve of his cheek and a smile twitched at the corner of his mouth. He was so handsome and sexy and always seemed to be happy. My attention drifted in lustful contemplation of a lifetime with him, which caused a flutter of contractions in my chest. I stole a second glance. His brow wrinkled in thoughtful creases as he consulted the piece of paper detailing the route. I imagined us snoozing on sunbeds on the deck of a cruise liner, ankles lazily entwined, white-jacketed waiters slaving away on our behalf. I imagined dozing on Rob's shoulder as we jetted off to some exotic destination for two weeks in a luxury beach house, and running into the surf, hand in hand, cavorting naked in the sea. I traced my finger along the edge of my hat and licked my lips. Suddenly, an apparition of Helen popped into my head. I screwed my Cossack hat into a tube. I thought of Rob caressing her naked body and his fingers jammed in her ribcage searching for a boob, and of—

'You're quiet, babe. You OK?' he asked, blinking like a sleepy cat.

I released the seat belt, and spun around to face him. 'Why did you do it?' I yelled.

He flashed me a look of terror and without dropping his speed, he swerved into a lay-by and hit the brakes hard.

'You spoiled everything,' I shrieked. 'And you're acting as if nothing happened, as though you didn't break my heart and, and, and . . .' I covered my face with my hands, and burst into tears. Hot, fat, salty tears slid between my fingers. 'Take me back to the hotel,' I said, weeping. 'This isn't going to work.'

'Come here,' he said in a panicky voice. He circled his arms around me and held me tight to him, forcing my head into the crook of his neck and tightening his hold. 'Don't cry,' he soothed.

I began to tremble. 'Why, why?' I sobbed repeatedly.

His hand stroked my hair. My heart lurched in my chest at his touch.

'I'm sorry, I'm so sorry,' he whispered, his voice warm. 'Evie, I know I have no excuse because there is no excuse, but I promise you it will *never* happen again. And OK, being drunk was my own fault but she, well, she . . .' He broke off.

I raised my head and looked up at him. He took my face

between his shaky hands and a sliver of blue blinked between long lashes that glistened with tears. He sighed and pressed my forehead on his damp cheek. When he spoke, his voice was thick.

'I love you,' he mumbled hoarsely. 'I love you *so* much, I need you to give me a chance. Evie, my heart clenches when I look at you. I made the biggest mistake of my life, and don't I know it? Not a day passes without me feeling heartsick at the thought of the mess I've made of things. Please, babe, let me put it right. I was stupid. I'm not blaming drink because I know that drunk or not, I was still responsible for my own actions, but Evie, I was stressed and worried I'd done the wrong thing buying the new coaches. I was wrong, I know it. But don't make me pay for it for the rest of my life. Please Evie, let me make it up to you . . .' He trailed off miserably.

I curled myself into him and cried my heart out. He pulled me closer. His strong broad shoulders arched and bowed as he cried with me.

We sat still for a while. Rob's hand gently and absently caressed my back. I rested my cheek in the crook of his neck and stared wordlessly through the car window. The comforting rhythmic thump of his heart made me feel weak and drowsy. He raised my chin and closed his mouth over mine.

'Evie,' he mumbled through the kiss, 'please take me back. Let's make a go of it.'

I loved him. What was the point of denying it? And after this weekend, after him coming all this way and trying so hard, I was sure he loved me with a passion and depth that matched my own. I blinked and smiled. Memories of our time in Paris flooded my mind, each memory happier than the one before it.

'OK, let's try,' I said in a scratchy voice.

He pulled me close. Air was suddenly in very short supply, in fact, I was choking.

'Rob,' I wheezed, 'I can't, can't breathe.'

'Huh? Oh sorry, sorry, babe.'

He held my face in his hands and kissed me hard, leaving my lips puffy and swollen. We grinned at each other.

'D'you think,' I asked, eyeing the unabating snowstorm, 'that we might get snowed in if we don't hurry up and move this car?'

He held my hands, his thumbs circling my palms. 'We might,' he agreed, 'but before we go anywhere, I want to ask you something now that we're friends again.'

'Ask away,' I invited.

'Will you marry me?'

My jaw dropped. I gawped in astonishment and my already soaring spirits rose even higher. I felt light-headed and breathless. I managed a snuffle of laughter. He clamped my hands between his and gave me one of his sexy smiles.

'Will you? Will you be my wife? I want to spend the rest of my life with you.'

I scanned his face. 'Yes,' I murmured with a watery grin.

He beamed boyishly.

'Yes,' I bleated a little louder. 'I will.'

There was an excited silence.

'Oh!' he exclaimed, frisking his jacket pockets.

I waited a couple of light years before he produced a blue box, a Tiffany box. I swallowed and managed not to snatch it. He flipped the lid. I stared in astonished delight at my new heart-shaped diamond solitaire. My left hand itched, hovered and trembled, whilst Rob fumbled clumsily to place the ring on my finger. My eyes flicked between his face and my sparkling bauble. I threw my arms around him and squeezed and squeezed and squeezed.

'You'll snap my neck or crack my ribs,' he joked. 'Forget Fort William, let's go back to the hotel.'

After the best shag of my entire life, I sat propped up against the pillows, admiring my ring. Rob, also propped up against the pillows, bashed away like billy-o on his laptop.

'Where will we live?' I asked him.

'Together,' he said.

'Together where?'

'Together wherever you want.'

'My flat,' I suggested.

'Fine, I'll relocate my office to London. My parents are moving to Spain in January so I'll be employing new admin staff anyway. But your flat's not big enough. Perhaps we'll rent the flat to Lulu and Vic and buy a house.'

I laid my head on his shoulder and watched his fingers dance over the keyboard. 'What are you doing?'

He gave me a lazy smile. 'Booking a holiday,' he replied.

'Where to?' I asked, squirming with excitement.

He turned to me. 'We fly home tomorrow, and two days later,' he paused annoyingly, 'we go to . . .' Another annoying pause.

'Where, where to?' I shot back impatiently.

'Barbados for three weeks,' he announced.

'Aaagggggg!' I yowled, clapping my hands.

He gave me a noisy kiss, and then another, and then another. PAYMENT CLEARED flashed up on the screen.

'Done,' he said, placing the laptop carefully on the bedside table. He turned to face me and pulled me under the quilt with him. 'Evie,' he began in a serious tone, 'let there always be honesty between us.'

I gave an indignant shuffle. 'I've never been anything but honest,' I told him.

He shook his head. 'I know that and I'm not implying other-wise.'

We spooned and my bum snuggled into his belly.

'This honesty stuff?' I asked.

He gave a sigh. 'I meant no secrets, that's all.'

'Right,' I said assertively. 'I agree that we should tell each other everything. Yes, why not? No secrets. Relationships are built on trust and honesty,' I said wisely.

His nose explored my shoulder. 'Did you apply for any new credit cards?' he asked, massaging my hip.

I flinched. My eyes grew wide. I swallowed a blob of panicky guilt. I know we'd just agreed on honesty, but he couldn't honestly expect me to be honest about that, could he?

'No, no,' I dithered. 'No I didn't,' I added firmly.

Technically this was true, because my Harrods card was a store card *not* a credit card. There's an enormous difference.

He tightened his arms around me. 'I love you,' he whispered, nibbling my neck.

'I love you too.'

'Thank you,' he said, lips curved in a smile against my jaw.

'What for?'

'For giving me a second chance.'

I shrugged absently.

'I'll make it up to you, I promise,' he assured me.

'I know you will.'

'We're lucky. The rest of our lives together, I can't wait,' he said, circling an arm around my belly and pressing his thigh against mine. 'Do you think we can put what happened behind us?' He faltered slightly. 'That we can move forward with no recriminations, no grudges and you won't for ever remind me that I let you down?' There was a pleading edge to his voice. 'I'm so ashamed. I want to forget it ever happened.'

'Yes,' I replied, giving a careless shrug.

'Say it,' he said.

'Say what?'

'That we can move forward with no recriminations, no grudges and you won't for ever remind me that I let you down.'

I gave an exasperated sigh. 'We can move forward with no recriminations, no grudges and I won't for ever remind you that you let me down,' I echoed.

He flipped me onto my back and held himself above me. 'I'm the luckiest man alive,' he beamed, teasing his knee between my thighs.

'So tell me, husband-to-be, did you have to put a pillow over her face when you were shagging her, because she's no oil painting, is she?' I asked.

Coming soon . . .

March 2012

IT HAPPENED in Venice

When your heart is broken, there's
only one place to go . . .

He cheated, but only once!

Evie Dexter has promised to forgive and forget,
to put everything behind her and fiancé Rob. And her
efforts to absolve his sins are paying off: in the past ten days
she's only called him a two-timing love rat eleven times.

Thank goodness for her flourishing career as a
tour guide. With trips to fashionable Dublin, in-vogue
Marrakech, cool Amsterdam and romantic Paris, what's not to
love? So when she's offered a luxury visit to the sensual city
of Venice, with its shifting silver canals and rose and vanilla
hued architecture, Evie jumps at the chance.

Four days in the city of light and love is just what
she needs. The sumptuous Grand Hotel, the gondolas, the
wine, the Italian men . . . Who knows what could happen?

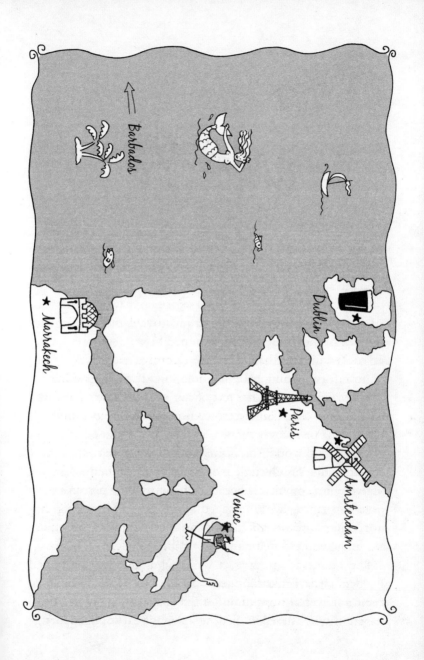

Chapter One

OK, he cheated on me but he couldn't be sorrier, and it was *only once*.

Sitting beside Rob on the flight from London to Barbados I pondered the amazing u-turn my life had taken over the past ten days. Rob and I were back together, after a separation of two long months.

I gave him an adoring look and nuzzled my head in the crook of his neck. He smiled, wrapped his ankles around mine and tucked my legs behind his. We've made a pact. We're going to move forward and put the whole sordid episode behind us. I am not going to ruin the rest of our lives because of one silly mistake on his part, a mistake I know will never be repeated. And I won't be for ever rubbing it in his face because I want this relationship to work. And it *will* work, because I love him. So I won't mention his silly little indiscretion, ever. It's in the past. I've forgiven him completely because I'm a forgiving person with a forgiving nature. We're engaged and I have a whopping diamond ring to prove it. I rubbed my cheek against his shoulder and snuggled in to enjoy the rest of the flight.

The hotel was amazing. It was a fabulous vanilla coloured wooden affair flanked by palm trees and a kaleidoscope of tropical flowers. I stepped out of the taxi, clasped my heart and gasped in awe. I stared in silent wonder as a turtle edged its way through the shrubs. I was about to bend down to have a chat with it, when Rob gripped my arm and whizzed me through the oak-floored, lavishly decorated lobby towards the reception desk. I gave a squeal of excitement when I spotted a glass display-cabinet full of handbags.

Rob followed my gaze without breaking his marathon pace. 'You *don't* need any more handbags,' he said stiffly.

'I'm only looking,' I shot back. 'But you're wrong. I don't have a purple bag.'

We halted at the front desk. He slid a menacing look at my new red Louis Vuitton Monogram Vernis bag, which I'd bought just before Christmas.

'Every time I think about how much you paid for that bag, I feel like clubbing you to death with the bloody thing,' he said.

I clutched the bag protectively to my chest. 'It was cheaper than therapy and better for me than Valium. What was I supposed to do? I was depressed. You'd gone off shagging behind my back and if it hadn't been for that, I wouldn't have been in the position where I needed to buy the bag, would I? It was your fault!'

A crimson stain spread up his neck to his cheeks.

'I could've ended up a Prozac addict,' I told him bitterly. 'Or a manic depressive, or addicted to gin or the horses. Anything could've happened to me. What were you thinking?'

He exhaled an infuriated sigh. The cheek of him! I thought. I'm the one with the axe to grind.

'You promised me that you wouldn't mention that again,' he said, measuring *every single* word.

My spine snapped upright. 'I've hardly mentioned it at all. In the past week, I've only brought it up eleven times,' I told him factually.

'Exactly!'

'Am I just supposed to roll over and accept the fact that you are a slut and I have a love rival? Am I?'

Quick as a flash, Rob's hand shot out and he grabbed my Lipsy waistcoat. He pulled my face to his and gave me a long hard lip-bruising kiss.

The receptionist coughed into her fist.

He raised me onto my tiptoes by my collar. The kiss lingered for a bit and then he ran his tongue around my lips.

'Evie, if you *ever* mention that singular moment of madness on my part again, for which I am eternally sorry, I'll pin you to the floor and pluck your eyebrows until they're non-existent.' There was a beat of silence. Blue eyes held mine. 'You'd look like an eejit without eyebrows,' he said, with a shoulder-shaking chuckle.

'You're choking me.'

'I'm not choking you but I admit I'm sorely tempted. So have we reached an understanding?' he asked, giving me another kiss. 'You agreed to put it behind us and you promised never to throw it in my face.'

I gave a non-committal shrug, privately regretting having been so amiable.

'A promise is a promise,' he said dolefully, tracing my cheeks with his thumbs.

I gave a congenial nod.

'Truce?' he asked, cupping my face.

I sighed and blinked a yes.

He kissed my forehead, and then turned to the receptionist who pushed the registration card in front of him. I quickly turned and took a picture of the display-cabinet on my phone. I would check out the handbags later if I had time.

That was all a whole week ago. We've now been holed up in a luxurious private beachfront villa on this beautiful island for eight glorious days. In that time, Rob and I have encountered only two other human beings. There was a maid who Rob catapulted from the room when her lips quivered suspiciously, as though she might've been about to strike up a conversation, and there's the waiter who delivers our room service meals. Rob said he wanted me all to himself and I'm more than happy to comply with that sentiment.

Robert Harrison is the love of my life, my *raison d'être*. An invisible cord draws me to him, heart and soul. This randy, handsome, ridey Adonis is my destiny, of that I am absolutely positive. I simply cannot get enough of him. Every nerve ending in my body tingles and jives when he puts his arms around me and a cascading torrent of excitement erupts and percolates in my chest when he kisses me, leaving me breathless. My obsession with him is both physical and psychosomatic. I'm driven by and demented with lust. I've been behaving like a sex-crazed lunatic, even waking in the middle of the night with this fierce ache in my groin that only he can satisfy. My fiancé, Robert Harrison, doesn't have a normal willy like any other bloke I've ever known. Robert Harrison has a bloody magic wand.

This obsession of mine is showing no signs of waning, which frankly has me worried, because I'm exhausted and I don't feel very well. I have a vicious throbbing twinge in my tummy as though I've done two hundred sit-ups. OK, I've never actually done a sit-up, so perhaps a more appropriate metaphor would be to say that I feel like I've had my appendix removed. My lips are bruised and I've ruptured a muscle in my inner thigh that I never knew I had, the result being that I now have a limp. I'm dragging my left leg around as though it had a clubbed foot. And as for my hair, I can hardly bear to look at it. Sweat and friction damage has morphed my long, shiny brown extensions into a frizzy, matted beehive affair. In short, I look like a hairy goblin.

This cannot go on, so this morning I showered, straightened my hair, put on my white bikini with a matching sarong and a wrapover top, and accessorised with a bit of silver bling. I'm going to wake Rob and *insist* we go out. I will not be swayed. I'm resolute and determined. I whizzed some Glam Shine around my lips and peered in the mirror. I looked quite normal, not like the haunted, knackered, sunken-eyed slut who woke up an hour ago. I've also got a bit of a tan because a fair bit of our shagathon has taken place on our bit of private beach. I stood at the foot of our four-poster canopied bed and nipped Rob's toe.

'Get up.'

He blinked like a drowsy bull and curved an arm above his head. 'Why?'

'Because I want to do something different!'

He sat up slowly. The sheet fell around his waist and he wore nothing but a lazy smile. 'You do?'

His face shone with the promise of possibility, his eyes were pooled and glazed and his smile beatific. He looked like he'd seen an apparition of the Blessed Virgin or the Angel Gabriel. Obviously he thought I was talking about sex.

He Mexican-waved the sheet and looked below for signs of life. His already wide smile grew wider. 'I'm game,' he boasted.

I snorted inwardly. 'I want to go out.'

'Fine, we'll go out.'

I crossed my arms defiantly and jerked my chin at the open window. 'No, I mean out to the hotel pool or the beach bar.'

He lifted his eyebrows. 'Why?'

'I want to meet other people. You know, do the holiday type of thing where we get chatting to someone and they ask where we're from. I'll say, "London" and they'll say, "Oh, my sister lives in London. Perhaps you know her? Her name is Mary Smith, she lives in Staines." And I'll scrunch up my face and pretend to think hard, and then say, "No, I don't think I do" and they'll say, "Never mind" and then we'll strike up a conversation and maybe have a drink and—'

'Evie, shut up and get back in this bed.'

I held up the flat of my hand. 'No.'

He threw back the sheet and padded, naked, towards me.

'Rob, a shag is off limits. Tonight perhaps,' I said, in my ward sister voice, 'but not now!'

He flashed me a manic smile.

'I don't want my holiday filled with raunch and porn and precious little else.'

He loomed above me. 'I do,' he said, lifting a long strand of hair and tucking it behind my ear.

He held my shoulders, pulled me close and bent his blond head to mine. His tongue tickled my forehead, then slowly travelled the length of my cheek. He stopped briefly to nibble the lobe of my ear before exploring my neck and hairline. My groin flashed on high alert, my spine stretched and my back arched, pushing my pelvis towards his.

'That's a shame . . .' he whispered, his voice warm on my cheek.

I felt a rush of excitement. He slipped his thumb inside my bikini bottom and did that fantastic little cartwheely thing he does that activates the lust bubble volcano in the pit of my tummy.

'Because I was going to spoil you . . .'

My eyes followed the hum of the ceiling fan in contemplative diversion.

'But you might not be interested . . .' he said.

The problem was that my mind and my erogenous zones had completely different principles.

'Really spoil you,' he said, rugby tackling me to the bed.

I wriggled free and pointed a stern finger. 'Right, Rob, I'm telling you and I mean it, a quickie as a favour to you. And then we're out of here,' I said primly.

Evie's Helpful Travel Facts

✤ Parisian women have a higher metabolic rate than the rest of us. This is obvious because they can consume vats of wine, lots of bread and enormous lumps of cheese without gaining weight. (Do not try this at home; you will go up four dress sizes).

✤ French men are dead sexy and really good in bed; this must be true because all French men say so. (Try this at home if you can find one).

✤ Parisian women can wear miniskirts even if they have fat legs and still look good. This is a scientific fact. Do not think you can do the same.

✤ No one in Paris can park a car; this is fabulous if you can't park either. If you are a really bad driver, you might like to drive to Paris, just so that you will look good in comparison.

✤ Most gift shops in Paris sell condoms. They are beside the keyrings and the postcards. And are in a white packet with a red love heart on the front, and have a caption that says, I love Paris. They are all the same size and quite good quality. They sell them as singles and as packs of three. (Not that I bought any).

✤ In the South of France, a sun bed costs ten euros. If you take your top off, it's free. (Not officially you understand, so don't hold me to that).

- Do not buy your own drinks in Monte Carlo if you can help it. A glass of champagne costs the same as a Karen Millen jacket.

- The Scottish Highlands has the same winter as Siberia. You should just be aware of that.

- There are approximately only two and a half million people in the expensive Paris city area, with another eleven million living in the more economical satellite suburbs. This is because the women spend their money in Chanel and Dior, and so obviously have to cut back on frivolous, unnecessary expenditure such as rent and mortgages.

- There are approximately five million people in Scotland. Everyone has two coats, three hats and hundreds of odd gloves. I don't blame them one single bit.

- Cannes, in the South of France, is the place to go if you want to buy a designer outfit and can't really afford it. Not because it's any cheaper than anywhere else, but because you can't help yourself and nor can anyone else. So obviously you don't feel guilty about spending money you don't have, because most people shopping in the boutiques around La Croisette and Rue d'Antibes, like me, should be looking in New Look.

- Scottish men really *do not* wear anything under their kilt. This scientific fact has my sexual antenna operating on super-high alert 24/7. I can't help but stare. (I walked into a pillar at Inverness Airport; I have a lump the size of a boiled egg on my head). My peripheral vision can now detect a kilt through brick walls and around corners. I chose to shut out of my mind the fact that the sub-zero temperatures may well affect the pictorial magnificence of what I'm actually fantasising about. I can't help but wonder why more countries don't adopt the kilt as a national costume. Namely the French.

The Alternative Travel Quiz

1. How many storeys does the Paris fashion store Galeries Lafayette have?
   a) Five
   b) Four
   c) Ten.

2. Apart from being the first Empress of the French what else was Josephine Bonaparte famous for?
   a) Writing poetry
   b) Being a devoted shopaholic
   c) Her singing voice.

3. Who took impressions of the decapitated heads of victims of the Revolution?
   a) Madame Tussaud
   b) The Duke d'Orleans
   c) Marie Antoinette.

4. Which film is *not* set in Paris?
   a) *The Da Vinci Code* starring Tom Hanks
   b) *Amelie* starring Audrey Tautou
   c) *When I Fall in Love it Will be in Paris* starring Cheryl Cole and Simon Cowell.

5. What do you do in Paris if you return to your car to discover you have been double parked?
   a) Sit it out in silent fury
   b) Look for a message from the offending driver on your windscreen
   c) Check to see if the handbrake of the car is off.

6. How many Avenues radiate from the Arc de Triomphe?
   a) Twelve
   b) Six
   c) Eight.

7. What is another name for the Champs Elysées?
   a) Oxford Street
   b) The Place of the Blessed Dead
   c) Broadway.

8. Would you like to win a two-night stay on the Boulevard Peripherique?
   a) Not sure if I would
   b) Definitely not
   c) I'd love to stay there for two nights.

9. What amazing gift did the French people give to America?
   a) The Statue of Liberty
   b) The Empire State Building
   c) The Golden Gate Bridge.

10. Who was married to Francis Dauphin of France and reigned as his queen consort?
    a) The Duchess of York
    b) Mary Queen of Scots
    c) Queen Victoria.

Answers

1(c)   This explains why Parisian women always look fantastic, because who could resist ten storeys of shoes, bags, jewellery and makeup? And frankly why should women have to? People's jobs depend on their spending.

2(b)   Josephine was amazing! Not only did she amass an enormous wardrobe, she bought crowns and houses and all sorts of fantastic stuff, and only ever admitted to half of her debts. She was a true inspiration. You should read her biography. (And she had affairs. Not that that was amazing or anything, you should just know).

3(a)   What a grim job! She even took wax impressions of decapitated heads of people she had known. Imagine it! Eeek . . . Mind you, if you hadn't actually liked the person . . . No! No! . . . It would be awful under any circumstances.

4(c)   Although maybe Simon will consider breaking into film one day . . .

5(c)   This is a simplistic yet effective solution to an inner-city parking problem. I can't help but wonder why the Mayor of London hasn't had posters or something printed to suggest we do the same. You leave your handbrake off so that the driver of the car you have blocked in can shunt you out of the way. Someone will show you how to do the 'shunting' – it's easy.

6(a)   Twelve, and unfortunately they all look the same, which is probably why drivers occasionally reverse on the roundabout if they miss their turning. Not that I've done it.

7(b)   Which is rather disappointing because any of the other two answers would have been better. It's not as though you would say 'Oh! I bought a skirt on The Place of the Blessed Dead,' is it?

8(b)   The Boulevard Peripherique is a dual carriageway ring road, the Parisian equivalent of the M25. Why can't we give our motorways fabulous names like that?

9(a)   And the designer Frederic Bartholdi moulded the face on his mother Charlotte, which surely makes him the mummy's boy of all time.

10(b) I can't help but think life dealt her a bad hand somewhere along the line. She would have been better off staying in Paris, and not coming back to the UK to go to prison and have her head chopped off.